The Lions and the Wolf

The Orphan Cub

By

Garrett Pearson

Published by Morepork Publishing

Cover Design: More Visual Ltd

Beta Reading: Scott White

ISBN: 13: 978-0473437442

This Book is for Marilyn.

Authors Note

When committing to this book it was my intention to create a tale relating to the Second Punic War, fought between the cities of Carthage and Rome from the years 218 BC to 202 BC.

Although historical records abound for this precise period from the classical scholars such as Livy and Polybius through to modern day writers, BH Liddell Hart and Ernle Bradford, it has always been concerning the commanders or "Giants" of that age, the political machinations of the two powers locked in the struggle and the big picture view of what occurred. The truth of which in fact needs no embellishment from the storyteller's pen.

I have followed the major steps of the war faithfully, changing neither the events nor their outcome, the chronology too I have left as history renders it to us.

The true historical characters such as Hannibal Barca, his brothers and Generals: the Roman Consuls, Generals and the Scipio family are all as they were, in both place and deed. I have but injected character into them using what we do know of them from history and with storyteller's licence as to what kind of men I think they would have been.

This book aims to see the war from an ordinary man's eyes, he and other everyday people with their struggles, triumphs and losses and their parts to play in the great scheme of things as they unfolded in this larger than life period of history. The would be lesser or more humble men of this book such as Baldor, Armaco, Gestix and Balaam etc. are inventions of my own along with their characters.

Garrett Pearson

Principal Character List

Adharbal Samilcar* Second son of the prestigious Carthaginian family of judges and business people. Brother to Serfina, Carthalo and Sakarbaal.

Ahaggar Bola* Professional mercenary soldier with Balaam's company.

Aiticia Targa* Wife to Baldor.

Armaco Salamar* Professional mercenary soldier with Balaam's company.

Asmilcar Targa* Veteran of the first Punic war. Husband to Melandara and father to Baldor, closest friend of Gestix.

Balaam* (Carthaginian mercenary Captain) Veteran of the first Punic war and old comrade in arms to Gestix.

Baldor Targa* Young Carthaginian man born into the Targa shipbuilding family and sole surviving family member.

Carthalo Samilcar* Eldest son and principal heir of this prestigious Carthaginian family, brother to Serfina, Adharbal and Sakarbaal.

Cornelius Publius Scipio (Roman Optio) Son of Publius, nephew to Gnaeus.

Gaius Laelius (Roman Centurion) Commanding officer, friend and mentor to Publius.

Gestix* A Gaul by birth and a veteran from the first Punic war. Comrade to Baldor's Father and family friend to the Targas.

Gnaeus Scipio (Roman General) Brother to Publius and uncle to Cornelius.

Hannar* (Captain) Captain of the Guard for the city of Carthage.

Hannibal Barca (Carthaginian General, Commander in Chief of the Army) Brother to Mago and Hasdrubal.

Harbro* Professional mercenary soldier and second in command with Balaam's company.

Hasdrubal Barca (Carthaginian General) Brother to Hannibal and Mago.

Mago Barca (Carthaginian General) Brother to Hannibal and Hasdrubal.

Maharabal (Carthaginian General) Hannibal's cavalry General.

Malo* Professional mercenary soldier with Balaam's company.

Marko* Professional mercenary soldier with Balaam's company, veteran from the first Punic war and friend to Gestix.

Publius Cornelius Scipio (Consul and General of Rome) Father to Cornelius, Brother to Gnaeus.

Strabonus* A judge in the Carthaginian senate.

Serfina Samilcar* Daughter of the prestigious Carthaginian family. Sister to Adharbal, Carthalo and Sakarbaal.

Tiberius Sempronius Longus (Consul and General of Rome)

*Denotes fictional characters

Glossary

Siege Machines

Ballista A bolt or stone throwing siege machine. Manufactured in a range of sizes, small for use in open battle or larger for use in siege warfare.

Catapult or Mangonel A stone throwing siege machine, again manufactured in different sizes, also capable of hurling fire pots. (Naphtha)

Vineae Mobile troop shelters, made of timber and covered in un-tanned animal hides to help prevent attack from fire.

Weapons

Caetra A small skirmishing shield or buckler, favoured by the Light Spanish troops (Caetratus) and from which the warriors take their name.

Falcata Carthaginian short sword, albeit Spanish in origin.

Gladius Roman short sword, with a heavy, straight blade.

Hasta Roman fighting spear, 8 – 10 ft. in length.

Naphtha Liquid chemical, a sticky burning fluid, water will not quench the flames.

Pike Long spear 16 – 18ft in length used en-masse in phalanx formation by the Carthaginians.

Phalarica Spanish javelin, wooden shafted with a soft iron head.

Pilum Roman javelin, wooden shafted with a soft iron head.

Scutum Roman infantry shield, large and oval, curved to fit around the body of the user.

Soliferreum or Saunion Spanish javelin made solely of iron.

Spatha Cavalry sword or long Gallic broadsword approximately 30" in length, a straight bladed, slashing weapon.

Troop Types

Caetratus Spanish light infantry

Equites Roman cavalry, approximately 300 attached to each Legion.

Hastati Roman medium/heavy infantry, the first line of defence after the Velites, armed with the pilum.

Princeps Roman medium/heavy infantry, the second line of defence after the Hastati, armed with a fighting spear (hasta) rather than the missile pilum

Scutaris Spanish heavy infantry

Triari Roman heavy infantry, the third line of defence after the Princeps. Again armed with the hasta, these soldiers were the eldest and most experienced of all, used as reserves and as a steadying influence for the front ranks.

Velites Roman light infantry or skirmishing troops, also used as foragers.

Musical Instruments

Carnyx. Gallic war horn

Cornicen. Roman war horn

Country & Place names

Carthage Founded by the Phoenician's, now within modern day Tunisia. The people were of Phoenician stock mixed through with native North African.

Cartagena Nova Modern day Cartagena in southern Spain

Drepanum Near modern day Trapani in western Sicily

Gades Modern day Cadiz in southern Spain

Gaul France, Belgium, Switzerland etc. most of western, mainland Europe except Germany, Spain and Greece

Icosium City in the kingdom of Numidia, now modern day Algiers.

Iberia Modern day northern Spain.

Igilgili City in the kingdom of Numidia, now the modern day city Jijel in Algeria

Lilybaeum Modern day Marsala in western Sicily

Massilia Modern day Marseilles in France

Nubia Modern day southern Egypt and northern Sudan

Numidia Modern day Algeria.

Placentia Modern day Piacenza in northern Italy

Rusucurru City in the kingdom of Numidia, now modern day Delles or Dellys in Algeria

Saguntum Modern day Sagunto in the province of Valencia in eastern Spain

Salamantica Modern day Salamanca in western Spain

Saldae City in the kingdom of Numidia, modern day Bejaia in Algeria.

Tarraco Modern day Tarragona.

Tarascon Provencal, southern France, near to the Rhone River.

Victumulae Outpost or township somewhere in the Po valley (the exact location is not known)

Units of measure

Cubit Ancient unit of measure, 1 Cubit equals 24 Inches or 2 Feet

Stade Carthaginian unit of distance, 1 Stade equals approximately 175 meters

Loss

I hear the Skylark whistle and sing
Soaring high in a cloudless sky of blue
Beneath, the summer blooms sprout bravely forth
Dotting the meadows of Emerald hue
This beauty that surrounds me stirs my heart
And turns my thoughts to you.

But you're no longer here for me to love
The memory of you is all that I now possess
Your chestnut hair and flawless skin
The sweetness of your caress
Your laughter and your loving
My very own Goddess.

Why did you have to go my love?
My heart is broken and spirit sore
This cold sword hilt has replaced your fair hand
As I turn towards my cities war
Please look for me, I pray you
When I approach the Lord Baal's door

Prologue

The port of Gades, southern Spain 228 BC

The frenzied knocking of scores of wooden mallets and the rasp of saws carried across the harbour mixing with the shouts of men and the coarse, screeching cries of the ever present wheeling, diving seagulls. The usual smells of fish and the sea that carried on the morning breeze mixed with that of freshly sawn timber, animal bones being boiled into glue and the rancid, bitter odour of human sweat, as hundreds of men laboured under the baking Spanish sun to build the new ships.

Vessels of many differing sizes in various stages of construction stood on the slipways. Some nothing more than a skeletal rib cage frame of timbers, some partly clad in planking; others decked out and their masts pointing skyward, one or two having the heavy cloth sail dragged into position by the riggers who swarmed up the masts and ropes like ants from a disturbed anthill.

"So many ships father! I thought we were busy in Carthage but this! ... How is it possible?"

The man ruffled the boy's hair, smiling to himself at the lad's excitement, at the same time shifting his weight from his damaged leg and grasping his walking staff tighter.

"I wanted you to see this Baldor, there is a huge world outside of Carthage and travel broadens a man's experience. This port of Gades as large as it is now, started from nothing. These yards were not always as big, they too had modest beginnings and this here is but one small part of Spain! Can you picture now perhaps where our business could go?"

The olive skinned, and black curly haired boy gazed up at his father, the look on his face of wonderment at the scene before him suddenly replaced with concern.

"Is your leg hurting again father?" The boy's hand tightened over the man's as he spoke. "Mother and Gestix told me I have to look after you while we are away."

The man smiled at his son, "You always look after me Baldor, and you're a good lad! But I swear I am married to two wives, what with your mother and Gestix chiding and worrying after me!" Baldor missed the adult humour in the exchange and replied with all the honesty and sincerity of the ten-year-old child that he was.

"It's because they love you father!"

The man laughed gently at the forthright words and drew the lad close,

"I'm a lucky man." He said lightly, smiling warmly. "Now! Let's find this Demetrius and see to business eh?"

The man arranged his cloak over his tunic, covering his ruined leg. Grimacing slightly, he placed his free hand on the lad's shoulder as reassurance for his balance and father and son walked into the shipyard proper, in search of their contact.

As the pair entered the shipyard, Baldor's gaze darted here and there, his mouth dropping open in awe at the scale of it all, his father intent on signs of his business contact. Within a short while both were met and guided to the buildings housing the administrative and management people for the yard. Cool, watered wine was offered and meat, fruit and bread brought for them while servants scuttled off to announce the visitors presence to their masters.

Baldor drained his wine cup quickly and poured a little more in to it.

"Slowly lad, slowly now!" His father chided softly while passing a fresh orange to his son.

"Father, can I go and look around while you have your meeting?"

"I would prefer you stay here Baldor, the yard's a busy place and you know it not."

Baldor looked crestfallen,

"I would have liked to have seen the different ships and there is much which looks strange, I cannot believe the size of the place!" Baldor's eyes had all the sparkle of a child in awe of his surroundings, his small face complete with the irresistible appeal of childish innocence.

The man gazed lovingly at his son and beckoned him close, glancing around as if there was a need for secrecy.

"Not a word to your mother or Gestix then … promise!"

Baldor's eyes lit up. "I promise father!"

"Warriors honour?"

"Warriors honour!" He said, placing his closed right fist to his heart and bowing his head.

"I will be done by noon, be back here." His father barked, imitating a General addressing his officer

"Yes sir!" Came from Baldor departing for the door at a run.

Out in the sun again he made for the nearest ship under construction, biting at his orange and spitting the bitter skin out as he went. His eyes looking everywhere devouring the scene of ships, lumberyards, colossal dry docks, high, stone wharfs and hundreds of men. His father's yard had seemed large to him but the scene before him dwarfed anything he had ever seen before.

Walking around the stone quays and docks finally brought him to a slipway where a vessel was preparing for launch; men were busy greasing the slipway from huge vats of animal fat, the stench of which caused his nose to wrinkle. As the greasing reached completion, men at the vessel's bows knocked the timber holding blocks clear with blows from huge, double-handed wooden mallets. The vessel started to move, slowly at first, heralded by cheers from the men on the ship's deck and alongside the slipway. She gathered speed and rumbled down the wooden slip with protesting creaks and groans from the timber, turning to a quiet scrape similar to that of a carpenter's plain shaving timber, as the whole of the keel lubricated from the pungent fat. The ship hit the water with a huge splash, ploughing her bows at first then rising up like a wine cork to ride the foaming bow wave she made, the awkwardness from the slipway replaced by a graceful swan-like glide on the green water. The men's cheering quietened and they looked to the next tasks of fitting out and preparing the vessel for sea trials.

Baldor looked for the next wonder.

His eyes came to rest on a small group stood in a circle on the top of a wharf from which occasional cheers and bursts of excitement flared up. His interest caught, he walked over to the group to see what was causing the commotion. As he approached, he saw the group consisted of boys much the same age as him; he paused a little way off and watched. The boys stood around a large flat-topped stone that served as a stevedore, upon which brightly coloured, round pieces of glass or stone were placed; one of the boys took a turn at aiming then rolling a larger coloured stone at the rest. Baldor watched intently, his eyes locked on the myriad colours of the pieces, his boyish demeanour fired. Eventually one boy turned and noticed him, the lad quickly brought Baldor's presence to his peers, the largest one of the group stood up, looked Baldor up and down then shouted,

"Do you want to play?"

"What are you playing?" He asked, walking towards the group,

"Marbles! … What's it look like!" This raising laughter from the boys.

"I don't know what marbles is!" He replied sheepishly.

"Come here then, we'll show you." The tallest shouted while beckoning Baldor over.

Baldor peered over the shoulders of the boys, there was much excitement, fingers pointing and advice being given to the boy who was to take his shot at the main group of marbles, followed by ooooh's and groans when the shot didn't have the desired result. Baldor had never seen such beautiful, brightly coloured things so perfect in shape and was so engrossed that he had to be tapped on the shoulder and asked twice if he wanted a try.

After a brief demonstration followed by a multitude of explanations and advice he tried his hand, his shot collided with the main group of marbles and pushed most out of the chalk drawn circle.

"Are you sure you haven't played before?" Came from the smallest of the group, his tone suspicious.

"No, no! But I would like another try."

"What have you got to play for then? Do you want to play for keeps?" Baldor looked confused, he gazed at the multi-coloured baubles before him and at the excited younger player who harangued him further.

The boy was quite striking in appearance compared to his compatriots. Where they were for the most raven-haired and swarthy skinned, he was pale or creamy of colour with hair the colour of ripened wheat. His eyes were of the deepest sea green, his face dusted with freckles across his nose and chin. The small pink lips parting in a smile showing even white teeth.

"Keeps! Do you want to play for keeps? … Come on!"

"I don't have any of …those …"

"Marbles! They're marbles! Surely you've seen them before!" Came from another boy shaking his head in mock disbelief.

"Tell you what?" Said the smallest boy again "I'll play you for that bracelet you have?" He pointed to the metal bangle around Baldor's wrist.

The group buzzed with excitement, advice been offered both for and against the odds and what the bracelet was worth compared to the marbles. The small boy reached into a leather pouch hanging from his belt and produced a marble larger than all the rest, holding it aloft for all to see.

"I'll play you for your bracelet and I wager you this." He said.

The appreciative sounds from the group confirmed to Baldor that which his eyes told him, the marble was beautiful to behold. It was deep blue like a summer sky but flecked through with small crimson specks like fireballs, giving the appearance of raining fire, a treasure!

"I'll hold the wagers!" Shouted the tallest of the group.

The small boy handed over his marble, the taller boy turned to Baldor with his hand out.

"Come on! Game on! Are you in?"

"Your bracelet against my Vulcan's fire?" The blonde boy badgered.

Baldor fingered his bracelet of copper and brass wire twists, all eyes watching him. He grinned and pulled the bracelet from his wrist giving it to the wager holder.

The group were beside themselves now. Chatter, whoops and shouts rose to a crescendo when the wagers were held up for all to see.

"My friends!" The wager holder began. "We have a match! I have a fine copper and gold, yes gold! Bracelet wagered against Vulcan's fire. Winner takes all!"

He gave a flourish as he finished, aping men, he had seen dicing and gambling.

The boys cleared back from the playing area and the new game was set up. Ten regular sized marbles were placed in a smaller, inner circle scribed centrally within the larger one, Baldor and the small boy being offered larger marbles to shoot with.

"Best of three games, dice for who goes first, highest number starts." Said the wager holder who seemed to be the games master too now.

Baldor won the throw with two sixes showing on the yellowed, bone dice and so began the match. Winning the first game and narrowly losing the second while the boys looking on advising, decrying, encouraging and cheering, all excitement and laughter. The third game could not have been closer with both contestants holding four marbles each. The remaining two marbles stood close together, a well-aimed shot could claim both and the wagered treasures, it was Baldor to play.

As Baldor looked for the best angle, the self-appointed games master busied himself shouting at and moving the group to give the players room. Baldor lined his shot, the boys fell silent, all eyes fixed on the remaining two marbles, breaths held. He took aim and sent his marble straight towards the remaining pair. He could hear his heart pounding in his ears, his breath held as the big marble headed towards the target. It missed by a hair's breadth. His heart sank, there was an audible gasp as breaths were released followed by sighs and much head shaking.

The smallest boy came forward, his face tight in concentration; the crowd broke out again in excitement and had to be silenced once more by the games master.

Taking aim, much the same angle as Baldor, he sent his marble careering towards the target. He knocked one of the pair straight out of the circle, the other travelling slowly, almost reluctantly towards the chalked line that was the boundary. The boys watched the path of the sloth like marble, cries of yes! ... No! ... Yes'ssss as the glass ball just crossed the line.

The group went wild, shouting and capering, disputes began over how the shot had been done, followed by re-enactments of the technique.

"Gentlemen ... my friends ... I give you the victor ... rrr." The wager holder shouted, holding aloft the small boys hand in triumph. He then passed over the bracelet and marble treasures to the winner.

The small boy slipped Vulcan's Fire safely into his pouch and pushed the bracelet onto his wrist, then holding his arm and prize aloft in triumph, turned to Baldor offering his hand.

"You played well." He said with a warm smile.

Baldor, somewhat despondent did not know what to say but he grasped the offered hand and smiled back as best he could.

The reverie was cut short by a gruff shout from a large, burly man who approached the group from the beach adjacent to the wharf with his fist raised and a large stick in his hand

"I already told you lot once! ... Get down from there! ... I'll tan your bloody hides!"

The boys snatched up their possessions and started to scatter, the tallest boy however could not resist stopping to make faces and hurl abuse,

"Try to catch us you old goat!"

The man broke into a run with a turn of speed that both surprised and frightened the scattering group. In the heightened sense of panic and need to get away from the beating they knew they would get, boys bumped into each other, pushed and jostled some tripping and stumbling in the race to get off the wharf before they were cornered. As the group burst apart, the small boy with his treasures was knocked clean off the wharf, his head smacking the stonework edge with a sickening thud and his body falling towards the water far below.

Some of the boys noticed him fall and hesitated while pointing and shouting. Most, too intent on their own safety and salvation just ran, looking for escape. Baldor, being the closest to the boy, was all too aware of the fall and found himself looking directly to the water trying to see the lad amongst the splash, bubbles and turbulence that marked his entry into the pale green water. He was dimly aware of the shouts to scatter and run and the harsher, angry tones of the approaching man. After what seemed like forever to him the little body floated up, trapped air from the fall caught in the boy's tunic acting as a buoyancy aid. The lad however was motionless and face down.

Baldor hesitated only for a moment then leapt from the wharf, clearing the floating body and hitting the water hard. The water came over his head in a boiling rush, his body seeming to go deeper and deeper, all sounds from above gone, just the roar of bubbles in his ears. He kicked hard; his arms flailing trying to pull himself back to the surface. As he broke from the watery embrace, his lungs sucked in the precious air as he looked about for the boy. Spying him close by, he rolled into his swimming stroke and closed on him.

Wrapping his hand in the boy's tunic, he drew him close, treading water and fighting to keep them both afloat. He rolled the boy over onto his back and pulled the freckled, bloodied face into his chest. The blood ran freely from the gash above the flickering eyes and mixed with the water that washed over them both. Baldor was now gasping with the effort of supporting them both, his free arm thrashing the water as he tried to swim. He was aware of shouts from the wharf, cries for a rope and men running down the steps to sea level and encouraging him to kick-out towards them. Swallowing the salty water, coughing and slipping under the surface, he fought doggedly to keep the pair of them afloat. Slowly, with lungs heaving and body aching with the effort he propelled himself and his rag doll bundle, stroke by stroke towards the steps. Just when he thought he could keep them afloat no longer strong hands lifted the boy from him, himself being dragged clear of the water a moment later.

Deposited roughly on the wooden landing at the base of the steps, his tunic plastered to his body, heart racing and lungs gasping he started to shake, not from the cold but from the shock of it all. The small boy began to stir, coughing and spitting water, vomit and mucus, his eyes rolling and eyelids flickering. Pandemonium ensued, men and boys shouting, fussing and arguing the best course of action, the two boys pushed this way and that in the mayhem.

A commanding voice carried from the top of the steps to the water's edge, the noise and argument ceased as all eyes looked skyward.

"I said; get the boys up here now!"

"Yes Sir, right away sir!"

The two sodden boys were picked up and carried quickly up the steps. Baldor shaking and the small boy coming to his senses between further spasms of coughing and vomiting.

The commanding voice was shouting for cloaks to wrap the boys in, the man removing his own to wrap Baldor. Both boys were propped sitting up while being rubbed and dried through the cloaks, each assessed for damage by probing hands, the small boys split head covered and bandaged with strips of cloth cut from another cloak. The man issuing the orders helping as well as directing, when he was satisfied with the state of the pair he turned to Baldor and spoke softly.

"They tell me I have you to thank for my son's life." He smiled warmly at the ashen faced Baldor "That was very brave for one so young, you have my eternal gratitude. Whatever is in my power to give, you have but to ask and it will be yours."

Baldor could only smile faintly, his frame still shaking slightly.

"I think… I'm going to be sick." He said, gagging as bitter bile came up into his throat.

The man leaned forward drawing Baldor close and supporting his head as he brought up seawater, wine and the remains of his orange.

"That must feel better lad! Now, what's your name?"

"Baldor … Baldor Targa, I'm from …"

"Father … father!" Mumbled the small boy.

The man drew the cloak tight about Baldor and moved to his son helping him to a more comfortable position, all the while explaining to him what had happened and reassuring him that all was well now, thanks to young Baldor. The boy's senses were returning along with some of his colour. He looked at Baldor, the same warm smile on his small features.

"Thank you! I …" He broke into another bout of coughing and vomited up more seawater and pieces of food. "I … I am in your debt." He bowed his head slightly. As he raised his head, his hand went to the small pouch on his belt. He rummaged in the leather bag then produced his treasure, 'Vulcan's Fire.' He coughed again then paused to collect himself before addressing Baldor.

"Bal … Baldor, we're now tied, this is my greatest treasure and I want you to have it." As he spoke, he pushed the fabulously coloured glass ball into Baldor's hand. "I will keep your bracelet to remind me of our tie." He added quickly.

Baldor felt the surge of excitement in his heart and tried to answer but could not think of anything to say. The two boys looked at each other intently, as if peering into one another's soul, a life bond made.

"Let me through damn you! Out of the way! Where's my boy? Baldor … Baldor?" Pushing his way through the group of men and boys came Baldor's father looking frantic. He stared at the two bundles in front of him, recognising his son he bent down as best as the ruined leg would allow to pull the lad close.

"You have a brave lad there, friend! A son to be proud of already, I thank Jupiter that he was here today or I would have lost my son, of that I am sure."

"Your son, he will recover well? No lasting damage?" Replied Baldor's father as he turned to face the small boy's father who offered his hand.

Baldor's father went to accept the hand while shifting his weight to his good leg as he turned to stand but seeing a gold dress ring on the man's thumb, shaped into the image of an eagle with spread wings, he recoiled from it as if diseased.

"Roman! Are you Roman?" He hissed through tight lips.

The man looked bemused and somewhat taken aback. The group of men and boys stunned to silence

"Yes, I am Roman … I am …"

"I've no interest who you are!" Baldor's father spat as he forced himself to his feet, his face twisted in hate as much as in pain from his leg. He reached down to Baldor and helped him up.

"Come Baldor." He said gruffly, removing the cloak from the boy as he spoke, pushing it into the hand of the astonished Roman.

"The lad still needs care, keep the cloak and keep him warm!"

"Lecture me not Roman! See to your own son and I will see to mine, leave us be!" He snarled, removing his own cloak and wrapping a horrified Baldor in it as he spoke.

He strode off as best and proudly as he could, away from the shocked group without a backward glance, his son held close and swathed in the cloak. When the pair were clear of the wharf and in a quiet corner of the yard he stopped and squatted down to his son throwing his arms round him, hugging him close.

"Are you alright Baldor? No cuts? No bruises? No damage?" He opened the cloak to examine the boy.

Baldor was tearful, still in shock and now confused, he had never seen his father so angry and distraught.

"No … I'm not hurt, I just feel sick."

He wrapped his arms around his father, his mind a whirl of questions, reasons and outright confusion.

****

"Mother, mother!" Baldor cried bounding up the villa steps two at a time and throwing his arms round the very serene and beautiful woman waiting in the cool shade of the portico.

She returned the embrace, kissing him gently on the brow, and ruffling his hair, all the while whispering endearments to him.

Her husband followed, he however forced to take the steps individually, his face lit into a smile on seeing his wife.

"Melandara!" He said holding out his hand to her. "I've missed you lady!"

Gently untangling herself from her son, she stepped toward her husband, her arms outstretched in welcome and love.

"My Lord's." She said, smiling warmly. "Welcome home! Come, I have food and drink prepared for you, I trust business was good?" She winked at Baldor.

The family entered into the cool of the villa and were met by servants with water and towels, the man and boy washing before partaking of the meal, father and son relaying the things they had seen and the details of the business accomplishments. Baldor's father however made no mention of the incident with the Romans, Baldor himself deciding not to broach the subject either, at least whilst his father was present.

Early evening gave Baldor a chance to speak to his mother alone. Showing her is new won treasure he told her of the game, the small blonde boy and the fall, as well as his father's reaction to the strangers and the total confusion in which he now found himself. Had he not been taught from earliest childhood to be courteous, considerate, and brave, to help when he could? Why had his father dismissed the episode and been so angry? The boy's father had been thankful, caring and polite; he had never seen his father behave so toward anyone before as he had to this Roman.

At the mention of the word 'Roman', he noticed a change in his mother's face, a look of bitterness and sadness played on her features. She paused briefly to gather her thoughts then drew him close, embracing him gently, placing her finger under his chin she lifted his head to look at him.

"The war Baldor, the war with Rome." She said in a hushed whisper. "Your father and Gestix both, they carry a hatred for the Romans which I don't think will ever diminish. They both suffered much, your father still does, he …"

"Should I not have helped mother? Was I wrong? I did not wish to upset my father, I …"

She gently hushed him, placing her finger on his lips. She smiled, a look of pride and love on her features, her fingers tracing over his face teasing his lips into a smile.

"The smile suits you better, come." She said, drawing him close and hugging him, speaking softly in his ear.

"What you did was right, of that I am sure, and it was noble as it was brave. It is a great thing to give a life, for that is what you have done and I know there will be a mother somewhere in Rome now who would tell you the same. She too would want to hold you and thank you for your courage and for her son's life. Your father too will be proud of you, only his hatred of Rome prevents him from showing you that pride; we have a brave young man for a son."

Baldor hugged his mother, a little more reassured, his mind eased somewhat.

"What would Gestix say mother? Will ..."

"I am sure he would tell you as I have." She said confidently, her face however did not emanate the same surety, her son with his face on her shoulder blissfully unaware of his mother's concern.

"A man without love, honour and courage is no man at all"

Anon

Part 1

Chapter One

The military harbour in the city of Carthage 219 BC

Baldor and the Shipmaster grasped hands firmly and shook.

"It's agreed then Baldor? You complete the fit out of those last three galleys within the next forty days and I'll ensure the full cost owing to you, plus settlement of the retention fees on the same date."

Baldor's face creased into a smile then a full grin. Receiving full payment was more than he could have hoped for in such a short time but to have the retention fee waived and paid went beyond any expectation the young man had.

"Thank you Sir! Thank you! I don't mind telling you that this will put me in a stronger position than I hoped to gain so quickly."

The two men walked as they talked, the Shipmaster the elder of the two ushering Baldor before him guiding him in the direction of the yard's administration buildings. Baldor stood a head taller than the Shipmaster and had to lessen the gait of his long legs so not to leave him too far behind. Barely twenty summers old, he was narrow waisted, lean and lightly muscled, his frame only needing the muscle to thicken and harden to transform him into a powerful man. The pair were in stark contrast to one another, both physically and in character. Baldor was quiet and of a serious disposition, the Shipmaster quite the opposite being jovial, light hearted and somewhat loud. The elder was rotund and thickening about the hips with middle age, his body having lost its shape as the muscles slackened. He limped along in the lee of the young man, his heavy jowled face atop his double chin wobbled as he went, too much good living and perhaps contentment aiding the ageing process.

"The workmanship from your yard is excellent Baldor, we have no problems with build quality or sea trials on your ships, we only wished your company were larger and could produce more of the same. Many of the other suppliers, as big as they are, produce inferior work, miss delivery dates and then spend weeks adjusting and refitting what should have been there all along." He gasped for breath as he spoke, the brisk walk and his overweight frame punishing his lungs.

Baldor grinned again, his white teeth standing out against his olive skin; his dark hazel eyes all of a sparkle. He ran his fingers through his thick, black curled, collar length hair, his hand hooking into and running around the leather thong tied about his neck from which a brightly coloured glass sphere hung. The orb encapsulated within gossamer, gold wire, netting and suspended from the thong by a thick gold loop; it caught the eye with its crimson tailed, fireball like shapes, vivid against its deep, sky blue surface. His long fingers rubbed and caressed the bauble, then remembering his wife's words, berating him for his nervous action quickly returned his hands to his sides and made to close the conversation and meeting.

"My thanks to you Shipmaster for your faith, this news will …" The Shipmaster waved a hand and interrupted.

"Your father would have been proud of you Baldor. It's no easy task stepping into the family business and making it work. Come! Share a goblet of wine with an old man before you leave."

Baldor would have sooner departed for home as Aiticia complained bitterly of the time he spent working which took him away from her, though she admitted honestly of her selfishness in wanting him home and near her. He smiled to himself when he thought of the love she bore him and the welcome he knew he would receive when he arrived home. He just wished she would understand that he needed to run the business.

Aiticia however, came from a wealthy merchant family where an army of retainers, servants and slaves worked to manage and run the family interests on a day-to-day basis. She was also used to the bustle of city life, numerous social appointments and gatherings that released her from any house bound monotony. Married and living now in the Targa family home and far from the city, he surmised she felt isolated and perhaps a little bored. Baldor's family, although of the merchant class themselves, could not compete in the same vein as Aiticia's, with their city and country villas, servants beyond count, and wealth beyond worry. Baldor however had always made it clear as to what he was and where the family stood in the social scale. Aiticia had willingly accepted him and for the first few months of their marriage, they had been both carefree and happy.

Baldor's father however, had died shortly after their wedding, finally succumbing many believed to a grief-stricken and broken heart from the loss of his wife, Baldor's mother Melandara. The lady herself having died some two years previous. A late in life and difficult pregnancy had claimed both mother and unborn child after the woman had tripped and fallen in her seventh month, bringing on a premature birth. The baby girl had been stillborn, the distressed woman surviving her child by only two days before loss of blood from a haemorrhage that the physician was unable to staunch, claimed her life. Thus with his father's death and being the only surviving child, Baldor fell to heading the family business.

He had been ill prepared to have this mantle cast upon him. He had worked with his father, but young love, pleasures and zest for life had found him placing work and business second, after all, he had thought his father would be there for years. The sudden death left him reeling from the loss and working long and hard to hold and consolidate the family interests.

The Shipmaster ushered Baldor into the office; the whitewashed stone building shaded by a high wall to its rear and refreshingly cool, away from the baking heat of the late afternoon North African sun.

"Come … sit please!" He puffed. "Let me pour you a wine, it is excellent, all the way from Persia. A little sweet but we can suffer it!" He broke into raucous laughter.

Baldor took the wine and raised the goblet.

"Here's to good business."

The Shipmaster guffawed loudly and tutted.

"Baldor! Baldor! Here's to life, pleasure and happiness! May the Gods smile on us and keep us all."

The goblets clashed and the men drank the cool wine.

"So my young friend, are you for home after this? Surely the ride will take you until after dark?"

Baldor grinned wolfishly. "I'll be home just after the sun has set!"

The Shipmaster burst into laughter again, nodding his head vigorously; his large portly frame shook with the effort.

"Youth! Youth! What it is to be young! Always speed, no time! Live a little Baldor enjoy life! Oh yes, I was young once and thought much the same as you do now but the war changed my thinking … your father's too, may the Gods hold him close! We returned wiser men."

"I didn't know you served with my father."

"Yes! Yes! With your father and big Gestix, being a Shipmaster did not prevent me joining the cavalry! I like to build ships, but I don't want to fight from them, I can't swim!" Again, he burst into laughter.

"How is Gestix anyway? A fine man that … for a Gaul!" He giggled again enjoying his own wit. "Looking out for you no doubt? And helping keep hearth and home together for you all."

Baldor smiled widely, his thoughts flashing to the big man.

"Yes, he is well, and as ever works hard, loves me like a brother … or a son even! He has always been there, since before I was born, he …"

"Oh I remember!" the Shipmaster cut in. "He would not leave your father's side as we came home from the war, that last skirmish at the foot of Mount Eryx it …"

The puzzled look on Baldor's face prompted the Shipmaster to explain further.

"Mount Eryx? Eryx, you know on Sicily, on the western side, General Hamilcar's fortress?"

Baldor still looked lost, the Shipmaster undeterred continued.

"Anyway during the fight, call it fate or the will of the Gods, your father and Gestix met. Your father saved Gestix's life and before the turn of battle, Gestix had returned the debt. It saw a special bond form between them. As you'll know your father fell wounded with his horse dead on top of him, Gestix stood over him and would not leave him." The Shipmaster paused again seeming suddenly sad; Baldor however was hanging on every word.

"Ah, forgive me Baldor; forgive an old man that talks too much as the wine loosens his tongue, enough talk of war and death!"

"No, please! Continue if you will. I know little of what happened. My father and Gestix, neither would say much, I know they fought together but I did not understand a Carthaginian and a Gaul fighting in the same division?"

The Shipmaster made to pour more wine and settled himself in his chair; he eased his head back as though he needed to think. After a short pause the older man began again, the younger, all ears.

"Well, as I said we were operating from the fortress up on the mountain, those Roman bastards couldn't get us out of there!" He paused again and sipped his wine. "We were returning from patrol." He said slowly, as if the mists of time needed to roll back for him to see, as much to recount events. "We were still some fifteen or sixteen stades from the fort, your father's and I's troop that is, some thirty men in all. We were tired, our mounts more so, a day of hard riding behind us. We were just about to exit a small wood when we almost ran into a Roman cavalry patrol chasing a handful of mounted Gallic scouts across the plain. We watched for a while trying to gauge the situation, we being still hidden among the scrub at the tree line. Had we waited longer and seen the true situation I believe the fight wouldn't have taken place. Our Captain however, seeing the Romans numbered only twenty or so judged it looked like an easy win. Ever a rash, pig-headed bastard he was and eager for glory, he ordered us to the attack.

We exited the trees and had to move to full gallop to catch the Romans and the remaining scouts. It was the best kind of fight for cavalry, a running fight, no tight charge into an unmoving enemy flank, just a high-speed pursuit dodging bodies along the way. Some of our men went down though as their horses tripped on the fallen, such was the speed at which we moved. When we closed on the Romans we had the advantage of both surprise and spear length, it's hard to fight to your rear when mounted and at the gallop."

The Shipmaster paused to smile and nod to himself as if reliving the moment; sipping his wine he began again, Baldor perched on the edge of his chair, soaking up the story.

"So, imagine a running fight." He stopped again and picked some green grapes from the bowl on the table and placed them in a group, then placed some figs in a strung out line behind them, following these with black grapes. "See, the green are the Gallic scouts, the figs Romans and the black us." He pointed to each in turn, as he spoke. "Way out front we could see one or two Roman horses going rider-less, as we and the fight moved forward we saw Gestix." He placed a small orange in the middle of the figs.

"Not that we knew who he was then mind. His mount dead, he on foot and facing the oncoming Romans. Two were already dead in front of him, a third screaming in the dirt with his horse hamstrung on top of him.

Most men would have tried to run had they been unhorsed, tis natural to want to get away from being crushed or ridden down, but I tell you Baldor, he just stood there, like some great tree weathering a storm. Calm he was, but full of fight, as we came past he'd taken another Roman down, he was, is a brave man, a formidable warrior."

The Shipmaster shook his head gently, not in disbelief at his words but in sad respect at the events he recounted. Baldor's attention was acute, he was about to ask questions when the Shipmaster began again, moving the fruit as he spoke.

"So, most of the scouts are dead." He said removing nearly all the green grapes. "The fight is moving past Gestix as we closed on the last of the Romans." He pushed the figs and the black grapes past the orange.

"This is where the trouble really began, as I said, the fight would never have taken place had we waited longer, because in our rear there appeared more Roman cavalry or Equites as they call them. Heavy cavalry anyway, close enough to a hundred of them, that's about a third of a Legion's strength in horse!

We'd had the best of the current fight, most of the Romans dead or down by this point, with one scout still mounted if I remember correctly, our own troop not in too bad a shape. We knew we had no chance in the fight that was coming so we turned for the fort. Speed was of the essence with the fresh Roman cavalry spilling onto the plain and coming for us at the gallop. We milled about collecting our injured and looking to remount those that were unhorsed, men were frantic to be gone; your father called to me and pointed back to Gestix. He was collecting javelins and sticking them in the ground in front of him, I'll be honest I thought him mad. He sheathed his sword and picked up a fighting spear turning to face the Roman cavalry, he intended to sell his life dearly. I urged your father we needed to be away, instead what does he do?"

The Shipmaster looked to Baldor as if wanting an answer; Baldor just stared at him wide-eyed.

"I'll tell you what he did lad; he galloped back towards Gestix and the oncoming Roman horse! Madness, madness! It was." The Shipmaster shook his head and closed his eyes as he spoke. "The distance and time to reach Gestix and away again were too great, but the bravery of it, aye the bloody bravery of it! … Your father told me later he couldn't leave the big Gaul to be ridden down, his courage in the face of the odds merited salvation, he said. Anyway, the Captain ordered us away; we thought your father lost as he wouldn't listen to our shouts and calls." The Shipmaster paused to drain his cup. "I tell you lad, the pair of them are two of the bravest men I have met."

He poured more wine for himself and offered Baldor who held up his goblet without taking his gaze from him.

"What happened from there Sir? Please, tell me the rest!"

"Well lad, here's where the Gods took a hand I say." He paused to sip his wine. "We had not gone more than a stade or so in the direction of the fort when we ran into more of our own cavalry coming towards us. Apparently the movement of the Roman horse had been reported back at the fort and the General, may Baal bless him, had dispatched our heavy cavalry to intercept them. Well that changed things! Our heavy cavalry were thundering towards us moving from column to line as they came, filling the plain and preparing to roll up the oncoming Roman column."

"What of my father, sir and Gestix? What …?"

The Shipmaster smiled at Baldor, cutting him short as he raised his hand for silence.

"We turned about and fell in, in front of our cavalry, merging ourselves into their ranks at the gallop. What a feeling that is, moving at break-neck speed, spear canted and shield locked. The ground eaten up before you, your horse at full stretch beneath you and the noise! Oh the noise! It rises up like thunder till it deafens you, the pounding hooves, the war cries the rattle of metal and the creak of harness, you feel as if nothing can stop you, you are invincible!"

The Shipmaster was excited at his own tale and almost breathless from the telling, in his mind's eye revisiting that day so many years before.

"I could see your father coming towards us too, he had Gestix in pillion behind him but they could not put enough distance between themselves and the Romans. The horse, tired from the day's patrol, pushed into battle then forced to carry two men and arms went down, your poor father beneath it and Gestix thrown clear."

Baldor bit his lip in anguish, his face showing the pain and concern at what he heard. The Shipmaster continued, the story coming out quickly now as if he needed to be free of it, to tell what had happened and ease the burden of carrying it with him.

"The Romans deployed at the gallop as we had done, moving from column to line, both them and us on a collision course. Between both lines was your father and Gestix and the distance was closing quickly. Gestix was trying to help your father clear of the horse but he couldn't get him from under the beast, his leg was trapped to the top of his thigh."

Baldor shuddered as he remembered the ruined and wasted leg his father had dragged around while imagining the pain and the horror of it all.

"Our line and the Roman's was about to clash, all Hades about to break loose! I tell you lad those Romans looked formidable. Heavily armoured in mail shirts with huge shields and crimson cloaks billowing behind them like sails, sun glinting off their helmets as they thundered towards us spears canted. I saw Gestix run from your father and in truth I thought him human at last and seeking his own salvation, I thought your father doomed. Gestix however, went no further than to pick up a shield and spear, he ran back and stood next to your father, his back to us and the spear levelled at the Romans.

The gap between our line and the Romans closed quicker than the telling and we came together like the meeting of two ocean waves. The thunder of the hooves surpassed only by the deafening clash of metal and flesh and bone colliding, along with the groans of men and the cries of horses as battle joined, your father and Gestix disappearing from sight into the mayhem. The impetus of the charge slowed and eventually stopped as men and horses absorbed the impact and crush before dissolving into flowing, eddying chaos, spilling men and animals to bloody ruin."

"How do men survive such Sir? What do…?" Baldor was interrupted again before he could finish.

"By the grace of the Gods Baldor! What else could it be? I surmise a man's time on this earth is decided by greater powers than his own and with Baal as my witness, if you survived such carnage, you would believe it too."

His voice tailed away as he finished speaking. He gulped his wine making a physical effort to control his feelings, upset at the memories he'd resurrected.

"Tell me sir, what went on from there … if you will?" Baldor badgered.

The older man sighed deeply, cleared his throat and smiled warmly.

"Aye lad, I will tell you. Forgive my upset, I grieve for your father and for friends we lost that day, but I judge you should know what happened, if only in tribute to Gestix and your father's bravery." He wiped his hand across his mouth, sniffed and topped his wine again offering a refill to Baldor. He settled back in the chair again.

"The fight had developed into a sizeable one, perhaps a couple of hundred men all told. With the initial charge over it dissolved into a push and shove of horseflesh. We were so tightly bound together for a while that the dead could not fall to the ground. By rights, the Romans should have had the better of it being the more heavily armoured. However, their weight tired them and their large shield reduced their manoeuvrability in the press. It was a big shield to hide behind and men will do so when combat comes close. A man tires quickly wrestling with his horse, a cumbersome shield, a mail shirt and having to fight as well. Thus, men wearied, died and went down. Eventually flesh and resolve gave way and the Romans tried to disengage, slowly at first, followed by a general retrial. As both sides parted from the mauling, we recovered quickest and regrouped carrying the fight forward again. The Romans, already broken, scattered and a rout began. Our troop for the most did not join the chase, the few of us that still survived that is, leaving it to the heavy cavalry as our horses were spent and us weary. As the field cleared of the living and the carnage of battle became apparent I saw that which I would never have thought possible. Gestix was still on his feet, like a lone blade of grass sprung up after the passage of a forest fire, his shield gone, sword and a broken spear shaft still in hand. I tried to guide my horse across to him seeking your father but the animal shied and skittered; the bodies so thick on the ground it could not walk without stepping on them. I dismounted and had to walk then climb over to where he was. I expected to find him dead, no one on the ground could have survived, or so you would think. I found your father semi-conscious though his breathing was shallow; Gestix had laid a shield over your father's head and upper body leaving him battered and bruised but alive! Gestix looked like an apparition from Hades, his nose broken and bleeding, the helmet missing a cheek guard where it had been hacked away, the cut had opened his face through to his jaw. He was bleeding from both ears; the physician told me later it was the result of severe blows to the head. The remains of his tunic hung in shreds, his face and upper body spattered in blood and sweat, his sword arm red to the elbow."

Baldor shook his head gently as if in disbelief.

"It took four of us to get the horse from off your father's leg. I believe it was the speed of moving him to medical care that saved it from amputation but alas the breaks were many and complicated, the damage ... well, the rest you know."

Baldor nodded gently, his lips tight and face drawn as he thought of his father. After a moment or two of silence between the pair, Baldor asked further, his voice respectably low.

"What of Gestix? How did he fare? What of yourself ...?"

"Gestix refused to be treated until your father was away to care, then and only then would he allow us to help him. For myself I was luckier than most, see!"

The shipmaster held up his left hand to show a little finger missing, a wry smile on his face.

"You would not believe it would you?" He said waving his hand in the air. "All that carnage and I walk away with just this! It was my own doing too. I lost my shield when it was hacked to pieces, I fought with my sword and good luck only. Anyway, this Roman closed on me, full of fight he was, screaming and hacking like a madman. We ended up opposed with his sword arm, directly against mine, so a shield was of no use anyway. Remember I said that the press was such that the Roman shields became trapped, well that's what happened, this distracted him and perhaps he surmised someone had grabbed it? Our blades were parrying on high when he glanced to his left as his shield became jammed, time enough for me to punch him, hoping to catch him in the throat or under the chin. Well, as he turned back my fist collided with his face instead and my finger somehow hooked under his cheek piece. He ended up unconscious then dead when I stabbed him and I had my finger ripped off! ... As I said I was luckier than most."

The Shipmaster's voice tailed away as he finished his account, the pain in the telling evident on his fleshy, weathered face. He coughed and cleared his throat, his eyes moist.

"So Baldor, that's how it was, Gestix came home with your father as you know, the war was finishing then anyway. They've been inseparable since that day, a strange companionship I grant you but one forged from bravery and nobility of the soul, for each has held the other's life in his hand."

Baldor finished his wine, swilling the last of it around his mouth, savouring the taste.

"So my young friend, that is what I know of your father and Gestix and how they came to be the friends they were. War does strange things and sometimes some good comes of it, you have a loyal and trustworthy friend in the Gaul and I am sure he will care for you as he did your father."

"Yes … yes, you are right. He was there for me when my mother passed on and again when my father followed. In truth he has been or is, parent, friend and guide, he is I deem, the elder brother I never had."

The Shipmaster nodded sagely his eyes looking into space still remembering the events of long ago.

"More wine Baldor?"

"No thank you Sir, I'm for home as my wife awaits and I would share this good business news with her. I thank you for your trust, your hospitality and knowledge of my father."

With a rattle of chairs across the marble tiled floor, the pair rose from the table and out into the last rays of the sun. The stifling heat of the day replaced by a warm, humid evening; the crickets whirred and clicked competing with the cicadas for the rights to the evening chorus.

"Time's running late Baldor! Will you not consider staying at my house tonight? Darkness will fall before you make home, we can easily find one more place for supper."

Baldor hesitated as though he was about to acquiesce, he enjoyed the older man's genial company and the thought of a good supper without a late ride home appealed.

The Shipmaster, seeing Baldor's indecisiveness continued.

"Right Baldor! Supper it is and …"

"Thank you sir, but I … err, Aiticia will be expecting …"

"Come on lad! You're most welcome, its stuffed quail and I have some more of that Persian wine, enough …"

"Thank you sir but I must say no." He replied more confidently this time. "Aiticia will have looked for me long since, she …"

The Shipmaster burst into laughter again, his body shaking and his face creasing in mirth, he waved his arm as if in understanding.

"I understand Baldor!" He said between fits of laughter. "I understand! I was young once too! Nowadays though a good supper and a decent wine has more appeal for me."

Baldor smiled while looking bashful and blushing slightly.

Chapter Two

The two men crossed the courtyard, the Shipmaster bellowing for Baldor's horse to be brought.

A servant appeared leading a horse as black as night itself, the animal tossing it's head as it caught scent of its master, it's hooves prancing and raising small dust clouds as it twisted and stepped sideways.

"By the Gods Baldor! That's a spirited animal and a fine beast to boot! Who leads who my young friend?"

Baldor grinned. "In truth, sometimes I am not sure, but we're good friends, Risto and I."

Baldor took the reins and smoothed the crimson, padded blanket that lay across the animal's back. The horse turned its head into his chest pushing him gently as if in greeting, sniffing and snorting as it did so. Baldor stroked the shiny black face and whispered quietly, calming the animal ready to mount.

"Safe journey Baldor." The Shipmaster called, raising his hand in farewell.

Baldor threw his leg over the horse and swung himself onto its back.

"My thanks again sir! I will see you ere the forty days comes nigh."

Raising a hand in salute, he wheeled the horse about and trotted out of the courtyard.

Man and horse wound their way along the cobbled road as it snaked away from the shipyard, passing huge stone warehouses, animal holding pens with their accompanying stench and then through the now empty slave market. Leaving the waterfront behind he entered the outskirts of the city, passing through stifled, narrow streets lined with shops, inns and brightly canopied market stalls that spilled out onto the road. Vendors were closing up from the day's business and clearing their wares as he passed, some hopefuls still offering to sell him everything from fresh fruit to lucky charms to keep him from evil. Beggars rattled their bowls calling for alms while offering blessings and prayers in exchange and from balconies and street corners, the whores called to him with promises of wine and journeys to paradise. The streets opened out into grand, stone-flagged plazas and here the temples of Baal Hammon and Tanith the mother Goddess stood in white marble carved splendour. Their heavy cedar doors thrown open and flanked by braziers that smoked and smouldered grey clouds of sweet, heady incense. From within, acolytes and priests chanted and sung calling the faithful to worship. Exiting the plazas, he came to the residential quarter and the magnificent city residences of the aristocracy, diplomats and politicians. Many of the houses rose from the street to three and four stories in height, the grander of which boasted large, high walled private gardens to their rear or ornate plant and shrub lined roof terraces.

A patrol of heavily armed city guards marched past him, resplendent in burnished bronze helmets and carrying white-faced shields with the crescent and horse emblems of Carthage emblazoned across them in gold paint, the cadence of their feet echoing along the road. As the sun dipped behind the tallest buildings and the light faded, oil lamps were flickering into life and casting golden pools of light from windows across the road. Cooking smells drifted on the air as servants and slaves prepared the evening meal for their betters. Nearing the city limits the buildings were replaced by market gardens and trees. In the distance, beyond the now dusky hills, the moon eased into view at the beginning of its nightly journey across the heavens, the face full and deep copper-gold in colour, a harvest moon. It bathed the land in a silvery spectral glow, lighting the road ahead for the man and his horse and picking out the features of the land in luminous brilliance or casting them into shadow and silhouette where the light did not fall.

Baldor eased his mount into a trot. Feeling Risto stretch beneath him, he moved to a gentle canter, at the same time patting the flanks and whispering words of encouragement to the animal. The gardens and trees gave way to olive groves, planted in orderly rows. Grape vines also stretched in long lines away from the road and disappeared up the hillside into the gloom. Moving into a crouch across Risto's back, he took it from a canter to a gallop. Crouching and gripping the smooth flanks with his legs, he wrapped the reins in his hands then into the long silky mane as he tucked his face in alongside Risto's neck.

Trusting to the horse to keep to the road Baldor gave the animal its head, the horse stretched itself into the pace and hurtled along the cobbled road relishing the freedom and delighting the man on its back, the two melting together, becoming one fluid being.

****

All was silent in the evening air, only the pounding hooves and the strong steady breathing of the horse disturbed the peace. Feeling and smelling the horse's sweat Baldor began to ease the pace, whispering softly.

"Steady Risto! Steady! Almost home. A rub down for you, some oats and fresh water, for me a bath and a jug of wine methinks!"

Seeing the lights of his villa twinkling in the distance, he slowed the horse to a trot. The gentle breeze rustled the leaves of the fruit trees in the nearby orchard carrying the sweet fragrance of orange blossom on it; peace and tranquillity seemed to emanate from the surroundings. He eased into a sitting position, breathing the heady scent and relishing the thoughts of home. Resisting the need for urgency now, he slowed Risto to a walk, allowing the animal to regulate and slow its breathing and to relax the hard worked muscles. As he approached the gate in the courtyard wall, a voice called out in challenge.

"Hold and state your business!"

"Tis I ... Baldor! Can a man not come to his own gate without being questioned?" He laughed as he finished speaking.

"Sir? ... Sir, tis you! You're late come. We looked for you before dark!"

"Well open the gate good Hator, else we be here till gone sunrise!" He answered sarcastically while grinning to himself.

Baldor heard the old man shuffling down the steps from the wall then busying himself sliding bolts loose and easing one of the heavy timber gates open amidst creaks and groans of old hinges. All the while gently scolding the young man for his lateness and the worry caused.

Baldor slipped from Risto's back and led him through the gate.

"Hator, peace! … Peace! I beg you! I'm not a child anymore!" He laughed gently. "There's no need to stay up and wait for me, to your bed and …

"Sir, I promised your father, Baal bless him that I would serve you as I did him, I haven't watched you grow to manhood only to lose you to some accident on the road or find you murdered in the dark!"

Baldor clasped Hator on the shoulder and squeezed affectionately, smiling as the old man pushed the heavy gates closed and refitted the locking bar; all the while continuing to mutter about the impetuousness of youth and how no one ever listened. Baldor crossed the courtyard, leading the horse by the reins heading towards the stable block.

Hator caught up with him and made to take the reins,

"Sir, I will rub him down. Please, my lady awaits you … please!"

Baldor made to resist then saw the devotion in Hator's eyes, old eyes but bright and warm with love for the young man whom he had known since swaddling.

"Thank you Hator, but then to your bed! Tis late and old men should be at their cups not running after foolish youths with no sense of day or night!"

This time it was Hator's turn to smile and nod his head.

Baldor paced towards the torch lit steps of the villa, stretching and freeing up his muscles as he walked. At the base of the stairs, by the weathered and bronze, greened statue of Baal he paused, bowing his head reverently and touching his fingers to his lips then to the feet of his God.

"Thank-you O Baal, for the blessing on my fortune this day, and for bringing me safe home again." He whispered as he mounted the first stair, then turning and bowing his head again in deference as he reached the landing.

He took the last flight of stairs two at a time, his news lightening his heart and tread, tiredness forgotten for the moment. Reaching the top of the stairs, he was met by Lucia, one of the young house servants with a bowl of scented rose water and a towel.

"Sir, welcome home!" She said, smiling then dropping her head in shyness.

"Thank you Lucia, It's good to be home! I will see my wife immediately if she has not retired?"

Baldor talked as he washed the sweat and dust from his hands and face.

"Yes Sir, I will announce you. The mistress is entertaining Lord Carthalo and awaits you … anxiously."

Baldor's face suddenly darkened, the happy visage replaced by furrowed brows and sombre, black looks.

Quickly drying his face and dropping the towel over Lucia's arm, he turned on his heel marching towards the open corridor leading towards the villa's living quarters. Lucia ran after him, the water slopping from the bowl and the towel falling from her arm as she went.

"Sir, please! My Lord, I must announce …"

Baldor stopped abruptly. "Lucia … it's alright! Go to bed, I'll announce myself." His sharp tone and stony look prevented any retort.

"Yes sir." She replied as she backed away before stooping to pick up the towel.

Baldor was already striding down the open corridor his fists clenching and unclenching with temper and his mind whirling. Pulling the door open to the family's private quarters he stepped inside onto a mezzanine landing which led on through an archway, down a spiralled flight of marble steps to the open plan family rooms below. The room was large and well-lit with an abundance of oil lamps giving a warm, homely atmosphere. The contents and furnishings however were neither grand nor luxurious but practical. Simple chairs, large floor cushions, occasional tables and couches, some with colourful material throws over them nestled around the hearth. The fire was laid with kindling of twigs and fir cones. Flowers and plants covered the front of the dog grate, screening it whilst unneeded. Rugs of various shapes and sizes were scattered over the creamy tiled floor, with the more intricately patterned and brightly coloured ones hung from the wall. A large table complete with dining couches was placed near the un-shuttered windows which looked out over the family's private garden. The warm evening air bringing the scent of daphnes and sweet woodruff into the room. Outside, torches mounted on poles the height of a man blazed amongst the foliage, lighting the front of the house and casting the dancing shadows of breeze stirred palms and shrubs onto the path.

Baldor paused to compose himself. Clearing his throat and calming his breathing, he looked down the steps to the living area. He saw Aiticia perched on the edge of the settle holding a cushion across her stomach, which she hugged closely. A man stood in the middle of the floor with his hands hooked into his robe at the shoulders, his head up and chest puffed out, an air of superiority and self-importance emanating from him. He was tall, slim of build and dark haired; his close cut beard lined his jaw and came to a small point at his chin. His features were sharp as if chiselled from granite, his eyes dark and insidious like those of a hawk.

"So, those are the facts my dear Aiticia, hard I know but never ..."

"Carthalo Samilcar!" Baldor hissed through tight lips, his tone far from civil. "What do you want? You arrive unannounced and unwelcome!" His mouth curled into a snarl, the blood-pounding drum-like in his temples as he started down the stairs.

"Baldor!" Aiticia exclaimed in relief.

"Well ... Baldor Targa! ... You return!" Carthalo sneered in an oily tone. "And that's no way to talk to a guest, especially one to whom you are indebted."

The hostility and dislike between the men had Aiticia squirming on the settle, looking first to her husband and then back to Carthalo. Baldor reached the bottom of the stairs pointing an accusing finger at Carthalo.

"I owe money to your father, nothing else!" He spat.

"What else is there?" Carthalo said while raising his hands in a hapless gesture and shrugging.

"I have a contract with your father which is no concern of yours! Now, I will thank you to leave my house."

"I will not! Whether you like it or not Baldor, we have matters to discuss. I was busy telling my lady here of such and the unfortunate position you find yourselves in." His words came out precise and clipped his voice nasal and rasping, his tone effeminate.

Baldor's face twisted in anger but before he could summon a reply, Carthalo continued.

"My father has taken ill, seriously ill. The leech thinks it is his brain, affected some way. We know not? He lies … and babbles!" He rolled his eyes as if it was all too inconvenient.

"I'm sorry to hear this of your father." Baldor replied quietly, making an effort to keep his voice steady, the sincerity however, was genuine. "He and I were, are good friends, I had not heard of his altercation, my prayers go out to him."

"Aye well, life goes on, as does business." Carthalo said dismissively. "Which brings matter's back to you and me. As the eldest son I now handle my father's affairs, so you owe 'me' money!"

Baldor's temper flared, unable to get his words out, Carthalo continued.

"The new law forces my hand Baldor." He said, trying to sound regretful. "What with this pending war with Rome and the increasing tax levies, the city empowers me to call in any loans owed and …"

"I know of the law Carthalo, lecture me not! You're father and I discussed it, he obliged me kindly not to call in my debt, we have …"

"I make the decisions now Baldor and I have a business to run, what passed between my father and you now passes to me. Believe me; it gives me no pleasure to see you in this position." Carthalo failed to disguise his sneer and enjoyment of baiting Baldor.

"Baldor, my father will settle the loan for us." Aiticia cut in tentatively "He …"

"Stay out of this Aiticia!" Baldor snapped, not meaning to sound as harsh but the words flooded out as hot as his temper. Aiticia visibly flinched for he'd never spoken to her in that vein before.

"A good idea my dear Aiticia." Carthalo said smugly, turning to face Aiticia and ignoring Baldor as if he no longer existed. "I would be happy to accept the settlement from your father my dear, seeing as your husband cannot service his debt."

"Bastard!" Baldor shouted as he closed the distance between them, his fists rising as quickly as his fury.

Carthalo, caught out by the surprise of the sudden movement could only manage a half turn towards his assailant. Baldor's fist connected hard against Carthalo's nose. As he rocked back on his feet, the fist smashed again bursting his lips and loosening teeth, the force of it knocking him backwards to the floor. Aiticia screamed and leapt up from the couch attempting to hold Baldor back from further destruction.

"Stop it! Stop it! Baldor, enough!" She cried, her arms encircling her husband her tears flowing and body shaking.

Carthalo regained his feet albeit a little unsteadily while wiping the blood from his face and beard and spitting broken teeth on the floor.

"You base-born dog! You'll die for that!" He spat the words through his bloodied mouth, the flecks of blood and spittle falling onto his robes. Pulling a dagger from his belt, he advanced on Baldor.

Baldor was still trying to disentangle himself from a now hysterical Aiticia and too slow evading the dagger that drove deeply into the top of his left shoulder. He grunted as the blade pushed into his flesh, the pain hot and searing. He rolled backwards taking Aiticia with him and both landed heavily. Baldor was on his feet almost instantly with Carthalo advancing on him with murder in his eyes. Baldor snatched up a wooden stool and used it to fend off the dagger strikes, he backed up guardedly as Carthalo advanced; the dagger pushed ever forward probing and jabbing. Baldor glanced briefly to his side, seeking a weapon. Carthalo rushed him; the stool however became wedged tightly between them saving Baldor as the dagger lodged deeply in the seat top. Baldor pushed hard on the stool and Carthalo fell backwards, knocking the wine jug and goblets from the table as he hit the ground for the second time. Aiticia meantime was recovering from the fall and trying to regain her feet. Carthalo pulled himself from the floor using the table to aid him while looking about for his dagger; Baldor however had reached the rear wall, pulling down a hanging sword.

Aiticia shrieked. "Baldor! Stop it! … Please … please! For the love of Tannith, stop it! … Gestix, Help! Gestixxxx!"

As Baldor advanced across the room with the sword pointed in front of him, it was Carthalo's turn to give ground now that his dagger was gone. Aiticia stepped in between the men once more, hysterically beseeching her husband for peace. At that instance, Carthalo snatched up the wine pitcher from the floor and hurled it with all his strength at Baldor to keep him away. The heavy bronze pitcher collided with Aiticia's head, hitting her temple with a sickening thud and she fell as if pole-axed.

Baldor dropped the sword and ran to her, scooping her up in his arms, the blood from his wound dripping onto and wetting her white dress.

"No, no, no! ... Oh no! Aiticia! Aiticia! ... Oh nooooooo!"

Carthalo, equally shocked by the sudden turn of events remained rooted to the spot just staring.

Baldor frantically sought signs of life in Aiticia, putting a hand on her heart then holding his cheek near her nose and mouth as he felt for her breath. Holding her close he whispered her name over and over, shaking her gently as if trying to wake her. His heart sunk like a lead weight and his senses reeled. Sheer disbelief at what he was seeing washed over him, his mouth suddenly dry, his stomach hot and heavy, his temperature soaring.

"I didn't mean it to hit her, I ..." Carthalo beseeched, trying to find the words.

Baldor looked up from Aiticia cradled limply in his arms. "You've killed her! She's dead, dead! Baal almighty, she ... you murdering bastard! ... Murderer!" Baldor shouted, his voice breaking with emotion.

Hearing the word murderer, shocked Carthalo to his senses. Accident or not Aiticia was dead, slain in her own house! Moreover, with her husband also wounded, the authorities could only view this dimly. As powerful as his family was and despite the influence they carried in Carthage and the senate, he did not like his chances before a law court. Seeing the anger and menace in Baldor's eyes told him the time for talk and reasoning had gone anyway. He must get himself out of this predicament and tell his story to the authorities with no one to say different. Seizing his moment whilst Baldor was still in shock, he ran to the hearth pulling another sword down from the wall, retrieving his dagger from the stool he advanced quickly on Baldor, both weapons outstretched.

Seeing Carthalo's intent, Baldor eased Aiticia to the floor then did a backward somersault towards the sword he'd dropped. Carthalo was on him quickly, just as he came up onto his knees. Baldor's sword timely parrying the vicious downward stroke. Sparks flew as the blades scraped together and the men grunted and strained. Carthalo pushed in low with his dagger to stab Baldor's side but Baldor twisted quickly evading the blow. With both men's power opposed on their sword arms, the sudden move with the dagger shifted Carthalo's weight and failing to connect, he overbalanced. He stumbled past Baldor trying to regain his balance. Baldor swung his sword in a downward arc catching Carthalo behind the knees slashing through ligaments, muscle and the hamstring. Carthalo fell like a wind-broken reed. Baldor powered up from his knees, spinning on the balls of his feet. Raising his sword in both hands as he turned he cut downwards viciously. Carthalo looked up, unable to counter the descending blade it chopped into the side of his neck. He looked surprised as the blade cut deeply, stopping only as it hit his spinal column. He collapsed in a bloody heap to the marble floor without a sound. Plum coloured blood pumped from the wound and his twitching lips forming growing pools on the white stone.

Baldor, breathing heavily and swaying unsteadily on his feet grasped the table for support while looking down at the ruin that was Carthalo. He dropped the sword by the body and walked trance like, back to where Aiticia lay. Bending down he gathered her up in his arms, nuzzling his face next to hers and crying softly into her hair. Outside, footsteps sounded followed by shouts and at the stairhead, a huge man appeared. Tall and broad of statue his blue eyes darted around the room, his body in a fighting stance ready for any perceived threat. His bull-like neck rested on a massive, bared chest his arms heavy with thick, corded muscle finishing in huge gnarled hands, one of which held a long Gallic broadsword. He was dressed only in green and black checked trousers of the Gallic style fastened around with a wide, leather belt; a baldric slung over his shoulder supported the swords scabbard. His chest was heaving from the run, his face set in a scowl, the long drooping moustache of blonde whiskers adding a look of savagery to his formidable physique. His mane of long, dark blonde hair hung loose framing his broad face; his stooped crouch as he advanced gave him the appearance of a golden lion entering an arena.

"Baldor! Baldor! Are you all right?" He shouted, running down the stairs now, as he perceived no living threat remaining in the room. "What in Hade's name …?" He stopped himself short as he saw the carnage in the room.

Totally lost in his grief Baldor did not reply. The big man reached down to Aiticia first, looking for signs of life in her small body to find only death. His eyes wandered over a stupefied Baldor, inspecting and assessing, his fingers quickly checking the wound on his shoulder. He looked over to the body of Carthalo, the growing pool of blood telling all he needed to know.

More footsteps and shouts came from the stairhead; Hator and a few other servants peered into the room,

"Hator!" He cried. "Keep everyone back, send Malik to check the gate and keep it locked! No one leaves! No one enters! Do you have it?"

"Aye Gestix!" Hator turned to usher then shoo the gathering servants away from the stairs. Talking quietly, he dispatched Malik to the gate.

Gestix turned back to Baldor and spoke quietly.

"We need to see to that wound Baldor and Aiticia should be moved to a ... more seemly place." The big Gaul's expression was stony and his eyes wet. He sheathed the sword and wiped his hand across his face, gathering himself before he spoke again.

"Baldor ... Baldor!" The young man did not move, had not moved, his head still against Aiticias, his body rocking gently back and forth, shaking with sobbing. "Baldor, sir!" At the formal naming Baldor finally looked up, a blank, unseeing stare of shock and disbelief.

"She's dead Gestix, dead!" He said in a hushed whisper.

"We must take care of her and treat your wound ... come, come." Gestix spoke softly and made to help Baldor to his feet and take Aiticia's body.

Baldor came to his feet unsteadily, still holding Aiticia's body close as if she would slip away from him. He gazed at Gestix but without seeing.

"Come Baldor." Gestix led the young man and his precious burden across the room to the base of the stairs then up towards the bedchambers, he pushed the door open and Baldor trudged woodenly crossed the room laying Aiticia gently on the bed.

"I'll call Lucia to help." Gestix said, moving towards the door.

"No!" Came from Baldor, his tone emphatic.

Gestix did not contradict but instead stood to one side and bowed his head.

Baldor busied himself straightening Aiticias dress and smoothing out the folds then tearing a piece from his tunic, wiped his bloodstains from her skin. Taking her comb from the table and tidying her hair he retied the ribbon that held it, he gently ran his fingers over her still open eyes, closing them for the last time. Taking the water bowl from the bedside and squeezing out the small sponge, he carefully washed her face, dabbing gently around the large blue-black bruise on her temple. He finished by washing her hands then slipping off her sandals and washing her feet. Refitting her sandals, he bent over her head kissing her gently on the lips, eyes and brow.

With his task complete, he stood back from the bed. Though a little unsteady on his feet he bowed his head and closed his eyes, his mouth mumbling a whispered prayer between sobs and gasps of breath.

At the side of the room, Gestix quietly shook with sorrow and rage, his tears falling silently to the polished wooden floor. Aiticia had made a huge impact on the Gaul's life and the Targa household in general. She'd helped fill the gap left by the death of Baldor's mother years before, her affection for the men of her new family, Baldor aside, had been unstinting and without reserve. Her kindness and thought for others was similar to that of her husband but where he was quiet and serious by nature, Aiticia was vivacious. She had brought life and laughter back into the house again, as well as the much-needed woman's touch. Gestix in especial had been the target for much of her teasing and joking, his revelling in it being to the dismay of both Baldor and his father.

The room was silent now except for the ragged breathing of the two men.

Time passed but Baldor remained statue like, his head still bowed and hands together below his waist. His tunic and arm now heavily stained with blood, some of which dripped steadily from the ends of his fingers. Gestix placed his hand on his shoulder.

"Baldor, we need to decide what to do and I need to tend your wound."

There was no movement from Baldor or even recognition that he had heard his friend.

"Baldor, you must address your people, they'll want to pay their respects to Aiticia and to know what to do… come, and I'll help."

Baldor raised his head slowly and looked at his friend.

"Summon everyone to the reception room, I will address them there … thank you." He said quietly.

Gestix nodded and slipped silently from the room seeking the servants.

Baldor left the bedchamber closing the door quietly behind him, forcing himself down the stairs towards the reception room. As he entered, he heard the distressed chatter and weeping of the women, the men standing quietly with heads bowed, sorrow and tension filling the room. He walked to the front of the assembly and leant forward on the table with both hands, his head bowed. With a tremor in his voice, he began.

"Good … good people." The words tumbled out in a rush and he paused to gather himself, fighting to control his voice and emotions.

"Good people, evil has befallen my house, my wife is dead, murdered! Our lives and yours are undone." He paused to wipe his face with a shaking hand and to compose himself again before continuing, raising a bloodied finger to point.

"I have slain my wife's killer; he lies dead in yonder room but I have brought ruin upon us. I ask forgiveness of you all but I cannot and will not ask it of the Gods for they have forsaken this house."

Baldor seemed to drain further as he neared the end of his address; Gestix stepped over and held him.

"Baldor, I must tend your wound, it is deep … the blood loss …"

Baldor seemed to draw strength from the big Gaul and pulled himself erect, clearing his throat and gently pushing Gestix away.

"Gather up your possessions, Gestix will share out what I have between you all, take what you wish from here for I have no further need of it. Begone far from here before the dawn for the man I have slain has powerful family and connections, vengeance will come swift and hard to any found here."

He slumped back into a chair, exhausted. Gestix approached but Baldor waved him away.

"See to my people my friend, they are lost, you must help them first."

Gestix turned to the assembled folk, quietly and efficiently he gave out instructions, behind him Baldor watched with unseeing eyes, his thoughts and mind elsewhere.

Hator and his wife approached, the old man patting Baldor on the arm and shaking his head, the distress evident on the lined, weathered face, his eyes red. His wife, taking the scarf from her hair bound it over the wound on the young man's shoulder, her hands shaking and her tears falling freely. Malik knelt and taking Baldor's good arm placed his hand on his head in deference. Others came to offer their respects before filing out quietly into the darkness.

When the room emptied, Baldor rose to his feet and walked back towards the bedchamber with Gestix flanking him. The young man stopped and turned slowly to his friend.

"Go Gestix! See that all are away now, and that they have what they need, yourself included … Thank you for that … go now my friend."

Gestix nodded back at Baldor then disappeared, following the servants out.

****

Baldor reached the bedchamber and closed the door behind him, leaning back against the door he gasped for breath, his balance and legs unsteady. His shoulder ached as if gripped in a vice and his head spun; fresh blood still trickled from the makeshift bandage adding to the already large stain on his tunic. He looked across to the bed and Aiticia's body, his heart surely broken. Going to the window, he tore down the drapes. With difficulty he laid the material shroud like over his wife's body, his left arm hindering him as he could no longer lift it or grip with his hand, cursing quietly to himself at the disability he persevered. Using his good arm, he dragged the wooden furniture alongside the bed then laid linen over all before collecting the unused oil lamps, tipping the liquid contents over the bed, wood and linen. With a final effort, he picked up the stand that held the lighted lamps and tipped it over the makeshift pyre.

Flames sprang into life, slowly at first then greedily eating into the cloth and spreading quickly across the bed devouring the oil soaked linen. He sunk down in the corner of the room his energy gone now his task was complete, the desire to spend longer in this world no longer there. He closed his eyes, his breathing uneven and heavy from his exertions, his heartbeat pounding louder inside his head. Unconsciousness crept up with noises coming and going and bright lights flashing and dancing in his head, he heard the crackle of the flames and the heat of the fire on his face, then nothing.

Chapter Three

With consciousness slowly returning Baldor stirred, albeit groggily. His mind a jumble of conflicting information and his senses swimming as he tried to understand where he was and what had happened. He became aware of a gentle rocking motion and the pungent smell of hessian mixed with the strong odour of horse sweat. He found himself on his side and in the strange half-light, he saw his chest mummified in linen sheets; he was confused and suddenly afraid, where was he? If this was death, it was a strange place.

A sharp, searing pain in his shoulder jolted him, bringing him to a sense of reality. Still unable to move, confused and in pain, completely lost as to where he was he tried to call out. All he managed was a muffled cry of agony from his parched throat as his wound announced its presence with another bolt of pain. Big fingers hooked into the side of the sling-like wrap that held him tightly to the side of the horse and Gestix peered into the bundle, smiling.

"Good morning Baldor" He said genially. "It's almost light so we'll be stopping shortly. I'll have you out of there, your wound dressed and some warm food in your belly."

Baldor's senses and memory slowly began returning to him, his mind drifting back over the previous events, his heart suddenly stone heavy as he thought of Aiticia, had he dreamt it? The agony and throb in his shoulder and arm once more reminding him that it was real, all of it, the fighting, the deaths and the burning but why was he still here? His stomach knotted and his eyes filled again, a lump formed in his throat as the image of Aiticia's lifeless form became terribly vivid in his memory.

Before he could ponder further, strong hands undid the securing ropes lifting him effortlessly like a swaddled babe from the side of the horse gently to the ground.

"Stay wrapped Baldor, keep warm! I'll see to the horses and get us some food."

Baldor tried to reply but his mind, victim to confusion, uncertainty and questions was too numb. The pain in his shoulder racked his body with a steady relentless throb; mercifully, he drifted back into unconsciousness.

The smell of warm broth and a gentle shake brought him back to a hazy, semi-reality, his eyes trying to focus, his head struggling to clear.

"Come on lad, eat now!" Gestix coaxed. "Then I need to take a look at that shoulder."

"Where… am I … we …" The words were a dry, husked whisper, disjointed and almost incoherent.

"Hush Baldor, eat! Time enough for talk later … come … its good, eat!"

Baldor looked at the spoon of broth as though it was poison and then at the fixed, determined gaze of the big man holding it. He opened his mouth and took in the hot steamy liquid.

"Good! Now let's get all of this into you."

Baldor opened his mouth mechanically accepting the broth, his body at least relishing the warmth transferring through to his grumbling belly. The sun was just climbing into the sky and the land still tomb-cold from the departing darkness, his joints stiff and aching from the confinement and the night's chill, his arm burned and his head spun.

"Once you've eaten and I've cleaned that wound we can talk …well, I'll talk, you can listen. You've lost much blood and I don't want you overtaxing yourself." Gestix said firmly while spooning more broth into Baldor's mouth.

Baldor ate without relish and made no other attempt to speak, Gestix however, smiling and nodding satisfactorily as he fed his friend.

"We'll rest up while it's daylight and then move once darkness comes, just to be safe eh?"

Baldor chewed slowly on the tough, stringy meat in the broth, saying nothing and staring blankly. The meagre repast over, Gestix removed the makeshift bandage from the wound. Baldor's tunic was stained in various shades of red, from ochre through to bright crimson where the wound had bled, dried and bled again. The wound was deep and fresh blood was once more leaking.

"We need to stop the bleeding Baldor; it requires stitching then binding so you don't open it up when you move."

Baldor looked about disinterestedly, his mind again elsewhere.

Gestix lifted a small pot of hot water from the fire and brought out some clean strips of cloth from his pack. He cut away the ragged tunic sleeve and began cleaning away the old dried blood before working his way towards the wound proper. Baldor flinched as the hot swab contacted the raw flesh, the agony etched on his face.

"Bear up lad, I have to clean it, otherwise you risk an infection."

When Gestix produced a fine bone needle and gut thread, Baldor found his tongue.

"Leave me be! … Leave it!" He spat, the words forced out with great effort.

Gestix ignored him and carried on with his work. Baldor tried to twist his shoulder away from Gestix's ministrations, the sudden move causing him further pain and his face contorted.

"Damn you Gestix! … Damn you to Hades! Leave me be … I want none of it!"

"Baldor, sit still! I'll dress this wound with or without your help. We can make it easy or hard. But with the God's as my witness you will have that wound treated."

Baldor knew from past experience and the look on Gestix's face that further resistance was futile. When the Gaul decided to do something he would do it come what may and he resigned himself to his misery. As Gestix finished his ministrations, Baldor was again falling back to unconsciousness. The fresh pain, combined with the continued blood loss mercifully taking him into the warm blackness away from hurt and woe, for a time anyway. Gestix stood back from his friend, wiping the blood from his hands with a fresh cloth, his heart heavy, Baldor was in a bad way both physically and mentally.

Why? He wondered, why the lad? Had he not had his share of heartache and death already? What perverse game had the Gods devised now?

Carefully wrapping Baldor back in the linen sheets and hessian sling again and placing the damaged arm uppermost, he ensured neither the stitches nor the bandage could be disturbed, then laid the limp bundle next to the small fire. Calculating travelling distances in his head as he worked, he looked to the sun climbing steadily out of the east relishing the early warmth on his face.

'So, westward methinks.' He mused as he tied his hair into a loose ponytail. 'Numidia then Spain, you will have a little peace lad if I have my way, but first some sleep.'

After a final check of the camp and the horses, he rolled himself in his cloak and lay down next to his friend.

****

Time slipped steadily by, coming close to almost fourteen days since the fateful night at the villa. Baldor still slept a lot, either dozing atop the horse or if Gestix could contrive it, slung from the animals back, rolled in the hessian where his body was fully supported. Despite the careful ministrations, a fever had set in as the wound knitted and Baldor shivered uncontrollably while sweating heavily at the same time. Gestix changed the soaked clothing, as Baldor had neither the strength, much less the inclination to care. The Gaul washed him, dried him and strived to cool him when he was hot then wrapped him warmly against the cold night air. The physical tasks did not bother him; however, the cries and tortured mumblings from Baldor as he wrestled in delirium drove him to distraction. His own emotions ranging from black anger at the cause to outright, heartfelt pity for one so young having to bear such heartache.

Thankfully, the fever broke and despite all, Baldor grew stronger as the wound began to heal. Baldor's mind was the main concern now, he never spoke he just did as he was bidden then retreated within his own dark world. Gestix however cared for him unstintingly, tending the wound, feeding him and talking to him regardless of the one-way conversation.

Having followed the Middlesea coastline westward since leaving Carthage, Gestix calculated they had crossed the border into Numidia some five days back. Initially he had stayed well back from the coast road but feeling safe enough to move by daylight now, was content to travel nearer the road and even on it when it ran through the quieter country areas. He'd avoided the first large coastal towns of Igilgili and Saldae which he judged to be still too close to the Carthaginian border. Now, still heading westward he surmised they were three, maybe four days from the town of Rusucurru, from there a further two or maybe three more days would bring them to Icosium. There, well away from the border and any jurisdiction of Carthage, he thought it would be safe enough to seek a ship's passage across the Middlesea to Spain and Baldor's relatives. They had met no one other than travellers on the road and nobody had taken any interest in the pair, other than to exchange a greeting or confirm directions, there had been no sign of any soldiers or anyone else searching for them.

Gestix alternated from riding and walking, in between times making regular checks of his precious charge. Baldor woke occasionally, the big man taking these opportunities to get water into him and giving him strips of dried beef to chew. Baldor said nothing but accepted the water and the meat as bidden, his brows furrowed and still lost in his misery. Gestix dressed the wound morning and evening, nodding to himself with satisfaction as it healed and Baldor's health steadily improved. He still tried to strike up conversation but received only blank looks and stony silence by way of return.

The silence gave him time to think at least. He wondered about events back at the villa. Some form of search would have been made for them no doubt, questions asked, vengeance and recompense sought, for people like Carthalo Samilcar did not die in anonymity. Despite the unpopularity and hatred even of the man in and around Carthage, he came from a powerful family of senators and judges, people powerful enough to seek out those they sought, at any cost. Carthage would be too hot for Baldor and himself. Thus, he reassured himself of his decision to leave but what would Baldor think of that? Well, he would cross that bridge when he came to it, restoring the lad to health and sound mind were his first priority.

One early evening Gestix halted near a small copse of tall, leafy marula trees, which were set back and up on a hillcrest some way from the road. Liking the elevated but sheltered position, he set up camp for the night. The two men sat opposite one another over the small fire, Baldor dozing with his back against a tree and Gestix watching over a pan of frying bread and lamb strips. He was about to make yet another attempt at conversation when the sound of hoof beats came from along the road. Judging the tempo and speed at which the horses moved and the late time of day, he reasoned these were neither travellers nor merchants, such folk were off the road well before dusk. He tried to throw sand over the small flames to smother them but in his haste knocked the pan over, tipping the contents into the fire, it roared into life spitting, crackling and sending fierce yellow flames and black smoke skyward. There was a sudden reining in of the horses on the road followed by exited shouts.

Swearing under his breath, he made no further attempt to put the fire out, instead, he loosened the long Gallic broadsword in its scabbard while assessing the area for space and manoeuvre.

"Baldor!" He hissed in a rushed, harsh whisper, startling him to wakefulness. "You sit still and say nothing, do you hear? ... Do you hear me?"

Baldor just stared blankly back at him. The horses had turned from the road now and were threading their way up the incline towards the treeline and the men's camp. The animals were already snorting and blowing hard from their exertions along the road and whinnied in protest at being forced uphill, clods of earth flying high in the air from their hooves.

"Stand to and declare yourselves!" Bellowed one of the riders as the horses neared the camp.

Gestix made no reply. Glancing at Baldor, he shook his head slightly while motioning silence with a finger on his lips, his expression grim. In a heartbeat, the riders were in the camp area, bringing their horses to a sharp, vicious halt amidst dust and sweated steam from the animals. The rattle of metal and creak of leather seemed all too loud in the small space, the reek of horse sweat filling the air. The foremost rider was a man of Gestix's age, his bronze helmet hugging his face and pushing his badger coloured beard to a point where the cheek pieces closed tightly along his jaw. He was heavily built and well-armed.

Gestix felt his heart sink when he recognised Carthaginian weapons and garb. His blonde hair and height plus the injured lad, this deep in Numidia could not be explained away to such as these.

"I said declare yourselves, damn your hides!" The rider snarled, lowering his fighting spear to point at Gestix.

His comrades were both younger men, one no more than Baldor's age; both were casting wide-eyed, nervous looks about the camp, as if the trees might come alive around them. The horses sensing the tension, skittered, neighed and tossed their heads.

"It's … it's, them sir!" The youngest rider called nervously while dropping his spear level with the still sitting Baldor and kicking his mount forward.

In that moment of surprise, recognition then distraction for the riders, Gestix grasped the spear shaft that was levelled at him and pulled hard, dragging the warrior towards him while drawing his sword. Surprised by the lightning quick move, the man pitched forward off balance as the broadsword came up and struck him in the neck just below the chin. Hot blood splattered shower-like over Gestix as the man's jugular cut open. The surprise was still evident on his face as he fell, Gestix finishing him with a swift over hand cut to the side of the neck. He was dead before he reached the grass.

The horses reared and stomped, frightened and wild-eyed from the sudden action and the iron stink of fresh blood. The youngest rider was struggling to control his mount as it reared. His spear hand clutching at the reins and the weapon pointed skywards again as he fought to maintain his seat atop the horse, his attack on Baldor undone. Gestix pushed past the rider-less mount and seized the panicking rider by his flailing cloak; dropping his sword to use both hands, he pulled him to the ground. Spear, shield and man landed in a heap on top of the fire, scattering sparks and burning sticks across the camp area. Gestix was on him before he could move. His fist smashed hammer like again and again into the open helmeted face beneath him, breaking the nose and teeth turning the features to a bloody, misshapen pulp. When the soldier ceased to struggle, Gestix stood quickly and turned to snatch up the fallen spear. Spinning back around, he drove it down hard, skewering the man across the fire and to the ground beneath. The youth let out a loud groan and laid still. The third rider, stunned by the lightning actions of the Gaul and the reversal of odds, turned his horse back down the hill and galloped away.

The fire crackled then roared as the flames hungrily devoured the man's cloak and hair.

Snatching a spear from the ground as he went, Gestix ran to the edge of the trees seeking the fleeing man. The rider however was already down on the road and headed eastwards, back towards Carthage, the sound of hooves already fading. Gestix tuned back to the camp cursing, he crossed over to Baldor who had not moved from the tree.

"Are you alright Baldor?"

Baldor was deep in shock at the speed and ferocity of the fight and did not reply. Gestix knelt alongside casting his eye over him assessing and checking. When he was content with Baldor's condition, he busied himself dragging the charred and smouldering body from the fire dropping it casually to one side.

"You should have let them take me and be done with it! Let them have me... I am through with this life; go your own way, just ..."

Gestix squatted again and pushed his face close. Splashes, spots and streaks of the dead soldier's blood covered his brow and cheeks and stained his blonde eyebrows a vivid red, his face grim and his jaw set.

"Listen to me Baldor and listen well!" The words were said quietly but firmly and with a dire seriousness about them.

Baldor's attention was caught.

"I refused to let you burn or perish for many reasons: firstly, because I love you like a son. Secondly, it won't bring Aiticia back nor take you to her." He held up his hand to silence Baldor as he saw an interruption coming. "She wouldn't want you to die like that ..."

"How do you know what Ait ...?"

"I'm not finished!" Gestix snarled, hot with anger. He paused, struggled to compose himself then began again but quieter. Baldor remained silent, unnerved by the Gaul's flash of temper.

"As I said, it won't bring Aiticia back." He paused again considering his words.

"You're worth more than a dismal passing on a pyre lad, vengeance taken or not. I cannot believe the Gods would have it so. Tis a sore thing to bear, the loss of loved ones. Your home, your life changed beyond knowing but life's a precious gift, live it!"

Baldor was about to speak but a glance at Gestix's face kept the words from coming.

"I know you've had your share and more of heartache lad, but it'll pass, ease ... you'll become whole again, trust me ... I know! You've honoured both Aiticia and your family with your actions and the world's a better place for Carthalo's death. Nevertheless, I could not, will not, let you sully yourself and your good name with suicide because of it. You're my friend's son, my son even! And I'll kill anyone or anything that tries to take you from me." Gestix lowered his voice again. "I grant you that at this moment in time things are hard, difficult even but you have something that many men would give much for; youth, life and a friend that will never turn his back on you, hurt you, or abandon you come what may? Honour your wife, your family and yourself and live! For death will find us soon enough, hasten not to Charon! Now come."

Gestix stood and held out his hand to Baldor whose eyes dropped towards the ground as if seeking an answer, then, looking up to the still extended hand, he placed his good one in it. Gestix grinned, tightened his grip and pulled him to his feet.

"Now, come on!" He said, smiling.

As Baldor straightened and found his balance Gestix pulled him close, embracing him.

"It'll be alright lad, I promise you! Give it time eh, just give it time."

Gestix felt him shake momentarily.

"Come now, we need to get these men out of sight and ourselves well away from here." Placing both his hands on Baldor's shoulders, he held him at arm's length, studying the sad face as he spoke. "Their comrade's moving fast and I don't know how far he has to go for help. Go fetch the horses, they won't have wandered far, salvage what gear you want from the bodies. I didn't have time to bring much for you when we left and we have a deal of travelling to do yet."

Turning away, he shook his head while muttering to himself. "I still can't believe they dared cross the border under arms let alone venture this deep into Numidia."

Baldor did as he was bidden, managing as best he could with his good arm to round up the two wandering horses and tying them alongside the others. Gestix busied himself cutting and collecting branches and fronds to conceal the corpses. Baldor looked over the bodies, the older man first. The large pool of congealing, plum coloured blood was vivid against the dry grass; the glassy eyed, shocked stare of the dead soldier unsettled him and forced his attention away and to the other corpse. The younger man's corselet was in ruin, the spear shaft sticking proud from the chest, the broad head hidden deep in the flesh from the force of its entry. Baldor unbuckled the baldric holding the sword and pulled it free, then collected the helmet and shield that lay on the grass where they'd fallen.

"Forget the helmet and greaves Baldor, we won't need them. Just take the weapons and any food or money you can find and let us be gone."

"We can't rob these men, Gestix!" He protested weakly. "We're not thieves! They died doing their duty."

Gestix thought to remind Baldor of the fact the men had been murdered doing their duty and their weapons looted, what difference did the money make? However, with Baldor at least talking but perhaps temperamental, he let it pass.

"Very well!" He conceded. "Help me cover the bodies then we're off."

They dragged the corpses from the clearing into the undergrowth, heaping branches and foliage over them. Baldor wretched dryly as Gestix pulled and twisted the spear from the soldier's chest amidst wet sucking sounds. As the flesh reluctantly released it and pink lung tissue followed, he vomited. Gestix laid the spear down and patted him on the back.

"Bear up lad!" He said softly. "It's always the worst when the fighting's over, tempers cooled and nerves are frayed. Men harden to it in time, here's hoping we've seen the last of it."

Baldor hawked and spat then wiped his mouth on his tunic his face ashen, his body shook and he shivered with the cold now the rush of sickness was over. Gestix walked to the horses and pulled a blanket from the back of the nearest, wrapping him in it.

"Go on!" He said gently, pushing Baldor towards the horses. "Mount up, I'll finish here."

Baldor walked woodenly to the horses and managed to pull himself up onto the back of the nearest, tightening the blanket closer around him. Gestix finished concealing the corpses then mounted smoothly, reining the animal around he urged it on, bringing the two extra mounts along behind him. Baldor fell in alongside but rode with his head down huddled deep in the blanket. He made no attempt at conversation and Gestix sensing his need for silence turned his gaze to the path ahead. Gestix's apparent content demeanour however, was in sharp contrast with the thoughts inside his head, Baldor's mental state although somewhat improved was still a concern. The fact he hadn't asked where they were going or what the plans were worried him. Still, Baldor was talking a little, the shock of the killing would pass he felt sure of that. Gestix contented himself to some degree that he and Baldor were on better terms than they had been since leaving the villa. Time and a little peace would go a long way to helping him; all that stood in the way was the need to leave North Africa behind them. He realised this was not going to be as easy perhaps as he first thought, for he'd surmised once they'd left Carthage's domain and borders the authorities would have had to leave them be. To find Carthaginian warriors this deep in Numidia was more than he had bargained for, the authorities obviously wanted them very badly indeed, the two dead soldiers bore witness to that.

Still they were alive and free, for the moment anyway, another few days would see them to Icosium and from there by ship to southern Spain. Looking to the sinking sun for his westward direction, Gestix kicked his horse into a trot and then on through to a canter, with four mounts between them they could now afford to press on harder.

Over the next few days, they avoided the road all together, keeping parallel to it but back out of sight from it. Gestix, keener than ever to put distance between themselves and Carthage dug his heels into his mounts flanks and the horse moved to a canter. Looking at Baldor he found him already bringing his horse on, this was a good sign; the lad was thinking and responding without having to be told. Some hard riding would keep him from contemplation over the last few days and keep him active. The pair made good time, swapping their mounts to rest them throughout the day and finally walking them as evening drew in. Walking towards a glorious sunset they watched as the sun began slipping beneath the horizon in a blaze of scarlet, pink and deep orange; the very sky seemed to be on fire.

"Where do you think it goes Baldor?" Gestix asked, attempting to strike up conversation.

Baldor gazed at the fading glow and shrugged.

"No thoughts, no ideas?" Gestix prompted, smiling.

The sun disappeared into the ocean and the blaze of colours faded in intensity as if the sea itself was quenching the fire from the burning plaint.

"Can we eat now?" Baldor asked.

Gestix was perplexed; Baldor didn't want to talk but the request for food was a positive sign. The lad had asked for nothing since the start of the trouble, at least with food on his mind it was a step in the right direction, surely?

"If you see to the horses I'll start supper. I still have some cheese, wine and bread left over, courtesy of our uninvited company. Not much of a feast I'm afraid but at least we won't be hungry."

Gestix noticed a small shudder from Baldor at the mention of the soldiers and wished he had left the reminder of the encounter out. Reasoning Baldor was still traumatised from the fight and perhaps like battle shocked troops may respond better to a firm command, he continued quickly, his tone changing from conciliatory to direct as if giving orders.

"Rub the horses down. There's cloths and brushes in the canvas bag and give their tails and manes a combing while you are at it, then tether them loosely and let them graze. We'll take them down to water once they're cooled and rested."

It seemed to have affect as Baldor obeyed without question. Reassured, Gestix busied himself with the supper preparation.

'Time; just time, that's all is needed to bring the lad right.' He thought.

Chapter Four

Gestix and Baldor guided their horses through the copse of dazzling, yellow-blossomed acacia, horses and men ejecting clouds of breath vapour into the cold morning air. The sun was slowly rising above the tree canopy promising to warm the night's chill from both the men and their mounts. Gestix halted beneath the tree and snapped a piece of blossom from the nearest bough sniffing it and nodding. Baldor seemingly oblivious carried on, Gestix dismounted calling for him to wait. He wandered around the tree boles using his foot to push through the dead leaves and sparse grass.

"Aha, this will do!" He said lifting a lump of coarse, brown bark from the ground while sniffing again and rubbing it with his fingers.

Baldor just looked on, neither interested nor curious.

"Once this is dried and powdered it can be used to treat wounds. I'm not sure how it works but it seems to kill any badness in the flesh and keep it from infection, strange eh?"

Baldor just gave a blank look prompting Gestix to try a different line to gain conversation.

"It was your mother that showed me this you know! She said if you grind the bark adding fresh, clean water to make a paste then apply it to the wound it should take away any infection."

Baldor, his face morose just turned away.

"Clever woman your mother!" Gestix called after him.

'A fine, clever woman, your mother.' He said to himself though his heart sunk a little with the lack of response. 'I'll get him well

Melandara, I promise you! I'll care for him as you cared for Asmilcar and I after the war, don't you worry lady.' He mumbled a blessing and smiled.

Riding onto the beach the sunlight dazzled their eyes as it shimmered and reflected back like quicksilver from the tiny ripples on the water's surface, causing them to lift their hands as shades. Just back from the beach grey-white smoke rose from the roofs of huts and buildings as the first meal of the day was prepared, cooking smells, burning wood and the waft of fish carried on the gentle breeze, a peaceful scene of beach, calm water and settlement.

"Well Baldor here we are, Icosium. We need risk the port to take ship but this will be as safe a place as any methinks. Mind you, this far west in Numidia we should be clear of any trouble … for sure this time!" Gestix smiled then urged his horse on gesturing with a nod towards the red, mud brick wall that surrounded the town.

Baldor stared vacantly; he was still quiet, far from himself but eating and recovering well. Gestix was happier with his physical condition though the wound still needed care; he reasoned Baldor's mental state would come right eventually. Outside the perimeter wall, a shantytown had sprung up with simple palm frond, roofed huts mixed through with cloth and animal skin tents and awnings, though the town itself, the wharf and harbour areas were built of stone. The harbour and town was scattered across a broad, flat beach sheltered from the sea by a natural breakwater of rocks, this safe haven the main reason for the town's existence. Within the harbour, a thick forest of masts, like trees denuded of their boughs and leaves pointed to the heavens. One or two pennons flapped lazily in the light offshore breeze, the spars and furled sails easing up and down in time with the ships rising gently on the swell.

The horses trotted along the dirt road leading to the town, their hooves raising small dust clouds and scattering pebbles as they went, their heads tossed as they picked up the new scents of animals and habitation. As the riders approached the shanty dwellings children appeared from around the crude abodes; small dark faces framed by mops of blue-black hair peered from around the corner of huts, their dark eyes big and curious. Perceiving no danger from the advancing men, the children edged forward surrounding them jabbering and pointing, some giggling, others holding out their hands for coins. Gestix raised his arm pointing back to the huts.

"Begone! Away damn you! We have nothing! Begone!" He shouted.

The children paid no heed and if anything pressed closer to the horses.

Gestix dropped his hand to his sword and part drew it from the scabbard, the gaggle of children jumping back from the horses and the now angry looking man, the laughing ceased, hands no longer outstretched, faces showing caution and fear.

"Away I say! I'll tell you no more!"

The children melted away to the relative safety of the huts and tent shadows, the older ones holding the younger and whispering urgently, some pointing to their waists and gesturing the drawing of the sword and leaving Gestix and Baldor to ride on un-accosted.

As the town proper began the number of people multiplied slowing the men and horses to almost a standstill. Having to thread their way through the crowd the men guided the horses around market stalls, wares laid out in the street, lame and blind beggars, groups of slaves chained and hobbled together and small herds of ragged looking goats and sheep. The people were a cosmopolitan mix of native Numidians with swarthy skins, raven hair and sharp, hawk like features, white Phoenician merchants and tall, heavily muscled, black warriors from the interior, toting painted ostrich feathers in their hair. Also, Spanish and Greek traders and some desert folk, robed head to foot and closeted in swaying platforms atop dromedaries of various hues. A multitude of smells emanated; spices, oils, fish, horses, animal dung and unwashed humanity. Baldor's nose twitched appreciatively as it caught the aroma of food being prepared for breakfast.

"Hungry Baldor?"

"Yes and whatever we can find has to be better than that boot leather beef!"

Gestix turned quickly his face lighting into a smile; this was the best response he'd had from Baldor in days.

"Let's eat then!"

The pair guided their mounts through the crowds seeking breakfast and a welcome rest from travelling. They headed deeper into the town, Gestix still vigilant for signs of trouble, Baldor intent only on breakfast. As they entered the town square, a voice hailed them.

"Gestix? ... Gestix! What in the name of Baal Hammon are you doing here?"

Gestix felt a shudder pass through him as he looked in the direction of the shout and saw a warrior with his arm raised in both salutation and recognition. Who on earth would know them here? The warrior's Carthaginian garb giving him further concern. However, he rationalised, wanted men were not hailed in the street in the friendly manner that emanated from this man and he relaxed a little.

"Gestix! Get over here and tell me what you're about man! What brings you this far west? Come man, come! It's me, Balaam!"

Gestix was still unsure but keen to reduce the amount of attention fostered on him from others nearby and made his way towards the warrior having to push his mount through a meandering flock of sheep; Baldor looking about nervously fell in behind him. As the pair approached the warrior, two others appeared on the street behind him, wine goblets and pitchers in hand. Baldor reined up, his face anxious. Suddenly Gestix laughed and shouted,

"Balaam? Balaam! By the Gods! I could ask you the same question, I thought you'd be married off to some rich widow and raising a herd of snot-nosed brats by now!"

Baldor physically relaxed when Gestix slipped from his mount, he and the warrior coming together amidst much handshaking and backslapping. Baldor remained mounted watching all.

"Baldor!" Gestix urged him forward motioning him to dismount. "This is Balaam, he served with your father and I in the last war."

Baldor eased the horse closer and took a moment to study the warrior. The man was of medium height and build and aged much the same as Gestix, he was dressed in a plain black leather corselet fastened over a grubby white tunic. He was armed with an ivory handled falcata and a broad bladed dagger nestled at the hip. His cropped raven hair and small, well-groomed goatee beard indicated a Mediterranean heritage though his eyes were hooded and of deepest blue, the colour of the ocean on a sun drenched day. His nose was twisted and flattened a little at the end, testimony to more than one break. His lips were thin and down turned at one side where an old wound had left a thick scar across the cheek and mouth, the beard unable to grow over the scar tissue. There was an air of ruthlessness about him, albeit subdued and controlled at this moment in time. The two men continued talking loudly and excitedly as Baldor slipped from the horse and went to join them.

Other warriors were spilling from the tavern and collecting in small groups, some drinking and eating others trailing scantily clad women with them. Baldor was formally introduced to Balaam, a Captain now it seemed and of this, his own mercenary company. As the three men talked, one of the warriors disentangled himself from his giggling woman and tapped the Captain gently on the shoulder. Gaining his attention, the man nodded to where the road entered the opposite corner of the square. The trio turned to see mounted soldiers pushing through the throng and heading directly towards them. The Captain raised his eyebrows and flicked his head gently to the interrupting warrior then turned to face the oncoming horsemen.

Gestix glanced at Baldor and then to Balaam. As if sensing flight the Captain placed a steadying hand on his shoulder patting it gently as if reassuring.

"Stand where you are! Hold there, I say!" The foremost rider pointed and bellowed.

The horsemen pushed towards the three men in the middle of the square scattering people and animals as they came, the Captain and the two friends turned to meet them. Gestix cursed softly and stepped in front of Baldor while slowly moving his hand across his waist towards his sword hilt. Balaam again placed his hand gently on the Gaul's shoulder and squeezed, Gestix stopped his hand short, hooking his fingers into his belt instead. The foremost rider was an older man in his late fifties, his face all but hidden beneath a bronze helmet, broad cheek pieces and dancing red horsehair plumes, he pulled his mount up sharply and spoke.

"These men are wanted criminals, I will relieve you of them now sir."

Balaam lifted his head slowly, eyeing the speaker while displaying an irritated, piqued look.

"Captain Balaam's the name and you sir are, who? …" He said slowly and quietly, his tone matching his look.

"My apologies er, Captain … Captain Balaam, I'm Captain Hannar of the Carthage city guard, I …"

"Well! You're a long way from home then, Captain Hannar!" Balaam Interrupted somewhat jovially. "And this isn't Carthage, or at least it wasn't the last time I looked!" The comment drawing guffaws, laughter and ready agreement from the nearby warriors and their women.

Hannar pulled on his horse's reins as the animal skittered, his cheeks flushing from the casual rebuke, he gathered himself for further speech but was cut off again by Balaam.

"Well, good Captain! Pray tell me what have these men done and what brings you across the border, hotfoot and on such a hot day as this?" More laughter came from the assembled men.

Hannar looked as if he were about to explode, his eyes now big and bulbous, his cheeks scarlet and in stark contrast to his white beard.

"Captain Balaam! These men are murderers! They …"

"You lie!" Spat Gestix.

Balaam held up his hand with the palm-facing Gestix, motioning him to silence.

"Captain Balaam!" Hannar continued sensing progress. "Hand over these men now or I'll arrest and take them anyway and yourself for obstructing justice and the laws of the city!"

Balaam sneered then replied in a slow, quiet, mocking tone. "Captain Hannar! Before you waste breath further, I suggest you study the facts. These two men are mine; they enlisted this morning in my company in response to General Hannibal's call for men." Seeing Hannar about to interrupt, Balaam continued quickly. "Also … also, this as you well or should know is Numidia, not Carthage, and thus you have no jurisdiction here."

Hannar's face went almost purple with anger.

"Arrest them all!" He shouted.

Swords pulled from scabbards, the noise like the hissing from a multitude of snakes. People scattered as warriors pushed back for room, horses stamped, snorted and whinnied.

"Hold! … Hold men!" Balaam shouted while lifting his hand in a halting motion, the first time he'd raised his voice during the exchange.

"Captain Hannar." He said quickly. "As I said, study the facts." His arm outstretched and palm open, gesturing around the square and the assembled men. The mounted men and their purple faced Captain looked about to find they were surrounded by more than thrice their number by the mercenary company. Whilst the verbal exchange between the Captains had progressed, the mercenaries had quietly fanned out in the square in response to their Captain's earlier signal. The mounted soldiers looked at the well-armed, encircling men and then back to their Captain for direction. The square fell deathly quiet, the very air charged, more than one man held his breath else whispered a quick prayer. In this moment of pregnant silence Balaam continued, again in the same quiet mocking tone.

"So Captain, the facts would seem to be; you are surrounded, outnumbered, outwith your jurisdiction and shall we say … out of luck!" Balaam raised his hands in a no hope gesture and smiled wolfishly at the fuming man atop the horse. "And" He added flatly. "I don't think I'll let you arrest these men today!" His smile replaced by an icy stare, all pretence at niceties gone.

Hannar wheeled his horse about assessing the situation, his head-bobbing cockerel like. Finding things exactly as Balaam had said, he found voice.

"You haven't heard the last of this you mercenary dog!" He pointed accusingly. "You'll all be hunted down! Crucified! You …"

"Captain Hannar! Do your duty and arrest this filth." One of the riders shouted while pushing his mount forward into the conversing group. Although not uniformed as a soldier he was dressed in the full panoply of war.

"My Lord, I'm sorry but we can do nothing! You can see we are … err, ill disposed, there will be another day."

The man sawed on his mount's reins, pulling it around sharply so he could see Baldor more clearly.

"Bastard!" He shouted at Baldor. "You murdered my brother! You'll pay for that!"

Baldor was shocked by the outburst and recognising the rider stepped nearer to him and his horse.

"Adharbal! Listen to me … listen! Yes, I slew your brother but it was a fair fight, I didn't murder him!"

Adharbal however was past listening, his frustration combined with anger and hatred for Baldor etched on his face. Tension heightened amongst the warriors in the square as all eyes focused on the two men and their personal feud.

Adharbal's temper gained in ferocity, his horse feeling the tension, skittering, he in turn pulling harder on the reins to maintain control while he cursed Baldor again.

"You murdering bastard! ... Bastard!" He spat on the ground emphasising his disgust.

Baldor stepped closer trying to speak above the noise of the horse and the rattle and creak of the riders harness.

"It's the truth Adharbal! I tell you! Carthalo slew Aiticia and ..."

Baldor was now close to Adharbal who lashed out with his foot, the heavy, cavalryman's boot catching Baldor in the face knocking him off his feet onto the dusty street.

Gestix grabbed for his sword but as quickly as he moved, Balaam was faster, pushing the Gaul's hand away from the weapon and at the same time shouting to all.

"Hold! Hold I say! Let them fight, let the puppies fight!"

Balaam was very much aware that many men would die if this fracas developed into open battle. The mercenaries would be the victors, of that there was little doubt but there would be high casualties on both sides and he had no desire to lose men needlessly before they even left Africa.

All eyes remained fixed on the two men. Adharbal was struggling to control his horse whilst Baldor dragged himself from the dirt, blood pouring from his nose and lips.

"Your whore's life was not worth that of my brother, you bastard!" Adharbal shouted again.

At the derision of Aiticia, Baldor exploded into action. In the blink of an eye, he was at Adharbal's mount launching himself up at his tormentor dragging him from the horse. The men hit the ground heavily, the pair wrestling and straining, each intent on destroying the other. The crowd cheering and encouraging the combatants, wagers on the outcome being offered. Adharbal managed to disentangle himself and dragged his sword clear of the scabbard. Baldor scrambled up from the dirt putting distance between them and reaching for his own weapon, only to find it was left with his horse. Adharbal dropped into a crouch, the blade extended in front of him, grim satisfaction on his face,

"Now you'll pay, murderer!"

Baldor to his credit didn't run but crouched ready to counter his attacker.

"Bets are off!" Shouted one of the mercenaries. "Unfair fight! Bets are off!"

"Split them up lads, if they're going to fight, let's make it fair." Balaam motioned some of his men to intervene between the combatants.

Adharbal was quickly disarmed and Baldor held back from setting about him again, the pair struggling and verbally abusing each other. The rest of the mercenaries and the mounted soldiers looked on with great interest, the tension between them eased for the moment. All eyes following the young men as weapons were brought for them to fight anew.

"Balaam, stop this now and let us begone!" Gestix said. "The lad's still carrying a shoulder wound from the last fight."

"They will fight Gestix! Men's lives are at stake here! I'll not lose good men over two striplings and their quarrels."

Gestix was about to argue but the icy stare from Balaam had him hold his tongue. Sighing deeply he walked towards the young men; both were being offered a choice of weapons and shields. Pushing Baldor gently to the side and away from the crowd, he spoke quietly.

"Two blades Baldor. Forget the shield, it's too heavy for that shoulder. Fight as we've taught you! Offensively! Fast arcs! Carry the fight to him, do you have it?" Baldor nodded as he picked out two falcatas of similar weights.

"Keep your temper Baldor! Do you hear? He'll die just as quick and be just as dead once you're done! Keep your mind on what you are doing; remember what you've been taught." The Gaul gripped Baldor's arm tightly emphasising his point. "He'll bait you; he wants you angry, angry men make mistakes. Baldor! Listen to me!"

Baldor however was lost in his hatred, Gestix reasoned the put down and slight of Aiticia to be the cause so tried a different tack.

"If you want to do justice to Aiticia's name listen to me."

The mention of Aiticia caught Baldor's attention. Gestix lowered his voice.

"Two blades as I said. Keep him busy with your right and then swing low with the left but watch that shield. He's not injured so may be stronger than you, catch his blade with both of yours, trip him then finish him before he gets up. Do it quickly, no quarter, you have it?"

Baldor looked intently into Gestix's eyes. His brows furrowed and the hatred etched into his face but he nodded grimly. Money was changing hands between the onlookers as bets were laid, the earlier trouble forgotten for the moment, excitement replacing the tension. Only Captain Hannar remained aloof from the crowd, fuming silently beneath his helmet while the two combatants were offered advice both verbally and physically from the crowd. The onlookers pushing and jostling to see the action formed a rough ring around the two enemies, who glared at each other with death in their eyes. Gestix managed a hearty pat on Baldor's back in reassurance. Although he would've willingly fought in Baldor's place the lad's pride and honour was at stake. Also he reasoned, if he and Baldor were to have a future after this, they would need support and thus credibility with the mercenaries. Gestix knew they cared for little except money but courage and martial prestige among them were also big factors in mercenary life.

Before turning his attention to the fight, Balaam ensured some of his men did not deviate from their encircling position around Hannar's guards. He was leaving nothing to chance, should the duel end unfavourably for this Adharbal and the guards thoughts turned back to arresting people, he wanted to be in a position to dictate his terms. Content that it was so he turned to the pair now circling one another like prowling lions, each seeking an opening and the other's destruction.

A light wind blew through the square swirling dust from the baked ground, all went momentarily silent, then the rush. Loud cheers came from the crowd as Adharbal attacked Baldor at speed his shield up and sword high. Baldor met the attack, catching the downward sword arc on his left hand blade then swung in viciously with his right beneath Adharbal's shield. Adharbal narrowly averted being hit above his knee as he twisted to one side, the blade hacking the hem of his tunic and removing one of the leather pteruges from the bottom of his corselet. The pair moved apart to regain their stance and think anew.

"Two weapons! That's not fair!" Came from one soldier.

"Shut up! They had their choice; he has a shield doesn't he?"

The two circled again, each seeking the smallest chance or mistake of the other to get in and kill, while the encouragement and excitement of the crowd grew.

Adharbal attacked again though more cautiously this time, his shield lower and his blade pointing forward just to the side of it, probing and pushing. Baldor edged back seeking a weakness to exploit the aggressive but well-guarded attack. Back, back he went with the point of Adharbal's sword pushed ever at him, the shield locked in good defence over his torso.

"Those two blades are no good to him now."

"He should have taken a shield! Who does he think he is? … Two blades!" Scoffed another.

Baldor pushed forward quickly, his right hand blade clashing on the locked shield; Adharbal's ever-present sword point jabbed again driving him back. He sidestepped but again Adharbal counter moved, closing and jabbing all the while. Baldor attacked to the front again but Adharbal's sword beat his down while ramming the shield into his chest, taking the breath out of him before he could bring his second blade into play. This was followed by a whistling crosscut at his head that nearly removed it.

"Ohhhh!" Gasped the crowd

Adharbal stepped quickly after Baldor trying to take advantage of his momentary off-balance. His shield no longer in front but to one side as he pushed forward with the sword aimed at Baldor's throat. Although unsteady on his feet, Baldor took his chance in that moment of the shield being lowered. Sidestepping, his right arm shot out, the tip of the sword striking like a cobra and piercing Adharbal's shoulder. The sword was there and gone, with Baldor back in a defensive position ready for any counter attack. Adharbal was stunned by the speed of the strike and the change in fortune from attacker to the attacked; he could only look at the shoulder pumping blood, bewilderment on his face.

"Finish him boy!"

"Come on, it's only a scratch! There's bloody good money at stake here, kill him!"

The two circled again with Adharbal struggling to hold the shield in place on his damaged arm. Baldor content now to stand off and let his adversary tire further. Adharbal attacked again, knowing he must finish quickly as the shield was already becoming too heavy to hold. Baldor too pushed forward in a high-speed attack with both swords moving in synchronised, shimmering arcs, one hammering the shield down the other beating Adharbal's blade down. As the blades scraped with a hideous screech and a shower of orange sparks, Adharbal pushed with the shield but the effort was only enough to move Baldor back slightly. In that brief respite he tried to drop the shield, Baldor seeing his moment, attacked again. Adharbal caught trying to disentangle his arm from the shield straps, only managed with great effort to prevent Baldor cleaving his head open by parrying high with his own blade. The crowd cheered and roared with excitement. With Adharbal's right side open to attack and the shield dragging his wounded arm down to his left, Baldor cut low to the right thigh and felt his blade slice into flesh and muscle then jar hard against the thighbone.

With a howl of pain, Adharbal collapsed amidst a gout of blood and a cloud of dust. Whoops came from some in the crowd, sighs of disappointment from others.

"Go on boy, kill the bastard!"

"Are you going to pay up now?"

The crowd bickered, Baldor gasped for breath sucking air in great lung fulls, his shoulder felt as if it was on fire and the joint ached terribly. Trying to ease the pain, he bent from the waist, his hands resting on his knees the sword hilts still firm in each fist. Adharbal lay on his left side but leaning up from his waist, his head lowered to his chest also gasping for breath. His left arm still entwined in the shield straps the other trying to hold the slash on his leg shut, his face contorted in agony. Baldor straightened up and stepped across to his opponent,

"Kill him!" The crowd began.

"No quarter! Kill him now boy!"

"Finish him, finish him! I want my money!"

With only the odd glance at the fight, Balaam had discreetly watched Captain Hannar for any sign or command to his men, more than ready to counter any move he might make.

Baldor slipped the falcata point under Adharbal's chin forcing his head up.

"I'll have my wife's good name back now." He said slowly, his breath ragged and his arm shaking slightly. Adharbal, himself breathing hard merely glared back at Baldor, his face ashen.

The crowd fell silent all straining to hear what was said, many suddenly curious to know what it was all about, money and wagers forgotten for the moment.

Baldor pressed harder with the blade point drawing a little blood from Adharbal's throat and forcing his head back further.

"I've no real desire to kill you Adharbal for we were friends once." He paused to regain his breath. "But if you don't retract your insults to my wife's name, so help me I will end you now!"

To emphasise his demand, Baldor brought the second blade up to Adharbal's throat who swallowed nervously as it nicked his skin. Not a sound came from the onlookers as the tension rose another degree.

"I am …" Adharbal began, he stopped as his words faltered and faded, moistening his lips, he began again. "I'm sorry that I spoke ill of you wife." He gasped as his face contorted in pain.

"Aiticia! … Aiticia! You know her name damn you!" Baldor spat.

"I'm sorry that … that I spoke ill of Aiticia."

Baldor lowered the weapons from Adharbal's throat. He turned away dropping the weapons and walked back towards Gestix. The crowd became vocal, calls for wagers to be paid along with loud discussion as to the tactics or the lack of them, what did 'wet behind the ears' boys know of combat anyway? Gestix met Baldor and shook his hand, his other arm slipping around his shoulder his pride in Baldor evident.

The guards and mercenaries turned to watch each other as Captain Hannar detailed four of his men to help Adharbal, two to treat his wounds and two to prepare a litter to transport him back to Carthage. The guards began mounting up with Balaam all eyes, watching every move. Captain Hannar walked his horse across to Balaam and was about to speak when Balaam pre-empted him.

"The matter appears to be settled, so I'll bid you good day Captain and wish you a …"

"You haven't heard the last of this you …"

Balaam's lips curled into a snarl. "You interrupt or threaten me again, Captain and I'll cut out your tongue before I hack off your pompous head and piss on it! Now get out of my sight before my good manners give way to my better judgement."

Hannar was about to reply but the icy look from Balaam gave him pause. Instead, he pulled his horse around savagely, muttering under his breath and calling for his men to move out.

"I must be getting old and soft." Balaam muttered to Gestix. "Time was, I'd have killed that old bastard and warned him after, bloody city guards, all uniform and attitude!" He turned to Baldor. "That was a reasonable fight you put up boy, you've got balls I'll give you that! With a little practice you could go a long way."

Baldor looked at the Captain but said nothing.

"A long way is where we need to go." Said Gestix. "Thank you for your help Balaam, we were in trouble there."

Gestix nodded his head to the Captain by way of gratitude, respect and farewell then taking Baldor by the arm began to walk off.

"Not so fast Gestix! Not so fast!" Balaam caught the Gaul gently by the elbow. "I think you owe me an explanation at the very least, and your young friend here … well! … Let's say I am curious?"

Chapter Five

City of Saguntum, southeast Spain

The pale glow in the east forced a wedge of hazy light between the night sky and the distant sea announcing the sun from beneath the edge of the world. This dawn on the eastern coast of Spain, found a small assembly of heavily armed and grim looking men outside the command tent of their General. They waited quietly, the only sounds coming from the creak of leather and chink of metal as weapons and harness scraped and rubbed from the movement of the wearer. These Carthaginian and Spanish officers wore painted leather or bronze corselets with strips of leather pteruges hung from a waist belt that covered their thighs to the tops of their knees. Their weapons supported from leather baldrics, their helmets held under the crook of the arm sporting multi-coloured feather or horsehair plumes. Most were black bearded and olive skinned, their hair cropped short or loosely curled after the Greek fashion.

Some among them however, marked out by their height differed both in colouring and dress. Their hair the colour of rusted iron, mousey-brown or blonde and worn long, bound into ponytails or plaits, their faces adorned with thick, drooping moustaches. Some had shorter, brush like hair teased up into thick white points using wetted, powdered lime, the tufts standing out from their scalp like hedgehog spikes. These Gauls wore trousers of check or plaid and either a mail shirt or metal studded, leather corselet. Long broadswords and daggers hung from wide waist belts of bull hide or metal loops joined and twisted. Their Bronze helmets also differed, instead of plumes and feathers for adornment they had pointed domes, rounded knobs or in some cases effigies of animals or birds. Large oval shields faced in bronze sheet completed their attire and reflected the rays of the new day's sun. This mixture of Carthaginians, Spaniards and Gauls as different in culture and dress as they were, all quietly awaited their General and his orders for the day.

Behind the group, still hidden in shadow, the besieging army was slowly coming to life, cooking fires kindled, men dressing and strapping on weapons amidst yawns, stretches and moans. Beyond them, the wreckage of the outer suburbs of Saguntum lay quiet. High above them on the escarpment the main city stood encircled by fortress walls, which now resembled broken teeth where rocks and bolts from siege engines had smashed sections of the stone away.

"Hail Generals!" Said a man who approached the group from behind.

Clanks and scrapes of equipment sounded loud as the men turned quickly.

"Hail Sir."

"Good morning General Hannibal, sir" Replied the group, many bowing their heads or holding a fist to their chest in a warrior's salute.

The man before them was raven haired, his curled locks fastened around with a headband of purple cloth, he was of medium height and swarthy skinned, his eyes warm and dark, almost black. He had a straight nose and a firm sculpted jaw, scraped clean of bristles. Dressed in worn but serviceable armour he smiled at his officers, the warmth of it and his tender years seeming at odds with the older, stern looking group before him. For all his youth there was a presence about him, an aura which emanated extreme confidence and surety of both himself and his actions but also a magnetism, a warm, enticing friendliness which drew men to him like moths to a flame.

"Sir, your orders for the day?" Asked one of the dark skinned warriors.

"The orders for the day General Maharabal are that we take a morning stroll around the walls." He replied genially. "And whilst enjoying the air I will put my new plan of attack to you all, as usual speak freely, all your thoughts and ideas, for we need this city taken and to be on our way, we have lingered here over long."

"On our way to where? General Hannibal." Asked the tallest man, his rust-mopped head tilting to one side like a questioning child.

"Take this city for me Sergatatonix and I'll show you." He replied smiling broadly. "Oh yes, I will show you!"

"I'd rather you showed me my breakfast, I don't like fighting on an empty belly!" Quipped a bull of a man, this raising laughter from the group.

"Get us into this city, General Mago and we can eat it behind those walls, up there in the shade." He pointed toward the citadel as he spoke. "But for the moment come walk with me, it's a beautiful day and good Mago, it will give you an appetite!"

The group moved off laughing and talking, clustered tightly around their General.

Saguntum was nestled on a hill above the bay; the overspill houses below and outwith the walls raised on a plateau that lifted them just above the beach and sea. Most of these buildings lay in ruin; some partly demolished others blackened from burning. On the hillside that overshadowed them, the remains of what had been well-tended gardens, olive groves and orchards stretched in parallel rows towards the walls that crowned the hilltop. The trees stood out stark and black charred against the grass, which had been trampled from the thousands of feet which had passed through on the way to assault the walls above.

The group wound their way through the trees, one or two of them slipping on the dew-wet grass. Turning westwards, their necks craning back to look up at the walls rising above them; they saw sentries peering from behind the battlements. The sentries followed the group as they progressed with their circumnavigation of the walls. The occasional arrow flew towards the group, falling just short of them but forcing them to keep distant. Hannibal stopped where the ground was less steep and levelled to some degree, here the walls stood higher again to counteract the land change and at the promontory of the adjacent walls, a huge conical tower overlooked and commanded the area.

"Here! It has to be here!" Hannibal thumped his fist into the palm of his other hand as he spoke, his words full of enthusiasm. "Three attacks simultaneously along the length of this wall! I want the battering rams brought up and the ballistae and mangonels placed in support for covering fire on that tower. We'll use archers and slingers to keep the wall clear of defenders."

The men scanned the wall and the terrain, studying, assessing and weighing up the odds of success or failure.

"I have thought much on it and I deem this the place! We cannot afford further time to starve them out; you have seen the options for attack, so objections? … Thoughts? … I'm all ears!" He smiled genially at his officers, he could have been asking them the outcomes of a dice throw so casual was his manner.

The men consented by their silence; in truth this was the only option for a frontal assault. Hannibal looked around each seeking opinion or argument, instead he found grave and sage like nods.

"Well, as we are all agreed let's to breakfast."

****

By the following dawn, siege machines had been dragged into place and the three-pronged attack commenced. The thump of timber throwing arms against thick leather padding heralded the departure of boulders city-bound as the mangonels released, the rocks arcing skyward to smash into the city wall or over it. Crews of men sweated and strained to operate the huge catapults, heaving the windlass' to bring the empty ladle arms back before loading them again with stone. The weight of the boulders was such that they had to be lifted using small wooden cranes. Ballistas twanged, sending wooden or iron bolts longer than a man, on a collision course with the battlements, tearing at the wall or skewering any defender that dared show themselves above the parapet. The ballistas, akin to a crossbow in shape but in giant proportion, were tensioned by a windlass set at either side of the long horizontal beam that was the bed for the bolt, the required trajectory adjusted by the crew. The bolts whistled and whined as they flew, surreal and terrible in speed and size as they hurtled towards the walls. Where the bolts collided with the crenulations, it blew them apart, scattering fragments amongst the defenders and exposing more of the parapet denying refuge and cover.

The rams were mounted on huge wheels, their roofed shelters covered in un-tanned animal hides as defence against fire, a giant bronze-tipped timber shaft protruding from each one. The men inside powered the mobile shelter forward by brute strength, while the ram remained out of bowshot, warriors aided the trundling monstrosity forward, pushing from the outside. Once it came under fire, the men fell back leaving the internal crew to propel it onward. Once in position at the wall the huge ram was retracted along its bed of greased rollers before being pushed forward at speed to pound the wall again and again.

To the rear were ranks of archers, serried and screened from fire from the city by wicker screens. These screens were placed together to form a fence, from behind these the bowmen used powerful composite bows to release salvoes of arrows skyward. Howling like the winter wind the shafts fell on and behind the wall, killing and scattering defenders. Hades had come to Saguntum.

The bombardment continued relentlessly all day, shifts of men were changed at the rams, these being brought up under cover of mobile shelters or vineae and the tired crews taken back. Despite the heavy missile fire, the defenders still picked off the slow or unlucky warriors as they changed from one shelter to another. Darkness fell but brought no respite in the battle; rocks from the mangonels replaced by earthenware jars full of naphtha, which was ignited prior to release. Shattering on impact and splattering their contents, the flames roaring and burning brightly, sending dense clouds of smoke into the night sky to hide the stars. The flames illuminated the scene casting giant shadows while beneath it all men strained, screamed, fought and died.

The following morning saw the archers assembled again and pouring their deadly rain over the wall once more. One of the rams however, was no longer operational, for during the night, grapnels had been dropped from the wall to hook and upend it, hauling it bodily upwards exposing the entrance were the ram protruded. The defenders bombarded it with fire pots and boiling oil to encourage the flames. The crew inside, already in disarray could not escape and became human torches within the burning machine that became their pyre. Their screams and howls rose above the roar of the flames and the assault, the hellish din mercifully short as life gave out. The smell of the burnt flesh however remained, filling the nostrils of those nearby with a sickly stench that churned the stomach and clung to the clothes and lungs of those continuing to fight. The other two rams had remained doggedly at work, the walls displaying the damage done with holes in a dozen places.

A triple blast of a horn saw the rams cease their pounding and reversing away from the walls. Archers appeared from behind the remaining battlements sending arrows through the front of the ram, bodies that appeared from under the machine confirming the effectiveness of their aim. With the rams clear, the catapults and ballista's began firing again, rocks and bolts once more smashing at the ruined wall. Suddenly, a long section of the wall, complete with three towers seemed to ripple and buckle like a collapsing ocean wave, tumbling masonry and men earthward. The earth shook, enveloping all in close proximity in a billowing cloud of white dust covering the ground and the archers in choking, blinding grime.

In the chaos that followed the archers were called to withdraw allowing assault troops through to exploit the breach, unfortunately the breeze blew the giant dust cloud towards the Carthaginians blinding their advance. The defenders, recovering quickly and less hampered from the dust, quickly marshalled into ranks and locking shields readied for the attack that would come over the ruins of their wall.

As the air cleared, the coughing, dust covered archers withdrew, helping their injured and bleeding comrades, many being victim to flying debris of stone fragments. Trumpets blared and the 'advance' called and repeated along the length of the assembling assault troops ranks, the line closers quickly shepherding the last of the warriors into formation.

"Shields!" was followed by a loud clattering of metal as men locked their shield to their comrade's and lowered their fighting spears before moving off towards the breach amidst the thud of thousands of feet.

The first ranks to the edge of the rubble came under heavy fire from arrows, javelins and the dreaded phalarica, this iron headed, heavy javelin with its small point punched through shields skewering men and armour. Where it failed to penetrate the shield, it bent from the weight of its shaft and pulled the shield down exposing the warrior behind, rendering him vulnerable to the next missile. Some phalarica shafts were swathed in pitch-soaked fabric and set alight, the air fanned flames adding extra horror as they struck home and turned men into human torches. The attackers encountered further trouble as the ranks were forced to break while the warriors scrambled over the rubble, the defenders missiles tearing into the open ranks

The archers reformed behind the assault troops and a missile duel began with a steady torrent of arrows falling on the defenders forcing them to huddle and raise their shields. Taking advantage of the easing fire, the assault troops increased their speed over the rubble and the bodies of their wounded or dead comrades. The Carthaginian arrow storm intensified, gradually pushing the defenders back though they maintained good order with shields held aloft and spears pointing forward. The assault troops cleared the wall debris and making level ground began forming their ranks again. The fire from the defenders, though less fierce still saw bodies falling into the dust and the lines continually adjusting to close the gaps.

The Saguntine ranks were now tightly closed and resisting the Carthaginian arrow storm with the front ranks kneeling, shields held roof-like and spears outwards. Just before the assault troops were fully assembled, the Saguntine shield wall parted to reveal ballistas, which had been dragged into position behind the screen of men.

The assault troops seeing the danger fell into confusion. Some hesitated, while others pushed forward to close the gap, the officers however, bellowing for the line to hold until it was complete. The moment the ragged shield wall started to move the ballistas dispatched their bolts, some skewering two or three men at once so tight was the press. These gaps had javelins, arrows and slingshot loosed into them and at the shortened rage the affect was deadly. Bowmen up on the edges of the breached walls added to the maelstrom, loosing arrows into the advancing assault troops flanks, adding to the carnage and dropping men in swathes like scythed wheat.

The assault troops, tormented and stung, finally charged. Colliding with the Saguntine front rank with an ear-bursting clash of metal and wood, shouts and shrieks, as they broke like a wave against a stout sea wall and forced to ebb back. Arrows came at them at almost point-blank range, penetrating and pinning shields to bodies or spinning men about with the force. The defenders held steady and from behind large shields, swords and fighting spears probed and stabbed at heads, legs and groins. Blood, guts and limbs covered the grass as the wounded went down to be trampled by their comrades or speared by the Saguntines as they edged slowly forward forcing the attackers back.

The Carthaginians fought doggedly contesting every step but their un-readiness for the breach; the scramble over the wreckage and the deluge of missiles left them disadvantaged. As they were pushed back to the rubble a rout began with men panicking and peeling away so to clear the obstacle. The thinning ranks were pushed faster and faster and practically hurled over the stone and timber debris. The defenders forming their line at the edge of the breach and pouring missiles into the backs of the fleeing Carthaginians.

Watching from his siege lines, Hannibal called for the cavalry to be assembled, the young General all action and direction. Strange looks from the command group were allayed as the citadel gates burst open to disgorge cavalry. The column turned to line at the gallop to attack the retreating assault troops in the flank.

The Carthaginian heavy brigade now raced towards them with spears canted the thunder of hooves adding to the bedlam of screaming, dying men, whining missiles and trumpet calls. The Saguntine cavalry reacting to the danger appearing on their flank, turned from attacking the infantry, attempting to reform before the charge of the fast approaching heavy brigade.

In this respite, Hannibal reformed his lines, sending slingers forward to help prevent any sortie from the breach while the light infantry advanced to screen the siege machines and protect the camp. What had begun as success for the Carthaginians had now turned into a massive counter attack from the defenders, which was becoming more determined and aggressive by the moment. Out of the city gates, in the rear of the cavalry there appeared heavy infantry in column ten abreast, bodies hidden behind huge oval shields and fighting spears bristling. Instead of helmets, they wore sinew caps over which leather hoods had been fitted enveloping and protecting the head and neck. The hoods, decorated with tufted horsehair from the brow across the top of the skull and down the nape of the neck. Following their horsemen, they rushed forward to widen and exploit gaps in the swirling cavalry battle.

At the breach, the Carthaginian archers found themselves under determined attack from the ballista's and massing ranks of archers and slingers. Despite the addition of their own slingers, they were losing the duel. Suddenly vulnerable, they began to back away. The

Carthaginians having gone from attackers to the attacked reeled from the onslaught. The heavy brigade holding the Saguntine cavalry in check found the supporting Saguntine infantry filling the gaps in the melee of horseflesh and pulling warriors from mounts. They hamstrung and disembowelled the horses before wreaking bloody ruin on the thrown riders.

The Carthaginian Generals surprised at the sudden turn in events shouted orders into the confusion, neither of them in any coherence or harmony with the other. Hannibal took command and grasping Maharabal bodily as he spoke, ordered a screen of light cavalry thrown out on both wings. The right flank to unsettle the Saguntine cavalry and heavy infantry, the left to threaten the defenders at the breach and bolster the resolve of the Carthaginian archers and slingers. Turning to Mago, he ordered the pike phalanxes to sweep the field and drive the defenders horse and infantry units before it.

The retreating assault troops melted to one side as trumpet blasts heralded the huge phalanxes of pike-men marshalling for the advance. Each phalanx consisted of two hundred and fifty six men in ranks sixteen wide by sixteen deep, the men heavily armoured in bronze helmets and chain mail shirts. Each warrior carried a small round shield and a pike twice the length of a fighting spear. As the huge formations began to move, some ten phalanx's in all, orders rang out to lower pikes. Amidst a rattle of metal and wood, the first six ranks levelled their weapons to the front, the next five angling pikes to forty-five degrees with the rearward five ranks still held vertical. The formations took on the appearance of giant porcupines, which slowly closed together becoming a giant block of men and iron.

With the light cavalry spreading to the wings and the phalanx advancing, Hannibal ordered the disengagement of his heavy cavalry. The Saguntines, seeing the oncoming phalanx and the danger to their flanks found themselves threatened and out manoeuvred. Unable to combat the phalanx and with the now added risk of attack on the wings and being cut-off from the city, saw an almost consented disengagement between them and the Carthaginians.

A tense backing away began, like dogs parting from a bone, some insults still audible as personal fights and blood lust still ran hot. The subdued noise as combat eased and stopped seemed strangely odd. The two sides left a trail of dead men and animals, the wounded crawled from the carnage, dragging broken limbs or spilled guts along the red stained ground. Cries for comrades, mothers and help drifted over the field. Injured horses tried to stand with legs that were hamstrung or broken, snorting and wild-eyed in fear they collapsed again twitching and kicking, knocking the wind from themselves and raising cries of agony from any wounded trapped beneath them.

The phalanx advanced with a steady thump of marching feet, officers and line closers bellowing to maintain the dressing and formation. Indomitable and solid, the iron wave slowly swept the field driving all before it and trampling bodies underfoot. The regrouping assault troops followed in its wake, dispatching enemy wounded and aiding injured comrades. The Saguntines were forced back towards the city by the magnitude of the Carthaginian advance. Their orderly withdrawal spoke well of their discipline, the cavalry rescinding first but still screening the infantry from the Carthaginian light horse waiting on the wing. The Saguntine heavy infantry, once more in block formation retired city-ward but maintained their front to the enemy as they backed away. Both sides were severely mauled and shaken by the turn and turnabout of the battle and now seemed content to part with out further confrontation, salvation and survival taking precedence over heroics and slaughter.

The Carthaginians were left where they had started, outside the city amongst the company of the dead, the huge gates once more slammed closed in their face, the open breach lined with ballistas and archers. Hannibal, ever watchful, directed his troops to reinforce and consolidate their positions in front of the battered walls. In front of the rubble, the Saguntines scattered caltrops, these three-pronged pieces of iron designed to leave a sharp metal point sticking skyward, no matter which way up it fell. Crippling to men and horses they were sown thickly on the grass over the full width of the breach, thus any further attack would have to clear the obstacles while under fire from the walls. Rearward of the breach labourers and builders toiled to raise a new wall. As the day ended, the gut wrenching work of tending the wounded and dying began. The badly injured were dispatched and the bodies removed to be burnt. Some of the dead horses were butchered and the meat taken for the evening meal.

Amidst the funeral pyres that lit the evening sky and the stink of burning flesh, a tense and pacing Hannibal called a council of war. Before the arrival of his Generals, he gathered his composure. When the guard announced the command group, he welcomed them while taking over the pouring of wine from the servant, waving the man away.

"Come sirs! Come." He said genially while ushering them to the seats.

The warriors fresh from the field were filthy, smoke blackened and bloody, their mood matching their countenance. Hannibal handed wine to each in turn

"Tomorrow… tomorrow is another day." He said, raising his goblet in salute.

The despondent looking men nodded and mumbled quiet agreement.

"We're sorry sir, we …" Mago began; his brows furrowed and face looking groundward.

"Enough Mago! Enough! No fault here … other than my own." Hannibal replied.

The group replied with loud denial, Hannibal raised his hand for silence, nodding his head gently.

"But I tell you!" He looked around them as he spoke "I tell you, we held our own today and I have learned … learned how these Saguntines fight and how to defeat them and take this city!" He swilled down his wine as he finished speaking.

The warriors sipped their wine; Maharabal cleared his throat to speak,

"Seven months we've tarried sir, trying to starve them out, then take it by storm. This sortie today, we were not ready, too sure that once the wall was breached the city would fall. I for one did not look for that, we would have lost this day sir, but for your intuition!"

Hannibal waved the compliment away, patting his cavalry commander on the shoulder; he smiled warmly and pointed to the map on the table and a model of a wooden siege tower.

"There will be no more sorties, we'll be ready and will give them too much to think about. See!" He pointed with a small dagger to the map

"The breach is here and the caltrops they've sown prevent us penetrating it. However, it also prevents them sallying out. Therefore, we'll go to the other side of their round tower and bring the wall down there. Our engineers report the wall is not mortared at this point, being made in the old way of mud bricks, here we will mine beneath it, prop it, burn it and collapse it. Now, this tower!" He tapped the model with his blade. "This will keep them busy along with the remaining rams and siege machines. It will drop men over the parapet while the ballistas mounted on each level will give fire as it approaches. The pike phalanx will stand just out of bowshot and threaten any cavalry thinking of venturing out. Bottled up these Saguntines are and bottled up they'll stay!"

"How long will this tower take to build sir? It will be huge!"

"Three days from now. The timber sections are already complete; we have but to erect it."

The group became vibrant, questions, looks of amazement and excitement showing on the tired faces,

"But how? Who did …?"

"I have to do something while you're busy hammering the city gates!" Hannibal replied, shrugging his shoulders and smiling.

The warriors grinned then laughed, the tension of the day's disappointments easing.

"Hannibal the carpenter!" Mago growled from under his beard. "Well little brother, you can be the builder of the family. Get us in there and I'll do the demolishing."

Laughter broke out, the warriors revelling in the camaraderie of the two brothers, the grim joke and the new prospects to come found their mood lightening and their setbacks fading. Hannibal called for supper to be served while outlining his plans for the morrow.

"We eat then circulate amongst the men. They have had a sore day and will need encouragement. Let them rest until the tower is built, issue extra wine to them for their efforts today but hold the siege lines tight. I want casualty numbers, both dead and injured; what we can't eat from the dead horses leave to rot then send back to the Saguntines via the mangonels, we don't want them going hungry!"

Somewhat heartened the men started supper; Hannibal hid his worries and concerns with his good company, inwardly however, his mind was elsewhere, planning evaluating and quietly worrying.

The following morning Hannibal took his officers to view the siege tower and then walked the walls once more pointing out his new plan and positions for attack. He drew them closer to the walls, wishing to be precise as to where the mortar was missing and where he wanted the mining to begin. Watchful for movement on the wall the men approached closer. Suddenly a shower of javelins arced from the tower top, thudding into the men and the ground beside them. Shields raised instantly, grunts and oaths coming from the warriors as they absorbed the javelins impact. Hannibal covered one of the men who had fallen with a javelin to the shoulder, twisting to cover him, he exposed his leg and a javelin transfixed his thigh. His leg buckled and he rolled to the side breaking the javelin shaft as he collapsed.

"Form up tight! … Lock shields!" Mago shouted, taking command of the situation.

Under cover of the shield roof, he bent to examine his brother, grasping his thigh, blood oozing between his fingers and puddling on the grass. Tearing the sash from his waist, Mago bound it tightly above the wound just below the groin.

"What of? …" Mago asked.

"Dead sir!" The warriors said looking up from examining the man with the javelin in his shoulder.

"We leave now! Maintain formation." He shouted above the noise of javelins and stones smashing into the shields. He bent down and picked Hannibal up, transferring the body weight to his right shoulder as he regained his feet, grunting and cursing with the effort. With Hannibal passing out from the pain the men backed slowly away from the walls. Fortunately, some archers standing nearby had seen the trouble and were sending arrows towards the battlements, forcing the defenders to seek cover and easing the fire that fell on the retreating men.

Hannibal was laid on the table in the surgeon's tent. Mago stood over him brows knitted and his face contorted into a black scowl. His shoulder and arm covered with his brother's blood making him a fearsome sight, he growled orders for the army to stand to.

Hannibal reached up from the table grabbing Mago's forearm in a vice-like grip.

"No attack Mago!" He hissed through gritted teeth.

"No attack? By the Gods Hannibal, I'll raise this shit-hole of a city to the ground and slaughter everyone in it."

Hannibal flinched as his wound was examined but his grip on his brother grew tighter.

"Listen to me Mago! Listen! No attack, I command you! Do you hear?"

Beside himself with pain, the veins in his neck knotted. The sweat breaking out on his brow, but his eyes stared, fierce and bright.

"Promise me Mago! All of you promise me! No attacks!"

Maharabal leaned across. "Rest Hannibal, rest! We promise we'll wait, it will be as you wish."

Hannibal's eyes flashed back to Mago.

"Very well brother, as you wish." He said sullenly. "I promise."

"Get this javelin out of me, rest the men, finish the tower, the …"

Unconsciousness took him as the surgeon went to work.

Chapter Six

"So …oo! Quite a tale my old friend! Quite a tale! You two don't do things by halves it seems! The boy here guts the son of one of the most prestigious families in Carthage, damn near kills another and you send two city guards to Hades when they try to stop you!" Balaam said, shaking his head in mock disapproval. "Sounds like just the men I need. Gentlemen we need to discuss plans, contracts and money!"

"Look Balaam, I'm grateful for the help back there, we were in trouble I grant you, but …"

"Trouble! …" Balaam sniggered. "You would be half way to being crucified by now if I hadn't intervened! Now listen to what I have to say before you waste further breath! We take ship on the morrow for Spain and Saguntum. As you will be aware, the city is under siege from General Hannibal and has been these last few months. He calls for more men, has a bulging pay chest from what I hear and would welcome men of our skill and renown to his banner."

Gestix appeared not to be listening, however Baldor's attention was caught and Balaam switched his conversation towards him.

"This siege will set loose the hounds of war, boy! Do you think Rome can do less than make war with Carthage now?"

"Well … Saguntum falls under the protection of Rome, all know that!" Baldor replied.

"In that you're right boy, but Saguntum see, is slap bang in the middle of Carthaginian territory and we didn't give the Republic special dispensation to offer their protection! Bloody Romans! Always pushing their noses into matters that don't concern them, just like the last war! Eh Gestix?"

"Whatever Balaam! I don't know! What's more, I don't care! The lad and I want nothing of your war, your General Hannibal or this Saguntum."

"I don't hear the lad here saying that, just an old man huffing and puffing and making excuses!"

"Balaam, you're going too far!" Gestix's voice rose, the flush of temper on his face.

"Calm down Gestix, no harm intended, just rattling your cage a little is all." Balaam grinned wolfishly and tut tutted softly. "Same old touchy Gaul eh? Ready to start a fight over a name or two, but can't see where there's money to be made!"

Gestix took Balaam by the arm and eased him out of earshot of Baldor.

"Look Balaam, the boy has had more than his share of trouble, let him be! Let me be! You have plenty of men; go set the world on fire but leave us out of it!"

"Baal almighty! You're like a mother hen with one chick! When we were his age we were already at war!"

"Aye! And did it make us better or wiser men? It damn nearly killed his father! And Rome as you know is no milksop to make war on."

"What are you going to do then Gestix? Grow old beating metal into shape or tending crops?"

Gestix shrugged. "I intend to see the lad safe to his relatives in Spain; I know not what from there!"

"I'll go with you Captain."

Gestix and Balaam turned to find Baldor standing just to their side and in earshot of what had been said. Gestix was dumbstruck and looked at Baldor as if he had two heads, his words failing him.

"Now that sounds like the most sense I have heard today, boy!" Exclaimed Balaam.

"Baldor, we have it … I have it … it's all planned. We're going to Spain, once you're whole again things will be better mark you! You are still not right from your wound and that kick to your head has addled your brains!"

Baldor took time to wipe some of the congealed blood from his nose and mouth before replying. Balaam standing back and listening intently now the seeds of doubt seemed to be sown between the two comrades.

"You're right Gestix; I'm not myself and doubt I ever will be. Yes, the physical wounds will heal but for the rest, well …" Baldor faltered and then clearing his throat continued. "It's not for either of us Gestix, this house and hearth, wife and family, mine have been taken from me and by your solitude and silence, I judge you to have suffered the same?"

Gestix folded his arms and looked at Baldor, not a hint of his thoughts showing on his face. Baldor however saw a momentary sadness in his eyes as he hinted at the past.

"I am already weary of looking over my shoulder and hiding. I would have ended it but for your care and kindness and for that I am thankful, more than, but enough now, that life is gone. I would change tack and see what fate throws at us, what have we got to lose Gestix? Do you really want to eke out our days on my uncle's estate in Spain?"

Gestix looked perplexed; Baldor had hardly spoken in the last weeks and now suddenly was all decisions and reasoning. He hung his head and shook it gently.

"The lad has the rights of it Gestix, I …"

Gestix raised his hand motioning silence; for once Balaam held his tongue. Taking Baldor gently by the arm, he guided him a few steps away from Balaam and spoke quietly.

"Is it truly what you want, this war? Don't listen to Balaam; he makes it all appear worthy, heroic even! It isn't, believe me!"

Seeing the concern etched into his friends face, Baldor answered quietly.

"I'm not sure but I don't want to go back to the life we had, I don't believe I could cope with estate living again. However, I am sure that I never want to be without you. You have always been my family, now you are all the family I have and I owe you my life …"

"You owe me nothing Baldor! Families don't have debts! All I ask is that you consider your decision carefully don't be rash."

"I have thought on it, all these weeks and in truth I didn't have a decision until today. Many people want us dead, me for my crime and you for being my friend. Do we wait for the next guards to come along or the next Adharbal? They will get us in the end, you know how powerful a family we have crossed, but we would be harder to find in an army of thousands, what say you?"

Gestix went silent again, deep in thought. With the city guards gone the square was returning to normal and hard to believe that only a short time ago two men had been engaged in deadly combat, life just went on, with commerce beginning again and the street people coming out to beg.

Baldor watched Balaam inspecting his men, stopping here and there to pass a word or two. Standing rigidly to attention the men were drawn up in three rows, the sunlight reflecting from helmets and weapon hilts. He wondered about the lack of shields, an infantryman was never usually far from his shield, looking closer he noticed the bow-legged stance and slight slouch of the seasoned cavalryman.

"Cavalry! They're bloody cavalry!" He exclaimed aloud.

His heart skipped a beat and a childlike excitement flooded through him, he went to shout to Gestix but seeing him still lost in thought he held back. Instead, he walked across the square to examine the men more closely.

He could hear Balaam clearly, briefing his men on the orders for the day as well as berating one for tardiness then praising another, what was very apparent was the respect with which the men held their Captain. He could feel it in the air almost; proud men with a prouder Captain, these men were mercenaries of the highest order. Baldor examined the faces, not all were young. Many had the look of veteran warriors about them, some carrying whitened scars as proof to their experience. They aged from late twenties to men of Gestix's age and one or two perhaps older. Their weapons a mix of swords of the falcata type and the spatha, the longer, slashing sword of the cavalryman. Most carried a dagger, some two; others had smaller knives attached to their baldrics. All had leather or mail corselets over their tunic and a short skirt of leather pteruges covering their thighs with cavalrymen's, calf-length boots on bare legs.

Baldor surmised their spears and shields must be in transit or with the horses. He wondered at the whereabouts of the animals as he counted up the men, eighty in all, that's a lot of horses to feed and manage he thought. Baldor had seen many soldiers and warriors before but never nurtured the desire to be one; as good as he was with the sword. Now, he wanted more than anything to join these he saw before him, with the ties to a life of normality gone, he had nothing to give him pause to consider. Except Gestix, he would not abandon his friend, so he must convince him into coming with him. He gazed across at the Gaul, his arms still folded and chin cupped in his fist, thinking … thinking. For the first time in weeks, he was clear in his mind as to what he wanted from this world, now to put it to Gestix.

"Gestix, Gestix! Do you think we should go with Balaam?" He said with less confidence than he would have liked. "Do you not think our path lies with them?"

Gestix turned to face Baldor, a wry smile on his face, his drooping moustache giving him the look of sadness that his heart genuinely felt.

"I think Baldor that you have already decided; you merely look for my approval?"

Baldor faltered, any pretence at confidence gone, the big man always seemed to know what he was thinking. From lessons learned in the past, Baldor deemed honesty was always the best policy when wanting something from Gestix.

"Er, yes … yes! I think we have nothing to lose by joining these men. As I said earlier I am weary of being hunted like an animal." Baldor felt his confidence growing as Gestix did not interrupt his reasoning. "You always told me to go after what I want, to live life fully because it's all too short!"

"That's true lad, very true! Life is short. However, are you keen to shorten it further? For that is what you risk if we embark upon this venture. If we go to Saguntum don't think that will be the end of it, no, no! This Hannibal is Hades bent on war with Rome and that is what will follow, as sure as night follows day. Rome cannot take this attack as anything else other than a declaration of war and when the she wolf howls let all beware."

"I'm not afraid Gestix, and I know you fear nothing!"

"It is not fear that I speak of Baldor, I know you're brave, resolute and as sound a companion as any man could ask for." Gestix patted Baldor's shoulder and smiled warmly. "But let us be clear about what we are getting ourselves into. Rome is an expanding empire and I believe she will embrace this war. Carthage is competition she can do without in her bid for supremacy in and around this Middlesea.

When Rome commits to war, she will come with men beyond number, huge monies, resources, and a ruthlessness to win. This war won't be measured in weeks or months lad, but years! This is what you must consider and if we join Balaam it will not be easy to walk away, we will enter into a contract of service, on pain of death if we break it! So consider well."

Baldor looked shocked.

"Do you think that will be the way of it? So big?"

"Think on it Baldor, Rome goes to war with Carthage over Saguntum, this brings in the Spaniards whether they wish it or not. Now, how does Carthage fight her wars?"

"Well, listening to you and my father talking, the city seeks and employs allies and mercenaries to complement our own men."

"Exactly! So add in, Gauls, Spaniards, Numidians, Moors, and Libyans, even Greeks maybe? Then if the war progresses favourably for Carthage, other states will join, for the hatred and fear of Rome runs deep. Many will seek to throw off their yoke and rebel; Campanians, Samnites, Lucanians, to name but a few; do you see where it's going lad?"

Baldor was dumbstruck and merely nodded his agreement; he rubbed at his Vulcan's fire and bit his lip. This war could involve most of the countries and people in the world that he had heard of.

"So think well lad, ere we throw in our lot. However, I tell you this; whatever you decide, I will abide by it. You have the right to determine your own destiny, you're a man grown. I have been wrong to push my plans for what I think is best for us both."

"No Gestix, not wrong! Never wrong! You had to make decisions when I could not, would not! The Gods alone know what I would have done without you. Well, I would not be here having this conversation, but for you."

"Tis sore what you've had to bear Baldor, you but needed time was all. So consider well but worry not for I will never leave you, whatever you decide we go together … alright lad?"

Gestix clapped Baldor's shoulder, smiling broadly.

"Now! I'm for a drink in yonder tavern. You can ponder our future and let me know whether it's to be war or peace? That old dog over there will want to know too no doubt." Gestix flicked his head towards Balaam.

He smiled again then crossed the square to the inn.

Balaam finished addressing his men and dismissed them. As they fell out and filtered away, he spun on his heel looking for Baldor and Gestix.

Seeing Baldor, he strode towards him hailing him as he came.

"Well boy what's it to be? Moreover, where in Hades name is Gestix? Typical Gaul that, never there when you need him."

"He's gone for a drink, he leaves the decision to me and …"

"Ha! Bloody Gauls!" Balaam started to laugh. "Typical, bloody typical!"

Baldor looked anxious fearing Gestix may somehow have overheard.

"Don't look so worried boy; I say that because I can, I know the prickly fellow and his pride from way back. He knows me well enough as to when I'm serious and when I jest. Now, what have you decided in lieu of our barbarian friend?"

"Well, I … we …"

"Don't hesitate boy, in our business there's sometimes only a moment to decide! Well?"

"We are in, pending the contract."

Balaam roared with laughter again. "Contract! Well, you're shrewd for a boy! I shall have to watch you!"

"Don't mock me!" Baldor bridled and flushed with anger.

This only made Balaam more jovial; he slapped Baldor on the back good naturedly, laughing heartily.

"Baal protect me!" He said. "You're as prickly as the Gaul, save the anger for later. I meant no harm, now contracts, let me see. It's simple really, you sign for a season's campaign under me, what I say goes and you do what I say. See, simple!"

"How do we get paid?"

"When I get paid! Ordinarily at the end of the term of service, not counting booty and spoils of course, we take those as we go. I'll pay you in gold or silver coin; anything you loot along the way is to be shared between us all, that's fair eh? Let me see, what else is there? Ah yes, you need to make a will and give it to me if you want anything to go to relatives or anyone in particular. Other than that, no will, see's what you leave divided amongst the company. Finally, I deduct from your wages a small amount for your funeral fund, just in case it comes to that, in our business life can sometimes be a little uncertain. Hmm, I think that covers it all, simple eh? Now, if you see Marko, he will sign you both on and that's it."

"Very well Balaam, you have a deal." Baldor extended his hand and the men shook

"One other thing boy! From now on its Captain Balaam or sir to you, Got it!"

Slightly taken aback he managed. "Yes Sir"

"Good, I can see we're going to get on! Now let's find the Gaul, I need a drink!"

Inside the inn was refreshingly cool and full of mercenaries, women and men from all cultures and creeds. Scantily clad women danced to a wailing flute, swaying and teasing the male audience, some falling prey to groping or slapping hands. Hoots of laughter and capering drunks added to the atmosphere, in the quietest corner was Gestix, drink in hand but his mind elsewhere.

The pair pushed across the crowded room to a bench next to Gestix. Balaam hailed a serving woman for a pitcher of wine. At the arrival of the two, Gestix came back to reality smiling warmly at Baldor and nodding to Balaam.

"Well lad, what's it to be?"

"Saguntum, we have to sign on with one, Marko?" Baldor looked to Balaam ensuring he had the name correct. "We are paid at the end of the campaign season and …"

"Save your breath boy, he knows the conditions, eh Gestix?"

Gestix nodded and turned to his wine.

"Balaam, er I mean Captain Balaam wants us ready to leave on the evening tide."

"Well, Captain Balaam!" Gestix said with just a trace of sarcasm. "Do we bring the horses with us or sell up and buy at the other end?"

Balaam didn't rise to the hinted sarcasm. "Bring them with you; Spanish horse flesh is poor to say the least. Ours have already left by ship, twenty of the lads went with them the day before yesterday, and they'll meet us in Spain. What have you in the way of weapons and equipment?"

"Swords, two spears, a shield apiece and some daggers. We'll have to negotiate for helmets and armour when we make Spain, there will be precious little of that ilk to be found here I surmise."

"We have a spare helmet and corselet that may fit the boy, see Marko when you sign on." Balaam turned to Baldor. "If it fits you, I'll deduct a fair price from your first payment."

With business settled, they turned to their wine and the atmosphere became more relaxed. Balaam questioned Gestix on his doings since their last meeting but it was a conversational, sociable questioning of one old comrade to another. Baldor was content to listen for the men had been friends longer than he had been in the world.

As early afternoon crept in the men ate, Baldor eating as though he had not been fed in days, Gestix noting with quiet satisfaction the change in his friend. Balaam quaffed his wine and stood to leave.

"Leave plenty time to get the horses aboard and settled before the evening tide, I'll see the Captain for extra berths. We have enough provisions to see the both of you through, so don't bother bringing anything other than your personal kit. When we make Spain, training starts. Which means personal fitness, as well as moulding us all into an effective cavalry unit. Most of the lads have had some time together already and all are professional warriors, which means boy, that you have a …"

"I can fight!"

"Yes, I saw. However, fighting as a cohesive unit and combat experience will be new to you and very different from a brawl in the street with some spoilt city whelp. Furthermore, don't interrupt me again when I am speaking. Do you understand?"

Baldor stared at Balaam incredulously.

"Do you understand me boy!"

Baldor looked rankled and was about to retort but Balaam's icy stare stayed his ire.

"Yes sir."

"Good! I'll see you both at the wharf this evening."

Balaam pushed his way out of the inn, not pausing to look back. Gestix smiled at Baldor.

"Bit of a shock the old bastard eh? But he's a good man to be with when things are looking rough!"

Baldor still looked crestfallen and merely nodded.

"Listen Baldor, life will be very different from now on. I …"

"So it would seem. What have I got us into now?"

Gestix grinned and broke into laughter.

"Baldor, Baldor! Enough, you've got us into nothing. It's the way of the Gods, fickle they are, they play games with our lives! We are but pieces on a game board; let's see where the play takes us? Come on, let's find this Marko and sign on. We had better be sorted ere the evening tide or we will get a telling."

Downing their drinks Baldor grabbed the last of the bread, stuffing it into his mouth as they followed in the wake of their Captain.

The sun was setting and taking the fierce heat of the day with it. The street life changing, merchants and vendors were packing up their wares, their customers also heading for home. In their place came the night people, the whores, the off-duty soldiers with money to spend and a more desperate looking breed of beggar. Following the smell of fish and salt air, which carried on the breeze, the pair found the dock areas. Gestix pulled the swords from the horse's baggage and passed one to Baldor.

"Here Baldor, strap it on. Get used to it, for it'll become part of your life." He slipped his own weapon and baldric over his shoulder. "She's a cold companion but like any wife, she demands regular attention and maintenance! I wish I had let you bring those helmets and greaves, it would have saved us a little money!"

Walking from ship to ship and looking for signs of the mercenaries or Balaam himself, they were hailed by a tall man standing next to an upturned barrel with papers on top held down by a sword.

"Gestix? … Gestix? Is that you?" The man asked while taking a flaring torch from another warrior beside him and walking towards the pair. Peering through the light he exclaimed. "By the Gods, It is you!" He said shaking his head in disbelief and smiling broadly.

"Marko! After all these years! When Balaam said your name, I never imagined it to be you!"

The two, shook hands then embraced amidst backslapping and exclamations of how each had changed over the years. Gestix turned Marko to face Baldor and made the introductions.

Balaam appeared at the head of the gangplank. "Move it along there! Save the small talk for later, we are underway once the tide is full. Marko, sign them on and have done! Get those horses on-board, move it!"

101

Marko pointed out where they needed to sign or make their mark on the parchment while pushing a silver coin into each of their hands.

"That's it then! Simple as that, may the Gods keep us all! We must catch up later Gestix; we'll have time ere this voyage is done. Now, let's have these horses aboard before the Captain gives us a swearing."

Baldor unloaded the few possessions they had from the horses then led them across to the ramp. Gestix pulled the blanket from the back of his own mount and gently laid it over the horse's head, talking and patting the animal all the while to reassure it. Marko scattered straw up the ramp then came back to help coax the beasts up it and into the ship.

"Baldor, cover Risto's head and bring him on, the straw under his hooves will reassure his step, quietly and steady does it now."

Baldor took Risto by the bridle, easing the animals head close to his own talking quietly and coaxing him up the ramp. Once clear of the ramp they were led to the lower deck where a cordoned off area had been prepared with straw scattered on the floor and hay hung from the wall in rope nets. Baldor and Gestix busied themselves rubbing the animals down and settling them into their temporary stable.

"Well, we're aboard. A few days will see us to Spain; let's pray for a smooth and quiet crossing. No doubt when we land the Captain will be knocking us in to shape, mark my words on that." Gestix talked as he brushed his horse.

"Is there anybody you don't know, Gestix?" Baldor asked referring to Marko.

"Truth is it's a small world lad. I'm surprised myself how people and things are coming together. It strikes me as strange after all these years ... people I never expected to see again." He paused from his work and leant against the horses his thoughts drifting to the past.

Baldor finishing his work and playfully pushing the still thoughtful Gestix to one side took over where he had stopped.

"Looks like I have to do the horses myself." He chided. "Work harder Baldor! Attention to detail Baldor! And I will stand and bloody watch you Baldor!" He laughed and looked at the big man who was just returning his thoughts to the present.

"Eh, what's that? Why, you cheeky whelp!" Gestix took a playful swipe at Baldor who ducked quickly.

"Not only idle but old and slow!" Baldor quipped again.

"We'll see, and you have to sleep sometime!"

The pair laughed, enjoying the camaraderie and relishing the first feeling of security in a long time.

"Do you want to eat when we are finished?" Baldor asked.

"I don't know what we'll find but Balaam did mention we'd be provided for and I am hungry!"

Completing their work, Gestix gave quiet thanks to any God that cared to listen for the change in his friend. The lad had a long way to go but he was coming right, time just time and perhaps the action he craved as salve to his wounds. Gestix had no doubt that action aplenty would greet them once they arrived in Spain.

Chapter Seven

The Samilcar villa, the outskirts of Carthage

The gate watchman squinted into the sun, shading his straining eyes with his hand to see who approached up the tree-lined road to the villa. Out in the heat shimmer he could see it was horsemen and armed judging by the glint of the sun on metal, three riders possibly more and moving at speed from the size of the spiralling dust cloud left in their wake. He sent word to the lady of the house announcing the unexpected visitors. Prudently, he also turned out the small troop of house guards and called up some of the stable hands armed with cudgels into closer proximity of the gate, just in case of trouble. The horsemen closed the distance to the villa quickly, scattering peasants and travellers from the road in their haste. They drew rein at the gate, the horses flecked white with sweat and spume, snorting and breathing heavily, the men covered in grime from the road. Their dust cloud caught them, swirling around about almost obscuring them from view.

"Captain Hannar, to see Lady Serfina!" Bellowed the leader of the group while beating dust from his clothes. The watchman flicked his head in signal to a servant who disappeared at the run to announce the visitors. The horsemen were ushered through the gate into the paved courtyard, the horses bridles held by servants. Captain Hannar dismounted stiffly, trying to ease some of the ache from his muscles as he was escorted across the courtyard up the steps to the villa's living quarters.

"The old bastard will get it now! I don't envy him having to tell her Ladyship that we haven't got the boy, nor that her brother's the worse for trying." The mounted warrior smiled grimly and wiped the sweat from his face as he spoke to his comrade.

"Which means we'll catch it off him, you know how it works? The shit's always passed down the line! Mind you, I wouldn't like to have missed that fight, I've never seen two blades used so well before, impressive!"

The men dismounted and walked into the shade of an awning, a blushing serving girl came with a tray bearing watered wine, bread and fruit. Slipping off their helmets, they reached for the food, all the while grinning wolfishly at the girl and engaging her in small talk.

Inside the villa, the Captain was ushered to a waiting room, rose-scented water and towels were brought as well as a tray bearing a goblet and a jar of wine. As he unfastened his helmet, he rehearsed the explanation of events in his head for the hundredth time then splashed water on his face, towelling it quickly dry. He quaffed the wine and poured himself another as he paced up and down the room.

Eventually, a pompous and very effeminate steward, bearing a carved staff as his badge of office strode into the room. Having difficulty hiding his disdain for soldiers and filthy ones at that, he curtly announced the Captain would be seen and that he should leave his weapons then follow him through to the Lady's quarters and be sure to touch nothing. Biting back a rebuke the Captain un-slung his weapon baldric, thrusting it and his helmet forcefully into the hands of a startled slave, then fell in behind the mincing steward. He followed the man down a marble floored corridor, into and through another magnificent reception room and out across a beautifully manicured garden complete with fish ponds, ornately clipped miniature trees and tall shading palms. A small army of slaves swept and tended the vista, working quietly deigning not to raise their eyes to the visitor as he was escorted briskly through it. Peacocks pecked and scratched amongst the short grass before looking up at the approaching men, the birds adding their own majesty to the scene when the male bird fanned its plumage as a demonstration of dominance as the men came close. The beauty of the display however was lost on the two as the steward hurried and the Captain quietly fumed. Above them, pigeons cooed softly from a small dovecote and the heady, sweet scent of jasmine drifted on the afternoon air.

Finally, climbing granite stairs to a pillared balcony, the steward tapped on an ornately carved wooden door before admitting himself and summoning the Captain inward. The coolness of the room was refreshing and took some of the heat from the Captains face. Within, the white plastered walls were decorated and painted in rich colours, depicting Gods and mythical animals. On a wall of its own, rendered in mosaic, a map of the Middlesea and surrounding countries. The furnishings were rich and luxurious, tables made of dark hardwoods and couches upholstered in sumptuous fabric upon which plump cushions were scattered. Tall, ornate lamp stands held a multitude of tiny brass oil lamps, ensuring darkness would never rule or pervade the room. The smell of cedar within the chamber was overlaid with a sweet, heady fragrance that steamed gently from small bowls of heated oils, bunches of fresh blooms further softened and added to the feminine feel of the room. To the rear of the chamber on a slightly raised, carpeted dais, in a throne like chair, an elegant yet austere young woman sat. The steward announced the Captain, bowed low to the woman and backed towards the door, bowed again and left.

"Captain Hannar! I expected you days past. I trust you bring good news?" The woman's voice was flat and monotone; she didn't look at her guest but continued staring into space.

"Err ... my Lady ... I, things have not ... not gone well."

"Not gone well? What pray was the problem?"

"There were complications ... difficulties ..."

"You left here with over a score of men, good leads as to the direction or likely whereabouts of my brother's killer and your word, your word, Captain! That you would return with Targa in chains! There were further bodies to the mark the way for you, was there not?" She maintained her lost gaze, never once looking at him.

She was dressed in a high-necked, sleeveless, black gown that reached to her ankles; it was cut from the hem to just above her knees to allow ease of walking. It was fastened at each shoulder with silver broaches set with haematite stones. A waist belt of intersecting silver rings gathered the material, accentuating her full breasts and narrow waist defining her hourglass shape. Her sandal straps criss-crossed delicately over her arches, around her ankles and half way up her shins. Her raven hair was gathered into a high ponytail, bound in a ribbon also of black. Her mourning jewellery of black pearls and bracelets of silver inlaid with obsidian and jet, stood out from her pale skin adding to her severe countenance; the only hint of colour about her was her rouged lips. Serfina Samilcar was a beautiful woman but grief, anger and lack of sleep had darkened and sunken her eyes lined her fine features and left her complexion pallid.

The Captain cleared his throat and began his rehearsed tale, trying to calm his voice, reminding himself that he was a Captain of some thirty years' experience, veteran of more than one war and she a mere woman. The comfort was fleeting for this 'mere' woman was a member of a powerful house and with her father incapacitated, an elder brother dead and another badly wounded, effectively the head of it. Careers greater than his had crumbled to dust from the displeasure of such people.

Serfina listened calmly as he reiterated his tale of tracking the fugitives to Numidia and the confrontation in the square at Icosium. She never once looked at him nor interrupted as he spoke of the fugitive's enlistment in the mercenary company and their intended destination of Saguntum. Only when he mentioned the fight between Baldor and Adharbal, did her head turn quickly towards him. She rose from the chair to stare at him.

"My brother, is he …?"

"No! No, my Lady he's alive but wounded …"

"Wounded! Wounded?" She screeched. "Damn you man! Damn you to Hades! You stand before me unscathed! Where were you? Your men? What were you doing?" She screamed as her fury broke.

"My Lady, we were surrounded, we could …"

She swiped a tray of drinks from a small table, the noise of smashing crockery and metal reverberating around the room. Quick footsteps and loud shouts from the corridor could be heard coming towards the room. The door burst open, slamming against the wall. A muscled leg stepped inside preventing the door swinging back on its hinges, the steward and two huge men armed with swords forced their way in. Before they could speak, Serfina screamed at them to get out, her snarl and anger driving them back whence they came, closing the door quickly behind them. She paused, breathed deeply, making a physical effort to regain her temper and composure then looking the Captain straight in the eye she said quietly.

"Tell me of my brother."

Settling back in her chair, she allowed him to continue his tale, he mopping at the sweat on his brow and face with his neckerchief. Though she didn't interrupt he saw her face change as a terrible anger built within her again, her hands closing into small fists as he described the fight. He attempted to placate her, describing Adharbal's valiant attempt to avenge his brother then tried to soften his tale telling of Baldor sparing Adharbal's life. Serfina cut in dismissively, asking about the condition and whereabouts of her brother and assuring him that this Targa would receive no mercy, supposing she had to drive the nails home herself when they crucified him. With that, she called her steward to see the Captain out. Dismissing him while he was still trying to explain further, he was unceremoniously shown out of the room back to the courtyard and his waiting men.

The two guardsmen looked at their Captain and his scowling red face and deigned not to ask how it had gone. They held his horse as he snatched the reins and mounted then scrambled for their own as he wheeled the animal about, brutally kicking its flanks towards the gateway and Carthage, raising dust as he went.

Serfina barked orders to her steward to find and fetch her scribe, the pair to meet with her immediately. Shortly, both men arrived, breathless and damp with sweat about their brows, their haste evidence that this woman was not one to be kept waiting. Serfina turned to her steward first, she asked for a progress report of the Targa property assimilation. The man swallowed nervously his reply tumbling out in a rush, the facts all disjointed and out of sequence, he, clearly terrified of the woman's displeasure. Serfina however, listened quietly; the man finding a little confidence continued finishing with a bow of his head and a nervous. "My Lady."

Serfina summed up and clarified for herself. "So, though the property itself is part burned it is quite repairable, both it and the estate has been ceded to us. The business interests of the boatyard also pass to us, the servants and slaves are long gone and his wife's family have claimed her body or what's left of it for proper funeral rights."

"That's correct my Lady." The steward managed through a still dry mouth.

"Good." She replied quietly to herself and the steward relaxed a little. "Which brings me to you and what I require next." She turned, pointing a manicured finger at the scribe who fidgeted nervously, picking at his ink-stained nails.

"The warrant for the arrest of Targa and his pet Gaul which was given to that idiot Hannar, you have a copy?"

"Yes, yes, m … my La … Lady." He stammered. "I but need add … add the additional charges of Mur … Mur … der of the guards slain on the Numid … Numidian road."

Serfina nodded her gaze again elsewhere.

"Make the addition! Then the warrant copy is to be read to the senate once more, after which I want it taken directly to this General Hannibal at Saguntum. He's to root out Targa and the Gaul and have them returned here for trial forthwith. Prepare an accompanying message to him instructing such. Attach my father's seal to it and I will sign it."

The scribe fidgeted again whilst nodding his head vigorously.

"Well! See to it!" She snapped. "And no mistakes! I've suffered enough fools with Hannar and his guardsmen."

Both men immediately made for the door, colliding with one another as they bowed quickly before closing the door behind them.

****

Far across the Middlesea near the city of Rome, in a villa no less grand than Serfinas, two men sat enjoying the warmth from the evening sun. They shared a pitcher of wine that rested on a crisp, parchment map depicting the Middlesea and surrounding countries. The timber sunhouse in which they sat was covered in blooms of purple and red bougainvillea, which intertwined about the bleached timbers turning them into a living structure. Despite the ambience and the peaceful scene, there was an underlying feeling of excitement mixed with mild apprehension between the men.

"So Publius, you're convinced the Carthaginian is seeking war?" The larger of the two men rose to his feet as he spoke, hooking one hand in to the edge of his robe, the other grasping his wine.

"Undoubtedly brother, and like his father before him he bears watching. As a precautionary measure we are planning and gathering our strength, envoys have already been dispatched to Saguntum to demand as to Carthaginian intentions and to remind them that the city remains under the protection of Rome." Publius spoke quietly, but with deep concern. "This Hannibal Barca however, is no rash adventurer or plunderer seeking fortune or notoriety; I believe he has designs to humble Rome, possibly even seeking her destruction! Our spies tell us of a pious man, sworn to his Gods not to rest till we are no more!"

"Hah! He's nothing more than a boy, what does he know of war? He sounds more like a priest than a soldier. Moreover, these Carthaginians, they're barbarians. Wait until he has to face a Roman Legion in the field! Fighting Spanish savages is one thing, an armoured, disciplined Legion quite another!"

"Gnaeus, I pray you, don't underestimate this boy as you name him, I will not! I cannot afford to! He disturbs me greatly; he has similarities in age, ability and character with Alexander of Macedon. He demonstrates that same magnetism, that …"

"Publius, you go too far!" Gnaeus cut in, scoffing. "Comparing him to Alexander? You over credit this boy!"

"Do I Gnaeus? … This boy has been with their army and trained in the art of war since his father took him to Spain at the age of nine! By the age of twenty-six, he was voted in as commander of that army, voted in! Mark you! Like Alexander, he has strong personal qualities; he shares his soldier's hardships, his men love him and he's not afraid to fight himself. Can you not see the similarities?"

"Similarities are all they are, that doesn't make him the new Alexander!"

"No, it doesn't. However, his actions are also beginning to speak for themselves. He's already crushed a vastly superior force to his own at the River Tagus, shown that he is unafraid to use perilous night marches and swift, decisive manoeuvres are his trait. His tactics though and his thinking are well planned, he leaves nothing to chance. From the Tagus he went on to take Salamantica, now he's beating at the gates of Saguntum, I believe he'll not stop there, he will come for us!"

Gnaeus remained silent and sipped at his wine

"You will remember they were a hard enemy to best in the last war?" Publius began again, continuing before his brother could reply. "It was a close run thing; you will also recall his father, Hamilcar remained undefeated at Mt Eryx? The Lion they called him and my reports tell me his brood are equally as dangerous as he was; Hannibal is the eldest and most bellicose of them. There are two more siblings, Hasdrubal and Mago and they love and follow their brother as do his soldiers."

"Many soldiers love their commander and their city. They naturally follow success and courage and from what you say it appears this Hannibal has both, but ..."

"But here's the rub Gnaeus, his army is not pure Carthaginian, most have never even seen Carthage. This army is made up of Gauls, Spaniards, Numidians, and Libyans, to name but a few."

"Hah! The scum of the Middlesea!" Gnaeus quaffed his goblet of wine as he finished speaking.

"Exactly brother, scum! So what kind of man is he that can control, unite and lead such scum to victory?"

Gnaeus didn't reply he looked at his brother intently, himself now a little disturbed, he poured more wine for both, deep in thought but saying nothing. Publius sipped the wine then pointed to the map and southeast Spain.

"We need to stop him here, Gnaeus." His finger tapped Saguntum. "And to be doubly sure, here as well." His finger moved down the map and came to rest on the northern tip of Africa and the city of Carthage itself. "Two armies, two invasions, one to knock at his cities door for if anything will move him out of Spain it will be a threat to Carthage, men always return home, when home is threatened. The second army is to land in Spain to reconsolidate our interests there."

"Why divide our forces then? You know as well as I the risk in that. Just send them all to Carthage and let him come to us there, Spain will keep."

"I agree that splitting any force is risky but hear me out. I intend to make him do the same; Hannibal inspires leads and has to be said wins. However, he is only one man; he cannot be in two places at once. If he splits his forces the one without him will be the weaker, I'm gambling that he will return to defend Carthage and leave Spain under his brothers! We break them first; with the Carthaginian I need an edge."

"Divide and conquer then?"

"Yes, we can afford to split our forces for Rome has the man power. Thus, one army under my fellow Consul, Tiberius

Sempronius Longus to invade Africa and the other under myself to attack Spain."

"And if the Carthaginian doesn't return home?"

"If he doesn't return we will lay siege to Carthage anyway, she doesn't have the manpower to put another army in the field. If he doesn't split his forces and returns home with his whole army, we trap him between our army at Carthage, while I bring the other from Spain into his rear. However, if he leaves Spain with no rearguard, he is cutting himself off from the silver mines and one of the major sources of income with which to pay his men."

"And if he does divide his forces?"

"Then we will outnumber him on both fronts. I'm counting on him returning home with his Carthaginians and maybe the Numidians and Libyans, leaving the Gauls and Spaniards to defend their homes. Without him to hold them together they will be a softer target."

"You seem to have him either way Publius, as usual you have thought much on this! How soon do we move?"

"Sooner rather than later brother, before he sets the world on fire."

Gnaeus drained his cup wiping his mouth on the back of his hand, "And where do I fit into the scheme of things?"

Publius smiled. "You Gnaeus? ... You're with me, I need you! The Carthaginian may have his two brothers but I and Rome have you."

Gnaeus offered his hand to his brother, the pride of Publius's faith in him lighting his eyes. "Well Publius, 'lion's brood' they may be, but they have reckoned without the sons of the 'she wolf' and the Scipios!"

The two men smiled and embraced each other.

"Uncle! Uncle you are here!" The blonde haired youth called as he approached across the garden, his walk giving way to a run in his eagerness to greet his uncle.

"Cornelius! By Jupiter lad, you grow every time I see you!"

Gnaeus walked quickly to meet his nephew, the two shaking hands and embracing warmly. Cornelius was of medium height and slightly built, his fine, wispy hair the colour of old gold, cropped short in Legion style. His skin creamy and pale, though exposure to the sun had brought forth freckles and given him a healthy, glowing radiance. His eyes, as green as emeralds, sparkled and shone with life and the vigour of youth.

"How goes it in the Legion? They tell me you are an Optio already.

Cornelius looked bashful. "My rank is more a commission, than earned."

"Well lad, we need men from the right families and of the right pedigree to keep those Legionnaire's under control, we can't have rankers taking over and running the army altogether, that just wouldn't do! Anyway, you look as though you are thriving on it!"

"I am uncle; it's a hard life but a good one."

"No broken nose yet? When I was your age my nose had been broken thrice."

"He fights better and moves quicker than you do brother!" Publius quipped, the three broke into laughter.

Publius placed his arms around his brother and son.

"Your mother sent you to bring us to dinner?"

"Yes father, she said we are all to eat before you and uncle Gnaeus drink anymore!"

"She did, did she?" Publius replied in a jovial, mocking tone. "Well, we best not keep the lady waiting, let's eat but pray bring the wine pitcher as well!"

The three roared with laughter again and headed across the garden towards the villa. There was no mistaking father and son, both were blonde, though Publius now had shades of grey creeping into his temples and his hair was thinning. They were both slight of frame but lean and wiry muscled, time spent with the Legions having tempered and hardened their bodies. Publius, despite his position as Consul of Rome and an ascending career in politics had not succumbed to pampered living. The leanness and creamy skin of the pair strangely at odds with Gnaeus who was broad of stature, swarthy skinned and dark haired. Publius was a head taller than both Gnaeus and Cornelius, his height causing him to stoop and giving him a rounding of his shoulders. His facial features coarse with a large hooked nose a broad flat face and square jaw, the simple, earthy look of a peasant farmer. His face and carriage detracted from his well-dressed appearance giving him an ungainly, un-regal look. Many of his political opponents and enemies alike had mistakenly read his appearance as that of a bumpkin and physical weakness, political opponents had often paid with their careers and enemies with their lives for their poor judgement. Publius Cornelius Scipio the elder, head of the house of Scipio had a sharp mind and wits matched only by his ability with a sword.

Cornelius, or Publius Cornelius the younger was like his father both in character and complexion but his facial features differed, being of a finely sculptured jaw and high cheekbones, which he had inherited from his mother.

"Still wearing that old bracelet I see." Gnaeus said pointing to Cornelius's wrist and the bangle made of intertwined copper and brass wire. "It's almost too tight for you now; we'll have to replace it with one of more noble metals, as befits your station in life."

Cornelius lifted his arm and rotated the bracelet it was well thumbed.

"It's a simple thing I know uncle but dear to me all the same and a constant reminder of my life debt, one I'm sure I will be called on to repay some day." He replied sagely.

"Well, I have to say we were all grateful to that boy who saved you." Gnaeus pushed Cornelius's hair back from his temple where a thick white scar still showed, he tutted gently. "His father was a strange one though? He would have nothing of your father when he sought to thank him. Barbarians eh? They have no manners, if this war comes as your father surmises, it will change things. These savages will bend to Rome and learn to behave in a civilised manner."

"He seemed to be of noble bearing uncle, he asked for me, my state …"

"Pah!" Gnaeus waved his hand in derision. "If they are not Roman lad, they're savages! The world must and will become Rome. Anyway enough, come, let's see what your mother has for us to eat, she always keeps a fine table."

Chapter Eight

The mercenaries were crammed in alongside a cargo of ivory, exotic animal pelts, spices and amphora's of oil and wine. Their sleeping quarters dingy and cramped with an overlying stink of stale sweat. The beds, no more than cargo nets slung from the roof lined with dirty woollen blankets to wrap themselves in. Gestix and Baldor however, had slept like babes in their cribs, safe and secure for the first time in weeks. The creaking of the ship and the rhythmic dip of the oars had soothed them to rest, a full belly and a cup of wine aiding the process.

"We'd best see to the horse's lad, then what we can find for breakfast eh?"

"Come on then, let's feed the horses and eat."

The pair found the makeshift stable, the strong smell of horses and fresh dung aiding the location. They stuffed the nets with fresh hay and filled the leather buckets with fresh water. Just as they finished up Balaam appeared.

"Upper deck!" He barked. "Fall in with the rest of the men, there'll be a briefing and then we can eat, got it!"

"Yes Captain." Came from the two men. Balaam nodded and disappeared as fast as he'd arrived.

Gestix and Baldor made their way to the upper deck and joined the assembling warriors; the men parading in line as the deck space allowed. Above them, the square sail was filling with the freshening wind and drawing a groaning protest from the mast as it absorbed the force, the ship itself riding a gentle but building swell. The oars dipped, creaked and splashed droplets of water on the wind as they came clear of the sea again, throwing up a fine mist as the two elements combined. The men were in a more relaxed state of dress now, most in light tunics or leggings, one or two wrapped in short hunting cloaks against the cool breeze, some wearing leather forage caps. Helmets and corselets being stowed for the journey safe from the salt air, each however still carried his sword and most a dagger as well.

"Alright you idle bastards! Fall in!" Balaam roared, adjusting his balance to the up and down of the deck, his voice loud against the wind and the noise of the vessel cutting through the choppy water.

"Right! We have a few days on this rat-infested tub before we make Spain and you start to earn your coin! Rest while you can, for once we land we train as we travel to Saguntum. Meantime, I want no fighting with the crew or among yourselves and no drinking to excess, is that understood?"

A mumbled disjointed "Yes sir …Yes Captain." Came back from the ranks.

"Captain, sir will be fine. Now do you understand?" Balaam shouted.

"Yes Captain, sir!" Came clearer and together from the men.

"Good! I can see we are going to get on. Now, for those of you that missed the fight yesterday, our two new recruits are Baldor and Gestix of Carthage." He pointed out both men. "They decided soldiering with us is better than crucifixion. However, that remains to be seen!"

This drew some laughter from the warriors.

"Right, for everyone's benefit, remember you are now subject to my orders and that of my second in command, Harbro. Harbro! Step forward and make yourself known."

"Yes Captain, sir!" Came the crisp reply followed by a smart one-pace advance from the ranks of a man of medium height but broad build. Harbro wore a band of cloth wrapped around his practically baldhead; he was clean-shaven and deeply bronzed from the sun. His countenance that of a serious, no-nonsense man. A bull-thick neck supported his head from broad shoulders and a big chest, his narrow waist supported by thick powerful legs. The short black tunic he wore was sleeveless, showing heavily muscled arms and leather wrist bracers emphasising his big hands. He wore his weapons suspended from a wide leather waist belt instead of the usual baldric style.

"Thank you Harbro!"

"Captain, sir!" He replied stepping back into line

"Also!" Balaam continued. "Remember you are under military law, we are not levies, or regulars but are subject to the same laws and punishments. Follow orders! Work as a unit, Do as you are told and the God's willing you will return home wealthy men. Inspection will be morning and evening while we are aboard, I want blades kept sharp, rust free and lightly oiled. Any questions? ... No?   ... Dismissed!"

The men fell out, heading to the lower deck in search of food. Baldor stopped before the stairs and gazed back along the deck.

"Bit of a tub isn't she?" Gestix said, noting his friend's interest.

"Nothing at all like a warship but not bad for a merchantman. She sits as you say, like a tub! But I have to admit she's turning a fair speed, tub or not."

The ship had a single bank of oars and a double rudder handled by two sailors on a small raised deck at the stern. Below, on the oar deck the strains and heavy breathing of the men could be heard as they strived to maintain time to the beat of a drum. Up high, above the sail, a small wooden platform complete with handrail served as a crow's nest. The pair continued down the steps following the rest of the warriors, their noses wrinkling at the pungent, acidic odour of sweat that greeted them as they passed through the oar deck.

"Takes the edge of your appetite eh?" Quipped Gestix.

Baldor grinned and quickened his pace.

Breakfast consisted of goat meat strips, dates and bread washed down with warm milk, a hand-full of dried fruit completing the feast.

"We'll look to our weapons after breakfast." Gestix said while chewing hard on the dried fruit and pulling skin and pith from his teeth. "A dressing for all the edges and a light oiling I reckon. We need a bit of oil in the throat of the scabbard too, just around the edging there, this bloody salty air plays havoc with metal."

"Who else do you know here?" Enquired Baldor changing the subject. "There's Balaam and Marko so far, any other familiar faces?"

"I'll tell you better when I see them all a little closer, I doubt it though, the last war seems a lifetime ago and peace carries off men of my age as surely as war."

"Steady Gestix, you're almost admitting to old age!"

The pair grinned at one another and finished their breakfast.

****

Finding a sunny spot on the top deck near the bows and sheltered from the blustery wind, Baldor and Gestix made themselves comfortable on the coiled anchor rope. Gestix searched through his leather bag for the sharpening stones and flask of oil. Baldor deposited the weapons on the deck and selected the dagger for sharpening first.

"Right Baldor, here's where we have to think, a lesson if you like. We're no longer in a normal situation with the luxury of time or the absence of threat, so which blade would you deem the most necessary?"

"The swords I suppose?" Replied Baldor, looking puzzled.

"Exactly, so in readiness the swords take precedence … yes? Simple, but important."

"I hadn't thought of it like that."

"There will be many lessons to learn, mainly small things, things that in a normal world would not matter a pinch but from now on doing them right will ensure our survival."

Baldor picked up his sword and rubbed the stone along the blade from hilt to point in steady strokes, paying particular attention to the slight nicks and dents that resulted from the fight with Adharbal. He knew that blemishes in the blade, as small as they were, could be enough to catch on an opponent's weapon and hook his from his grip. The pair worked methodically, sighting and checking the edges as they dressed them before applying a coat of oil over the blade and into the neck of the scabbard.

"Something else we need to practice Baldor. Never be separated from your weapons or at the very least one of them. Whatever you do; eating, washing, pissing, sleeping, anything at all in fact, always have your weapons to hand. Men have died for that mistake, one moment off your guard and you could become another casualty and we haven't come this far to die so."

"I have much to learn it seems, with no room for error."

"We both have lad. I haven't been at war for half a lifetime, so you watch over me and I'll watch over you and what we both miss. May the Gods look out for us both!"

He laughed which eased the tension from the moment. Baldor grinned and started work on his dagger; his sword nestled against his thigh, the first two lessons of military sense in his head.

When the last blade was finished, Baldor stretched across the coiled ropes like a cat in front of the winter's fire, the sun warming his body and inducing sleep. He yawned and snuggled himself further into the coils relishing the peace.

"Get some sleep lad; I'll wake you if we're called."

Baldor closed his eyes; Gestix too, settled his back against the rail enjoying the sun and the contentment that Baldor was on the mend. The shoulder wound had healed without further infection and the lad's mental state had taken a more positive swing since their paths had joined with the mercenaries, even his sense of humour was returning. Gestix mused over how things were transpiring; here he was in his forty-third summer and off to war again but this time with his comrade's son, not many men could attest to that! It seemed like a myriad number of lives he was living. From his youth in Cisalpine Gaul followed by the first war against Rome, then a different life half a world away in Carthage. He had thought he would spend his days on the estate with Baldor's family, watching the boy grow and living in peace. It seemed the Gods conspired for a turbulent life for him. He smiled accepting his lot happily, life was for living and he would live it to the full and give the Gods an interesting saga to follow.

****

The following morning found the pair refreshed from another un-interrupted night's sleep. Routine was already becoming familiar as they rose at the same time, groomed and fed the horses and presented themselves for inspection.

Balaam walked up and down the ranks of men, inspecting, appraising, and questioning, some on well-being and others receiving a sharp rebuke for appearance. He paused in front of Baldor and eased the lad's tunic from his shoulder inspecting the wound, nodding approvingly.

"Healing well, boy. You need some light exercise though to get the shoulder fluid again."

"Yes Captain, sir!"

"Right!" Balaam shouted, turning back to the rest of his men. "This afternoon we will look to weapons practice and as there isn't much space it will make it all the more realistic." A few moans were quickly muzzled by a harsh bark of, "Silence!" Followed by a malevolent stare. "Now, seeing how you've all laid around sunning yourselves for the last couple of days growing fat and soft; be advised, the going is about to become a little tougher from tomorrow when we land in Spain, so some exercise won't do you any harm.

Any questions? ... No, good! Be on deck just after midday. Dismissed!"

The men fell out and headed below decks to find breakfast grumbling as soldiers do.

"Let's bring our food up here Baldor; it's too beautiful a morning to be stuck below."

"What kind of food would you like Gestix? Fresh fish lightly fried, perhaps some eggs and cheese? Or do you want good old dates and bread? Or old dates and old bread?" Baldor grinned while gesturing with his arms as if inviting Gestix to dine.

"I think old dates and old bread sound good." Replied Gestix. "You can fetch it while I save our place at the bows."

Baldor disappeared below and Gestix settled himself on the anchor ropes. It was Marko, who found him first. The man extended his hand and the pair shook firmly.

"One war not enough for you then Gestix? Or are you worried you grow old and fat?" Marko burst out laughing and settled himself on the ropes. He was olive skinned and black haired, his temples only just showing fringes of grey, his well-shaped goatee beard still ebony black. His nose was large and somewhat hooked; his eyes hazel coloured and full of life.

"What about yourself Marko? No woman? No home to call your own? Or do you still just love a fight?"

Baldor returned bringing an armful of food and a jug of warm milk.

"Baldor, this is Marko."

Marko turned and extended his hand, Baldor shuffling the armful of food to accommodate.

"That was well fought the other day, I've not seen two blades used so well before, you're skilled my young friend, where did you learn such?"

"From Gestix and my father."

Marko grinned and nudged Baldor playfully.

"Very sophisticated fighting to come from a Gaul eh? What happened to the chop chop, head off! Gallic tactics?" Marko laughed and nudged Baldor again.

"I can still oblige Marko and such base cuts are all I need for the likes of you." Gestix laughed loudly and Baldor breathed a quiet sigh of relief for he had seen the big man's ire rise to less; he surmised Marko had earned the right to the jest.

"In truth." Gestix began again. "Twas the lad himself that started it. He is equally clever with both hands, from learning as a child he would change from hand to hand with ease. As you saw it's useful when limbs are not as good as they should be." Gestix pushed Baldor's tunic back exposing the wound to Marko who nodded sagely.

"You must show me Baldor, it's never too late for an old dog to learn new tricks and I need to keep up with this old rogue here, especially if he has moved on from chop chop!"

Laughing between themselves, the three settled under the shelter of the rail to talk and eat.

****

Midday at the stern of the galley the ship's Captain caught up with Balaam leaning in thoughtful solitude on the creaking rail.

"Captain Balaam, sir."

"Yes Captain what can I do for you?" Balaam asked without turning around.

"This wind's freshening and cooling quickly; combine that with the hot weather we have just had and this building swell and I say we have a storm coming."

"What chance have we of making Spain before it hits?"

"Very little, I'll stake my reputation that it breaks before nightfall. I'd warn your men and secure the horses; I think we may be in for a bad night."

Balaam nodded, then grumbling beneath his breath found the nearest group of his men and dispatched them with orders to all for an immediate briefing on the deck. Already he could feel the wind strengthening and the bows rising higher on the swell. The mercenaries appeared in ones, twos, and groups, falling into line in front of their Captain.

"Come on! Move, you idle bastards, get in line, fall in!"

The last arrived at the run and quickly joined the assembled ranks; the men struggling to keep their balance as the deck heaved beneath their feet. The sea had changed from blue to a deathly grey, reflecting the colour of the storm clouds as sporadic raindrops hit the deck with a ferocity that promised a torrential downpour.

"Where in Hade's name did this come from? I've never seen a storm gather so quickly!" Marko muttered.

"Right lads!" Balaam shouted above the rising wind. "As you can see there's a storm coming." As if on cue, a crash of thunder peeled across the sky, its tone reverberating like that from a huge gong.

"Weapons practice will have to wait, Harbro take four men and secure our gear. Gestix, Baldor see to your horses, the rest of you below decks out of the way, dismissed."

The rain became a deluge, the heavy drops battering the deck like missiles. The men broke ranks heading off to allotted duties, else disappearing below deck like rabbits into a warren. Gestix and Baldor found the horses already skittish and stumbling in their stall.

"Give me a hand here Baldor." Gestix grunted as he lifted some cloth bales towards the stalls "We'll pad the stall out and lash the bales in place, the less room they have in there the better if this squall is going to blow us about."

Up on the deck sailors were swarming up the rigging to the cross spar that suspended the sail. They hoisted the heavy cloth up after them, lashing it secure then returning to the deck via the mast ropes as quickly as possible. The mast creaked and groaned as the vessel was buffeted from the waves, the ship teetering high on the swell then dropping stone like into the trough. As she ploughed in the boiling sea, the first of the wild water came over the rail and swilled down the deck.

"Bring her about you dogs!" The Captain shouted at the two men at the rudder. "Baal's beard! Bring her about! If we're caught broadside on we'll be swamped!"

The two men struggled to change the vessels position, the Captain running to aid them when he saw the enormity of the task. Two other sailors also ran to the stern to help take a hand with the rudders. The Captain, leaving the four men to their work descended to the oar deck where he began assigning the spare top deck sailors to oar work. Up in the crow's nest the lookout secured himself to the mast with a rope and called on all the Gods he knew to bring him safe through the storm.

Below decks, the mercenaries climbed into their net beds, reasoning that to be off the deck had to be safer than dodging moving equipment and trying to keep their feet. The ship rolled forcing protesting creaks and groans from the timbers, the mercenaries swinging in their nets like caterpillar chrysalis' blowing in the wind. One of the net ropes gave way dropping its occupant hard onto the floor, the others swinging so hard they hit the low-beamed ceiling. The men's angry and anxious curses mixed with the muttered but heartfelt prayers to their Gods to bring them through this ordeal. Few had been aboard a ship prior to this, let alone caught up in what was becoming a ferocious storm.

Balaam appeared in the cabin doorway his hands clawing at the timber frame for support and balance, at the same time making a concerted effort to remain calm for his men. He was soaking wet, his tunic sticking to him like a skin, behind him, lightning flashed and lit up the coal-blackened sky. A mixture of rain and seawater forced its way in past him, the spray carrying on the gusting wind and soaking the men nearest the door. Just as he tried to speak, the thunder crashed again and smothered his words. The ship dropped to the bottom of another trough, the men's stomachs following the rapid descent. Knocked off balance, Balaam's head collided with the framing, the impact rendering him senseless and dropping him to the floor. The ship suddenly rose and the netted bodies banged against the roof tipping another man onto the floor throwing him the length of the cabin and smashing him like matchwood against the wall. Men tried to disentangle themselves from their nets to help their Captain and comrade, more than one emptying his stomach either from fear or from the inevitable seasickness. Balaam was helped to his feet and attempting to issue orders, albeit in a slurred, drunken sounding voice. His forehead was split open, blood running across his face mixing with the rain, the bright crimson in stark contrast to his death-white, pallor.

"Get … oar decks … more men." He mumbled as his eyes rolled back in their sockets and the eyelids flickered.

"You two!" Harbro pointed to the nearest men. "Get the Captain into his net and tie him still, stay with him. The rest of you with me to the oar deck, move!"

They exited their quarters like rats from a burning barn, swarming across the deck and disappearing down the forward steps below to the oar deck. As the last few approached the hatch, the ship ploughed again and water came up and over the bows, wrenching loose and smashing the timber as it came. Broken timbers washed along the deck hooking men's legs from under them, the force and swirl of the water sending men, timber, ropes and anything loose on the deck tumbling and screaming towards the stern. The warrior nearest the hatch steps was the only one who managed to hold on. He was powerless to help his comrades behind him who were swept along with the water, timber and ropes, all mixing together like an infernal soup in some demonic God's broth bowl. Moments later nothing on the deck remained. Harbro appeared from the stairwell and dragged the warrior below decks to relative safety,

"Help there with the oars!" He shouted, pointing the man to the nearest bench.

The mercenaries had doubled up on the oars alongside the sailors and following their lead were heaving and lifting the oars in time to the still steady thump of the drum.

The ship pitched and rolled and men slid from the benches, water found its way down the stairway and sloshed around their feet. The stench of vomit, urine and sweat giving an acid taste to the air. However, the men sucked it in, in gasping lung-fulls, labouring to keep the ship on tack. The Captain teetered along the raised central walkway encouraging them to work their sweeps and keep time to the drum, while trying to calm and reassure them that all would be well. Seawater and rain washed down the stairs and entered through the oar ports, the deck boards disappearing under an ever-deepening froth of filthy, turbulent water. Men were dispatched from the overcrowded benches to bail out; helmets, buckets and bowls all finding use as men worked to keep the ship from wallowing. Baldor wondered whether this was to be the end for them all. The churning in his bowels and stomach making him flush hotly one moment and shiver the next, his mind a whirl of past events, his future seeming suddenly very short. He yawned uncontrollably, a sure sign that sickness was to follow.

"Are we keeping you awake over there Baldor?" Marko shouted from the opposite bench.

This ludicrous comment in the middle of the mayhem brought some strange looks that someone could jest at such time. Baldor gave a dozy grin then vomited hard.

"Actually, I'm sick and tired." He replied wiping his mouth on his arm.

Those that heard the banter had to laugh; some looked on wondering if madness had pervaded the ship, the Captain seized on the moment.

"Come on! Row damn you! Time enough for jokes when we're out of this mess. Stop puking and keep rowing."

This small respite seemed to give new life to the men and they bent their backs to the oars.

The Captain rotated his men from rowing to baling while allowing short rests when the water level came under control. He dared not let them rest too long as some looked physically and mentally spent; keeping them moving was the key.

Time wore on, early evening came and went then darkness fell and still the men laboured. The first sign of the storm easing was when the baling party found their workload slowing. The ship still heaved and tossed but with less ferocity than before, allowing the mercenaries to be released from the benches leaving the sailors to their work. Dawn found men asleep where they could, backs almost broken and arms numb from their efforts, their eyes sore from the saltwater. The stench from the vomit, urine and sweat the least of anyone's troubles, being alive was all that mattered.

Baldor and two mercenaries were dispatched for a damage report, the three gingerly climbing the stairs to the upper deck, their legs and balance unsteady, stomachs and heads not their own; the fresh morning air felt like ambrosia clearing the stink from their noses and filling their lungs. The eastern sky washed pink as the sun dragged itself from its watery bed. Pale, milky-light was pushing back the black-grey storm clouds while the wind dropped to a stiff breeze, though still strong enough to create white wave crests as far as the eye could see.

The sail was still furled but the spar to which it was lashed was broken in two, leaving it hanging at an obtuse angle to the mast. Above it, the lookout hung still suspended from his rope, his body swinging in time to the rolling of the ship like a broken puppet on a string. His arm at an awkward angle from his shoulder and his head smashed and misshapen from battering the mast, the timber itself splattered in dark blood and stained all the way to the deck. At the rudder the men leaned heavily on the handles, supporting themselves as much as holding to the course; one of them with a dislocated shoulder but his good arm still firmly gripping the tiller, his head resting on his chest with exhaustion. The deck itself was devoid of anything not fastened down; even the cargo hatches had been ripped away and sent seaward along with the wooden handrails.

Baldor leaned over the side and wretched hard again, with his stomach empty only traces of sour, sticky saliva came up. His stomach was cramping and sore and his head ached, his legs feeling very weak.

"Report!" Bellowed from the oar deck. "You're not up there to sun yourselves, damn you!"

The men trudged back to the stair to give the ship's Captain the damage assessment, while the Mate called the ships roll and Harbro counted the mercenaries.

Midmorning saw the crew and mercenaries patching and repairing the battered ship as best they might, the injured were treated and the damaged cargo thrown overboard. What food there was available was shared out and the fresh water rationed. Balaam was conscious but badly concussed. He constantly asked for casualty counts of his men and equipment losses, having to be told repeatedly of his three men lost overboard and one that died from head injuries after colliding with the steps. Harbro spared him the minor details of broken fingers, cracked heads and chronically seasick warriors. The oar crews were thinned out during the afternoon and men allowed to sleep when and where they could. Baldor found his net bed and collapsed into it, exhaustion inducing sleep and taking away the pain while the dry bread Gestix had forced into him eased the sickness and put a lining on his stomach again. As the light faded and the stars came out the ship was still out of sight of land, the ship's Captain calculating they could be as much as a day off course.

****

Gestix was awakened by Baldor shouting and thrashing in his net. He was out of his own net and beside his friend in an instant. Baldor shouted louder, calling Aiticias name over and over, tossing and shaking wildly. Gestix shook him gently, talking quietly to him coaxing him awake.

"Shut him up!" A slumbering mercenary called from another net.

Ignoring it, Gestix continued trying to wake Baldor by shaking him gently.

"By the Gods! Shut him up!" The mercenary shouted again now fully woken from his slumber.

"He's fevered, damn you!" Gestix snarled.

"Choke the bastard then, we need to sleep!"

Gestix spun on his heel heading for the complaining mercenary his face twisted into a snarl. The man heard him coming and struggled to free himself from his net, realising the need to defend himself from the enraged Gaul.

"Gestix! Leave it!" Harbro snapped as he awoke with the commotion.

Gestix stopped in his tracks, the complaining mercenary still struggling in the extraction from his net.

"See to the boy Gestix. Milor shut your mouth and go to sleep!"

Gestix returned to Baldor and had to shake him firmly to wake him from his nightmare. He sat up sharply grabbing hold of Gestix with a vice-like grip; his eyes wide in horror, his face beaded with sweat.

"Dead, she's dead, she's …"

"Hush Baldor, it's over, it's over!" Gestix said quietly though he gripped Baldor fiercely trying to bring him back to reality without too much fuss in front of the resting men.

"Gestix, here." Harbro whispered and passed a water flask over, motioning for the liquid to be given to Baldor.

Gestix pressed the flask to Baldor's lips and had him drink; he poured a little onto a piece of cloth and laid it over the lad's brow. Baldor was awake and looking about him, the look of horror replaced by bewilderment. Realising where he was he sighed deeply and laid back in the net his look that of a little boy lost. Gestix patted him on the shoulder reassuringly then headed back to his net.

The rest of the night passed quietly, the exhausted men and their injured Captain sleeping like the dead, the cocooned warriors swinging gently in time with the ship. Baldor however, lay staring at the wooden beams above him, all traces of sleep gone. His chest felt constricted and tight, the ache in his heart like a hot stone lodged in its place. His stomach was knotted and still nauseous feeling, a lump in his throat that he couldn't swallow away. He closed his eyes at times but the horror of Aiticia's death and the tumultuous events since haunted him, robbing him of peace and rest. His eyes were sore from lack of sleep and further aggravated by the quiet but copious tears that flowed unchecked to mix with the sweat on his face and neck. He lay quietly lost in his own misery, wishing once again to be no longer part of this world.

As the first fingers of dawn spread across the sky and dimmed the stars, Baldor fell asleep. However, before the sun was fully risen from beneath the horizon a cry came to waken the whole ship.

"Land ho, Captain! Land ho!"

Chapter Nine

"Right let's move!" Harbro bellowed, banging his fist repeatedly on the cabin wall.

The mercenaries tipped and slid from their nets, their feet still unsteady as they landed on the filthy decking. Stumbling and off balance their eyes bleary, heads aching and stomachs empty they gathered up their belongings. Weapon belts were adjusted and blades loosened in scabbards as they made their way from the stinking sleeping quarters to the top deck and clean air. With Balaam still incapacitated, Harbro was marshalling the men and rapping out orders.

"Baldor, Gestix, bring your horses. Danaar, see to the Captain and make sure his gear comes ashore."

Baldor walked unsteadily up the deck, Gestix following in his lee.

"Keep going lad, you'll come right back on solid ground." He pushed the sick looking Baldor gently along.

The thud of the gangplank hitting the wharf seemed to shake the ship as well as the heads of the warriors waiting to disembark. Harbro pushed past the pallid men and careered down the gangway, the timber bending and creaking to his heavy footfalls,

"Come on, move! We haven't got all bloody day, move!" He shouted back from the wharf.

The warriors fell in along the rickety timber wharf, the port no more than a fishing village.

"You'll get fresh water and breakfast. I know you don't feel like it but eat and you'll feel better. After breakfast we march, the horses will meet us along the way for we have missed our original disembarkation by a day, maybe …"

The men grumbled and muttered among themselves, clearly unhappy at the prospect of a march.

"Silence! I don't want your bloody thoughts! Eat and drink, for it could be a while before you have another chance." Harbro scowled, looking along the line as he spoke, seeking further complainers. "Dismissed!"

The men formed a line in front of two warriors who dished out bread, cheese and dried fruit. Harbro sought out Gestix and Baldor and dropped a heavy leather sack in front of them.

"The Captain said you needed some gear, helmets and such? The lads we lost in the storm have no more need of these, see what fits and return the rest. Usual rules, we deduct the cost from your payment."

He stalked off, shouting orders to unload and cursing warriors and sailors alike for tardiness. Gestix fished in the bag and pulled out a helmet and a leather corselet studded with flat bronze discs. The studs were green tarnished with verdigris for want of a polish. A further search produced three more helmets and two corselets, Gestix passed the items to Baldor.

"Anything fit? It's not bad equipment! Just needs a clean-up and some grease on the leather. Here, try this." He passed a bronze helmet to Baldor; it had large cheek pieces that covered most of his face and jaw. The conical bowl was decoratively embossed above the brim around to the ears. The top of the helm culminated in a brass tube from which black, horsehair plumes cascaded fountain like down the back of the helmet and the nape of Baldor's neck.

"Looks good, how's it feel?"

"I can hardly move my jaw."

"Good, you need it tight."

Baldor pulled at the cheek guards trying to ease the tension on his jaw.

"You'll get used to it … Hah! It makes you look even taller. Here, this is about your size."

Gestix pulled a grubby, white painted, leather corselet clear of the bag. It had a narrow red strip emblazoned across it near the base, with black triangles embossed into it like saw teeth; above this in the centre was a bronze ring for securing the large shoulder straps in place. These straps covered the shoulders, reinforcing the upper chest and back, embossed onto them in black leather was a circle surrounded by six triangles pointing away from it and looking like ebony sunbursts. Baldor removed the helmet and undid the straps before pulling the corselet over his head. Once in place he pulled the straps down, securing them to the ring on the corselet with the leather cords. Gestix punched at the corselet then tugged at it.

"It's a good fit Baldor. It'll do I reckon. Now, let's see what there is for me?"

He tipped the remaining items from the sack and picked up another corselet, assessing and testing the leather and the stitching. Baldor picked up a black leather belt from the pile, attached to it vertically were long leather strips, also black and about two fingers in width, there were two rows, one row shorter and laid on the top of the other. This skirt of leather pteruges was designed to be worn below the corselet, protecting the upper thighs and groin but flexible enough to allow full movement in battle or when riding.

"Eat up! Make the most of it, there's nothing else except water till nightfall, we move fast." Harbro announced as he took his ration and found somewhere to sit.

The pair, content with their acquisitions joined the queue for breakfast; Gestix collected his ration and returned the sack to Harbro.

"Did you find anything?" Harbro said between huge mouthfuls of food that he washed down with gulps of water.

"Two helmets, two corselets and …"

"Enough Gestix, enough." Harbro said, wiping his mouth on his arm. "Just settle up for those and that'll do, methinks there will be more than enough to go round shortly if what I hear is right."

"Things not going too well at Saguntum then?"

"The reports aren't good." He paused to lick the remains of the cheese from his fingers. "This siege could be a long drawn out affair and no place for cavalry I'll warrant. Still, we'll go like the good soldiers we are and earn our coin, there's also the rumour of rich pickings to be had and I would rather fight than spend another day on that boat puking! What about you lad?"

"I'm glad to be off the boat sir." Baldor managed quietly. He looked wretched, his face still pale and drawn and his eyes tired and bloodshot.

"Eat up then and get some water into you for we have a way to go." Harbro stood and brushed the crumbs from his tunic then patted Baldor on the shoulder. "We need your horse for the Captain, lad; he's still groggy from the smack on the head so I want him to ride."

"Sir." Was all Baldor could manage.

With breakfast finished, the warriors formed into column four files wide, packs and belongings over their shoulders, the men's mood black. Tired and discontent they trudged off northeastwards following the coast road, Harbro appointed a rear-guard while he led the group, his hand holding the bridle of Balaam's mount. Balaam, his head bandaged sat the horse awkwardly, his injury clearly causing him some discomfort. Leaving the marshalling to Harbro, the best he could manage was a wave forward of his hand and the column moved off.

It was tolerable going for most of the morning, the sun slipping in and out from behind the clouds and changing the colour of the nearby sea through a multitude of blue and grey shades. The onshore breeze cooled the warriors and dried the sweat that oozed from their pores. To the west and inland, the coastal plain went from flat grassland with scattered bushes to undulating hillocks. Well beyond the distant heat shimmer, the land rolled upwards into hills, which coloured blue and purple across the horizon. Clouds of white dust rose as the booted feet thumped up and down in time to the march legs and tunics turning white as the swirling powder stuck to sweat dampened clothes and skin.

"Company, Halt! … Water stop."

As the warriors stood at ease there was a noticeable gasping for breath, the cavalrymen unaccustomed to the rigours of the march made poor infantry, their mood had not improved and grumbling's were all too vocal. Harbro came back along the line bellowing and cursing, his face twisted in anger, men quietened and turned to drink instead of talk.

"That's better! Stop whining like a pack of brats. The horses will meet us along this road. Until then this exercise will do you good, so toughen up! You'll be in combat in the next few days against an enemy who has been fighting for months, they are experienced! Hard! And they won't give you time to draw breath!"

The men scowled and drank but no one ventured further complaints.

Evening found the men still un-united with the horses and forced to sleep in the open. Camp was set up next to a small copse, cooking fires lit and a meagre supper prepared. Harbro moved around the men and allotted watch duty, two men on guard at once with a given position of the moon indicated before change over, he checked warriors and weapons as he went.

"He's good. Knows how to be with the men, he and Balaam make a decent team, I'll give them that." Gestix said nodding sagely. "We shouldn't go too far wrong though we need some decent food, this fruit and bread has its limits!"

He spat some tough skin out of his mouth then rummaged through his pack, pulling out a small, cloth wrapped package passing it to Baldor.

"Here lad, it's cold, tough and probably dry as sticks but at least its meat."

Baldor opened the cloth to reveal a pile of smoked meat strips; he halved the meat between them.

"When did you get this?" He said, stuffing it into his mouth.

Gestix laughed tapping his finger to his nose.

"Chew it Baldor, get all the goodness out of it, eat it slowly and it'll take the edge off your appetite."

As they ate they spread their blankets, swords were un-slung and laid on the bedding near at hand. Gestix unsheathed his dagger laying it under the cloak he had bundled for a pillow; he nudged Baldor intimating him to do likewise. The exhausted men were soon asleep and the camp quiet as the grave, the watch keepers quietly waking their relief as their own duty period ended. Just before dawn, Baldor and Danaar took their turn, the retiring guards waking the pair with a gentle kick to the feet, followed by a nod of the head in the direction of the camp perimeter. The two rose, rubbing sleep from their eyes and stiffness from their bodies as they strapped on their swords. Baldor slipped his dagger back into its sheath and drew his cloak about him as he walked to the edge of the trees to watch along the road. Danaar joined him, rubbing his hands and body vigorously as he approached, trying to warm himself and rub life into his aching limbs.

"For the love of Tanith, It's colder than a hag's tit! Worst time of the night this, eh?" His breath left a vapour trail as he whispered.

"It could be worse, at least we've slept and the ground was still."

Danaar looked sour and paced backwards and forwards.

"I hope the horses are here by morning I've had enough of marching, I didn't sign on for this infantry shit!"

With some time until dawn, the men separated and moved off to cover the approaches to the camp. Baldor gazed northwards into the darkness; the sky was thick with stars and very still with just a sliver of moon to cast a light. The invisible sea gave a gentle roar as the waves broke on the beach, other than that peace and silence reigned. Baldor knew time to think and reflect would only raise ghosts and memories for him and he made a conscious effort to focus on the task in hand to prevent his mind wandering to past events. The likelihood of trouble was minimal but remembering the lesson already learned from Gestix, he slipped the sword from its sheath and held it beneath his cloak and listened intently as he walked the perimeter of the camp. As his eyes accustomed to the gloom he defined the shapes of the sleeping men, some huddled together for warmth while others slept singly. The small fire had long since been smothered, Harbro took no chances.

Baldor and Danaar met each other as they circumnavigated the camp, nodding to each other as they passed. Baldor's thoughts moved to the coming siege, he'd had no time to train with the men and although he deemed he could fight, he knew battle was going to be very different from just weapons skills and one to one combat. Gestix had impressed on him the need to fight as a team, to watch each other's back and to forget risky moves. Most important of all to give no quarter, he wondered at how he would cope with killing someone begging for mercy. Going over the advice in his head as he continued his progress, the seeds of doubt in his abilities began to grow. His stomach tightened, feeling both hollow and hot, his mouth dried and the lump seemed to grow in his throat again. This moment of panic passed as quickly as it came as he remembered the likely alternative to being here was crucifixion, that sobering thought quickly allaying the previous fears. Trying to lighten his thoughts, he picked up the pace as he patrolled but this demon-haunted time of the morning seemed to heighten and amplify his fears, sapping confidence and stealing his courage away. Collecting himself, he was relieved to see the pale glow in the east announcing the coming day, the light at last scaring away the demons of the night and giving promise of warmth to the land. As the pair passed each other again, Danaar caught Baldor's attention and nodded towards Harbro.

"Best wake them. Start with him."

Baldor quietly approached Harbro but before he reached him; Harbro, eyes still closed, spoke.

"I'm coming boy, wake the Captain, then rouse these laggards."

Baldor was taken aback by the wakefulness of Harbro and thought of the need to hone his stealth capabilities, while also learning to sleep lightly. The camp came to life as the warriors woke, stretched, yawned, broke wind and complained of aching limbs.

"Light breakfast! We eat and move! When we meet the horses we will train as we go." Balaam shouted, who seemed to have recovered his wits and be returning to his old self.

"Light breakfast! We have never had anything else, I wish …"

"Shut up Milor, put the food between your teeth along with your tongue and spare us your whining!" Bellowed Harbro.

As the men ate, Balaam addressed them. "We are further south than that idiot of a Captain surmised, so we will keep pushing along the coast until we unite with the horses. As we landed a messenger was dispatched northwards to bring the horses to us, until then you can stretch your legs and lungs." Seeing his stern look no one ventured complaint. "On the positive side, this extended journey allows us extra time to train, for the word is we will need it."

The last comment had everyman's attention; Balaam made to continue but was cut short by a shout from Danaar.

"Captain! Horses on the road coming from the north."

The men suddenly looked buoyant, smiles spreading over dirt-lined faces.

"Form up! Back to the trees, move the gear. Harbro, Danaar, go check, I want numbers!"

As the men fell back to the treeline, the large cloud of dust could be seen approaching quickly from the north, the billowing dust taking on an orange hue from the rays of the sun and creating the illusion of a runaway fire hurtling along the road.

"Weapons! … Be ready." The rasp of metal leaving sheaths sounded loud in the early morning. "This should be our horses but we take no chances, if its trouble, keep to the trees and stay in pairs." Balaam walked the line as he talked while drawing his falcata from its sheath.

Baldor's heart raced as he and Gestix dropped back to the trees, horses or trouble? Either way it was a break from marching.

"You keep near me lad, you hear? We're ill equipped to take on cavalry." Gestix said quietly.

The thunder of hooves built to a crescendo as the swirling dust trail came closer. Hands tightened on sword hilts, breaths held and men shuffled together, the absence of shields making their companions a source of comfort and protection. Danaar came running back seeking the Captain, swift words between the two saw Balaam nodding, smiling and turning to his men.

"The walking is over lads, the horses are ours!" Cheers drowned his words; he let the men have their head for a moment before raising his hands for silence.

"Enough, enough! I want this camp cleared, rub the horses down and rest them, then report to me here and we'll go over the training we'll be doing as we go, now move!"

Appraising hands patted, stroked and checked the animals, some of the horses tossing their heads, whinnying and even nuzzling their master when they picked up his scent. Rubbing down and removal of the white flecked sweat and spume began, blankets where thrown over the horses backs to prevent any chill. A rope line was ran out and the beasts tethered, some idly cropping the grass others sniffing on the breeze for fresh water.

"Gather around! Come on, the Captain wants a word; we'll water the horses once they've cooled down." Harbro walked through the men urging and pushing them in the direction of the Captain.

With the men gathered in front of him, Balaam squatted down and smoothed the dust with his hand clearing a small area. He produced a leather bag and tipped the contents onto the ground.

"Before any of you ask, we're not going to be playing games." He quipped as the cleared dust patch filled with brightly coloured marbles. Some men sniggered and others made mock groaning noises.

"Right, each one of you is a marble, this larger one here is me and the red one is Harbro." Balaam placed the marbles into a column of pairs with the large marble and red one to the front.

"This is us in column, the usual order of progress, got it? I relay orders to Harbro; he will announce the commands to you, either by voice or signal or both. To refresh your idle heads and for those who have joined us recently, these are the basic commands."

Getting to his feet again Balaam raised his right arm, holding it straight above his head; then brought it down in an arc, pointing forward and stopping it level with his shoulder,

"That means forward at the walk."

He pushed his arm out straight from the shoulder but to the side of his body and made a backward circle with it.

"That means move to a trot."

Next, raising his arm to his shoulder and bent upwards from the elbow at ninety degrees, his hand formed a fist. He pumped it up and down twice.

"This means we canter."

He paused checking for understanding or anyone seeking to question, seeing none he continued.

"As we move to the charge." He pointed the arm straight forward again and held it. "Questions?"

With no comment, he continued with the simpler, self-explanatory signals for turning. "Now, it becomes a little more complex! When I want you to move from column to line it's like this!"

He put both arms out straight from the shoulder and to the side of his body, and then dropped them like a bird flapping its wings.

"Alright so far? … Baldor?"

"Yes Sir!"

"Good, now the important one, when I raise both my arms thus."

Balaam lifted both arms above his head and made an apex.

"This is …?"

"Form an arrowhead or wedge sir." Said one of the men.

"Good! Now I'll demonstrate with the marbles."

The warriors pushed in tighter as he began arranging the marbles in the dust, talking them through the manoeuvres and the changing positions with the brightly coloured glass spheres. Baldor pulled at the marble hanging around his neck, rubbing it between his thumb and forefinger, his mind drifting back to the last time he had played marbles all those years before. His reverie interrupted by a dig in the ribs and a stern look from Gestix who nodded towards the marbles and he quickly refocused his attention. Once the briefing was complete and the horses watered, the warriors began attaching gear to their mounts. Helmets were hung within reach and shields slung on the men's backs, war spears were taken up as the men mounted. They fell in two by two behind Balaam, their humour changed from sombre to light and cheerful, at one with their mounts, the miserable and ill tempered, enforced infantrymen gone. Harbro rode up and down the assembling men dressing the ranks and amidst the rattle of metal and the creak of leather, Captain Balaam's mercenary cavalry finally came in to being.

Midday saw them still making their way along the undulating, dust-choking road. The warriors cast longing glances seaward to the sparkling water that invited rest, refreshment and a chance to wash the grime from their bodies. The road gradient steepened making the horses work, hooves flailing stones and dirt high in the air, riders leaning forward into the animal's necks and urging them on. As it levelled out Balaam signalled for a slowing of pace and the panting, snorting horses were walked. The height of the land from the sea brought a cooling onshore breeze that rolled up and over the cliffs giving comfort to both man and beast. Orders came back along the column for a short rest for food and water.

Balaam allowed a longer break than he'd intimated, this gave time for some of the heat to slip from the scorching sun and as the shadows lengthened, Harbro called to mount up and form column. The plain was gently undulating, a mixture of white sand and dust. In places, patches of pale green sward tried to establish itself amongst the bone-dry landscape, dotted amongst the sparse grass were stunted bushes, scorched from the wind and the swirling dirt. The remainder of the afternoon saw men and horses put through their paces. Harbro working amongst the ranks, guiding and coercing the men into position, in tune with the commands from their Captain. With the onset of early evening, the spume flecked mounts and the tired men were pushed into the last and perhaps most difficult manoeuvre of the day, the wedge or arrowhead.

Balaam's arms formed an apex, Harbro bellowed above the noise of the galloping horses to form a wedge. Others took up the call and the ranks sorted themselves from a line into a fast moving, compact triangle of horseflesh and men. Harbro called for tightness and the warriors closed up until their legs were touching the flanks of the mount to either side of them. Near the centre, Gestix urged Baldor closer to him, Baldor caught up in the euphoria and the breakneck speed of the manoeuvre grinning broadly. The press in the centre was such that spears were raised vertically and shields pulled to the front to make room. On the outer line, spears levelled and shields canted while Balaam drew his sword and pointed forwards, taking the armoured wedge to the charge. The flesh and metal wedge thundered over the ground leaving a blooming white dust cloud in its wake, the drum of hooves filling men's ears and carrying distantly over the plain. Finally, Balaam signalled a slowing of pace to a canter and then a trot, the wedge moving at a gentler pace began its change back to column formation. As the column slowed to a walk, Harbro reined in alongside his Captain. Collecting his orders, he pulled his mount around hard and cantered off back down the column, bellowing commands for a stop for the night and the usual rub down for the animals, watch duty to be appointed.

"Well Baldor, that's your first taste of cavalry work, think you can manage it?" Gestix grinned as he hassled his friend.

"I'll manage fine Gestix, it's old men like yourself that may be found wanting!"

Baldor ducked as a hand went to slap his head, he was about to reply with comments of old age and slowness when a booted foot hit his shins.

"Sharpen up Baldor, I'm twice your age but it would seem twice as fast!" Gestix tutted sarcastically and shook his head. "Boys, boys! It's going to be a long, hard war!"

"You have to sleep some time old man, I can wait."

"You should live so long!" Gestix replied, smiling. "And if I am so old and slow you can rub my horse down while I rest."

Baldor, struggling for a quick reply could only smile and shake his head as Gestix passed him his horse's reins.

The camp was set up near a dried stream bed, the long hot summer having reduced the flow to a mere trickle, enough for the men to replenish water flasks and slake their thirst but not enough to bathe in. The men had to scratch and dig some of the bed out to form small puddles for the animals to drink properly. The horses drank deeply, the exertions of the afternoon and the sweat loss creating the need in them for huge amounts of water. The men cleaned themselves as best they could then sought supper and an early night. Balaam called for a briefing before retrial.

"Tomorrow we make Saguntum." Cheers broke out which he quelled with raised hands demanding silence. "Rest well, for we could be in action the day after and remember, stay together and fight as a unit. We haven't had enough time to train together, so the less experienced among you." He glanced at Baldor and some of the other younger men. "Look to your elders for direction." Laughter and sarcastic comments broke out with some of the older warriors being jostled and harangued, this resulting with threats and playful cuffs of the heads and ears of the mockers. Again, Balaam called for silence.

"Don't laugh too hard young pups! You don't get to our age without being good at what you do. Mark my words, watch and learn." Balaam's words quickly sobered the younger men of the group.

****

The night passed quietly, the men rising at first light. Horses were made ready, equipment stowed and the men dressed in the full panoply of war. As the sun lifted to full view above the waves the column moved off, sunlight flashing and reflecting on helmets, spear points and shields. Horses skittered and stomped sensing the excitement from their riders, the animals as keen as the men to be on their way. Throughout the ride Balaam and Harbro constantly called up training formations, attack, flanking and general order of march, the men learning to come to terms with the heat and the full weight of their war gear. Skills between old comrades were re-honed and tentative bonds began to form between veterans and the latest recruits.

As late afternoon approached and the heat of the day began to slip away, Balaam called a halt to the manoeuvres and signalled the men into column. Then taking the lead, led them off the plain and on the final leg of their journey to Saguntum. Just after the light faded from blued shadow to blackness, the column crested a rise to see hundreds of small fires twinkling and flickering in the night, some scattering sparks high into the darkness as fresh fuel was heaped onto them.

The fires encircled the mound upon which the city stood, illuminating the walls above with an orange-red glow. The city showed no lights from the walls or from the buildings which reared above them. Like some grim leviathan, it skulked in shadow without signs of life.

The column weaved its way towards the camp, intercepted every now and then by sentries that materialised from the gloom to check identities with the Captain before fading back into the blackness. As they entered the camp itself, they had to slow their progress to weave amongst the campfires and the throng of warriors that squatted, ate or slept around them. Some singing could be heard, occasional laughter and sometimes raised angry voices, which were quickly shouted down by officers or comrades interceding to stop arguments escalating. Dogs yapped, mules bellowed, horses whickered and the mournful melody of a reed flute carried on the air, mixing with the rasp of whetstones honing blades. This apparent disorganisation seemed at odds with Baldor's ideas of an army camp and he looked about not quite knowing what to make of it all. Gestix, seeing his bewilderment ventured an explanation.

"Not like a real army camp eh, that's what you're thinking?"

Baldor nodding, prompted Gestix to carry on.

"It's not that different from any other really Baldor. Granted a Roman camp would have the tents in neat rows with equipment stowed, straight horse lines, and probably more discipline. But remember this is a mercenary army, there are half a dozen different nationalities here with their own ideas of war and relaxation. However, soldiers are soldiers the world over, you'll see. Come on, let's get settled in, I'm for supper then bed, what about you?"

Baldor nodded agreement as they weaved in single file through the throng of men and animals. Balaam led them to the outer edges of the encampment and away from the multitudes around the fires. Harbro called for a fire to be set, allotted watch duty and advised of a lengthy stay. The warriors spread sleeping mats and slipped off helmets and cuirasses, weapons however being placed next to them and within immediate reach.

"We'll set up camp in the morning, proper, I'll find out what the play is and where we fit in, you start earning tomorrow!"

Chapter Ten

Hannibal stretched his wounded leg; tentatively flexing the thigh he eased some of the stiffness from it, he grimaced when his manipulation sent a spasm of pain through the muscle.

The tent within which he sat was grubby, off-white in colour and blotched in places from old dirt and mud stains with the odd repair patch here and there. The entrance had dried rushes spread on the floor though this gave way to carpets and rugs in the living quarters themselves. The furnishings were sparse but practical; a low couch over which a black war cloak was draped and a small cedarwood table served as a writing desk with an old padded stool for a chair. The table covered with yellowed parchment plans, drawings and sketches with oil lamps as paperweights to keep the documents secure. A longer, trestle table complete with a dozen chairs stood in the centre of the tent and beyond it on an upright, cross shaped frame his armour, weapons belt and helmet were stored. In the yellow glow of the lamps, the armour took on the look of a spectre-like warrior waiting in the shadows. To the rear of the tent behind a curtain was another table draped in a scarlet cover, richly patterned and embroidered with gold thread and the only sign of opulence in the tent. Upon it was a miniature stone altar complete with a finely carved effigy of the austere God, Baal Hammon made of yellowing ivory. A lamp heated a dish of scented oil and water, giving off an aromatic smell, which sweetened the air and helped mask the musty smell of old cloth and rushes. At the very back of the tent, heavy curtains screened a simple camp bed.

Hannibal continued to massage and rub to aid the circulation, his mind, just as active, planned and calculated his next moves to take Saguntum and more importantly the future phases of his campaign. The guard announcing the arrival of his physician interrupted his thoughts.

Hannibal raised himself from his couch. "Synbolus, you are a wonder, see! I am much recovered." He stood as he spoke.

"General, please remain seated, it's more rest that you need for the wound was deep." The old man said gravely while tut-tutting and shaking his head, all the while gently pushing the young General back to the couch.

"Is the wound still dry? You haven't burst the stitches or ..."

"Synbolus! Peace man, peace! I am ..."

The old man waved the retort away still muttering to himself and ignoring his patient's pleas, his long bony fingers probing the thigh and pinching toes. Hannibal relented with a deep sigh and let the old man examine him.

As the bandage came clear, Synbolus finally nodded in satisfaction but continued muttering about youth, soldiers, and idiots and how one was indistinguishable from the other. He produced fresh bandages and set about his ministrations, the younger man quietly resigned to his fate.

The guard ventured in once more.

"Beg your pardon, General. There is an envoy here from the senate; he requests an audience with you."

"I need some time to prepare, delay him!" The guard saluted and left. "Synbolus, strap the leg, keep the bandage above the hem of my tunic and pass me my robe, quickly now!"

The old man speeded up his ministrations but carried on muttering to himself as before.

Hannibal called for his servants, commanding the tent tidied, plans and drawings folded and food and wine placed on the table. Synbolus was dismissed with a clap on the shoulder and a short word of thanks. On his feet again, Hannibal checked the bandage and that the tunic and robe covered it amply.

"Guard! Call my officers; I want them here, now."

By the time the envoy was announced, Hannibal and his staff were convened, all had been briefed as to the condition of his wound, which if mentioned was to be of no consequence.

The envoy entered the tent, bowing to the General and the assembled men.

"Hail General! Greetings from the senate."

"Hail envoy! What news from Carthage?"

"Sir, the senate wishes you well and looks for news of the siege; we have heard little of any progress."

A low snarl came from the men around the table followed by mutterings of sending more warriors and money instead of snivelling, pompous messengers. Hannibal quietened them whilst calling for his scribes to bring the latest reports to him. He gestured the envoy to the table offering food and drink, while dispatching servants to see to the envoy's escort and their needs. He conversed genially with the messenger, advising of the state of the siege and the estimated time of completion but without disclosing his plan as to how the city would fall. With no mention of his injury from the visitor, Hannibal also let the issue lie. He asked for the continuing support of the senate and the people of Carthage then offered a leather satchel containing his written reports.

"All news is within." He said, smiling warmly.

The envoy took the satchel and offered a similar one in return then reaching into his tunic produced a folded parchment heavily sealed with red wax.

"Sir, I am to place this personally in your hand, it is an undertaking from ..."

"My Lord Hanno Samilcar!" Hannibal, recognising the seal completed the sentence.

Growls and mutterings came from the officers at the table with Mago's voice the most vocal.

"From my Lord Hanno Samilcar's family, General." The envoy corrected. "The old Lord is sick, stricken with a palsy they say."

Hannibal broke the seal, his heart beating a little faster as he did so. The Lord Samilcar, senator and judge, head of the aristocratic party in Carthage had always been a staunch advocate against the expansionist policies of his own family, the Barca's. There would be no help or comfort in the letter, that was a given. Unfolding the parchment, he read it and shrugged. Quizzical looks from his staff prompted him to speak.

"We are to apprehend and return to Carthage forthwith a one, Baldor Targa."

"Who, in Hades name is that?" Grunted Mago.

"It seems this Baldor Targa has murdered the Lord Carthalo, eldest son of Lord Hanno then badly injured the second son, Adharbal in a brawl." Hannibal read to the officers.

"Ha! We should give the bastard a commendation!" Mago shouted, a disapproving look from Hannibal prompted him to finish "Before we crucify him, of course!" Hannibal's glower quietened his brother and quelled the laughter beginning at the table.

"Murder is murder. The man should stand trial for what he has done." Hannibal asserted.

Mago hooted, other than that, the table was now silent.

"But what has this matter to do with us?" Hannibal asked the envoy.

"The criminal is said to have enlisted with your army General, serving under a mercenary cavalry Captain named Balaam."

"Well that narrows it down to about ten thousand men or so!" shouted Mago. "Baal's breath man! Do you think we have nothing better to do but apprehend bloody criminals?"

"Just the one criminal is all we need you to apprehend, General Mago!" The envoy replied caustically.

Mago jumped up from the table, threats and curses on his lips his colleagues restraining and attempting to calm him. The look of alarm on the envoys face faded as Mago was gently but firmly pushed back to his seat. Hannibal placed the warrant on the table and brought the situation under further control by announcing the man would be found and dealt with.

"No General, you are to return him to Carthage for the senate to see justice done." The envoy corrected.

"Very well. It will be as the Lord Hanno's family desires." Hannibal consented, once more looking to the table to silence any retort. "Other than that, is there further business?"

"No General, with your leave I'll be on my way, I will carry your reply to my Lord's family."

The envoy pushed back his chair, collected the satchel, bowed eloquently to Hannibal and quickly to the still seated men then departed.

"Pompous, smug little turd!" Growled Mago.

"Thank you gentlemen for your time, we will reconvene at dawn tomorrow I will cover off my plans for the next and hoped for final phase of this siege. My leg is well recovered so we must be about this business in earnest, General Mago spare me a moment if you will."

The officers filed out of the tent leaving the brothers to talk. Mago, seeing his brother's furrowed brows and dark looks tried to pre-empt the anger he saw brewing.

"Hannibal before you say ..."

"General Hannibal, Mago! General! I command here sir!" Hannibal barked at Mago through gritted teeth.

"I am ..." Mago began again then corrected himself. "General Hannibal, I am sorry."

"I don't want you being sorry Mago, I want you to hold your tongue and listen sometimes! How do you think that looked to the envoy?" Mago looked downcast. "I'll tell you how it looked! It looks like I am not in command here, the siege goes badly enough without the message going back to Carthage that I can't control my officers!"

"I am not some slave to be told my mind!" Mago argued bitterly.

"No you are not! You are supposed to be my General, my support and a man of intelligence!"

Mago bridled again at the sharp rebuke but said nothing. Hannibal continued, though he lowered his voice somewhat and brought his temper under control.

"You're a fine warrior Mago and as good a field General as I could ask for but save your wrath for the battlefield eh. Old Lord Hanno is no friend to us but he is still owed respect. The eldest son I grant you is ... was, a fool and the world probably a better place for him having left it, but those thoughts are best kept to ourselves.

We have a siege to finish and a war coming that will set this world by the ears. I need a secure base behind us in Carthage but most of all a united front here in the field." He paused again his tone now conciliatory. "I know you're loyal! And I know you are entitled to your opinion and the freedom to express it but choose your time brother, choose your time!" Hannibal placed his arm over Mago's shoulder and hugged him roughly.

"Tomorrow we start this siege again. Channel your frustration into the battle, I want that wall taken, you are the man to do it. Now rest up, ready for the morrow."

The following dawn saw the besieging army preparing for combat. As the sun cast its first rays across the bay, the Generals and field commanders made their way to Hannibal's tent to collect the orders for the day. With the men seated around the table, Hannibal expounded his strategy.

"General Maharabal."

"Yes General." The slight framed man acknowledged as he scratched his greying hair. He sported a close cut goatee beard, which disguised a very pointed chin, his eyes were large and warm in contrast to the sharp features of his nose that was thin and pointed at the end but also crooked at the bridge. His lips were thin and his mouth small, the left corner of which drooped towards his chin. His left shoulder twisted slightly, giving him an awkward posture. For all his unimposing physical appearance, he was one of the finest commanders of heavy cavalry in the world, the numerous silver bracelets on his right arm, one for each campaign, showing the depth of his war experience.

"General, I want the heavy cavalry ranked obliquely to the siege tower." Hannibal pointed to a position on the plan, which was spread across the table for the men to view. "The cavalry will prevent any sortie from the city gate to attack the tower, behind them we'll place mangonels, ballistas and archers, their combined firepower should keep heads low on the parapet until we have the tower in place. General Mago, you will lead the assault from the tower and I want our assault troops in it, ready. Reinforcements will be supplied readily using the vineae for cover. Once the men are on the parapet we need to keep feeding troops up, no respite!

General Hasdrubal"

"Sir." The youngest officer smiled at his brother, the admiration and respect clear on his face. Hasdrubal was of the same build and had the smooth good looks of his elder brother. He wore his hair in similar fashion and like Hannibal went clean-shaven, the pair almost passing for twins. His devotion to Hannibal was that of blind loyalty, the elder brother looked upon in hero status.

"I want five hundred of our light troops with pickaxes and pry bars to undermine the section of wall that we viewed the day I was speared, which is here." Hannibal pointed with a small knife to a position on the plan.

"We need the wall undermining and propping. Pack the hole with kindling, faggots and timber and set fire to it. Once it's down, and the engineers estimate this amount will fall." Hannibal drew his finger across the plan; the Generals leaned in close to see, followed by some sharp intakes of breath and shaking heads at the expected breadth of the breach.

"What if it doesn't sir?" Asked Maharabal.

"The engineers are sure of their calculation. Remember; it is here we saw the mortar missing? The oldest part of the city wall, made from mud bricks, it will come down."

Questions and comments came all at once from the officers, Hannibal having to bang on the table to restore order.

"Gentlemen, gentlemen! Let me finish, your questions and arguments are most welcome, when I have covered the whole plan. Now, when the wall collapses the heavy Gallic infantry under Sergatatonix will force the breach, the Iberian light troops will follow in support to consolidate and hold the ground. Gentlemen, questions?"

The questions were many but no arguments were raised against the plan. A sense of excitement, hope for victory and an end to the siege filled the tent. Hannibal called the men to order while summing up and pouring a goblet of wine for them. He personally offered a drink to each, wishing them victory, honour and a safe day.

"Beg your pardon, General Hannibal." The sentry entered bringing a sweating, dirt-stained messenger with him.

"Can it not wait soldier, we'll be but a moment?"

"General, there are Roman envoys at the harbour; they demand an audience with you!" Blurted the messenger.

"Romans here?" Maharabal exclaimed, the shock evident on most of the faces within the tent.

"Why are you all surprised?" Hannibal asked. "We are pulling the 'she wolf's' tail, are we not? Does the wolf not turn to see who dares come to her den? Take this city for me while I will deal with the wolf!"

Smiling again, he took total command, bringing the room to order and dispatching his staff to mobilise as planned. As the men filed out, he summoned the messenger to ascertain further details of the Roman envoys.

"Now, I need these envoys delayed for ..."

Outside, the rumble of thousands of horses moving into position drowned his words, the ground vibrating as the cavalry passed directly in front of his tent. Having to wait to be heard, Hannibal had the messenger help him strap on his corselet. As the man fastened the lacings and buckles, Hannibal tied his purple sash about his waist then reached for his sword baldric, slipping it over his head and shoulder adjusting the weapons into place. As the noise of the cavalry subsided, Hannibal began again.

"I don't want the Romans up here; I need you to buy me some time."

"Yes sir." The messenger replied, finishing up the buckles.

"Find out who is here, I want names. I also need to know what power is invested in them. Most importantly, they are to remain where they are; I don't want them anywhere near the city. Tell them we cannot guarantee their safety."

"Yes General."

Hannibal cupped his chin in his hand deep in thought; he motioned the messenger to fit the bronze greaves while he contemplated.

"Tell them ... tell them, I will prepare letters of introduction for them to take to Carthage. They must go there and speak to the senate. However, this will take time." Hannibal paced the tent as he spoke.

"See they are given good and safe quarters but down near the quay ... it will take a day or two to prepare these undertakings ... I cannot at this critical time give them an audience. Do you understand? You must buy me this time."

Hannibal patted the messenger on the shoulder, the man saluted and slipped out of the tent.

"Guard!" A helmeted head ducked into the tent.

"Fetch Silensos for me and have him bring his writing materials."

While Hannibal waited for his chronicler he went to the small altar and dropped to his knees bowing his head in prayer, he was still praying when the scribe was announced. Silensos entered bidding him a cordial good morning, though he stopped short when the young man remained on his knees. Silensos bowed his head and stood quietly waiting for the other to finish his reverences. Silensos was a man of late middle age. His black curled hair cut to his collar and carefully trimmed beard cut thinly along his jaw line flecked through with grey. The absence of a moustache giving him a regal, almost kingly look. He held himself in a noble, statesman like poise, his parchments carefully rolled under one arm and a small embossed leather case containing quills and sharpening knives in his hand. Shortly, Hannibal stood up, bowed to his God and turned to greet him.

Outside, the loud thump of mangonels and catapults releasing their deadly cargos announced the fresh assault on the city. The air whooshed as archers loosed their shafts and in the distance, the dull crack of stone hitting stone told of the boulders colliding with the city walls. Creaks and groans like a giant tree bending in the wind emanated from the colossal tower as it began its progression on giant rollers towards the wall.

"Silensos, two tasks for you. Firstly I need letters prepared alerting our supporters in Carthage to the arrival of the Roman envoys. Secondly, I want letters of introduction done for these Romans. These letters will place them under the guidance and protection of our people for I need this delegation carefully handled." Hannibal stared into space deep in thought. "Yes, handled very carefully indeed."

He pulled out the stool and gestured Silensos to sit. The scribe tucked himself into the small table and opened his case.

Silensos looked bewildered. "We have Romans here sir?"

"I'll explain later." He said pacing the tent. "Suffice to say I have no time to see them, nor do I wish to. They will be in Carthage within the week but I need the way paved for them, if you get my meaning. The senate must be briefed and prepared for their arrival and make sure our people are on hand to receive them from the moment they dock. I want them kept away from our un-friends, they must be chaperoned to and from the senate.

I will have names of these Romans for you ere the day is out, prepare the letters and add the names later, questions?"

"The usual protocol General? And the same contacts in Carthage I presume?"

"Yes, the same. I need this done today Silensos, this is paramount to everything. You do understand that?"

"It will be done General."

"Excellent!"

Hannibal pulled his helmet into place and picked up his shield. Pausing briefly, he smiled and inclined his head to Silensos then ducked out of the tent, leaving him to his work. He called for his Standard-bearer and signaller as he strode out of the camp towards the city walls.

Silensos worked through the morning, carefully writing his General's instructions back to their supporters in Carthage. From time to time, he was troubled with a growling, grumbling belly. His temperature fluctuated making him sweat profusely then shiver with cold, he quaffed water to allay a sudden thirst and nibbled at hard, dry bread to line and settle his stomach. By midmorning however, he could no longer bear the churning, gaseous pains and dashed from the tent to relieve himself, having to stop short of the latrines to vomit hard and empty his bowels. Though weakened by his exertions he returned to the tent and between shaking, shivering and sweating he laboured. Finally, unable to bear the pain he called the guard to summon his young assistant to help finish the task.

A clumsy, wide-eyed, bumbling youth appeared in the tent, his excuses for lateness cut short when he saw the condition of his master.

"Damn you Aristides! Where have you been?"

"I'm most sorry sir, I was …"

"No matter!" Silensos waved him to silence. "Here boy, help me with these, I need them all done and then I must rest." He mopped at his brow with a damp cloth as he spoke and passed the letters he had finished to Aristides.

"Dry the ink and seal them, put them into the dispatch bag. Hurry boy!"

Aristides sprinkled fine sand over the script before blowing the surplus off then folded the parchments sealing them at the edges with wax and Hannibal's seal.

Silensos suddenly doubled up in pain clutching at his stomach, he rose from the table sending the stool tumbling backwards. Staggering like a drunkard then losing consciousness, he fell onto the writing desk scattering letters, writing equipment, maps and plans across the floor of the tent. Aristides screamed for the guard whilst trying to assist his master up from the floor. Only after rubbing damp cloth's over the man's face could they find signs of life returning to him. The agonised, befuddled chronicler grabbed at his stomach again as a fresh wave of pain wracked him, his body shook, his skin pallid with beads of sweat that stood out all over his face. The men gave him sips of water and as he nodded in gratitude, he gasped.

"Finish sealing the letters Aristides … they must! … Must leave here today that was the General's …" He folded in pain again, struggling to complete his words. "That was the General's instruction … they are to go to Carthage today, do you understand?"

The Guard was now calling for the physician with Aristides fussing over the stricken man. Silensos grasped Aristides firmly by his tunic pulling him close, hissing through clenched teeth.

"Let me be! Listen! These letters, they must go today, they…" His eyes rolled back in his head as he passed out.

Silensos was removed to the sick tent, Aristides being left to clear up the mess. He righted the table, sorting and placing the maps and drawings neatly back upon it. He packed the writing case and gathered all the scattered correspondence together from across the floor, some of which had been crushed and their heavy seals broken when Silensos fell. Fretting over the damaged work he quickly smoothed and re-folded the parchments. Heating more wax, he resealed the correspondence before placing them in the leather dispatch satchel. Calling the guard once more and giving instructions for a messenger to be brought, he closed the satchel adding a further seal to the catch.

Chapter Eleven

Way off in the distance, lost in the cold half-light of dawn, a cockerel crowed his greeting to the day. Gestix rolled in his blanket to find Baldor already sitting up, wide-awake.

"He shouldn't crow too loud, this could be a risky place for a cockerel! Mind you, where there's a cockerel there are usually hens and I could fancy me some eggs!" He grinned and winked at Baldor who just returned a wan smile, the rest of the warriors were still asleep or lying quiet, huddled in dew covered blankets and makeshift shelters.

"Up! Up! Move your lazy arses!" Harbro shouted his voice flushing some roosting wood pigeons from their high-branched retreats, sending them swooping low over the camp, their wing beats loud in the morning stillness. Harbro walked among the warriors as he spoke, shaking and kicking those that didn't rise quickly enough. Similar commands and shouts seemed to echo elsewhere in the camp as officers rousted men from their slumbers.

"The Captain will be returning with our orders shortly and I want you all in full battle dress and ready to move. I said get up!" The last command was screamed into a still slumbering, Milor's ear.

The sky was a blaze of pink and vivid hues of red, the sea still black, as the sun had not climbed from beneath the far horizon to bring the true light of day.

"Looks like the weathers about to change; red sky in the morning is always a sign of bad weather or a storm." Groaned a warrior.

"There'll be a bloody storm alright if you don't move your lice-ridden arses and make ready!" Harbro's final threat quietened the men and they set about dressing and arming themselves. "The first ones ready rekindle the fires for breakfast unless you want to go into battle on empty bellies!"

Gestix pulled his leather corselet over his head and fastened the shoulder straps. He fitted his weapons belt and was busy adjusting his shield straps when he noticed Baldor struggling with the lacing on his corselet. Gestix made his way over to him.

"Come on lad, let's have you laced up and then we can eat, I'm hungry!"

Baldor looked up from his fumbling; his hands were shaking preventing him from tying the knots in the leather cords. Gestix gently and without fuss took over the lacing.

"Fingers not working too well of a morning eh? We will have to get up earlier!" He said smiling.

Baldor feeling embarrassed blurted out in a hash whisper. "I'm not afraid Gestix! They just won't stop sh …"

"Shhh, Baldor!" Gestix cut him short, his voice low. "I know you aren't afraid lad; it's just nerves before battle is all. Men piss and shit themselves when they're afraid. I spewed before my first battle. So you are doing well!" He finished the lacing and patted Baldor on the shoulder reassuringly, passing sword and baldric to him as he did so.

"We'll prepare the horses then eat, leave your helmet off for the moment, don't don it till before we mount."

Gestix threw blankets over the horses while stroking and talking to them as he worked, he also fastened an extra sword onto the tack at the neck of each animal.

"Handy these, Baldor." He slid the weapon in and out of the scabbard as he spoke. "Just in case you lose the first one."

Baldor nodded and passed the round, bronze faced shields to him, these too were slung over the animal's flanks. They led the horses back to the hitching rope and went to breakfast.

"I've left Risto back today, use the spare mount instead. I want to see how this battle progresses, I don't envisage an open fight so we will keep the better horses in reserve. Come on lad smile eh! Live everyday like it's your last!" Gestix laughed helplessly at his grim jest, Baldor eventually smirked and broke into nervous laughter himself.

The men were eating heartily of fresh bread and fried lamb strips washed down with goat's milk when Balaam returned with the orders of the day.

"Bring your food and gather round." Balaam smoothed the dirt with his foot then used his dagger to scratch an outline of the city wall along with a square representing the siege tower. "Right, listen! We're to join the heavy brigade and flank the tower." His dagger drew more lines in the earth. "We act as a screen for the tower and help contain any sortie out from the city gates. No sortie, we don't move, our job is purely to protect that tower! If these Saguntines do venture out, we roll them up and force them back through their gate." He paused, looking around for understanding. "It could be cavalry or infantry, my silver's on a mixture of both. Watch yourselves if infantry emerge as we won't have enough time or space to charge them, if the fight becomes patchy stay together and watch for them tripping and hamstringing the horses. Give no quarter, for believe me, you'll receive none!" He paused briefly to allow his words to sink in. "This fight's become desperate and is hanging in fine balance but I think we have arrived in time to tip it in our favour." He changed tack a little and lightened his tone. "This city is ripe for the taking, it's reputed to be the richest in Spain and we all receive a share of the spoils as well as our fee!"

The men cheered at the last comment.

"Finish your breakfast lads then make your peace. We move into position once the sun is full above the sea, if the Gods will it I will see you all back here for supper." Balaam stood and saluted them all.

The men dispersed to finish eating and to pray.

"Eat up Baldor and then we should pray or make an offering." Gestix said, spooning the meat quickly into his mouth.

Baldor just stared deeply into his mess bowl. He pushed the food around with his spoon and said nothing. He watched as the Gaul moved off to the nearby trees and found a quieter place to get on his knees, close his eyes and bow his head. When the order came to mount up, Gestix dipped his head in reverence once more before fitting his helmet and tying the chinstrap tight.

"No prayers Baldor?"

"No." Baldor replied quietly. "I have neither the time nor the inclination for it, what good did it do Aiticia?" His tone suddenly bitter.

Gestix was about to retort with leaving the past in the past and not to blame the Gods for Aiticia's death but instead placed his arm around Baldor's shoulder and hugged him roughly.

"Well, I prayed to Epona for us both." He said quietly through a sad yet warm smile. "And I want you to have her to watch over you and keep you safe."

He pushed a very small but intricately cast bronze statuette into Baldor's hand. The effigy was of a beautiful maiden riding side-saddle with a small bird perched upon her upheld right hand. The metal was greening in places but on the outer edges, it was highly polished from rubbing by revering hands. Using his own hand to keep Baldor's shut he stared intently into his eyes. Gestix put his other hand to his lips signifying silence.

"Don't abandon the Gods lad! We need all the help we can get. I don't understand any more than you do as to why things happen or why the Gods let things happen." He continued quickly seeing Baldor was ready to interrupt. "This is my lady, my protector, Epona. She is the Goddess of horses and patron of all cavalrymen. She has always nurtured me, now I want her protection for you."

Baldor shook his head and again went to interrupt. Gestix cut in once more, a sombre look on his face.

"Humour me."

Baldor stared deeply into his eyes then eventually nodded; he took the small talisman and slipped it inside his tunic.

"Mount up!"

Gestix pulled Baldor close, embracing him tightly.

"You stay by me! Do you hear?" He whispered hoarsely.

"I will!" Baldor replied, the tremor in his voice betraying his nervousness.

With the sun full above the horizon, the thunder of drums and blaring trumpet calls heralded the Carthaginians into position. The white painted city walls dazzled the eyes as the morning sun reflected back from it, causing more than one warrior to shield his gaze in order to look upon it. The giant siege tower was already in slow rumbling progress towards the walls, spitting iron-tipped, wooden bolts city bound from the ballistas mounted on various decks within it. The tower was hauled from the front by oxen teams and pushed by men from the rear, wooden rollers being slipped under the base to slide the timber leviathan along. The tower's front covered in wetted, un-tanned animal hides as a means of fire proofing, into which arrows from the defenders thudded as they sought the openings of the ballista firing windows. An answering arrow storm from the Carthaginian archers began raking the wall, forcing the defenders to seek shelter behind their stone ramparts. The creeping tower steadily filled from the rear by heavy assault troops, these heavily armoured men with plumed or feathered helmets, corselets of thick leather or mail shirts and carrying large round shields. Their legs protected from ankle to knee with greaves of bronze or boiled leather, most carried heavy fighting spears, some, long shafted axes, all bore swords and daggers. The warriors swarmed up the ladders through the various levels of the tower, packing in tightly shoulder-to-shoulder and filling all the floors. On the top deck, the front wall was in fact a hinged drawbridge. Once the tower came within reach of the wall top, the bridge would drop and the assault troops would flow over the ramparts like a wave over a sea wall.

To the right of the tower, vineae crept forward under the direction of Hasdrubal. The inside filled with men carrying hammers, axes, picks and shovels, the mobile shelters heading for the section of wall selected as being weak and in a poor state of repair. The heavy brigade including Balaam's mercenary horse flanked the tower, easing slowly forward in time with its movement; their eyes fixed on the city gate to their left. Drums pounded, the tower creaked and groaned as timber stressed and bent, horses snorted and skittered, some wild-eyed and rearing at the noise. Oxen bellowed, men shouted and strained, some screamed as arrows found flesh. Above all was the howl of rocks as they flew through the air to break on the city walls into showers of fragments and raising clouds of dust.

The ferocity of the Carthaginian firepower kept the defenders behind the ramparts, however from within the city their own artillery replied with rocks, bolts and earthenware pots containing the feared naphtha or Greek fire. The pots shattered on impact, spilling glutinous, fiery liquid and burning all that it encountered. The first salvo fell short of the massed cavalry but the roar of flames and black, oily smoke terrified the horses and scorched the grass and ground. Animals whinnied, reared and kicked, throwing and trampling some riders, another salvo followed and this time the deadly conflagrations found their mark. Men and horses exploded into flames their agonising screams adding to the pandemonium, the sweet, sickly stench of burning flesh coating the air.

Balaam walked his mount slowly up and down the front rank of his men. Commanding calm and to hold the line. Gestix glanced at the city gate then back to the tower, it was almost up to the wall, its advance marked by a trail of dead men and oxen; in the distance, he could see the vineae already in position at the base of the wall.

"Get ready Baldor, if they're going to do anything to stop us, now's their time!"

A fire pot exploded close by, spewing oil and fire and turning two men and their horses into incendiaries. One animal collapsed instantly, crushing its rider and setting fire to the grass around them. The other animal bolted, the increased passage of air fanning the roaring flames brighter and hotter. The grim spectacle raced away only to fall, scattering flames and rider over the sward. The man remained mercifully still though the horse rolled and kicked, whickering in agony as it burnt.

"The gate! The gate!" Balaam shouted as he pointed to the wooden doors.

A trumpet sounded the advance and all along the line, horses and men began to move to the left, parallel to the city wall, towards the gate. All keen to close with the enemy and be clear of the fiery death raining from the sky. As they advanced, a crash to their rear told of the tower's drawbridge smashing onto the battlements, this was followed a heartbeat later by howls and whoops of bloodlust as the assault troops raced over the bridge onto the parapet. At the base of the tower, the queuing troops continued their ascent up the ladders towards the walls.

The vineae were stationary at the base of the wall and acting as shelters protecting the men that dug at the foundations. Back at the gate the Saguntine cavalry began to emerge, trying to form lines and advance before the Carthaginian cavalry closed on them. The heavy brigade came on, riding parallel to the city wall, moving from a trot through to a canter then into a slow charge. The Saguntine cavalry also pushed forward, their battle cries and screams adding to the rising noise as they closed the gap across the plain. Amidst the cacophony of hooves, shouts, and jingle of harness Gestix bellowed to Baldor to close up tight.

Gestix looked to the front calculating distance to the impact then glanced to his right watching the city walls for signs of danger. Suddenly, he began changing his shield from his left hand to his right, shouting a warning to Baldor and Milor as he did so; his words however, drowned in the noise. Baldor didn't understand and looked about confusedly as Gestix continued to shout.

Without warning, he felt his mount shudder then stagger before collapsing and throwing him hard onto the grass, knocking the breath out of him. Milor, not so lucky had his horse killed beneath him instantly, as defenders on the wall poured a salvo of arrows into the cavalry's flank, sheer desperation finally overcoming their fear of the Carthaginian barrage. All along the cavalry flank, warriors and animals fell, crashing and rolling on the ground, their bodies resembling pincushions as brightly fletched arrows protruded from them at every angle. Leaving the wounded and dying in its wake the charge thundered onwards to collide head-on with the Saguntine horse.

Gestix however had reined in and dismounted and was hauling Baldor to his feet, he badly shaken and sucking air in gulps.

"Come on! Move!" Gestix shouted, raising his shield to the wall, arrows thudding into it and the dirt around their feet. Baldor stumbled trying to regain his breath and balance.

"Lift your shield lad! Come on, we need to find cover!"

Milor also struggled to his feet his nose and face smashed bloody from the fall, his arm limp, dislocated from the shoulder. He staggered, disorientated and half-senseless, seemingly oblivious to the arrows falling about him. Gestix pushed Baldor back the way they had come then ran back to Milor pulling him by his baldric back towards the tower.

The rain of naphtha from within the city continued but was now ranged further back causing havoc amongst the Carthaginian archers. In typical archer style, they began to fall back, unprotected and vulnerable to the incoming missiles, their resolve to stand, weak. They scuttled rearwards seeking safety of the range limit.

Gestix, Milor and Baldor, having survived the arrows and naphtha reached the base of the tower, where they were ordered to climb by an infantry officer who was marshalling the queuing assault troops.

"Sir, we're cavalry. And this lad is injured." Gestix managed between gasps of breath, pushing the still senseless Milor in front of the officer.

"I don't see any horses … up!" The officer pointed skyward. Then to Milor. "Get yourself to the rear boy!"

Gestix resignedly pushed Baldor into the tower and Milor towards the camp. Milor staggered two paces then three arrows thudded into him, spinning him around and knocking him to the ground. Shields raised and men crouched trying to make themselves small behind them, Baldor looked on in shock at the twitching body.

"Keep moving! Up! Up!" The officer shouted while calmly walking alongside the bunched warriors.

"Come on." Sighed Gestix, steering Baldor into the tower.

Inside the dark timber rooms, the warriors squashed shoulder to shoulder. The acid smell of sweat mixed with the stench of vomit, excrement and the nasal piercing odours of urine and wet, un-tanned leather. Exertion from climbing the ladders in full war gear forced more salty liquid from the men's pores, stinging their eyes and trickling through beards to itch while sticking tunics to skin. The air was heavy and stale, leaving men struggling for breath as they climbed higher, fearful of what awaited them above but wishing to be free of the fetid air below.

The tower swayed slightly from the movement of the warriors climbing within it, the wood groaning and creaking. Sawdust fell from between timbers, slipping into tunics and eyes adding to the men's discomfort. The repeated thud of arrows hitting the tower, matched by the snap of the ballistas as they returned fire to the city with their long wooden bolts.

On the final ladder leading to the top deck, Gestix pushed in front of Baldor and heaved himself through the hatchway into the light then reached back offering his hand.

"Come on, the air's cleaner up here!"

Baldor climbed onto the top deck gratefully sucking in the fresh air, the breeze cooling and drying the sweat on his skin. Gestix turned towards the parapet drawing his falcata.

"Watch your footing lad and stay by me!"

Baldor unslung his shield and drew his sword. His heart thumped in his chest the adrenalin surging through his veins. Scared beyond reason he vomited hard as he and Gestix started forward stepping over bodies and discarded weapons scattered on the deck. Blood pooled brightly on the pale timber and crimson sandal prints trailed across the floor like some ghastly waymarker leading the attackers to the city wall. The wounded and dying crawled to one side to avoid being trampled by the fresh troops as they began their run across the deck to the parapet.

On the plain below, the cavalry battle was almost at a standstill and a tightly packed melee ensued. Men hacked and battered at one another, the press so tight the dead couldn't fall, leaving bodies lolling and flopping from their mounts. The sheer weight of the Carthaginian heavy brigade however, steadily eased the mass of Saguntines back towards their city gate.

In the shelter of the vineae, men laboured throwing dirt and stone up out of the mines, gradually burrowing their way under the walls foundations. Wooden poles, jammed in place supported the mine roof as men tunnelled ever deeper. The rain of rocks and boiling oil onto the vineae roofs had virtually ceased, the defenders realising the fruitlessness of the action. Contingents of Cretan archers placed in support, sent arrows raking across the wall top seeking any defenders brave enough to show themselves.

Back on the wall, Gestix and Baldor joined the hand-to-hand combat raging along the parapet walkway. Having gained a foothold the Carthaginians fought doggedly in both directions along the wall, while more troops emerged from the tower to join the push. Men slipped and fell, some being pushed or hurled from the wall while the dying and the dead littered the walkway, creating further hazards at the feet of the combatants. There was little room to swing swords and Gestix and Baldor locked shields, advancing as a pair, blades pointed forward held low to thrust. The Gaul keeping Baldor close to the wall whilst he protected the lad's right side.

All the while, the Saguntines sent more men streaming up the steps from the courtyards to the parapet, hoping to stem the advance of the attackers pouring relentlessly from the tower. A warrior swinging a two-handed axe battered Baldor's shield down, sending stinging spasms up his arm. Gestix's blade struck like lightning taking the man in the throat, the man gagged, blood spraying in arcs from his neck the hot liquid splattering Baldor's face and armour mixing with the vomit on his corselet.

"Alright lad?" Gestix shouted as he battered a space in front of them. "Get your bloody shield up! Stay with me!"

More Saguntine warriors rushed to the attack shouting hate and promising death as they came. Gestix stepped over the dying axeman and smashed the first backwards with his shield, knocking him into his comrades. He bellowed for a stupefied Baldor to step alongside him and add his blade to the fray.

Hannibal moved across the field directing operations and encouraging his troops, his small entourage comprising a Standard-bearer, signallers and a number of lightly armed runners. Above his head was the standard of Carthage, a golden disc embossed with the city name and the God, Baal Hammon. Above was a crescent moon of silver representing the mother Goddess Tanith, both devices mounted on a shaft of dark cornel wood their magnificence catching the morning sun sending a dazzle of light towards the smoke clouded walls.

As far as the eye could see thousands of men flowed and eddied around siege ladders like a restless tide, the cavalry fray had degenerated into a bloody push where flesh and bone now choked the gates. On the wall, archers and defenders poured arrows and rocks into the battle below, caring not whom they hit so desperate were they to deny access to the city. Defenders strained and pushed to close the huge gates but the volume of retiring cavalry was such that the doors couldn't close, the dead and dying becoming so deep the cavalry could no longer move forward, the riders dismounting to attack on foot.

Seeing the problems the heavy Brigade were facing, Hannibal dispatched his Spanish Caetratus who waited in reserve. These lightly armed troops went bare headed and wore no armour only plain white tunics after the Greek style. Their tunics were one piece, edged in bands of blue or red and fell to mid-thigh. Instead of greaves, they wore knee length, leather boots, their weapons were small javelins and the falcata. Each warrior carried a small round buckler or Caetra, from which they took their name. Like ants over a carcase, they climbed over the fallen slaughtering the injured Saguntines as they went, fighting their way in through the still open gateway.

At the base of the wall, grey smoke belched out of the ground, swirling around and into the vineae as they backed away. Tongues of deep orange flames followed a sudden roar from the tunnel mouth as the fire took a good hold, crackling and fizzing as it engulfed the oil-soaked faggots.

"Messenger, here!" Hannibal beckoned one of his runners.

"Have General Sergatatonix marshal his Gallic infantry; I expect that wall will be down shortly, I want his warriors ready to attack the moment it collapses. Understood!"

"Yes General."

Hannibal pressed a stamped silver token into the messenger's hand.

"This proves you speak for me, report back here once you have delivered the message, go!"

The messenger saluted and set off at a run to locate the Gauls.

Hannibal gazed at the battle, a tentative feel of success in his heart after the months of stalemate. He muttered a brief prayer to Baal Hammon to bring the wall crashing down, allowing the attack to progress on three points. Surely then the defenders must lose their resolve?

The assault troops gained control of the parapet, though some remaining Saguntines boxed into the corner of the wall fought doggedly on, selling their lives dearly. The fighting had moved down the steps to the courtyards below but was no less fierce or bitter, the withdrawing Saguntines reforming into ranks with shields locked, endeavouring to prevent the advance of the Carthaginians further into the city. The assault troops, howling their bloodlust and sensing victory slaughtered any stragglers too slow or badly wounded to make the safety of the forming shield wall. Thereafter, hurling themselves at the massed ranks only to be stalled and forced back; the defenders it seemed still full of fight. With the Caetratus joining them from the gateway, the assault troops were readying to charge the defenders once more when a trumpet call and a sharp command halted their attack.

"Hold! ... Form up! ... Close ranks!" Mago's gruff voice cut across the mayhem. Attired in black cuirass and helmet he prowled up and down the front rank like a great bear, directing and marshalling his men.

The file commanders coerced and shouted to form solid ranks, the Caetratus ushered in behind, ready to exploit and widen any gaps battered into the defenders lines. Baldor and Gestix found themselves in the third rank from the front, packed in tightly but at last able to draw breath. Sweat streamed down their faces mixing with blood splashes and vomit, their mouths parched and hands sticky on sword hilts. Gestix, quite out of breath nodded to Baldor then winked, the young man smiled grimly and managed a wink back.

A deep, scraping rumble came, followed by a ground shaking crash as the wall collapsed. The earth shook beneath the massed warriors and men looked on in alarm. A giant plume of dust spiralled skyward, swirling and mixing with the black reek from the fires. Loud cheering followed by yelps, whoops and battle cries and then the pounding of thousands of feet as the Gallic infantry surged into the breach.

Seizing the moment, Mago pointed with his sword towards the waiting Saguntine ranks and shouted to his assault troops.

"The wall's down! Take the cit…yyyyy!"

With spears bristling, the massed ranks advanced. Large brightly painted shields obscuring bodies and faces, nodding plumes all that showed above the rims. The defenders bunched tighter together, grim faces disappearing behind shields while sweat-damp hands tightened on sword hilts. Javelins flew from both sides clattering and ricocheting from shields, some slipping through the gaps to catch men in the shoulder or neck, screams and thumps sounded as bodies fell in the dust. The fight proved to be short but bloody, men stabbed under shields seeking thighs and groins else probed over the rims seeking faces and throats.

The defenders having been pushed back throughout the day and seen their gates breached, finally broke. Warriors streamed away seeking safety, the gaps quickly filling with Carthaginian and Spanish troops. With the shield wall disintegrating the slaughter began.

Chapter Twelve

The sun lengthened the shadows of the late afternoon and the stifling heat began to slip away. High in the sky, kites circled lazily and the crows and ravens perched on the wall anticipating the feast to follow, their harsh cries piercing the terrible quiet shrouding the city. Black smoke drifted from countless fires and the odour of scorched timber and charred flesh carried on the breeze to catch in men's throats and sting their eyes. The courtyard where the assault troops now stood victorious resembled a butcher's shop, bodies heaped and scattered amidst discarded weapons, blood and gore, the flies buzzing in black clouds over the dead flesh.

No living Saguntine troops remained in the courtyards; the few that had escaped now ensconced behind the walls of the inner citadel, leaving the assault troops masters of the outer walls and courtyards. The Gallic infantry had experienced similar success but like the assault troops, had paid a bloody price for their gains. Now, between ministering their injured they removed heads from the dead Saguntines as trophies of war. The heads would be washed, the ragged flesh trimmed away and hair and beards combed before placing them on spikes or spears. Hannibal strode across the debris of weapons and bodies, directing and pointing out the positions he wanted artillery placing and a screening wall raised. Behind him came reinforcing troops, engineering staff and a trundling column of siege machines, battle won the final phase was to begin immediately.

The assault troops, cheering both their General and their own success, were given the order to retire. Weary and hungry the warriors turned for the camp, some needing aid from their comrades, nearly all helping carry their dead back. A victory it may have been but the human cost had been high.

Back at the camp Gestix and Baldor were welcomed by a relieved Balaam, the pair presumed dead when they could not be found after the cavalry were recalled. He was visibly shaken at the heavy losses his company had suffered so early in the campaign, the long list of dead and wounded in his hand.

Baldor removed his helmet and weapons belts. Unlacing then shrugging out of his corselet he sat down heavily on his bedroll and cradled his head in his hands. Gestix patted his shoulder gently before walking to his own bedroll, Balaam following and sitting down alongside him.

"We did well today." He began quietly. "Our losses were terrible though …so many …so many! And not just us, the infantry took a hammering and we're not in the citadel yet! I've never seen an enemy fight with such ferocity." He shook his head gently his gaze empty.

"Would you not fight tooth and nail if it was your home? Your family?" Gestix asked reaching for a waterskin.

"Huh, what?" Balaam seemed to snap out of his reverie.

"These aren't regular troops or mercenaries fighting for pay; they're people fighting for their lives and their families, their home and hearth. It's bitter now but I vouch it will become more so, the nearer the city comes to falling."

Gestix sipped the water then tipped some over the back of his neck and passed the flask to Baldor.

"Drink lad, slowly though." He nudged Baldor urging him to drink. Baldor was ashen but he took the water and sipped it.

"You did well boy!" Balaam said quietly. "You'll come right! The first battle is always the worst."

"What happens from here then?" Gestix asked tiredly almost disinterestedly.

"We'll pound them some more and beat their walls down, this city will fall, no matter what."

"Here's hoping some of us survive to see it so." Gestix got up again to throw a cloak around Baldor's shoulders. "Sleep lad, sleep! Tomorrow's another day."

Baldor rolled tightly in the cloak, lost in his thoughts. He shuddered when he remembered his horse killed beneath him, bringing back stark memories of his father. His mother came to mind and he groaned inwardly when he remembered the promise made to her, never to take the path of the warrior. Feeling lost then guilty, his mind slipped back to the fighting and carnage he'd witnessed. Men and animals screaming and burning, the hacking and stabbing, the hate and the fear and the foul stench he could not get out of his nose. His head rang with the howls of agony, the begging for death from the injured, both friend and foe alike and the memories of the grisly mess of limbs, blood and entrails that had littered the field. He thought of those he'd slain, some wife or mother, sister or child would no doubt be cursing him, wishing him dead and his shade on the way to Hades in atonement for those he'd sent to the ferryman. He felt hollow, empty inside, and sick to the stomach.

Gestix was right, this action; nay slaughter did not ease the pain of Aiticia's passing. The folk he'd slain had done nothing to him; they fought for their lives and homes the same as he had fought Carthalo and he felt ashamed at what he had done.

"You alright lad?" Gestix leaned over him. "You're unsettled, do you want to eat or talk maybe, before we sleep?"

Baldor looked bleakly at Gestix, shaking his head. "I couldn't stomach anything … thank you for bringing me through that today, I don't …"

"Shhh, lad, you watch my back and I'll watch yours eh! That's the way of it!"

"I'm sorry I got us into this I should have listened, you were right!" He shook his head. "I thought this would fill my mind and ease my pain." His head dropped as he finished speaking.

"Listen Baldor!" Gestix said quietly, reassuringly. "This is not your doing; the Gods must want it so! We are here because we fit into the great scheme of things, I told you before we're just pieces on the God's gaming board." He shuffled closer to Baldor. "You will feel better lad. Right now, you are feeling sick and guilty and wishing to undo all that you have done and had to endure today. Remember, I said to you this visits a man after battle. When the killing is over and you feel guilty for not being dead. I tell you it's the way of the world, men kill and fight because it is in their nature to. Whether you fight out of hate, love or for money or even just for the pleasure of it, it's just the way life is. Take your father and me, he fought because the city asked it of him and he saw it as his duty. Me, out of pure hatred of Rome and all things Roman. We fight now for money, an honest enough profession. But a fight which I think would have become a duty too soon enough."

"What do you mean duty?"

"Look at the size of this siege Baldor, its huge! All these men, all this effort to reduce a city! This city allied to Rome! There's a war coming lad and Carthage would call you to serve her if you were not already here."

****

Hannibal returned to his tent calling for Silensos to be summoned. A nervous Aristides appeared in his stead explaining his master's condition but also of the completion of the letters for Carthage as instructed. Hannibal nodded in satisfaction giving Aristides the names to be added to the letters for the Roman envoys to complete for the following morning. Settled at his desk Hannibal sorted through his papers, eating dinner as he worked. He pored over the city plans, calculating his next moves late into the night; finally, with eyes stinging from lack of sleep and head aching he considered his bed. As he rose, he remembered the warrant of arrest for the criminal. Sighing and yawning he searched his correspondence for it, deeming it prudent to have the man found and returned to Carthage, thereby keeping the family of Lord Hanno placated and out of his affairs. Finding nothing, he cleared the table, carefully sifting through the maps and documents again all of which rendered nothing. With eyes almost closed he finally surrendered to his bodies need for sleep, making a mental note to ask Aristides in the morning where he had moved the warrant to.

He was awakened at dawn by a grim faced, Mago and urged to the doorway of his tent, where two guards waited with a large wicker basket. Mago grasped a spluttering torch then pushed the lid from the basket and pulled out a severed head. Hannibal's face darkened into a scowl. Mago continued picking from the basket; bloodied hands, feet, fingers and genitals.

"The remains of the recruiting officers we sent to the Oretani and Carpetani tribes! It looks like we have a revolt on our hands as well as a siege!"

"Enough Mago!" Hannibal snarled as he placed his hand on his brother's arm preventing the removal of further limbs. "See these remains receive a decent burial then convene my staff, I have additional orders for the day."

He gathered his cloak about him and ducked back into the tent.

****

The mercenaries rose as the cock crowed the new day. Most had slept little as the cries and screams of the wounded had continued throughout the night, chilling the marrow of the living and bringing nightmares to those who managed to doze. The men were stiff and sore from the battle; utterly exhausted, most had sought sleep immediately as they withdrew instead of rubbing themselves down with warmed oil.

"Form up!" The men snapped to attention as Balaam addressed them.

"We have a change of orders; we're not going into battle at the city today. We're to become a vanguard on a punitive expedition against two local tribes who have failed to support us."

Moans and gripes started up about being left out of the spoils when the city fell.

"Silence! All will receive an equal share, General's orders. You need to concentrate on staying alive to collect it!" He glowered darkly at the men, his look ensuring silence. "These tribes are large and savage but after our mauling yesterday I'd rather take our chances battering them into submission than that push and shove around the gates again. Moreover, who knows what the barbarians have? All men have gold somewhere, do they not?" The men's mood lightened somewhat at the prospect of plunder "The city won't fall within the next few days, time enough for us to quell this revolt and be back here to collect our share of the spoils. Be ready to move after breakfast."

Midmorning found the punitive force well clear of the city. The column headed inland, weaving its way through poppy dotted meadows then through scrubland leading towards a huge forest.

Local scouts were already in front of the column but orders came back for screening patrols of cavalry to be posted on the flanks as protection for the infantry. Balaam's men divided into two groups and sent left and right, he leading one patrol and Harbro the other, Baldor finding himself separated from Gestix.

Out on the column's flanks they were soon lost from view amongst the copses and gently undulating hills. As the trees became dense forest and reduced men's vision, Baldor's senses heightened. His ears strained and his eyes peered, he rode with his spear readied under his arm, his shield pulled around to cover his chest. He listened to the sounds around him, mentally ticking off those he recognised, the breeze blowing through the canopy, the creaking boughs, the cicada's and the crickets clicking and the gentle cooing of woodpigeons and far off, the bark of a fox.

Balaam called for a water stop and gathering the men close around him quietly gave his orders.

"Right, no talking from here, watch for my signals and pass them on. Close up the gaps and be ready to fight. If the murdering bastards are looking to attack the land doesn't come much better than this."

The warriors moved off again, only the hoof falls and the odd creak of harness betraying their passage.

Despite the coolness in the forest, Baldor sweated beneath his helmet, the salty fluid running down his face and back sticking his tunic to his skin. His thighs chafed, feeling hot and slippery against Risto's damp coat. He sniffed hard picking up the scent of horse, damp forest and wild mint, then listened again utilising both senses to compensate for the lack of vision.

The warrior in front of him held up his hand for pause. Passing the silent message back, Baldor held his breath and listened again, this time the silence seemed almost deafening ... nothing, only the wind continuing its path. Heads bobbed and flicked from side to side like chickens as they listened for the slightest sound, sweat damp hands tightened around spear shafts and shield straps.

Moments slipped by. Baldor's heart pounded in his ears, his mouth dry, more sweat ran down his body, itching and irritating beneath his tunic. A whistling of air followed by a dull thud and a grunt saw the warrior behind Baldor knocked from his mount. Bedlam ensued, shields raised, men shouted, the horses stamping and wheeling about with the sudden tension. The wounded man gasped, pulling at the feathered shaft deep in his chest then laid still.

"Steady lads! Anybody see the direction of the arrow?"

A nerve racking silence followed, nothing except the horses moved, men breathed heavily as the tension grew. Time dragged but no further arrows came from the trees. Balaam beckoned the men on and cautiously they urged their mounts forward. The tree canopy thickened reducing visibility further, the dimming light heightening tension and giving a claustrophobic, eerie feeling. Some warriors slipped their spears into their left hand along with their shields, drawing swords anticipating close quarter combat.

It was almost noon before the next arrow came. Again unseen and knocking another warrior to the forest floor never to rise again. Balaam called again for a sighting … nothing. Frustration and fear gripped the mercenaries, calls to come and fight echoed through the trees with silence the only reply.

"They daren't rush us! So there's only one, maybe two of the bastards at most! Dismount and walk tight to your horse, we'll be harder targets then." Balaam dismounted as he spoke the men quickly following suit. "Sheathe your swords, spears to the front. Malo! Track me this bastard!"

A tall, ebony skinned warrior slung his shield on his back, passing his spear to the warrior closest to him. Taking a composite bow and quiver of arrows from a case strapped to his horse's flanks, he passed his reins to Baldor then disappeared silently into the trees.

"Malo will get us a trail." Balaam said in a hushed whisper, "We'll have this archer's head before long."

Balaam gestured the men to squat whilst they waited for Malo to return. Bodies disappeared behind shields, the men drawing some comfort from the cover. The wind moved the canopy and time dragged again, the horses stood idle while the warriors waited quietly fretful, anticipating further arrows. Eventually Malo returned, materialising silently from the gloom, he spoke quietly to Balaam who motioned Baldor forward indicating for him to leave his mount.

"Go with Malo! Take these!" Balaam passed Baldor a quiver of white fletched arrows. "Do exactly as he says, got it?"

With a nervous nod, he followed the black warrior as he quietly slipped back into the undergrowth.

"Keep behind me boy and don't walk anywhere I don't, you might spoil any tracks see! Stick one of those arrows in the ground every thirty paces or so, it'll help guide the Captain and the lads."

The two men probed deeper into the forest, Malo crisscrossing the ground for signs. He examined depressions in the forest mulch and ran his hands over bare patches of earth that showed any kind of disturbance, trying to identify a boot or foot mark. He moved small sticks and checked fallen leaves, ensuring the dampened side was still facing the ground and had not been disturbed by a careless foot. After what seemed an eternity of bending and squatting Malo looked up, concern on his face,

"Nothing!" He said in a hoarse whisper. "Nothing! No one has passed this way today!"

"But, that's…"

"I know … impossible! Right boy, bring the Captain and the men forward to this position, meantime I'll search further and meet you back here."

Baldor slipped quietly away as Malo went forward deeper into the forest. The afternoon spent advancing in relays of Baldor and Malo scouting then bringing up Balaam and the men. With no trace of the enemy found, mumblings began of forest spirits or angered Gods venting their wrath on them. Balaam savagely quashed the men's malcontent shrugging it off as tales for frightened children.

"Whatever's stalking us is flesh and blood so it will bleed and die!" Balaam sounded convincing but deep down he too was troubled that Malo had found nothing.

"If its flesh and blood sir, how come it leaves no tracks?" The nearest warrior to Balaam asked.

"Because it's bloody smart is all." Balaam snapped, still in a hushed whisper. "Give Malo time, he'll find us this shadow."

As Baldor brought Balaam and the mercenaries up to a waiting Malo for the umpteenth time, the hunter held up his hand as they closed on him. Hands tightened on weapons and shields lifted again as men expected contact. Malo beckoned Balaam and Baldor forward but for the rest to remain, he pointed down the trail. Amidst a cloud of flies was a head mounted on a wooden stake. The head still wore a helmet of the type favoured by the Carthaginian's; the eyes however had been ripped out and lay on the floor at the base of the stake. The mouth was open showing smashed teeth and crusted blood where the tongue had been cut out, it being nailed to the stake. Baldor heaved and quietly vomited, Balaam cursed. Calling the men forward he had the head removed and laid in the undergrowth along with its remains. As a warrior stood up from covering the head he was knocked backwards, spinning in a half circle from the impact of another arrow that hit him in the chest.

"Sighting?" Balaam bellowed from behind his shield

The warrior writhed in agony trying to speak but all that came out was a wet gargle and choking noise as his lungs filled with blood. Baldor knelt alongside him covering him with his shield and trying to sit him up. The warrior gripped Baldor's arm fiercely, coughing blood and froth over him trying to communicate amidst sobs and gasps for breath. Malo peered from behind a tree trunk an arrow nocked on the bowstring; he looked to Balaam for any sign of the whereabouts of the shot.

"Anybody see anything?" Silence answered the question.

Marko moved alongside Baldor helping minister to the injured warrior. The man shook violently all over, his gargling had ceased and his mouth opened and closed like a dying fish. Marko looked at Balaam and shook his head gently; Balaam closed his eyes momentarily and nodded. Marko held the man's head up and spoke gently to him, the man mouthed then gagged as Marko slipped his dagger across the jugular cutting deep, the warrior twitched then laid mercifully still. Baldor looked askance at Marko then wretched dryly, horror etched into his already pale features.

No further attack occurred and Balaam dispatched two riders to locate the main column and advise of contact while the depleting scouting party pushed on. It was mid-afternoon when a quick, halting hand movement from Malo stopped Baldor. He pointed through the leafy boughs. Baldor peered to see what had caught the hunter's attention; eventually he identified a man's head and shoulders over the top of a stunted bush. His hand gripped his spear by way of reaction but as he continued to watch, something struck him as odd, the fixed stare, a lack of movement and more flies. Malo edged forward and beckoned Baldor on, closer and closer they came to the watcher. Malo scanned the area once more then walked right up to him, Baldor followed behind then gawped when he realised what it was. The man had been skinned and his flayed body stuffed with grass then crudely stitched back together. His uniform refitted and the severed head complete with glass-eyed stare, placed atop the body reuniting them in macabre union. Malo muttered a prayer and Baldor's skin crawled.

"What kind of people are they?" Baldor asked, his voice shaking from the horror of the scene before him and the nagging fears getting the better of him. Malo began searching the area again, suddenly he crouched, Baldor following suit instantly, expecting an arrow.

"At last! These bastards are real enough!" He said tracing his hand in the dirt. "I was beginning to wonder if we were tracking spirits. Look here!"

He traced a faint footprint with his finger; it would have been invisible to Baldor had Malo not pointed it out. Malo followed the short trail until it stopped alongside a large tree.

"The tracks stop ... they vanish!" The pair looked at one another, then to the canopy above, realisation dawning on both at the same time.

"They're using the trees! The cunning, devious bastards! Fetch the Captain quickly!"

Baldor turned back down the trail, only to find Balaam and the men almost upon them. Before he could relay the news, the leading warriors saw the dead man and panic ensued as the stress and fear of searching for an invisible enemy surfaced. Cries of demons and spirits ran through the ranks until Balaam barked them into silence, roughly handling those nearest him to restore order. Baldor quickly relayed their findings and Balaam, himself breathing a sigh of relief, turned to brief the men.

"Right!" He whispered. "Now the game's on! Malo has a trail; these savages are no more demons or spirits than we are. Come on! We'll catch this damned tree climber and nail him to it! Then we'll find the rest of these barbarian bastards and pay them back for the lads they've sent to Hades."

Late afternoon found the mercenaries deeper in the forest and though still nervous, no longer fearful of demons and spirits. As Malo and Baldor silently materialised out of the undergrowth their faces showing excitement, Balaam gathered his men close urging Malo to speak.

"One stade ahead sir, our phantom archer is hidden in a giant oak, half way up and to the left of the trunk."

The black warriors ebony beard flicked up and down as he relayed his news, his hazel eyes shining bright like a fox loose in a hen house. Malo slipped back into the undergrowth while Balaam formed the men into column, placing himself at the front with Baldor behind him and Marko bringing up the rear, he waved them forward.

Counting towards the one hundred and seventy-five paces in his head to gauge the stade, Balaam saw the giant oak on the edge of a clearing. Not daring to scan the tree too intently but also having to act normally vigilant, he advanced steadily. Going closer, he felt the hairs rising at the back of his neck and the sweat ooze from his pores, each footstep feeling as if it could be his last. He tensed his chest and stomach muscles and prayed to Baal almighty that Malo was ready. The whoosh of feathers on the wind seemed deafening across the glade and Balaam hefted his shield close to his body ready for the impact. Instead, the sound of rustling leaves and small branches breaking came from the oak. A body tumbled out of the canopy, head first, an arrow lodged deep in his chest, it came to a jarring halt as its foot hooked in the tree's foliage, within a blink of an eye another arrow thudded into the swinging body.

"Got the bastard! Malo to me! The rest of you stand to."

Balaam and Malo walked to the suspended body, Balaam grabbed the head by the hair and twisted the face up to his own, then turned it to the men. The man groaned then gulped blood, his eyes glazed over and he died.

"Spirits my arse!" Balaam spat as he let go of the head.

"Sorry sir, I was a bit over zealous with that second arrow, we may have got something out of him before he died."

"Better him than me Malo, eh? There will be others to question before the day is out. See if any more tracks lead away from here and take the boy with you to mark the trail. Find us a place to rest up ere its dark."

Balaam called the men to him while Malo and Baldor disappeared to look for tracks.

"This is your enemy lads, primitive looking but flesh and blood just like us! He's well-armed though and bloody hard to see!"

Balaam gestured at the body and the composite bow of horn, wood and sinew that lay on the ground. The man was wearing buckskin trousers and boots, his chest shoulders and arms were painted in green, black and brown streaks, his face daubed completely green with eyes shaded and blackened by charcoal.

The mercenaries stared at the dead man, relieved that their quarry was human at least. Many had seen painted savages before but not in colours that hid them from view. The way the man had travelled still un-nerved them and most needed to touch the body as proof that he was just a man. They pulled the body down, tying it over the back of one of the spare horses then Balaam led them from the clearing following the trail of white arrows.

The light faded early in the forest and with the shadows falling, Malo halted Baldor on a small rise the hunter had selected for the camp.

"This gives us a little height and therefore an edge if we have to fight." He said in between quaffing some water. "We'll rest up until the Captain and the lads catch up."

Baldor sat down heavily on the hillock physically and mentally drained.

"Uh, uh lad." Shaking his head, Malo motioned a confused Baldor up again.

"Look! … Like this."

Malo squatted, resting his arms over his knees, the still nocked arrow resting on the bowstring. Baldor tried the same position but his long legs made him uncomfortable and off balance, he fell to one side. Malo grinned, his white teeth standing out against his coal dark skin.

"Like this then." He knelt on one knee, "You are resting but still ready to move quickly, see?"

Baldor nodded and adjusted his position, another lesson learnt. As the light faded the black silhouettes of the mercenaries appeared, Malo giving his report to Balaam.

"Right we rest up here, Malo has seen tracks leading away, so we presume they know we are here, however they are as disadvantaged as us in the dark."

Balaam paired the men up, sitting them back to back in a line with the horses hobbled next to their riders. He set the watch rota and made himself comfortable against Baldor.

"Dry rations lads, no fires! You won't get much sleep but rest while you can, we'll return to the main column in the morning."

An uneventful but long night saw the men up and moving just before dawn and by midmorning, they had contact with the main column once more. The morale of the column was badly shaken for there had been sniping during the previous day but no enemy bodies to show. Balaam's men caused a stir when they produced the stiffened, painted corpse and again, heartfelt relief when it was seen to be of flesh and blood.

Asking the whereabouts of Harbro's column, Baldor sought Gestix, however by noon Balaam had the men together again and advised of the complete disappearance of his Second's patrol.

Chapter Thirteen

The mercenaries were stood down and given rest and respite within the safety of the column, other cavalry units taking their place. Baldor fretted the time away desperate for news of Gestix, an anticipated feeling of dread making his stomach churn and ache. Hot, bitter bile from his empty belly rose to his throat, the tightness of which made it difficult to spit away.

At the front of the column and lost from sight in the tall dark trunks came the rumble of hooves, followed by sounds of whickering animals and men crashing wildly through undergrowth, mixed with a cacophony of shouts and screams. As the far away noises drifted and echoed back through the forest the column faltered, some men stopped to listen others talking, some trying to march on. The officers barked for silence whilst checking the formations, closing up and dressing the ranks and pushing the column onwards again. Warriors glanced at one another nervously, the more experienced men trying to calm and reassure their younger comrades with winks, nods and smiles, albeit grim ones. However, all of them gripped their spear shafts a little tighter as rider-less horses galloped towards, then through the column, followed behind by a steady trail of wounded warriors.

The column split apart as it entered a large clearing, the men moving away from the centre track and marching around the perimeter. As Baldor approached, he saw the reason for the counter march, the middle of the glade was in fact a huge, gaping pit. Skirting the rim, he saw, amidst swarms of buzzing flies, the remains of over a dozen horses and men impaled on sharpened wooden stakes that rose upward from the pit floor. The tangle of twisted, broken bodies lay in a grotesque pile like a butcher's offal heap, some skewered on the pointed poles others killed from the fall or crushed from the weight of their comrades. The remains of the pit's false cover; broken branches, netting, leaves and cut turfs was sprinkled over the carnage and already covered some of those who had fallen first.

Risto skittered nervously along the crater's lip, the stink of death unsettling him. Baldor dismounted. Trying to calm his mount, he looked from body to body, his blood pounding loud in his temples. Horrified at the carnage and fearing to find Gestix amongst it a hollow, brittle feeling crept into his bones. A horse whinnied pitifully from the bloodied heap below, its head tossing up and down, eyes bulbous with fear. Unable to rise as its hindquarters were pinned to the ground by a bloodied timber, its forelegs scrabbled desperately in the dirt. The column filed past as he stared, other young warriors gazed as they drew alongside, some vomited others looking hurriedly away. A hand on his shoulder startled him from the horror below.

"He's not there boy, those men died only a short while ago. Come on, back on your horse, don't gawp, it will unsettle the rest of the lad's see!" Malo said in hushed tones as he pulled back his bow. The creaking of the flexing horn and sinew loud in Baldor's ear and followed by the whoosh of the released arrow. The shaft lodged high in the centre of the maimed horse's head, burying deep and mercifully silencing the injured animal. Nothing further moved in the pit and the flies settled back to their feast.

More bodies littered the forest track as the column advanced, some feathered by arrows others caught in pits or traps of various kinds, out front the screams and shouts continued. The enemy remained elusive and as the Carthaginian death toll mounted, their morale crumbled. Baldor scanned the dead as he passed, he asked the wounded for news of the mercenary scouting party, mostly he was ignored; at best he received a shake of the head.

The forest began to thin out, the trees giving way to a scrub-covered bank dotted with stunted bushes and saplings. The hill sloped steeply downwards to a small stream which cut through the narrow valley floor before the land rose sharply again with the forest thick and dark across the opposite hillcrest. In front of the timberline, arrayed along the contours of the hill were thousands of tribesmen, the sunlight reflecting and shimmering from helmets and spear points. At the sight of the Carthaginians emerging into the scrub, the tribesmen roared and howled their hate while their swords and spears began hammering shields. A tempo built as metal clashed wood, ragged and uncoordinated at first, then building to a deafening thumping rhythm which seemed to shake the very ground. The din abated as some warriors pushed from the ranks and shouted to the Carthaginians offering single combat. In response, the Carthaginian vanguard closed ranks and locked shields, spears protruding forward like porcupine quills.

The tribal champions, finding themselves ignored coerced the Carthaginians scornfully. Some spat in contempt and turned their backs, others threw down their shields in an effort to invite reaction or the acceptance of combat. Carthaginian officers rode up and down in front of their men evaluating terrain, enemy numbers and dispositions, the two forces separated now by less than a stade. A chanced arrow hit one of the officers sending him tumbling earthward, the rest moving back to observe from a safer distance.

As more and more Carthaginians spilled from the forest and marshalled along the slope, the tribesmen dragged captives from behind their lines towards poles set in front of their assembled warriors. The naked and bloodied captives were kicked and beaten into position between a pair of poles, their wrists secured to each upright timber. The hullabaloo of the tribesmen quietened and died away as their lines parted here and there to allow men dressed in dirty white robes to emerge. Wild warriors bowed their heads in deference and edged respectfully almost fearfully aside as the priest like figures passed through the ranks, coming to stop in front of the bound captives.

These men wore their hair long; down past their waists in some cases, some plaited others loose with just a headband to keep it from their eyes. All had small bones and pieces of shell or stone entwined in their matted locks, the elder amongst them bearing blue coloured tattoos on their hands and forehead. Each carried a bronze dagger in his hand. The tribesmen bowed their heads as the priests lifted their arms to the sky chanting prayers to their Gods for victory.

The only shouts came from the rank closers on the Carthaginian

The only shouts came from the rank closers on the Carthaginian side as they marshalled their men. Baldor found himself in the centre and front of the line with Balaam, Malo and Marko alongside.

"Prepare to advance." Shouted one of the Carthaginian officers.

On the other slope the priests began hacking at the captives, small cuts here and there, severing ears, fingers, genitals and blinding others but nothing to kill quickly. One priest made a cut to a prisoner's abdomen then pushed his hand into the wound slowly pulling out a string of intestine, he backed away some ten paces unravelling the man's gut, the prisoner howling and twisting in agony. The man lost consciousness or died and as his head slumped to his chest, the priest cut his bonds letting him fall to the ground.

A low growl rose from the Carthaginians as they witnessed their comrades being butchered.

"Advance!" echoed across the clearing and the Carthaginians started forward.

The priest crouched down beside his victim as if speaking to him before rising and pulling again on the intestine rope. The butchered man got unsteadily to his feet. Stepping woodenly, his hands trying to push his guts back in as the taunting priest led him like a dog on a leash. He staggered drunkenly behind his tormentor to the delight of the tribesmen and the horror of the Carthaginians.

"Advance! Advance!"

The Carthaginian line faltered and stopped, the men looking on in terror and disbelief at the macabre spectacle in front of them, murmurings of magic and necromancy becoming more vocal. Some of the officers began advancing themselves in a bid to encourage their men but within paces of the lines most were feathered by arrows.

"Bastards! Damn them to Hades! That's no way for men to die, butchered like animals!" Balaam muttered under his breath.

"Gestix!" Baldor gasped and pointed as more captives were dragged towards the killing posts.

"Shit! Harbro's there too!" Balaam spat.

Meanwhile, the Carthaginian lines were edging backwards up the slope, away from the enemy. Baldor wheeled a nervous Risto roundabout and pushed out of line to face his comrades.

"Come on!" He implored Balaam. "For pity's sake, come on!"

Balaam looked at Baldor then looked away, anger and frustration on his face.

"There's nothing we can do boy! ... Nothing!" Balaam snarled. "Do you think we would stand by if there was something we could do? Look about you, the men are terrified, they're falling back! Now get back in line!"

"Captain! ... Sir! We can't leave them!" He pleaded.

"Damn you boy! Don't tell me my business; get back in line, now!"

Baldor looked to Marko, his face changing from a mixture of fear and hope to anger.

"Marko, for pity's sake! ..."

"Baldor, get back in line! The Captain's right, we can do nothing!" Marko snapped from tight lips, looking wretched, his face grim.

"I can help." Came from a morose looking Malo as he nocked an arrow to the bowstring. "A quick, clean death at least!"

"Noooooooooooo!" Baldor howled as he realised the dark warrior's intent.

Baldor glanced left and right and saw the Carthaginian lines edging back. Fear etched on the men's faces, their eyes wide and nerves frayed from attacks by an enemy they couldn't see, finally, horrified by what appeared to be a dead man walking.

Baldor snatched hard on the bridle forcing Risto around to face the enemy then kicked hard on his flanks driving him forward like an uncoiling spring. With all reason and logical thought gone and his nerves frayed to breaking point, desperation and adrenalin took over.

"Get back boy! Get back you stupid bastard!" Balaam bellowed.

Baldor urged Risto down the slope, scattering clods and dead leaves as he went his heart ruling his head. He took his hands from the reins guiding the horse with his knees, pulling his shield around to cover him and raising his spear level with his shoulder. A sudden twist by Risto almost unseated him as the animal stumbled and lost its footing. An arrow thumped into his shield and another zipped past his face. Risto careered on, easing back on his haunches as his hind legs skidded down the steeper parts of the slope, horse and man drawing attention from both sides. Down on the level ground between the hills more arrows whipped about them. One lodging again in Baldor's shield, another breaking on his helmet and whipping his head back with the impact, his vision and balance momentarily askew. Cheers erupted from the tribesman as they expected him to go down. A sigh became a ragged cheer from the Carthaginian ranks as Baldor maintained his seat and the horse raced on. Acute interest focussed on them as they headed towards the captives and the priests. Seeing his intent some of the tribesmen moved forward to protect their holy men. Still shaken from the impact of the arrow but glimpsing an unnatural dip in the ground, he sensed another pit and dug his knees into the horse's flanks adjusting his approach. Pushing Risto hard to avoid it, the horse nearly fell underneath him, the pair only just managing to stay upright. More roars and shouts came from the onlookers. Part of the trap framework fell away and Risto whickered and shied, stepping precariously along the edge. Dangerously parallel to the enemy now, more arrows whipped past, miraculously none finding their mark. Cheers rose louder from the Carthaginians as more of them waited to watch the outcome, the men drawing pride back from the young man's bravery.

Clearing the pit, Baldor turned Risto sharply and rode headlong at the tribesmen advancing to protect the priest. The closest warrior was driven under Risto's hooves as his comrades pushed forward in eagerness to drag the rider down. Baldor impaled the second on his spear, losing it in the man's chest as he flew backwards under the impact, the others swarmed about him like dogs attacking a bear.

"Bloody crazy boy! Malo, can you even the score? Quickly now!"

Before the last word had left Balaam's lips, the first arrow was flying towards the battling group.

Tribesmen grabbed and snatched at Baldor, tearing at his shield trying to unseat him. Baldor slashed and stabbed downward, his sword arm a blur. All the while, he forced Risto around in tight circles to scatter the men, give space, and prevent the horse from being hamstrung. As his shield arm was finally clawed down, he slipped his arm from the straps letting it go, his empty hand snatching the second sword from the sheath on the horse's tack.

The Carthaginian's cheers rose to a crescendo as both blades wrought bloody ruin while two more tribesmen running to join the fight were killed by Malo's arrows.

As the tribesmen edged back from the stabbing, crushing death, Baldor drove Risto directly towards the priest nearest Gestix. As he closed on the man, disbelief at the rider's survival and fear of his deadly fury stalled his attackers and they gawped as the priest turned to defend himself. The man thrust upwards with his dagger as Baldor came alongside him. Baldor parried the thrust with one sword while decapitating him with the other, the head rolling and bouncing down the slope. Tribesmen stared as if expecting Baldor to be struck down or the ground open and swallow him. The other priests ceased their butchery and stared at the collapsing corpse still spraying blood from the neck stump. Baldor slashed the bonds holding Gestix, the Gaul collapsing to the dirt grunting in pain.

"Come on! Attack, Attack! They die like other men!" Balaam bellowed, raising his spear high and kicking his horse forward downhill.

Malo turned his horse to follow Balaam while sending another arrow whistling across the scrub, thumping into another priest's chest, knocking him to the floor. The mercenaries moved off down the hill followed closely by the heavy cavalry. The infantry also began to turn and form ranks to the front. The tribesmen recovering from their momentary shock also began advancing. Again, the men nearest Baldor rushed him, placing Risto as a screen to Gestix he prepared to defend himself once more. He urged Gestix up but crippled from the beatings and stiff from being bound, he could only raise himself to one knee, his hand holding his ribs. Baldor kicked Risto forward, scattering the oncoming tribesmen making them easier targets. The ragged charge of the Carthaginian cavalry gathered momentum as they reached the base of the hill, the horses flowing around the pit with more units following on in their wake. The infantry locked shields, edging and slipping down the hill in close support of their mounted comrades. The men attacking Baldor saw the oncoming enemy and drew away seeking relative safety in their shield wall. Behind the Carthaginian infantry, archers had appeared from the rear and were hastily assembling, within moments arrows arced overhead towards the advancing tribesmen. A heartbeat before the cavalry collided with the enemy ranks; the whistle of falling arrows announced their arrival and the tribesmen lifted their shields for cover. A moment later, the cavalrymen's spears pierced the unprotected bodies and men went down like ninepins, the horses riding through the suddenly crumbling wall. The first of the oncoming infantry moved up to double-pace and hurled themselves into the gaps opened by the cavalry. As the cavalry hurtled past him,

Baldor dismounted to help Gestix, the big man gasping as he straightened up, his arm clutching his ribs.

"See to Harbro lad; go on, I'm alright!" He managed between wheezing gasps.

Baldor pushed a bloodied sword into the Gaul's hand then ran to Harbro, cutting his bonds and helping him towards Gestix. A sudden whooshing roar caused all to look up to see fireballs flying overhead, sparks and plumes of oily black smoke trailing across the sky towards the dispersing tribesmen. The Carthaginian field artillery had deployed and moved into action alongside the archers. The first fiery salvo landed high up on the opposing hill smashing into branches and scrub setting both aflame. The second salvo, following only moments later fell into the densely packed tribesmen on the hillcrest as the artillery found their range. Tribesmen burst into flame as fire pots exploded on shields, men or the ground, spraying burning, glutinous liquid that would not extinguish. Hideous screams rose above the din of battle as human torches rolled on the floor, ran amok or tried to beat out the flames. The tribesmen's ranks began to crumble, men peeling away from the formations in ones and twos followed by a general exodus back through the trees. As the rain of fire ceased, Carthaginian heavy infantry attacked the tribesmen. Advancing quickly up the slope they slew any who still drew breath. No quarter given as men took revenge for their butchered comrades, venting their fury for the past days of frustration and fear.

Baldor, free of any threat from the enemy began cutting down the other captives from the stakes. Some were already dead, others savagely mutilated and dying of their wounds, one or two looking as though they may just survive their ordeal. He gently eased the injured men to the ground, wincing as some whimpered pitifully in their pain, others bravely biting back their cries.

A youth much the same age as himself was cut high and deep along his abdomen, his stomach gaping open. He shook violently and babbled blood as Baldor slashed through his bonds. His skin ashen, eyes glassy and unseeing. He spat and coughed blood as his mouth opened and closed, spraying Baldor with specks of crimson froth as he called repeatedly for his mother. Unsure of how to help, Baldor just held him as his calls for his mother repeated faster and faster. His hand tightened vice-like on Baldor's forearm, the finger nails digging deeply into his skin. The shaking slowed a look of peace replacing the pain on his face, a gentle whisper of 'mother' was the last sound he made and the hand fell away as the body went limp. Laying the lad gently on the ground Baldor retched dryly, his empty stomach having nothing to bring up.

As more infantry arrived, some were detailed to help Baldor in his grim task, more than one of the younger men retching and vomiting at the state of the injured. Free of the need to help others, Baldor returned to Gestix and Harbro offering water, his cloak and blankets to them. Gestix, despite broken ribs and difficulty breathing embraced him tightly, mumbling his thanks through broken lips and a face swollen to twice its size from the beating he'd received. The two held one another as if they were the last people on earth, Baldor shaking and sobbing quietly as the adrenalin soaked away. His relief at his friend's salvation balanced with concern at the state of his injuries. Harbro had fared worse, his ribs cracked and an arm dislocated, his eyes mere slits from swelling, his nose pounded into his face. Barely able to breathe he gripped Baldor's shoulder, muttering as best as he could through his destroyed face in husked tones.

"Baal bless you boy ... I ... thought that ..." He paused to catch his breath and moisten his throat with a sip of water "... that was the end of us, here's ... here's to you lad!" He raised the waterskin in salute, managed another sip then passed it to Gestix, saluting Baldor with his good arm and bowing his head.

The slaughter continued on the hill above them. Those who could flee had already left the field with the cavalry harrying and killing any they caught. The tribesmen that remained clustered in small isolated groups seeking strength in numbers. The Carthaginian heavy infantry paused briefly to reform then began a systematic destruction of the final knots of resistance. This fighting turned particularly savage as the tribesmen sold their lives dearly with no quarter asked or given. Balaam returned from the chase, his sword and the horse's flanks splattered with blood. He drew rein in front of Baldor and the injured men.

"You need to learn to obey orders, boy!" He shouted hotly, pointing a blood slicked blade at Baldor, anger clouding his face. "Or you won't remain in this world much longer! Either the enemy will kill you or I'll do it myself!"

Baldor looked at his Captain and said nothing.

"You're an insane, insubordinate, stupid … brave bastard!" Balaam's face split in to a grin. "I ought to kick your bloody arse but after this I am more than likely going to have to kiss it!"

Baldor dropped his head, not wishing to hold his Captains gaze and trying to hide his embarrassment.

"Harbro, Gestix! You two all right? We thought you food for crows for a while." Balaam dismounted as he spoke.

"Sir." Came in a whisper from Harbro as he struggled to speak and breathe, Gestix just nodded.

"Well you don't bloody look it. Have the orderly check you out, I'm not paying cripples!"

Balaam strode across to the injured men pausing to kick and spit on the corpse of the priest Baldor had slain. He stepped over the body then swung his sword down hard and fast, hacking off the priest's hand at the wrist. Stooping, he picked up a golden bracelet that had fallen from the arm into the dirt; wiping it on the dirty robe of the holy man, he held it up for examination. The bracelet, finely constructed from individual strands of gold twisted together formed a thick rope of gold. Balaam looked at the bracelet with deep appreciation before walking to Baldor taking him by the arm. More of the mercenaries returned, gathering about the former captives anxious to see who had survived, some just looking at Baldor, many quite in awe.

Balaam pushed the bracelet onto Baldor's wrist, lifting the lad's arm up straight he shouted.

"Hail warrior!"

"Hail warrior! Hail warrior!" He repeated, turning Baldor to face the gathering men.

The men took up the call, the chant growing louder and becoming more coherent as others joined in, many bowing their heads and saluting.

Baldor, embarrassed and shy of the attention forced upon him looked down to the ground, the acclaim however continued unabated then suddenly grew louder and broke into cheering. Balaam's hold on his arm became a squeeze drawing his attention to the new source of ovation. Looking up he saw a young man, just a few years older than himself mounted on a bay horse and drawing close.

"Hail General!" The warriors chanted pushing in close to the approaching rider, some drawing swords or raising spears in salute.

Hannibal reined in a few paces from Baldor holding up his arms for silence, the surrounding men's cheers slowly dying away. Hannibal unlaced his helmet and removed it, cradling it under his arm.

"Warriors, warriors! Praise me not this day is not mine. This warrior here is where thanks and credit should be given." He pointed straight at Baldor.

Cheers broke out again arms slapping Baldor's back. When the noise died down again, Hannibal dismounted and made his way to Baldor and Balaam.

"Get your helmet off boy! Quickly!" Balaam snapped beneath his breath.

Baldor undid the lacing slipping the black plumed helmet off, Balaam taking it from him. His hair was matted and plastered to his head. Sweat trickled over his brow, the salty liquid stinging his eyes and running into his mouth tasting bitter on his tongue and reminding him of his raging thirst. Hannibal extended his hand and bowed his head repeating. "Hail warrior." The two shook hands.

"That was bravely done soldier, bravely done! That's one of the most courageous deeds I've seen, your name and company if you please?"

Baldor's mind was in turmoil. Confused and suffering from the mental come down after the fighting the words would just not come.

"Your name boy! For the General!" Balaam urged. Silence held as the assembled men waited for Baldor to speak.

Clearing his throat and trying to settle his nerves, Baldor looked straight at his General.

"I am Bal…" His voice broke and tailed off, his tongue and throat parched.

Hannibal reached to his mount and lifted a waterskin down, passing it to Baldor.

"Drink warrior, you've earned it and then give us you name." He said smiling.

Baldor drank deeply, wiping the back of his hand over his mouth and clearing his throat.

"I am Baldor Targa, son of Asmilcar of the city of Carthage. Grandson to Hasdrubal Targa and great grandson to Hasdrubal the younger and great, great grandson to Hasdrubal the elder." He held his head up as he spoke clearly and proudly. "I serve with Captain Balaam's mercenary horse."

"Hail Baldor Targa! May Baal Hammon bless you and your house." Hannibal's words were echoed by the surrounding men, their subsequent cheers loud in the forest clearing. Hannibal leaned across to Baldor's ear and spoke above the din. "When we return to Saguntum Baldor Targa, come and see me. I would know more of you."

"Thank you sir but with respect I must decline, I ..."

"With respect Baldor Targa, that's an order!" Hannibal replied quietly, smiling warmly as he turned to his horse.

The remainder of the day was spent tending the wounded and clearing the field of the dead; the tribesmen's corpses being stripped of anything of value then hurled into the empty pits and dirt thrown over them. The Carthaginians built funeral pyres and burnt their dead, prayers offered to speed the men's souls to Elysium. The mourners suffering the stench of burning flesh as they farewelled their comrades. The weary men camped on the battlefield, crammed tightly into the clearing but thankful of the rest and free of the tension and horror of the past few days. Wine flowed freely as they honoured lost friends and celebrated their own salvation. Despite the mild autumn evening, men heaped wood on the fires and sat close to the crackling flames, happy at the light driving the darkness back and grateful for the closeness of comrades. Cavalry units returned throughout the evening, carrying bloodied heads atop spears else trailing stumbling captives from tether ropes with tales of an enemy slaughtered and harried for tens of stades.

Baldor, Marko and Malo spent the evening alongside Gestix and Harbro. The pair washed, bandaged and laid as comfortably as possible on the ground outside the medical orderly's tent, the more seriously wounded placed within. Harbro's arm was reset and strapped, both men wrapped like babes in tight cotton binding across their chests keeping their ribs secure. The blood was gone from their faces leaving the yellowing, blue-black bruising and swollen, broken lips. Despite the pain they were in, they smiled readily, having to hold themselves as the little group joked and laughed, Malo in particular causing uproar when he compared the two invalids to himself with their new colouring and large lips.

Baldor, the ever-reluctant centre of attention was given no peace, being constantly toasted and praised for his actions, no amount of pleading for quiet or attempted refusal of wine being allowed. Long before midnight, Baldor had succumbed to the drink and merriment, falling deep asleep where he sat amongst his friends. Strong hands gently lifted and laid him comfortably alongside the two injured men, covering him in blankets, a cloak folded as a pillow. Gestix smiled contentedly as a final toast was offered to the sleeping boy. Baldor now had respect, loyalty and a bond with men that would help ensure his survival as best as possible in this risky profession he'd placed himself in. He had a family again.

"Battles may be won on the bloodied field but true victory lies in the winning of the hearts and minds of men"

Anon

Part 2

Chapter Fourteen

Baldor leaned on his elbows resting against the ships balustrade, staring back at the distant coast of Spain as it wobbled amidst the heat shimmer before slipping from sight as the boat went deeper seaward. Fingering his Vulcan's fire, his thoughts drifted back to the last sea crossing and the near sinking they had endured. Thankfully, today was calm and bright, so much so that the huge square sail remained unfurled, the ship gliding over the mirror-like sea from the push of the twin banks of oars alone.

He'd never envisaged crossing the Middlesea again, let alone returning to Carthage. Yet here he was, doing just that in an attempt to clear his name, with letters of commendation for his bravery and a written testimony to his character in his pouch. In complete contrast to his departure, Baldor was in good health, well dressed and groomed, with money in his purse.

He was though without Gestix, who was still incapacitated but recovering slowly from his wounds. The savage beating had left him with cracked ribs, a broken collarbone, wrist, and his hearing impaired in one ear. Hannibal had mentioned quietly to Baldor that Gestix remaining behind might be an advantage; at least he wouldn't have to explain the deaths of the two guardsmen to the court. With Baldor was a man of letters and the law, to help lead and advise in his defence, also an escort of ten heavily armed warriors, a measure to show his personal worth in the eyes of the General and the army and also to ensure he would receive a hearing.

A pang of doubt to his journey led to a surge of panic and a feeling of dread swept over him like a hot desert wind. He may never leave Carthage alive if this deputation to clear his name failed.

After their return to Saguntum, Hannibal had questioned him regarding his background. The boy in him trying to hide his past and his pain, the man within however crying out for justice, for the laying to rest of Aiticia's shade and the restoration of his good name. The hot wind came again and with it the queasy, heavy feeling in his stomach as he remembered Aiticia, lifeless in his arms.

His eyes misted and filled with tears. Closing them tightly to stem the flow and blink them away, instead sent them running down his cheeks to drip onto the rail. He dragged the back of his hand over his face fearful someone may see his anguish. Sniffing hard he tried to compose himself for this was neither the time nor place to mourn his woman.

Forcing his thoughts from his misery and burying it deep in his heart, he went back over his meeting with Hannibal. The General had been genial company, asking of Carthage and how it had changed; he'd spoken quietly and smiled readily, putting his hesitant guest at ease. He dismissed the servants after they fetched dinner for both of them in his tent, choosing instead to serve Baldor with his own hand. He had laid much respect upon Baldor for his bravery in the forest and deemed Gestix and the other captives truly blessed to have another risk his life so willingly for their salvation. This action he said, undoubtedly turned the tide of battle in Carthaginian favour and for that he added his own thanks. This gratitude was followed by a formal presentation to Baldor, done in front of the army with an accolade in the form of a silver campaign bracelet, upon which was deeply inscribed *'For honour and courage'* A more reluctant and bashful recipient of an award however, had never been seen.

The similarity in age of Hannibal and Baldor, along with the aid of potent wine had seen the barriers of formality come down further and for a short time at least, war and death put to one side. Rather than soldier and General, they revelled in being just young men, enjoying good food, wine and each other's company. Initially Baldor held back the reasons for his coming to Spain, more than once he passed them off as that of adventure, which he consoled himself was the essence of truth. Hannibal however probed gently, returning repeatedly to the subject, wily enough to realise that the story did not add up. Adventurers came looking for riches and notoriety, Baldor had had both heaped upon him and seemed to shun them like leprosy. They had talked late into the night, the bond of friendship growing quickly between them. Hannibal's enigmatic charisma drew Baldor in, his warmth and affable nature giving Baldor an ease and peace he had not felt since before his troubles had begun. Eventually, whether it was the wine that loosened his tongue or the need to be rid of the dark secrets that haunted him, he'd divulged his sorrowful tale.

He'd recounted the events, his voice low and monotone, his eyes staring unseeing into space, his mind reliving the past. The tale told without pause as if he needed to be free of it but it was also told slowly, as if no single detail must be missed. Hannibal had listened intently and without interruption, watching as Baldor' emotions played out in his hands as they grasped and slackened on his goblet and in his voice as it dropped lower with anger and hate, as if the injustice would choke him.

When the telling was done, Hannibal picked up the wine pitcher and refilled the goblets, the silence in the tent ominous. Baldor sat quietly, his eyes absently searching the wine in his goblet, expecting at any moment for Hannibal to summon the guard and have him arrested. As time seemed to stand still, a strange relief came over him, he felt as if a gnawing, consuming disease had been driven from him, he felt light and almost wholesome but for the piece of his heart that had left him the day Aiticia died. The noise of Hannibal clearing his throat snapped him back to reality.

"So … it was your name on the warrant!" He exclaimed. "The warrant we never found! Synbolus or Aristides must have sent it with the letters by mistake."

Baldor not understanding just looked blankly at his General. Hannibal waved the confusion away and took a drink. He pointed to Baldor his hand still holding the goblet and said quietly but with conviction.

"I believe you've been wronged! You will go back to Carthage, clear your name then return to me here for I need you."

****

"Need you?" The words echoed in his head, why on earth would Hannibal need him?

Baldor noticed the chill and saw the sun was setting. Footsteps behind him snapped him from his reverie.

"Excuse me sir, we're having some food prepared, will you dine with us?"

The speaker was a man in his thirties, thick set and powerfully framed and almost as tall as Baldor. His raven hair cropped unfashionably short, his strong looking, tanned face, part hidden by a mud brown, leather patch that covered his left eye. Small white scars showed from the edges of the leather hinting at the carnage hidden beneath, his manner of speech was that of great respect, bordering upon reverence.

"Armaco." Baldor said genially. "Don't 'sir' me, Baldor is fine. You are this escort's leader, not me. It is I who should call you sir!"

"Begging your pardon sir, but I am entrusted to see you to Carthage and back again, General's orders. He thinks you are a brave man and with respect sir, so do I. Can I add you to the dinner table?"

Baldor smiled and nodded, "Only if you stop calling me sir."

"Yes si… er, Baldor." Armaco, his turn to smile turned away to see to dinner. Baldor returned to his thoughts.

The warriors squeezed in about a crude wooden table in the Captain's cabin, awaiting Baldor. Armour had been dispensed with and packed ready for the escort duties in Carthage and the men for most wore short tunics of various hues, some however still covered their chests with a lightweight, leather shirt. All however carried a dagger, one or two slipping sword baldrics from their shoulders, placing them over the arm of their chairs as they seated themselves. The cabin ceiling was very low, the room cramped and too warm with so many in it, the acid taint of male sweat strong. The mood of the men was light, an unexpected trip home with additional leave to boot keeping their spirits high, except for one.

The food was served and the men looked to Armaco to offer prayers and so begin the meal. He instead waited, stating no one was to eat until Baldor arrived. He dismissed the grumbling over the delay, instead pushing wine pitchers around the table gesturing for the goblets to be refilled.

"Seems like a lot of fuss being made over some boy that got lucky instead of winding up dead like he ought to have." Came from the one sullen warrior. The man almost spat the words, his disdain and apparent dislike of Baldor obvious.

Armaco picking up his goblet paused from drinking to reply. "He changed the course of battle Ahaggar, you know that! We were falling back until he broke ranks and went for the prisoners, he …"

"Hah! More like his bloody horse bolted and took him with it!"

Some of the men laughed. Armaco smiling a little at the jest himself, he sipped his wine as he quietened them with a wave of his hand.

"Either way." He said swallowing a huge mouthful. "Either way, he fought like a God amongst them, when a man has a friend like that he is truly blessed."

Men nodded sagely, others capered and made beseeching mock cries of 'save me' to their neighbour. Armaco grinned, nodding his head and shrugging.

"Is that why you are all over him like some cheap whore?"

The laughter and foolery stopped abruptly. Silence descended like a veil, frivolity replaced by tension, a deadly, nerve tingling tension. Heads tuned to face the bitter Ahaggar. Men watched, waited and barely breathed as Armaco slowly got to his feet placing his goblet on the table and resting both fists on the table top, leaning forward he stared at Ahaggar. Ahaggar held his stare, only a twitching nerve in his cheek betraying his nervousness. His hand moved slowly backwards from where it rested on the table towards his waist and his dagger.

"Move that hand further and I'll kill you!" Armaco said quietly, his words slipping from grimacing lips, the menace in his voice freezing further movement from Ahaggar.

"I … I, spoke out of turn, I meant no insult!" Ahaggar managed his mouth suddenly dry.

"You're a despicable, whining bastard!" The words seemed to sting Ahaggar as if being lashed. "Always you complain harking at others, spreading your spite and malcontent, can you not show some respect or civility to any? Perhaps you fear that none would risk their life for you?"

A warrior pushed the goblet of wine back into Armaco's hand, tentatively gesturing him to sit. Armaco continued to stare coldly at Ahaggar, forcing him to look down and away. Only then did he sit.

The same warrior, thinking quickly proposed a toast to leave, wine and women and smiles returned lightening the mood once more.

Baldor joined the group just as the goblets were recharged, the warriors rising to their feet when he entered. Bidden to sit, he added another pitcher of wine to the table, the warriors whooping and slapping the table in appreciation. A little embarrassed as usual, he greeted all quickly, though he missed the jealousy and hatred in Ahaggar's eyes, Armaco did not.

****

Baldor and his escort lodged in the town house of General Himilco. Though he was already in Spain with Hannibal, the General's name still held great sway in Carthage, his prestige and armed retainers also guaranteed Baldor would not be assailed or harassed before the hearing.

The morning of his hearing Baldor left his breakfast untouched, taking only a drink of water he dismissed the personal slaves that fussed about wanting to dress and groom him. His lack of comfort with everything being done for him, coupled with his need to hide his nerves found him choosing to attire himself. Tying the blue headband in place to hold his oiled and curled hair he looked at himself in the polished sheet of bronze, not out of vanity but to ensure he was carefully and respectfully dressed. Ankle length robes of creamy white replaced his short, warrior's tunic the side hems edged with a thick strip of ocean blue. The robe covered his left shoulder then swept around his body leaving enough material to be gathered and draped over his left arm, giving him a regal look. His right arm and shoulder remained bare, his bracelet standing out brightly against his tanned skin.

A gentle knock on the door was followed by Armaco, attired in burnished bronze and oiled leather, his helmet with crimson horsehair crest cradled beneath his arm.

"Good morning sir! Are you ready to leave for the senate? The men are standing to and the man of law … Strabonus, is waiting."

Baldor took a deep breath and nodded. His stomach announced its presence as it rumbled and churned, he felt somewhat nauseous, his bones hollow and brittle. Putting on a brave face, he smiled and fell in behind Armaco, his legs feeling quite wooden.

Outside in the courtyard his escort formed up, their harness and weapons gleaming, the early morning sun shimmering and reflecting from spear points and helms. In the centre of the formation, an elderly and very portly man waited, holding a leather tube beneath his arm containing his papers. Like Baldor, he wore a robe edged in blue but with an irritated, impatient look on his chubby, heated face.

"Come young Targa! Come, come! We should be gone ere now! We will go over it again as we walk, the morning air will clear your head and settle your nerves. How's your bowels? A court case is always good for the bowels, keeps you regular, hah! … Lead on." He said, flicking his head at Armaco.

The party moved off across the paved yard and out through the gate.

"How are your bowels, lad? It's important to be regular, you should defecate every day, get rid of shit, hah!"

"I am well sir … regular even." Baldor replied somewhat bemused.

"More than can be said for these senators then, full of it they are, shit that is! Shitbags, every one of them, hah!"

Baldor heard some of the warriors chuckling, he himself smiling.

As the column weaved its way through the streets, Strabonus continued in earnest with his diatribe on the intricacies of the bowel, to the amusement of all that could hear him.

"Have you prayed this morning young Targa?"

"No sir, no… I have no time for it."

"Well you should young Targa, you should! Be regular in all things, praying and defecating especially! If the first doesn't work the second will surely follow through, hah!"

Even the serious Armaco couldn't hide a smile. By the time Baldor managed to break into the seemingly one-way conversation to ask of plans for the day, they were already at the base of the steps leading into the senate. Strabonus merely waved his hand dismissively, advising Baldor to tell only the truth and leave the rest to him.

The senate steps were of smooth white marble and wide enough to admit two score of men marching abreast, they led up to a plaza and the senate portico supported by a dozen fluted pillars, each thrice the thickness of a man. The portico rose to an apex, beneath which carved in heavy relief was the inverted crescent of Carthage and a set of scales showing the weighing cups evenly balanced. Set beneath in its shade were two huge cedar doors, these were wide open and fringed on the inside with gathered crimson curtains.

The group pushed its way through the crowd gathered on the steps. Armaco jostling Baldor and Strabonus into the centre of his men, at the same time dispatching a warrior to find out what was causing the large crowd and to announce, 'Baldor Targa was here in answer to his summons, by the grace of Baal.' Before they reached the plaza however, the warrior was back, forcing people out the way with his shield as he came.

"Sir! … Sir, its Romans, Romans!" He paused to curse and push more folk out of the way, catching his breath and continuing. "Roman envoys are here and in the debating chamber! Their leader, a one Quintus Fabius Maximus is speaking now! All other cases are delayed for the moment until …"

"Get me in there!" Strabonus barked at Armaco, his face suddenly serious, his manner and speech direct and commanding. "Use the flats of your swords if needs be!"

The warriors closed up tightly and locked shields, Armaco shouted time and they marched off scattering anyone who got in their way using sheer weight and impetus. They broke ranks as they reached the entrance, alleviating the anxious looks of the senate guards. The warriors remained at the doors whilst Strabonus and Baldor slipped inside where the smell of over-heated humanity from the press of bodies hit them like the opening of an oven door. They stood in a gallery looking down into an auditorium where the centre of the floor was taken by a man dressed in scarlet robes, his hands hooked into the folds at his chest. Seated behind him were his colleagues, Romans like himself and dressed similarly.

The man appeared agitated, unable to speak further for the babble and noise of the crowd. He held his greying head high, an air of superiority emanating from him; his fingers tap, tapping in frustration on the lectern in front of him as he waited while the stewards called repeatedly for silence. Surrounding him, on tiered marble benches draped in crimson cloth throws and cushions, was a sea of Carthaginian senators all robed in white. They talked among themselves in groups, some discussions becoming heated with fingers pointing and some shouting, in order to be heard or endorse their point to unconvinced colleagues.

Finally, the stewards' voices aided by a banging staff prevailed over the hubbub and the noise died away. Men returned to their seats and all eyes turned once more to the man at the lectern. When all was silent, the head steward looked to the man in scarlet robes.

"Pray continue sir."

The man looked round the room in disgust. He took his time shuffling the parchments on the lectern as if to make the people in the room wait, as he had, had to wait. He cleared his throat and eyed around the room again, ensuring all now listened.

"We, the citizens of Rome, have laid our concerns before you. We ask once again, by what right you assail the city of Saguntum. This attack …"

Angry shouts and disjointed replies broke out again having to be silenced by the stewards before Quintus could continue.

"This attack by your General Hannibal upon Saguntum is illegal! The city falls under the protection of Rome. We demand that you withdraw your armies and raise the siege immediately, while offering up this General Hannibal for trial and paying …"

The Senate erupted again with booing and cries of "Arrogance!"

The staff banged again. "Silence! Silence! … Let the man finish! Ere I call in the guard and have order restored, forcibly if need be!" The head steward bellowed above the din. The hush that followed gave Strabonus his chance to join the debate.

"Sir!" He said politely, directing his words to the Roman at the lectern. "Sir, how can this siege be illegal? Saguntum lies well south of the river Ebro and thus within Carthaginian hegemony does it not? Moreover, we have a right to punish insurgents and rebels for that's what these Saguntines are! I advise you not to interfere here. These are domestic matters and with respect, no business of Rome's."

"My Lord Strabonus does not speak for all here!" Said a young man, who rising from his seat, supported himself on crutches. "Not all agree with General Hannibal and his actions!"

Some senators erupted from their seats with cries of. "Traitor!" and "Arse kisser!" Shouted at the man, along with rolled papers, scroll cases and small coins. He, having to retake his seat in order to use both hands to fend off the missiles aimed at him.

The stewards bellowed for order again, finally the marching in of armed guards quietened the crowd and normality and order returned.

The guards lined the outer perimeter of the circular floor area looking upwards and back at the seated senators and Roman guests.

"My Lord Adharbal does not speak for many here, I'll warrant." Quipped Strabonus, this raising laughter and shouts of "Hear! Hear!" from the assembly.

"Perhaps sir, you should consider the Lord Adharbal's thoughts and question your General Hannibal and his motives before they drag you into a war you cannot win." Interjected Quintus.

The mention of war seemed to have a sobering affect on the assembly and a taught silence fell. All around the room breaths held, colleagues looked at one another but none deigned to speak. Strabonus cleared his throat and looked at the Romans then stepped forward waving his arm for permission from the steward to speak. All eyes turned to him as he was granted the floor.

"Do I hear you aright sir? ... That you threaten us with war?" Strabonus sounded incredulous.

"This city is in alliance with us and thus under our protection."

"This city is in Carthaginian territory so your alliance means nothing here!" Strabonus's tone changed from politeness to firmness. "Now sir, I ask you again, do you threaten us with war?"

Even the arrogant and confident seeming Quintus faltered as the gravity of the question struck him, the very air of the room charged, nations and lives hung in balance. History was being made at that instant, the silence pregnant and suddenly terrible. Quintus, snapping out of his stupor made a melodramatic gesture placing his hand inside his robe next to his heart.

"In here I have both peace and war, which is it to be?"

Strabonus summoned a steward to him asking him to collect the most senior judges to consider the response.

"Bear with us sir, if you please?" He replied to Quintus.

Baldor noted the steward bowed deeply to Strabonus as he departed on his task and that other men who caught Strabonus's eye bowed their heads. He realised now that Strabonus must be one of the most senior and important men in the building and perhaps why, he had seemed so relaxed about Baldor's case. Hannibal it seemed had powerful friends indeed.

The judges disappeared into an anteroom. The heavy door closing with a definite thud that echoed round the chamber as if announcing the apocalypse. Men talked among themselves again in vibrant but hushed tones, the Romans themselves in deep debate, as all awaited the momentous decision from the room. After a surprisingly short wait, the doors opened and the group filed out. Senators rose to their feet, trying to read the decision on the faces of the judges as they made their way back to their seats. Strabonus however, strode directly to the centre of the floor opposite Quintus. His robes gathered in his left hand, he turned his corpulent body side on to the Roman, tilting his head back to look down his nose. Silence fell without being asked for.

"You say you offer peace or war ... we say ... you choose!" His tone un-conciliatory.

Quintus let go of the lectern, pushing himself up straight and tall and looking around the room, he said fiercely. "We choose war!"

"We accept!" Snapped Strabonus as he turned his back on Quintus, walking away without a further look.

There were no loud outbursts, cheers, groans or otherwise. Instead, a strange hush settled over the room. Seats began to empty as men made their way out into the sun, anxious to spill the news and contemplate the consequences for themselves. The two greatest powers around the MiddleSea were once more at war.

Chapter Fifteen

The following morning saw Baldor and Strabonus escorted back to the senate. Strabonus again enquiring after the condition of Baldor's bowels, Baldor replying in truth, that he was most regular and likely to remain so for the length of his trial.

Strabonus winked and chuckled, his heavy jowls shaking. "Best purge in the world the courts, eh!"

There were no crowds on the steps nor was there a full complement of senators at the benches inside, the whole city seemed to be in the throes of an anti-climax. The judges called the senate to order and Baldor stood forward to listen to the charges laid against him. As instructed, when asked of his plea he answered a clear 'not guilty' his head up looking proud, his tone though respectful and dignified. His stomach however in complete contrast to his look. The lack of breakfast forcing his gut lining to digest itself, causing pain with burning sensations and an oily, nauseous feeling. His bowels felt abnormally full, his throat dry and he was sure all could see his heart pounding in his chest.

As the prosecution began their opening speech, Baldor caught sight of Adharbal and the pair exchanged a long look. Baldor bore him no malice and his gaze was one of sadness for what had passed between them at Icosium. He was unable to read Adharbal's stare, his features betraying nothing, his thoughts remaining hidden. The pair had been good friends during their childhood years, the actions since of an older brother causing a loss for both and now a blood feud.

The charges against Baldor amounted to four; the murder of Carthalo, failure to repay monies owing, resisting arrest and the murder of two city guards. A quiet comment from Strabonus in Baldor's ear of. "May as well be hung for a sheep as a lamb eh?" Did nothing for his stomach despite the wink and chuckle that accompanied it.

Strabonus began the defence by responding firstly to the charge of murder of the city guards. At that time he stated, Baldor had been wounded and therefore physically unable to partake in the fray. He had Baldor stand and bare his shoulder, exposing his wound to all in the chamber, at the same time, he produced a physician to verify his argument from the nature and age of the injury. Furthermore, he argued pacing across the polished floor, these guards were deep within Numidia when the fight took place therefore outwith their jurisdiction and thereby technically illegal in their actions. By reason of this, the additional charge of resisting arrest was therefore nonsense.

He continued, uninterrupted so far. Concerning the monies owing, Baldor had not defaulted on his loan, he had been obliged with time to pay by the Lord Hanno Samilcar before the old man had fallen to illness. This had been a full written and legal agreement between the parties and thus the Lord Carthalo had no right to overturn it.

Finally, he moved to the rebuttal of the charge of murder of Carthalo. At this point senators straightened in their seats, ears straining so not to miss a word that was said. Of them all, only Adharbal remained statue like, his hand supporting his chin, still staring at Baldor. Strabonus shuffled his papers, took a sip of water and stared around the room then continued.

"The defendant admits he struck the first blow in response to a slur on his character. He did not however, reach for weapons first." Strabonus paused to let the statement sink in.

"He was forced to defend himself when Lord Carthalo took to him with a dagger. Further … it was the Lord Carthalo that began the killing he …"

"We object!" Shouted from across the room. A small man jumped up from his seat, his head bobbing chicken like as he looked around the benches, as if daring others to contradict.

"Silence! Let him finish." Came from one of the senior judges. "In truth the only survivor of the encounter is the defendant, therefore let us hear the defence out ... continue sir."

Strabonus cleared his throat. "The defendant's wife was slain by Lord Carthalo, which is fact!" Sharp intakes of breath could be heard and some muttering. "It was however an accident, the wine pitcher that hit the lady was aimed at the defendant, the ..."

"If it was an accident then why did the accused slay the Lord Carthalo?" The prosecutor got in quickly before the judges could silence him.

"If you keep your tongue between your teeth I'll tell you!" Strabonus quipped, this raising some laughter from the crowd before the stewards barked them into silence.

Strabonus began again, "Reason it out sir." He said pointing to the prosecutor. "Lord Carthalo arrives at the defendant's house, late in the day, unannounced and demanding monetary repayment. The wife is slain, accident or not and her husband, the defendant is sorely wounded. How would that appear to a court?" Strabonus looked about the chamber his hand open and gesturing, as if seeking a reply.

"Perhaps sir ..." The prosecutor replied. "Perhaps, the accused returned home and misconstrued the Lord Carthalos presence as that of a secret lover and ..."

Baldor snarled and jumped to his feet, a low voiced curse forcing through gritted teeth. Strabonus tuning quickly placed a restraining hand on Baldor's shoulder pushing him back to his seat. His stern looks silencing any retort from him.

"Sir!" Strabonus said turning to the prosecutor. "Without wishing to cast further aspersions upon the character of Lord Carthalo." He sighed as if regretting his words. "It's no secret, perhaps we should say well known that his sexual preferences were ... aimed at other than women." Strabonus added the statement with a quiet dignity as if he resented having to explain. He paused, allowing the words to sink in and the following silence to add affect before continuing. "As I was saying, the Lord Carthalo was then intent on murder to silence the husband. Thereby leaving only himself to answer in the courts, where he could pass events off as other than they were." He slipped the statement in quickly so the defence had no time to object.

Listening to the scenario, Baldor's mind slipped back to the terrible night. Unashamed tears slipped from the corner of his eyes as he thought of Aiticia, not daring to wipe them away or draw attention to them he bit his lip hard, tasting the bitter, iron taste of blood. The pain helping him to focus and maintain his proud composure.

"We have only the word of the accused on that!" Came from the chicken-headed prosecutor.

"Yes sir we do, that is true! We readily admit the death of Lord Carthalo … that is truth and fact but murder it was not! The wounds suffered by both men show only signs of a fair fight, no backstabbing! Furthermore. Ask yourself, does a man that commits murder then spare the life of an avenging younger brother when he defeats him in a fair fight? A fight I may add, that was to be to the death! … Does a man that commits murder then risk his life against insurmountable odds to save his fellow warriors? … I think not!" Strabonus paused again, glaring round the room as if daring a response. "Judges, senators the defence rests!" He collected his papers from the lectern and strode back to his seat.

Debate broke out amongst the senators. Whilst the stewards called for order Adharbal rose from his seat, struggling onto his crutches and made his way to the prosecutor. The pair spoke quietly; Adharbal turned and hobbled away making his way to the door. Finally, order was restored and the judges offered the floor back to the prosecution. The small man approached the lectern, bowed to the judges and the room.

"Judges, senators, the prosecution withdraws on two counts, that of the death of Lord Carthalo and the loan."

All around the room men stared at one another. Vibrant talk broke out, the judges and Baldor looking bewildered. Strabonus merely smiled contentedly to himself.

The stewards called for silence then advised a recess until the following morning where upon the city prosecution would begin regarding the charges for the slaying of the guards.

****

Back in court for the third day very much aided Baldor's constitution in line with Strabonus's predictions and apparently much to his delight. The man himself in excellent humour.

"Well, we'll soon have this matter closed now young Targa, then you can get back to the General and the very real business of this war. Tricky things wars! You never know which way it will go, that's why there are no fat soldiers, always regular, hah!"

Baldor mentally decided he would rather face the whole of the Roman army than go through this legal drama again. He felt sure Roman soldiers would keep his bowels in a similar condition as the courts but it was fewer traumas in his mind.

After the city prosecution finished reiterating the charges for the murder of the guards and the resistance to arrest, Strabonus once more took the floor. He took his time placing his papers upon the lectern, then clearing his throat he began:

"Upon whose authority were the guards given leave to invade Numidia?" He asked imperiously.

"Come sir, you miss-speak! This was no invasion and you know it! The guards were dispatched to apprehend the accused. There are no barriers to justice." The prosecutor replied.

"Sir, Numidia is a friendly power to us and as you know, currently supports us with troops in Spain! Now, did you seek permission to enter their country with armed men?"

"If they are as friendly as you say sir, surely they would not object?"

"Whose authority sir? Moreover, from whom the permission? Else, it is invasion! I would not come to your home with armed men without notice and your permission … and we are friends are we not?" This drew a few smiles from the senators. Strabonus peered down his nose at the prosecutor a teasing smile on his lips.

The prosecutor appealed to the judges. "The defence bandies with words, this…"

"Whose authority sir? Whose permission?" Strabonus repeated with mock weariness, he strode the floor as he spoke, his thumbs hooked in his robes.

The prosecutor edged to the benches to confer with his colleagues. After an agitated, whispered discussion but no reply, Strabonus began again, smugly.

"So it was invasion then!"

"The defence is basing their argument on technicalities." Replied the prosecutor as he finally found voice.

"Technicalities start wars sir! We all witnessed that yesterday! … The defence rests."

The prosecution then turned to Baldor and questioned him, Baldor did as he'd been bidden and answered truthfully. The prosecution then called for Gestix; instead, Strabonus took the floor once more.

"The Gaul cannot appear my Lords, he remains in Spain incapacitated. However, I must stress that this man defended his friend from an illegal arrest. Also, he fought at Saguntum for us and fell at the battle in the forest; we are told he is likely to die of his wounds." His voice lowered as he finished.

Baldor's head whipped around to look at Strabonus, his eyes wide with concern. Strabonus raised his eyebrows and carried on.

"Furthermore! He is not a Carthaginian citizen; you have no more right to summon him here than you had to attempt to arrest him." He said quickly.

Whilst the prosecution conferred, Strabonus again announced the resting of the defence and sat down. Eventually the prosecution also rested and the judges departed to the anteroom to decide the issues placed before them. Baldor sought Strabonus, pulling him sharply to one side speaking in agitated but hushed tones.

"What do you mean, likely to die of his wounds? I wasn't told! I should never have left him to come here! He wouldn't ..."

"Calm yourself young Targa, calm yourself! He is alright, he will be alright, trust me!"

"But you said he ..." Baldor looked totally confused.

"Yes, I know what I said and you and the rest of the court interpreted it just as I hoped you would. Listen carefully... like all of us he is going to die ... sometime. Those wounds will not have helped his longevity, which is a fact. That is what I said."

Baldor sighed with relief. "But that's being economical with the truth is it not?"

"Please! I prefer technicalities as I believe my prosecuting colleague over there called it."

Strabonus smiled and winked then broke into a chuckle while gesturing Baldor to sit, the two settled down to await the return of the judges.

The time seemed to drag for Baldor. In the end, he was unsure how long the judges had been gone; his stomach ached and burned his bowels suddenly full. His mind ranged from euphoria to black despair and horror as his thoughts jumped from winning his freedom through to losing his life on a cross the next. A dozing Strabonus was no comfort, his hands clasped together across his ample belly and his head dropped forward with his triple chin resting on his chest, little contented snorts being his only input.

Eventually, the court was called to order as the judges re-entered. Baldor nudged Strabonus who snorted quite loudly before opening his eyes and coming to his senses. He got himself to his feet quickly urging Baldor to do likewise.

The senior judge began. "Baldor Targa, son of Asmilcar, citizen of Carthage, herewith is the judgement handed down by this court." He paused to pick up his scroll, Baldor standing proud and straight felt his skin flushing and his stomach gripe, his legs frighteningly weak.

"On the charge of the death of the Lord Carthalo ... you are found not guilty, the prosecution having withdrawn.

Concerning the monies owed ... again, we find you not guilty, as you were not in breach of your contract. Your home and shipyard wrongly taken from you in lieu of that debt. These properties to be returned, though payment must be made for the cost of the repairs already made by the Lord Hanno's family. Alternatively, you can cede the properties and take a cash settlement instead. If you choose this path however, we require full settlement of the outstanding debt to be paid, as the assets of your property were guarantee of your loan." The judge paused for breath, allowing time for the verdict to sink in.

"On the charge of resisting arrest ... not guilty. This undertaking being unlawful. On the charge of the slain guards, again we find you not guilty. However, as this Gaul, 'Gestix' was acting in your interest, you must pay to the wives and orphans of the said guards, a one off maintenance payment which will be determined by the court and advised to you at a later date. These proceedings are closed, you are free to go."

Cheers broke out around the court. Baldor however, just stared, somewhat numbed, trying to absorb what had been said. A hearty slap on the back from Strabonus and a heavy arm thrown round his shoulder hugged him close. The portly man's laughter in his ears brought it home to him, he was free to go and rebuild his life.

As the court dispersed, Baldor and Strabonus made their way out into the sun to be met by Armaco and the escort. Armaco looked apprehensive, trying to read their faces.

"All done sir? ... All done?" Baldor was still dumbstruck but managed a nod and a smile. "I knew you would be alright, Baal looks kindly on the brave." The tall warrior's hand shot out to grasp Baldor's in a vice-like grip, shaking it vigorously. "The General will be pleased at …"

"Targa! Targa, you murdering scum!" Serfina shouted while trying to push through the warriors to Baldor. "You may have fooled those befuddled idiots in there but I will have justice!" Her face twisted in hate, her fingers hooked like talons as she grabbed at him.

"Murderer! Murderer!" Her shouts growing louder and more frantic as Armaco stepped in her way, restraining then pushing her roughly away as her nails gouged at his remaining eye. She staggered backwards trying to maintain her balance but the push sent her reeling across the plaza, her hair coming unbound falling in disarray over her shoulders. Momentarily shocked at the fracas, Strabonus stared then bellowed for calm and order. Finding himself completely ignored and his voice drowned by Armaco ordering his men to form up and lock shields, he ran as fast as his overweight frame would allow calling for guards, the scene descending into mayhem. The warriors closed around Baldor protecting him, swords scraping from sheaths as Serfina's escort of six, giant Nubian bodyguards began to fan out around the knot of warriors. Sunlight danced on their oiled, ebony skins as they glided like hunting panthers, advancing on the group while crouching low and freeing iron-tipped, wooden cudgels from their belts.

With his sword clear of its sheath Armaco stood forward of his men, beckoning with his empty hand at the Nubians.

"Come, if you want to die, come! I'll spread your heathen lites over the plaza!" He glanced at Serfina, "You want blood you demented bitch? Let your black barbarians loose and I'll spill some for you!"

The black giants eyed the bright blades and the grim faces of the warriors peering above the large shields. It would be a hard fight; they glanced at their mistress awaiting her orders. Serfina was about to command an attack but the rumble of sandaled feet and the rattle of harness and weapons coming close caused all to look up. A scarlet plumed officer with a score of guards forced his way between the parties.

"Throw down your weapons! Down I say! Or I'll arrest you all!"

Armaco wondered how the slovenly looking guards were going to affect an arrest but the added commands of Strabonus and now Adharbal, in support of the officer brought some restraint to the ruckus. Adharbal, hobbling on his crutches behind a panting Strabonus barked at the Nubians to back away. No one moved, the Nubians looking to Serfina, Armaco's men remaining immobile awaiting orders from him.

"Serfina! Enough! ... Call off your guards damn you! ... I command it!" In his haste, Adharbal lost a crutch to a pothole and went down hard in the street. Crawling to his crutches and struggling to his feet, he caught up with Strabonus. Bruised and hurt from the fall, almost breathless from his exertions he gasped his orders again. "Serfina! Stop this now! I give you my last warning, call off your guards!"

Serfina cast her brother a murderous look then glanced at the guards and the row of shields that almost hid Armaco's men before slowly motioning her men away. The Nubians backed off gradually, cudgels still raised, none taking their eyes from Armaco's men.

"Weapons down! ... Now!" The guards' officer shouted again, though not as confident as before as he assessed quality and numbers.

Armaco spat contemptuously at the retreating Nubians then slowly lowered his sword; his hand motioned his men likewise.

"You are all under arrest! Hand ..."

"Thank you officer! That is all we require, peace is restored." Came from Strabonus who gathering his composure was trying to speak genially but also take charge.

"Sir, I must arrest them all! Brawling and brandishing arms in the city is ..."

"I know I know." Strabonus said attempting to placate the officer. "Of course you are right and you should but all is well now ... save yourself the paperwork eh? These warriors are on their way back to Spain, the lady's guards a little over zealous ... a misunderstanding is all it was."

"That's right officer, that's all it was." Adharbal added.

The officer still unconvinced looked around as he thought, noticing for the first time the well-serviced but very used weapons of the warriors and their ready discipline. He looked at the silent but menacing Nubians seeing restrained violence ready to unleash upon command. Deciding he didn't need the paperwork or the aggravation, he nodded to Strabonus and Adharbal.

"Very well, I will bid you good day gentlemen." He marched off with his men falling in behind.

The two sides continued backing warily away like dogs forced to part from a bone, either party still ready to fight at a moments notice. Once at a safe distance Armaco asked of anyone who could answer.

"What in Baal's name was that about? Who's the bitch?"

"That was the sister of the recently departed Lord Carthalo and the Lord Adharbal; the man on crutches. We can take it she is not happy at the courts verdict. I suggest we return to General Himilco's villa and plan your return to Spain as soon as possible young Targa, are you alright?"

Baldor nodded to Strabonus though he looked despondent and sick to the stomach.

"Bloody crazy bitch!" Armaco muttered.

"Undoubtedly! However, a damned dangerous one never the less! Come Armaco lead us home, well done to you and your men, they're a credit to you, they gave those Nubians pause for thought."

Un-noticed by anyone, Ahaggar picked up Serfina's hair ribbon pushing it inside his corselet.

****

Adharbal reclined in his chair. Leaning on the arm with his head supported on his hand, his damaged leg elevated on a stool, he was both weary and sore. The physician had washed and cleaned the cuts he'd sustained from the fall and was busy assessing the old leg and shoulder wounds from the fight with Baldor months before. The door was suddenly and unceremoniously thrown open to bang back on its hinges as Serfina stormed into the room.

"How dare you! How dare you speak to me so?" She screamed at her brother, her eyes burning bright with anger her voice hot with venom.

Adharbal gave his sister a tired look. "Enough Serfina!" He said quietly.

The physician stood and hurriedly backed away as Serfina crossed the floor like an approaching storm. Adharbal nodded to the man and gently waved him away. Hesitating to pick up the water bowl and his bag, he suffered the full force of Serfina's wrath.

"Get out! ... Out!" She screamed, swiping the bowl from the man's hand then striking him hard across the face. "Out!" The liquid covered Adharbal, the bowl smashing into pieces on the floor.

The physician dropped his bag and fled. Adharbal's face darkened. He smashed his fist repeatedly upon the small table at his side, the wood splintering and collapsing. He snarled from tight lips.

"Serfina! I said enough! ... Enough! Enough!" His voice rising to a shout.

He tried to stand but fell as his leg buckled beneath him. He landed heavily, his fore head banging the floor, bright blood poured down the side of his face. The sight of blood seemed to bring Serfina to her senses and she ran to his side using the corner of her robe to stem the blood flow.

"I'm sorry brother, sorry! I didn't want you to be hurt; I just don't understand you? You drop the charges and let Targa walk away then defend him in the street! He, who did this!" She pointed to his leg.

Serfina's eyes filled and tears fell copiously down her cheeks, she sobbed as though heartbroken while helping Adharbal to his feet.

"Can't you understand me brother? I love you. Carthalo, Sakarbaal. You're my brothers, my family, no one must hurt you."

She settled Adharbal back in his chair again. "Let me call the physician back to tend you ..."

"No... no, not yet sister, we need to talk." He spoke softly again, smiling warmly. "Come sit." He reached over to drag a chair across for her. He wiped the blood from his temple as he spoke. "Listen sister, Baldor slew Carthalo that much we know and he has admitted. He didn't murder him; it was a fair fight ..."

"How do you know?" She interrupted her anger still raw.

"I watched his face as he answered the court and I saw truth." He paused to wipe blood away from his eye. "Remember, I have known him all my life, we were good friends as boys; he was ever honest and honourable, even then. Its true what Strabonus said about the fight between us, he could have slain me and in truth if I'd won, I would have slain him, for my temper ran hot ..."

"I would that you had and put an end to it, instead of us suffering this travesty of justice." Serfina replied bitterly.

"Better it turned out like it has. I want no more deaths over money."

"But he should be imprisoned at least, instead he walks away free as the birds!"

"His loss is every bit as great as ours and I for one would not swap places with him. He has lost his wife, mother, and father, his home and now it seems the Gaul as well. He is quite alone; at least we have each other. I think he's suffered enough."

Serfina said nothing

"It ends now sister, all of it! The hatred, thoughts of revenge, everything! We will stand by the decision of the court and sort out his property rights. Then … then perhaps we can get on with our lives."

Serfina said nothing she just hugged her brother.

"Do you hear me Serfina? It ends now!"

"I hear you brother." She replied quietly, her tear filled eyes however smouldered like fanned coals, her hatred a monster to be fed, any notion of forgiveness blackly opposed by thoughts of retribution. "Now you must rest, I will have the physician brought." She fussed around him making him comfortable, hushing him gently when he made to speak further.

****

Evening came with the air warm and balmy, the threat of a storm heralded by the growl of thunder in the distant hills. Serfina gazed into the burnished bronze mirror idly combing out her hair. Fresh from a fragrant bath and the ministrations of her body slaves she was relaxed, the soft caress of the silk robe on her skin adding to her comfort, the dramas of the day far away. She listened to the clicking cicadas and the call of the peacocks as she combed, strangely at peace with herself for the first time since the death of her eldest brother. A timid and quiet tap on her door disturbed her peace. "What is it?" She sighed.

The door eased ajar. "Mistress there is a man to see you, he says it's important."

"At this time? I'm expecting no one, tell him to leave a message with my steward and begone."

"I've already told him you're not to be disturbed mistress but he says you must see him, it's important and will be to your benefit."

"Get rid of him, I'm weary."

The door closed quietly and the slave girl's footfalls faded. Serfina had just stretched out on her settle when the knock came again.

"Mistress …"

"By all that's holy! Can I not have peace?" Serfina's temper rose sharply along with her voice.

"Mistress, I tried to send him away but he keeps saying, demands even, that you see him …"

"Turn out the guards, throw him out! I'll not be harangued in my own house!"

"Please mistress, he said to give you this, he said it would explain his visit so late in the day." The young girl, shaking just a little handed over a black ribbon. Serfina stared at the ribbon as if she'd been struck.

"Who is he? What does he look like?" Serfina shook the girl's shoulders, her questions not answered quickly enough.

"He gave no name mistress. He's well-dressed but not like a senator or a Lord, he wears the cloak and short tunic of a warrior."

"A name girl, get me a name! I see no one without a name." Serfina pointed to her robes as she spoke, the girl rushing to help dress her. Once enrobed, Serfina sent her scurrying away to gain a name, tying the robe closed herself. Her heart fluttered in her chest; surely, Targa would not dare come to see her? Who else could it be? Her anger flared again as the day's events came flooding back. She paced as her mind raced. Soft footfalls on the stair heralded the return of the now breathless girl.

"Mistress … mistress … his name is Ahaggar, Ahaggar Bola. He is a warrior with General Hannibal's army."

Serfina frowned the name meant nothing.

"I will receive him in the small reception room. Have Panhessy armed and posted within."

Serfina made her way to the reception room and settled herself in the chair. A titan sized Nubian arrived a moment later, his skin black as a moonless night. He wore a white, wool tunic from waist to knee held in place by a leather belt that supported a broad bladed dagger. Filling the doorway with his width, he entered silently on bare feet and bowed low to Serfina. She motioned him to one side and awaited her visitor.

The slave girl entered bidding the visitor to follow her.

"Mistress, this is Ahaggar Bola of Carthage. He has matters to discuss with you, if you please?" She bowed low and left, closing the door gently behind her.

Serfina studied the warrior before speaking. He oozed pride that verged upon arrogance, his smile laconic, almost a sneer. He was swathed in a scarlet, campaign cloak, fastened at the shoulder with a silver broach wrought in the shape of a crescent moon. The black corselet beneath was adorned with brass crescents and small pointed stars riveted in symmetrical patterns over the facings of the leather. The metal patterns designed to give an eye-catching look as well as practical protection from weapon slashes and thrusts. Burnished to a lustre like the leather, they sparkled and twinkled like real stars as they reflected the yellow light of the oil lamps.

He was of medium height and build, in his late twenties, and like most Carthaginians swarthy and raven-haired, his thin lips crowded by a close-clipped moustache and goatee beard. His eyes dark and fathomless, his manner that of a wily animal as he glanced about the room taking all in, especially the giant Nubian. He smiled at Serfina but there was no warmth in it.

"My Lady, what I have to say is for your ears only. I think we can dispense with 'Atlas' here." He nodded towards the Nubian, smiling at his own wit. "I am unarmed and mean you no harm." He opened his cloak further then raised open hands, smiling his winter smile.

"Panhessy stays! He's a deaf mute, so say what you have come for then begone for the time is late."

"I trust you received your ribbon back?"

"Don't bandy words with me; you didn't come here to return my ribbon! What is it you want? If you have something to tell me, speak and then go. I'm in no mood for games!"

Ahaggar shrugged. Realising his small talk was making no inroads he became bluntly direct.

"You want Targa dead. I can see to it but for a price." It was a statement not a question. He stared at her trying to read her reaction.

Shocked by his directness and the cold piercing stare, Serfina felt as if he was peering into her very soul. She subconsciously pulled her robe tighter closed across her breasts. She swallowed quickly, not trusting herself to speak while she tried to think. She felt uncomfortable, out of control of the situation and somewhat scared at the thought of killing now that it had been put so blatantly. She stood and poured herself a drink, turning her back on Ahaggar. Out of his stare, she recovered some of her composure. She sipped her drink buying more time then walked slowly across the room away from him trying to appear nonchalant, her mind scheming and calculating.

"You are part of his escort are you not? Should you not be seeing him back to Spain safely?"

Ahaggar shrugged. "Do you want him dead or not?"

"Yes I want him dead!" She said in a chilling snarl. "I want him dead and rotting but not here, not anywhere near here. Do it when you return to Spain. Kill him how you like, as long as it doesn't implicate me or my family. We have suffered enough on his account." She felt her strength and surety returning as she spoke, along with her anger.

"Aha! And you are going to pay me ... what?" He answered slowly.

"The weight of you sword in silver coin, take it or leave it? Now get out!" Serfina turned her back once more signalling the audience was over.

Ahaggar was about to haggle but Serfina was already leaving the room, the giant Nubian turned to face him, massive arms still folded across his chest. The expressionless black face studied him briefly before pointing with one huge hand to the door.

Ahaggar turned on his heel, killing Targa would be a pleasure anyway and any reward would be a bonus.

Chapter Sixteen

Baldor sat on the warm stone of the balcony wall. He shaded his eyes from the sunlight reflecting from the small green waves formed by the wind blowing against the rising tide. Below him the harbour mouth was busy with shipping of all sizes going about their business, fishing boats, galleys, transports and rowing boats all taking advantage of high water to slip over the sunken sand bar that gave protection for the harbour but also danger for the unwary. A loud crack drew his attention to a bireme or double sweeped war galley heading out to sea, the noise coming from a dirty-white sail flapping as it unfurled He smiled to himself at the sudden increase of the boats speed as the cloth bellied and filled with wind, the oars thereafter being quickly shipped.

"That'll save you back's lads!" He said, smiling to himself.

He could hear Armaco's warriors in the courtyard below him as he bellowed his orders, calling them to attention ready for inspection and orders for the day. With another day to wait before departing for Spain, he had time on his hands and he stretched out enjoying the early morning heat on his skin. His thoughts drifted as the light breeze blew about him, for all he had slept well the previous night he could feel the warm zephyrs caressing and soothing his body, gently lulling him back to slumber. With the court case over and the worry lifted from his shoulders, his body took advantage for rest after the previous months of depression, stress and combat. Within moments, the noises of the warriors and the sea faded, his mind drifted and sleep took him.

He was awakened by tentative calls for him and the light tread of bare feet moving over the wooden floor of his bedchamber. Rousing himself from the bench, he rubbed sleep from his eyes.

"Out here!" He yawned and cleared his throat to call louder. "I'm out here."

A serving girl bearing a silver tray laden with food pushed her way through the white drapes to join him on the balcony.

"Good morning sir! Your breakfast ... where would you like it? Out here in the sun or inside? There is fruit and fresh bread with poached fish; it was caught only ..."

The girl stopped abruptly when she noticed Baldor staring at her intently, his expression one of shock bordering on fear. She took a step back, still holding the tray with one hand whilst easing the breeze-blown hair from her eyes with the other, frightened a little by his wide-eyed stare.

"Sorry sir! Did I startle you?"

Baldor just carried on staring, saying nothing.

"Begging your pardon sir, do you want me take your breakfast away?"

"Err ... no, its fine. Fine, just leave it ... thank you."

The girl laid the tray on the bench and backed away; she smiled wanly then turned and disappeared through the drapes, almost at a run. Baldor put his head in his hands, he nipped his cheeks hard with his fingers and winced at the pain, he was awake then! The girl was almost the double of Aiticia! The same height, shape and hair colour. His stomach heaved and pulse quickened, his body flushed hotly and he felt sick. His loss revisited him and his eyes filled.

"Baldor? ... Baldor! ... Are you alright?" Armaco shouted from the bedchamber.

Baldor stood quickly, snapping from his misery and composing himself.

"Baldor?"

"I'm out here!" He sniffed hard. "Out here!" He managed a little louder.

Armaco pushed the gently billowing drapes to one side and stepped onto the balcony, pulling a very frightened serving girl along by her wrist.

"I was coming to see you when I was almost run down by her bolting out of your room like a frightened rabbit. She looked suspicious and after that bloody crazy bitch yesterday, well ..."

"No, I'm fine ... she's fine, well she should be, it's just ..."

"Just what?" Armaco picked up the tray, sniffing suspiciously at the food. "Smells alright, there's no taint. But here, you eat some." He said pushing the plate towards the girl.

"Let her go Armaco, it's alright!" Baldor said softly, turning to face the girl. "My apologies ..." He gestured for a name.

"Aspasia, sir ... I'm sorry; I think I woke you suddenly or ..."

"It's alright Aspasia, you haven't done anything wrong. It's just ... just that ... you remind me of someone, someone that ..."

"Alright girl, about your business." Armaco interrupted, letting the girl's wrist go sensing Baldor's awkwardness.

Baldor turned away, looking out to sea again. "Thank you Armaco I'll be fine, there's no need to worry, I just need to think a while."

"As long as you are alright! I tell you, I'll be glad when we're away from here and back in Spain. There at least you know the enemy is coming from the front. What are your plans for the day? Do you wish to go anywhere? If you are resting up I can stand the men down but maintain a couple on watch."

"No Armaco and thank you. Stand the men down, let them have some rest and peace before we take ship, I'll be fine."

Armaco left him to see to his men. Baldor leaned onto the wall resting his chin on his arms, deep in thought. With privacy and quiet once more his thoughts returned to Aiticia. Closing his eyes, he forced his memories to happier times rather than the last night of her life. As his thoughts drifted, he saw her in his mind's eye, so real, so beautiful! A Goddess! So perfect with her petite but siren like figure and lustrous brown hair, which when released from her ribbon-bound ponytail, fell to the middle of her back. Her dark, hazel eyes, which told of warmth and the sensuous, smoldering looks, she would give when they were alone or when she wished them to be so. He remembered her small, perfect nose that wrinkled when she laughed. High cheekbones that had lengthened her face and her delicately shaped chin giving her majesty and her perfectly shaped, slightly pouted lips ... beautiful she was and beyond compare. He smiled to himself recalling his admiration of her from afar and how he'd never dared thoughts of her having an interest in him let alone she could be his.

Despite his pleasant reverie, he found warm tears careering down his face wetting the hair on his arm. He wanted so badly to hold her again to tell how much he loved her, to hear her laugh; to undo all that had happened. His mood changed abruptly from pleasant longing to grief and finally to guilt. Guilt for his pride, his anger and his temper but also for his selfishness. He was not alone with his grief; Aiticia's family had been cruelly left to guess at what happened to their daughter and to pick over the threads of her demise. It was they, who must have seen to a decent funeral for her, her husband having failed in all these duties and then vanished like smoke on the wind. How had they fared? How would he have felt if it had been his daughter? With guilt and remorse eating him, he decided he must go and explain.

Armaco, still busy drilling his men looked up as he saw Baldor heading to the stables.

"Company, at ease!" Leaving the men, he cut Baldor off before he reached the stables.

"Sir ... Baldor, if you are going out the men are ready to go now."

"Thank you Armaco but no."

"No sir, I have my orders, the General said ..."

Baldor placed his hand on Armaco's shoulder and spoke quietly. "This is for me Armaco; I need to sort things out, here in Carthage and in my head before we leave, please! I'll be alright, just rest the men let them enjoy the peace while we have it eh?"

Armaco, ready to object and insist looked into the sad eyes. He chewed his lip. "Alright then but I need to know where you're going."

"No, it's personal!" That came out sharp and harsh causing Armaco to back away slightly. Baldor softened his tone again, "I need to sort matters out Armaco so I can find a little peace." He smiled sadly, as he spoke. Armaco looked at the full, watery eyes and nodded slowly then stepped to one side allowing Baldor access to the stables and turned once more to his men.

"Weapons practice! Into pairs." He hefted a leather bag from atop the garden wall and dropped it at his feet. Opening it, he handed out wooden swords to each pair in turn. The warriors finding a space took their stance trying their balance and footwork, swinging the swords in practice strokes flexing arms and wrists, testing the weight and balance of the training weapon.

"Commence!"

Swords slapped like breaking branches as the warriors engaged, feet shuffling on flagstones as men tried to outmanoeuvre their opponent. Armaco watched intently, walking from pair to pair, assessing.

"Come on, come on! Let's have this idle living sweated out of you." He called as he noticed a slowing in the fighting.

"Change!"

The men broke apart and sought a new opponent, relieved to catch their breath for a moment. He heard the clop of hooves behind him as Baldor departed through the gate.

"Commence!"

The clash of wood echoed again. Armaco continuing to drive the men harder until the clacking of wood punctuated with laboured breathing.

"Come on, work you laggards!"

Eventually calling a halt, he walked amongst them passing comments to each regarding their performance, drawing his own weapon to demonstrate points he made.

"Right, that's it for the day! Watch rotation as before. Check and sharpen your blades and clean your harness then the rest of the day is your own, be ready to leave at first light."

Whoops and cheers rang across the yard. Armaco sheathed his weapon and headed to the stables, quickly bridling and throwing a blanket over a horse he followed in Baldor's wake.

****

Baldor made his way into the heart of the city, riding through high, narrow streets choked with people, traders, beggars, warriors and animals. The heat and smell around the buildings growing steadily as midmorning changed to noon. He sweated freely but not just from the heat. As he turned off the last cramped street, he entered a tree-lined avenue that took him up a gentle rise to a magnificent town house and the city residence of Aiticia's family. Shading his eyes from the sunlight reflecting from the white stone, he reined in at the base of the steps that led up to a grand canopied doorway flanked by two heavily armed guards. His throat was bone dry and his nervous swallow caused him pain as his tongue pulled free from where it was stuck in his mouth. Gritting his teeth, he dismounted and hailed the guard.

"Guard! ... Baldor Targa, son of Asmilcar to see my Lord and Lady Maagbul ... If they please?"

The guard nearest him nodded and opened the door calling for the steward. After a brief delay that felt to Baldor like a lifetime an elderly, portly man stepped out. He looked Baldor up and down, frowned, then looked again as if not believing his eyes.

"Baldor? Baldor Targa? ... By the Gods ... it cannot be!"

"It is I, Aassur. I arrive unannounced and to what welcome I know not? But if it is possible I crave an audience with my Lord or Lady."

"Wait you sir, wait if you please!" He gabbled. "My Lord is not yet at home but my Lady is within, I will see if she will receive you?"

The steward hesitated, unsure as to whether to invite Baldor into the reception rooms, in the end he disappeared leaving Baldor in the street holding his horse, the two guards looking at him then away disinterestedly. He patted the horse and smoothed the folds from his tunic as he waited for the steward to return, his nonchalant actions belying his thoughts that spun and whirled through his head. He had no idea what reception to expect from his mother and father-in-law. All the times he had gone through this scenario in his head, he still found himself at a loss. They had loved him like a son, for they had none of their own, only daughters of which Aiticia had been the youngest and the apple of her father's eye. He knew not what they had been told regarding the night at the villa. It dawned upon him; they had been left to pick up the pieces of their daughter's life as well as her remains without ever knowing the truth, he being the only one who could give it. He felt ashamed for being alive, for being so immersed in his own grief that he had never considered theirs. His guilt and self-loathing deepened and he cursed the Gods again that he still drew breath. His anger flaring when he thought of Gestix saving him from the flames, wishing truly that he had died and that had been the end of it. Thinking to ride away before the steward returned, he punished himself further, calling himself a coward. What kind of man was he? He'd failed in his care of Aiticia and was ready to blame his friend for saving his life and was now preparing to ride away without giving his wife's family the answers they would so badly need. Aassur cut his dilemma short, appearing at the door, his face grim but he beckoned Baldor towards the steps, assigning the guard to take his horse. Swallowing the lump in his throat and feeling sick to his stomach Baldor followed the steward into the house.

He was still thinking how to explain events when the steward gently pushed open double doors ushering him into a large reception room. The room was refreshingly cool and the scent of sweet woodruff and dahlias drifted in through the open windows, complementing the fragrant oil that burned and bubbled beneath a polished bronze statue of Tanith. Standing to one side of the window, which looked onto the garden, was a woman elegantly robed in a long dress of midnight blue; she looked at him as if seeing a ghost. Her lip trembled slightly and she held her fingers across her mouth as if not trusting herself to speak. Baldor bowed his head respectably then summoning his courage looked the woman in the face. He was shocked to see how much she had aged since he saw her last. Her eyes were sunken and dark-ringed, her skin sallow and stretched across her high cheekbones. Grief had etched fine lines around her lips and chin and her dark hair had strands of grey creeping in to it, she was also much thinner than he remembered.

"Lady, I have come to tell you of your daughter … my wife … and to offer you my respects." The words came out slowly and quietly, he dropped his head before he finished speaking.

The woman's chin quivered and her eyes filled as she fought her emotions, trying to maintain her dignity. She raised her head and straightened her shoulders, looking regal despite the tears that ran freely down her cheeks.

"Tell me then, Baldor!" She began in a raspy, broken voice. "Tell me how my daughter died and why you did not come to us? Tell me, why you were not there to share our grief? Why you were not there to help us mourn Aiticia?" Having gotten the words out, she wept, then walked towards Baldor repeating between sobs. "Why? … Why?" Stopping in front of him she raised small fists, drumming them against his chest between catching her breath in gulps and sobbing she repeated again. "Why…"

Baldor, not knowing what to do just stood motionless; he could not speak above her weeping. The woman finally sunk against him as if her strength had drained away, he felt her hot tears soaking his tunic and the sticky skin of her brow on the base of his neck. His own tears fell freely and his chest heaved, he put his arms around her holding her as her heart broke. They stood together in their grief with neither one speaking, as Baldor felt her crying ease and her breathing settle he whispered softly.

"I'm sorry Zaalana … truly sorry!"

The woman slipped her arms round his torso and hugged him. He lifted his cloak and very gently wiped her tears away.

"We lost you both Baldor and we knew nothing … nothing! We … we got Aiticia's remains …"

She wept again, un-consolable.

Baldor guided her to the settle and eased her on to it; he poured a cup of wine and crouched down offering it. When Zaalana collected herself and her weeping had degenerated to sobs and gasps for breath, she sipped from the cup. Baldor sat beside her and hugged her gently; he began his tale in a quiet voice beginning from the moment he had entered his villa to learn that Carthalo was ensconced within. He left nothing out; he had to pause to console Zaalana again when he told of the wine pitcher hitting Aiticia, the woman reduced to racking sobs. Finishing his explanation they sat for a while, neither speaking, her weeping had stopped though tears still fell. Outside in the garden birds whistled and called and the crickets joined in, inside the house was quiet, with only the slow breathing of the pair punctuated with Zaalana's sobbing.

A timid knock at the door broke the peace

"Leave us!" Zaalana managed in husky tones.

The door remained closed but Aassur spoke quietly from outside.

"My Lady, your husband has come."

Zaalana sat up as if struck, her face ashen.

"You must go Baldor, now! Magon will not listen; he blames you for all the woe. His love for you has turned to anger, he will not suffer to listen and hear what you have told me. Please, go quickly."

"No Zaalana, I cannot, will not! I did things wrongly when Aiticia was slain, I would set things right."

"Please Baldor I want no more grief, please go! You have eased my mind that is what you came here to do, quickly now …"

Outside in the corridor brisk footfalls could be heard and the tapping of a staff on the stone floor. Zaalana got to her feet pulling at Baldor's arm.

"Into the garden Baldor, you must go!"

Baldor got to his feet, straightening his tunic and adjusting his belt as he did so. He smiled as best he could to Zaalana.

"I must explain, I owe you both at least that."

Zaalana looked at him beseechingly, her eyes wide. He smiled again and leaned to kiss her gently on the brow. His quiet confident behaviour belied the racing heartbeat and tensing muscles as he turned to face the doors. The quick footsteps and the tapping stick were closer now, suddenly the doors were thrown open and a thin man of late middle age entered. He was as tall as Baldor but stooped a little as an old injury bent his shoulders forward; he leaned on a plain wooden quarterstaff topped with a ball of silver. His hair had a pepper look where the grey and white was overtaking the black, his badger coloured beard close cropped along his jaw line the rest of his face clean-shaven. Seeing Baldor, his eyes narrowed and his mouth twisted into a snarl.

"You! … How dare you come here?" He forced the words past closed teeth. At the same time walking towards Baldor.

"My Lord …" Baldor began.

Before he could speak further, the staff whirled in Magon's hand and hit him across his shoulder. "Magon no!" Zaalana screamed as Baldor grunted in pain.

As his shoulder and body gave to the impact, the staff was already coming back for a second hit, this time it struck him on the neck. Baldor staggered, holding up his hand to fend off the next blow. Zaalana pushed between her husband and son-in-law, only to be shoved roughly to one side by the older man as he attacked again. The staff struck the side of Baldor's head changing his vision into bright then dark flashes, when another blow hit his temple he collapsed; he heard the screams of Zaalana fading as his senses closed down. He didn't feel the next blows rain across his back.

The sharp piecing odour of smelling salts brought him back to consciousness, his eyes flickered opened and closed again. The odour came once more, stinging and burning his sinuses. The feeling of a cool, wet cloth applied to the back of his neck saw his eyes open and he looked about him. He was still on the floor but raised to sitting position and supported by a muscular, black servant. Zaalana was holding the salts in front of his face while Aassur was helping another servant restrain a breathless Magon on the settle amidst curses and threats of dire consequence if they didn't release him. Baldor's shoulder was on fire, his head throbbed and rang, and his ear dripped blood steadily onto his tunic from a split that left it almost in two pieces. He felt sure something was broken in his back, as he couldn't breathe without the pain bending him double. Watching his father-in-law frantically struggling with the steward and servant, he saw the blind hatred and fury in his eyes and knew the time for explanation was long past. He struggled to his feet, steadying himself against the servant's shoulder then staggered as his balance failed. The commotion in the room stopped as he looked as if he was about to collapse again. Summoning final reserves of strength and finding a tentative balance, he drew himself up proudly, ignoring the stabbing pain in his back and drumming in his head, he looked his father-in-law in the eye.

"I have lost my wife and you ... you have lost your daughter ... I was wrong to have done things the way I did and for that I am truly sorry, I ...."

He felt a roaring in his ears and his body teetered as his balance mechanism went awry; he stumbled, having to grasp a table to prevent his fall. Steadying himself, he continued.

"I had hoped to set ... set things right between ..." He collapsed before he finished.

The next thing he knew was being dragged along a corridor by the two guards towards the door onto the street. He was vaguely aware of Zaalana crying hysterically and the harsher tones of Magon shouting her protests down. At the doorway and stair-head, he was physically hurled out. He landed heavily, rolling down the last few steps into the street, the wind knocked out of him. He was trying to pick himself up when the boot of the first guard caught him in the stomach knocking him sideways and driving what was left of his breath from him.

"Get the hell away from here boy!" The boot landed again rolling Baldor with the force. "And stay away! If you know what's good for you." The boot drove in once more, hitting his ribs this time. He heard the second guard laughing as he came down the steps.

"Save some of him for me!"

"It's alright, he needs a good lesson." The guard nearest Baldor said, stepping closer swinging his foot back to kick again.

Baldor lashed out with his leg desperate to keep him away, hitting the man just above the ankle taking the legs from under him, he went down cursing.

"Right you bastard, you're for a real beating now!" The second guard growled as he dodged around his sprawled comrade.

Out of nowhere came the noise of drumming hooves and a man urging a horse on. Baldor looked up from the dirt to see a rider coming down the street at breakneck speed, his falcata drawn.

"Armaco … Here!"

The two guards unsure as to what was happening just gawped. The rider aimed directly for the group his weapon pointed forward and arm locked straight, a savage roar breaking from his lips. Realising the man intended to ride them down the guard on the floor struggled to his feet, his comrade still looking around for his spear when horse and rider drove into them. The horse hit him hard sending him spinning then crashing earthward again. The other received a smack to his helmet with the flat of Armaco's sword sending him staggering across the street. Dismounting as he spun his horse savagely around, Armaco closed on the fallen guard struggling onto his hands and knees. He kicked him hard on the side of the head; the man fell back to the dirt and laid still. Turning on the other, he found him regaining his balance and drawing his sword. Armaco closed on him, his blade arcing and whistling through the air as he advanced driving the other back; finally, the guard's sword came up. Armaco smashed it down and the street rang with the metallic ting of blades as every defensive stroke the man made, Armaco beat away. Seeing the grim look on Armaco's face and recognising superior skill driven by savage ruthlessness, fear gripped the man and he backed away throwing his weapon down hands up in surrender.

"Enough, enough! I'm done … for the love of Baal … I'm done!" He panted.

Armaco closed the last two paces pointing the weapon to the man's throat.

"Not so easy when it's a fair fight eh? … You piece of shit!" He snarled.

"Quarter … quarter! I'm only carrying out my orders … just doing my job."

Armaco kicked the man hard between the legs and he collapsed to his knees holding his groin. Stepping in closer again, Armaco slammed his knee into the man's face knocking him on his back.

"Just carrying out my orders ... just doing my job!" He said as he stamped hard on the man's open sword hand. Hearing the bones snap he spat on the man then sheathed his sword and went to help Baldor who had pulled himself to a sitting position.

"Come on Baldor, let's go!" Armaco hooked a hand under his armpit pulling him to his feet, the lad groaning as he was helped towards the horse.

"Can you ride?"

Baldor nodded, resting his head and bodyweight momentarily against the horse's flank as he wrapped a hand in its mane. Armaco helped him mount, he slumped forward groaning with pain then slowly pulled himself erect. Armaco looked about for signs of further trouble as he took the bridle. Seeing people gathering on the steps of the house he shouted.

"Anybody else want a try? ... Anybody?" He spat on the road in contempt when eyes looked elsewhere. "Bring the lad's horse and get this shit off the road!" He flicked his head at the two unconscious guards.

Aassur brought the horse, his corpulent body wobbling as he ran the animal across the street to Armaco's outstretched hand, he whispered quietly while discreetly pushing a small package into his hand.

"Give this to the lad sir, I'm sorry ... sorry!" He said in a hurried, hushed whisper then turned on his heel walking quickly away.

Armaco kept the object in his hand as he mounted and ushered Baldor off down the street in front of him. Turning his mount about, he slipped the package into his tunic and walked the horse across to the steps.

"If anybody follows us I'll kill them." He cast an icy, one-eyed stare over the assembled crowd, none deigned to meet it let alone return it. Muttering further disgust under his breath, he turned his mount, showing his back and contempt then trotted after Baldor. As they turned the corner into the street Baldor slumped forward, Armaco caught and steadied him. He reined in both horses and pulled his water bottle from a hook on the horse's trappings, tipping it slowly over Baldor's neck until he showed signs of coming round.

"Come on lad, hold up! Let's get you back to the villa before you get yourself killed and me crucified for letting it happen. I tell you! From now on, supposing you go for a piss I'm coming with you."

He took a drink and tipped the rest over his head shaking it like dog.

"That's better!" He hung the bottle back on the hook and fished in his tunic. "Here! That fat old goat gave me this for you." He passed the package to Baldor. "I hope it was worth your trouble."

Baldor fumbled with the wrapping and a piece of oval silver fell into his palm. Puzzled, he turned it over, Armaco watching in interest.

He gasped as he saw the other side. "Aiticia!"

The detailed relief chased into the flat silver cameo showed her head and shoulders and the thick lustrous hair he remembered so well.

"Your wife?"

Baldor nodded without looking up.

Armaco leaned in for a closer look and whistled softly. "Worth dying for!"

Baldor shuddered slightly as the words weighted the memory, then with an unexpected lightening of his heart tucked the cameo into his tunic and urged the horse on.

Chapter Seventeen

Returning to Spain in the early winter Baldor, Armaco and his warriors rejoined Balaam's mercenaries and the army in its winter quarters at Carthago Nova. Saguntum had fallen to the Carthaginians in the autumn amidst terrible slaughter, rape and looting, the usual fate of most cities that defied or kept an army embattled outside its gates. The Saguntines had rejected the terms set down by Hannibal, being that each citizen was to leave with only the garments they wore and that all gold, silver and riches were to be delivered up to the Carthaginians. Instead, they had built a fire in the centre of the city and set about burning everything of value, some of the citizens had then committed suicide rather than surrender to the besiegers. With confusion and horror abound within the city, many defenders left the parapets to see to the safety of their families. The Carthaginians seeing the defenders departure and raging fire within stormed the walls once more. A battered section had crumbled quickly and the assault troops charged over the rubble-strewn breach into the city. Hannibal, quick to exploit his chance reinforced the advance and by early evening, the city fell.

Few were spared; the order to kill any male old enough to bear arms carried to the letter. Any remaining folk refusing to leave their homes or attempting to defend it found themselves locked in and it burnt about their ears. The spoils had been huge as the wealth of one of the Middlesea's greatest cities was stripped bare. With the warrior's appetites for slaughter, women and monies sated and the Barca war chest filled, the surplus was sent on to Carthage, a gift from her absent son.

Baldor was fully recovered from his beating and Gestix too was in better shape but not quite the man he was. His hearing was almost gone in one ear and he still suffered pains in his lower back, his ribs had repaired though chest pains gave him trouble during the colder days. As ever, he never complained nor admitted to his ailments but Baldor saw the occasional grimace and noticed a physical slowing down of the big man. Harbro was also back from the dead but like Gestix had not been fit enough to take part in the final assault. Balaam on the other hand was effervescent as ever, now richly robed and clad in expensive, looted armour, and further delighted with the addition to his command of Armaco and his men.

****

With an unseasonably dry and hot spring here at last, the army was on the move, heading northeast following the coast, they were now almost as far north as the River Ebro. Balaam's command was working as outriders, guarding the western flank of the huge army of twelve thousand cavalry and ninety thousand infantry as it snaked like some giant, lethargic serpent across the river plain to the fords on the Ebro.

Baldor guided Risto along a narrow goat-track. It cut across the sward and through the stunted bushes and gorse of the small hills that rose on the edge of the vast plain, the horse's hooves raising small red-brown dust clouds as they slapped the dry earth. The track ran parallel to a shallow stream, which gurgled over its gravel bed and twisted its way around the base of the brown-grassed hillocks. He walked the horse into the stream, letting it drink while easing his arm from the leather straps that held his shield in place, hanging it on Risto's harnessing before dismounting. Relishing the water washing over his boots and knees, he bent down and scooped some to his mouth using his hands as cup. He was practically cooking in his corselet despite its reflective white colouring, so unlacing his helmet and using it as a bucket; he filled it with water and tipped it over his head. The chilly liquid snatched his breath but refreshed him and he risked another helmet-full before refitting it. The day was stifling hot and very still, the air strangely heavy and humid, swatting at the buzzing flies that constantly followed man and horse he looked north of the Ebro to the sky above the distant Pyrenees. He saw huge black and bronze coloured clouds rolling and banking up then heard a faint rumble of thunder followed by a white flash of lighting.

'Please let it rain!' He thought, the land needs it the men need it. He splashed water over Risto then washed away the dried sweat; the horse whinnying and twitching its coat in appreciation. Squatting down he washed the horse's legs up to its belly.

"How does that feel Risto?" Again, the shiny black coat rippled as if in gratitude. He left the horse in the stream to drink and waded to the bank, hitching up his short tunic to relieve himself beside a gorse bush. Sighing, he sat down with his feet in the water, his upper bodyweight leaning against an old manzanita stump. His body weary and aching from another full day on patrol, his skin chaffed and sore from the edges of the corselet and sticky from the sweat soaked tunic. The weight of two falcatas slung and crossed over his back, along with the broad-blade dagger fastened at his waist adding further discomfort.

The mercenaries were working in pairs along the flank of the army, he and Armaco had split again to scout the small hills and agreed to meet somewhere in the middle, he reckoned he had a few moments to spare before Armaco caught him up. He allowed his body to relax against the stump, the dry timber creaking as it took his weight. He closed his eyes briefly, relishing the comfort it brought. The stream gurgled softly by him and the lazy drone of a passing nectar-seeking bee all helping lull him toward an exhausted sleep. With a huge effort, he flicked his sleep-heavy eyes back open, looked around and promised himself he would get up shortly … just a little longer! Hearing a cuckoo call somewhere in the distance and the sweet twittering of a skylark hovering way above him, he drifted again, his eyes flickering and closing once more.

He heard nothing else as exhaustion took him off to sleep, not even the warrior who arrived quietly behind him. The newcomer stopped his horse and scanned the area carefully, watching Baldor for a while, noting the steady, rhythmic breathing of a sleeping man. Smiling to himself, he dismounted and walked with a silent, stealthy tread towards him. Risto looked up from the stream and whickered softly when he caught the scent of the other horse, Baldor dozed on, oblivious. The warrior slipped his dagger from its sheath as he drew closer, grimacing slightly at the hissing rasp the blade made as it came clear of the sheath. When he was less than ten paces from Baldor, the sound and scent of another horse pushing through the bushes brought a curious Risto from the stream and as his hooves stepped up on to the bank, the vibration woke Baldor. He awoke with a start, sitting bolt upright and looking about him, one hand instinctively reaching to his shoulder for a falcata. By the time he turned fully around the approaching warrior had slipped the dagger back into its sheath and changed his gait from stealth to a more normal, natural walk.

"Ahaggar! What in Hades are you doing here?" Armaco growled in suspicious tones as he guided his horse through the last of the bushes.

"Looking for a drink." He said sounding amiable.

Armaco walked his horse to Ahaggar's mount and unhooked his waterskin from it. He threw it, aiming it purposely short so it fell at the man's feet, landing with a heavy thump.

"Try drinking the water you have if you're that thirsty." Armaco's lip twisted as he spoke, the words coming out in a suspicious sounding snarl.

"I wanted a cool drink, that water is warm."

"Get a drink and get back to your section! What do you think this is, some casual afternoon ride with chilled drinks for your comfort? Baldor! Get off your lazy arse and mount up … move! … The pair of you … now!" Armaco balled as he kicked his horse past them and on through the stream.

Baldor mounted and reined in next to Armaco, embarrassed at his shortcomings he offered his apologies. Armaco disregarded the remorse and looked over his shoulder before turning to speak to Baldor.

"I don't like that bastard!" He spat in the dirt then looked to the front as his horse moved to a trot.

Ahaggar squatted down at the side of stream muttering under his breath.

"Next time Targa, next time! Old Cyclops won't be there to watch your back forever … and then, then I'll trade your corpse for silver."

As he gazed into the water, he mused as to where his hatred for the boy came from; in truth, the lad had done nothing to him. He absently pushed his fingers in the moist dirt of the bank as he thought; he reasoned he hated the boy because of his easy and unassuming manner, for his popularity, for his goodness and childish innocence. He hated him for his courage and his ability to fight, for it had to be said the boy was fast and skilful. He hated him for his friendliness and … he found his fingertips bleeding from the agitation and decided he had enough to hate the boy for and that justified killing him. That was enough!

Armaco and Baldor rode out of the hills to a panoramic view over the wide river plain. Like ants pouring from an anthill, the army spread as far as the eyes could see in long multi-coloured columns of horses and men. Box shaped regiments of infantry beneath forests of pikes and spears, followed by ox carts, pack animals and off to one side on their own, a single line of plodding elephants. The sun flashed and reflected from the metal on the men's harness while the thump of thousands of hooves and sandaled feet rumbled like thunder. A huge dust cloud hung motionless above with not a breath of wind to move it. The two men reined in to take the view,

"By the Gods Baldor! That's a sight is it not?" Armaco patted his mount as he spoke.

"Unbelievable! The whole world must be here! The columns must stretch for hundreds of stades?"

"All of that and then some I reckon." Armaco shielded his eye as he spoke. "You can't see the end of the columns and it's a clear enough day; Baal knows how far they stretch."

"Come on then, let's head down to the river for a closer look. We should catch up with the Captain there and report. I warrant we'll camp at the ford tonight then cross in the morning and I'd like to see those elephants."

"Bloody elephants, they stink! I wouldn't mind a swim though. With a little luck the Captain might stand us down."

The pair dug their heels into their mounts flanks and the horses trotted onto the plain raising dust as they went. Working their way along the front of the columns, they found Balaam, Gestix and Harbro. Saluting their Captain, Armaco gave his report as he and Baldor fell in alongside, Baldor smiled at Gestix and Harbro, bowing his head in respect.

"What do you think of it all then lad?" Gestix asked.

"Incredible! I knew the army was large but this. … Can Rome field as many?"

"Aye, near enough, more given time and they've had plenty of that."

"Rumour has it their fleet's marshaling at Pisa under the Scipios." Balaam interjected. "Once we cross the river it'll force their hand altogether for they claim anything north of the Ebro is theirs and they're territorial bastard!"

"What will we do once we cross the Ebro?"

"Occupy I imagine, I think the General is for making Spain his own." Replied Balaam.

"I'm not so sure." Gestix said. "It's a lot of men and effort just to make northern Spain another province of Carthage and it's not worth antagonising Rome over."

"What, then?" Asked Armaco.

Before the conversation could go further, a dust covered rider galloped up to the party.

"Captain Balaam sir, the General requests your presence and reports' this evening; you can stand your men down sir."

"Right lads, you're stood down, I'll see you at dawn."

"Swim, then food?" Baldor asked hopefully.

As Balaam trotted on the others turned for the river. Finding a flat piece of ground, they hobbled the horses leaving them cropping the lush grass beneath the willows that lined the bank. They spread their bedrolls and stacked their weapons to hand. Stripping off armour, helmets and sweat damp tunics, they enjoyed the caress of the air on their skin. They looked a little strange with faces, arms and legs all tanned and weathered but their torsos still pale. As they headed to the river, all picked up a sword depositing them by the waters edge. Armaco was the first into the water with a huge splash, he surfaced quickly, blowing hard and gasping for breath. Full of laughter Baldor followed him, and suffered the same skin tingling, breath stealing shock. Harbro and Gestix, shaking their heads waded in thigh-deep before gently washing water over arms and chests, accustoming their skin to the cold. Baldor slapped the water hard sending spray over both of them.

"Hey! You're not too big to slap!" Gestix said, pointing his finger.

Harbro shook himself like a dog and raised his fist. "You've got to sleep sometime boy!"

Armaco smirked and Baldor laughed. "Getting old are we?"

Eventually all four managed a swim and the water though cold was refreshing once accustomed to it. Finishing their swim, they headed to the bank but as Gestix's feet touched the riverbed, he stopped still, looking intently into the water.

"Get me a spear, quickly!" Without looking up, he extended his arm, hand open.

Harbro being the nearest to the bank padded silently to their camp returning with two spears, he threw one to Gestix who caught it whilst still maintaining his gaze into the water. The two younger men watched intently as Gestix gently immersed the spearhead then struck like lightning. Hefting the spear clear of the water, it shook and bent with the weight of a large, wriggling fish impaled on the point.

"Harbro joined the hunt and moving stealthily lined up his quarry ready to strike. Gestix flicked his spear and the fish flew off the end landing on the bank slapping and flipping on the grass for a moment, before lying still, mouth and gills opening and closing. Harbro struck next with a soft splash, he too produced a squirming fish on the spear point.

"Well that's the old men fixed for supper, what are you lads having?" Harbro chuckled as he made his way to the bank.

Baldor and Armaco were already making their way to their spears; fresh fish would be a treat after the weeks of the same fare. Gestix speared two more throwing them onto the bank where Harbro was now busy gutting them. As Baldor and Armaco waded back into the water spears in hand, they heard the sound of thrashing water downstream.

"Look! The cavalry are crossing already." Baldor pointed.

"It makes good military sense lad." Harbro said looking up from the fish. "The crossing is undisputed so best establish yourself on the other bank, and then if trouble does eventuate you can be reinforced easily. Believe me; you don't want to be forcing a river crossing under fire."

Baldor leaned on the spear to watch. "Numidians aren't they?" He asked, looking at the mass of small sand coloured ponies and riders churning the shallow water to white foam. The riders were lithe, brown-skinned men crowned with black-blue curled hair and clothed in sleeveless cotton tunics. They rode with neither saddlecloth nor bit; the only adornment the horse had was a piece of plaited rope about its neck. For armament, each warrior carried two or three short javelins and a round leather faced shield, some carried short swords or daggers at their belts.

"Aye, Numidians alright, wicked little bastards they are too! They don't look much but they can cause serious trouble along the flanks of an army, hitting and running all the time. Once they've driven the enemy to distraction and their ranks break the heavy cavalry carves them up." Harbro talked as he worked.

As the ford choked with horses, the three fishermen returned to their work, Gestix continuing to catch and throw fish up to Harbro. Baldor and Armaco, despite grunts and muttered oaths produced nothing for their efforts, the trick of aiming below the fish in order to hit it clearly unknown to them. Harbro looked up occasionally to watch their attempts chuckling to himself at their clumsiness; he shook his head when they looked up scowling.

As the cold water took its toll, the men retreated to the bank, Armaco and Baldor still fishless. Harbro had a fire going with the fish suspended on a wooden stick and sizzling and spitting oil onto the flames, the smell tantalizing the taste buds. At the ford, more cavalry were crossing. Baldor looked up and Gestix answered his question before he asked it.

"Spaniards!"

The Spanish warriors wore bronze helmets with wide, hinged cheek pieces some topped with coloured feathers others with a plain knob, slung on their backs they carried small, circular wooden shields. Armed with fighting spears and javelins, all had a falcata and dagger slung from wide waist belts. They wore short white tunics in the Greek fashion but with V-necks rather than the classical square, the material edged in a vermillion red or a pale blue, on their feet, they wore soft, calf length, leather boots. They rode with sheepskins over their saddle blankets atop dun coloured ponies, the ponies themselves were not well bred having flat rumps and big heads. Their poor shape and ungainly looks however was made up for with stamina and toughness,

"Are they good warriors?" Baldor asked.

"Can be, once they decide which side they're on. Different tribes will fight on different sides and they will change allegiance if things look shaky." Harbro pulled a bit of fish off as he spoke and pushed it into his mouth. "It's good Gestix! Lacking some herbs methinks but it'll do for old men!"

Armaco and Baldor eyed each other but said nothing.

The men gathered around the fire grateful of the warmth as the early evening brought a chill. The elder men ate their way through the fish while complaining greatly of being full, Baldor and Armaco chewed on dried beef strips eying the fish longingly but saying nothing. Orders shouted from the ford drew their attention, the Carthaginian pikemen were now wading across the river their feet churning the water white. Some warriors stumbled over the slippery gravel, their pikes twice the length of a fighting spear clattering and rattling with those of their comrades, the noise like branches banging in the wind. They were heavily armed with mail shirts or bronze cuirass and a small round shield. All carried short swords and daggers and wore a bronze helmet; on their legs from ankle to knee, they had bronze greaves.

"There's some weight going over there, imagine all that on a bridge! They should be a match for the Legions alright; the bastards won't be able to get close with those pikes to keep them away." Ventured Armaco.

"As long as they're on level ground you're right." Harbro said his mouth full of fish. "They'll break up the Legions, the difficulty comes if they have to operate over broken terrain and the formation becomes disjointed, if the Romans get in amongst them then, there'll be trouble."

Gestix yawned then took a long drink from his wineskin. "Well I'm for bed, no doubt the Captain will be kicking our arses awake in the morning and it's going to be another long day. We'll save that fish for breakfast Harbro, eh? There's plenty left." He couldn't resist a wink to Harbro as he spoke.

Baldor donned his spare tunic and wrapped his blanket about him slinging a sword over his shoulder.

"It's a while till dark, I'm going to take a walk to see if I can find the elephants, I would like to have a closer look, stink or not."

"Just follow your nose lad." Harbro said rolling in his blanket.

"I'll come with you Baldor I just need to take a piss first." Armaco slung his weapons baldric over his shoulder and picked up a wineskin as he walked towards the trees. He wasn't interested in the elephants at all but concerned as to where Ahaggar was, for he was convinced the man meant Baldor harm but until he could prove it … Baldor wouldn't think to look for a knife in the dark so he must watch Ahaggar and if the man looked like trouble, well he would take care of it. Finishing his ablution, the pair walked back to the ford sharing the wine as they went. Regiments of troops were now queuing along the riverbank and spilling back onto the plain waiting their turn to cross the river.

They passed more Spaniards as they walked, this time it was infantry, both light and medium classes; all dressed similarly to their cavalry counterparts.

"See the light infantry Baldor? They're Caetratus; they named the buggers after that small shield they carry." Armaco pointed before gulping from the wineskin then belching loudly. "They are good skirmishing troops mind and can upset infantry formations with missiles else menace their flanks like wasps around a bull." He passed the wine to Baldor.

Baldor guzzled the potent wine, grimaced and nodded thoughtfully. "What of the others then, the medium infantry, those with the big shields?"

"They're Scutarius, they support the skirmishers as they come up against heavier armed opposition or support the phalanxes and heavy infantry as they smash holes in the enemy lines. They fill gaps and cause havoc, preventing ranks closing, they are light enough to move quickly but well-armed to hold their own against heavy troops once their ranks are broken." Armaco tore then chewed a beef strip as he talked; spitting some of the hardest bits out he gulped more wine. "Baal's breath! That beef's salty stuff! Do you see the logic of it Baldor?"

"Yes, but who's our heavy infantry? Apart from the pikemen I haven't seen anybody else."

"In truth we are a bit light in the heavy department." Armaco laughed at his wit. "Some of the Gauls can be classed as heavy infantry, the lad's with mail shirts, helmets and such and there are some Carthaginian heavies but not many, our men tend to make up the heavy cavalry so it will make for interesting combat if we meet Romans."

"Have you fought Romans before?"

"No, but from what I'm told their strength lies in their heavy infantry. They are piss-poor cavalrymen though and their light troops or Velites aren't rated very highly either." Armaco pulled at the last of the meat with his hands and teeth, his face twisting with effort. "Shit Baldor! I wished you hadn't splashed the old men, we would have had fresh fish instead of this sandal leather!"

"You shouldn't have sniggered!" Baldor snatched the wineskin and took a long drink.

"You know, Gestix is right, you're not too big to slap!" Baldor ducked and felt the wind from the swinging open palm pass his head.

"No, but way too fast!" He answered smugly then pointed to where large grey shapes silhouetted against the sinking sun. The elephants were hobbled in rows and busy eating their way through bundles of dried grass. As the men drew closer Baldor stopped, his expression one of disappointment.

"They aren't very big! ... Just over spear height to the shoulder, I thought they would be huge! You can't fit a turret onto them, how do you fight from that? I was told Alexander used elephants with turrets on their backs to house the warriors and that they were monstrous beasts."

Armaco gargled the wine before swallowing and twisting his face at the raw taste.

"Different breeds Baldor; these are bush elephants from the north of Africa. They're small in comparison to the Indian elephants the Macedonians used. Malo speaks of even larger creatures which he has seen in Kush, with ears larger than the biggest shields, true monsters!"

"How do these bush elephants work in battle then?" Baldor reached for the wine again.

"The animal itself is the weapon, their smell terrifies horses untrained to their presence and small or not it's a brave man who'll stand and face down a charge from them. When they go into combat, they carry a rider, mahouts I think they call them, with an archer or a javelin man placed behind him. The mahouts steer the elephant but also carry a mallet and a wooden spike, which they will drive into its head if it looks like going out of control. They have their own armour, a mail blanket over the forehead and brass points fitted on the end of their tusks. They fit metal hoops onto their legs to prevent infantry slashing tendons and hamstrings and on their backs goes a giant saddlecloth of quilted leather, which hangs down to their legs to deflect arrows and spears. Believe me, when they are all decked out they look quite something."

"Have you faced them in battle?"

"Thankfully not, I heard about elephants from an old warrior that frequented the tavern where I was raised. He'd served in numerous wars but harked on about the battle of Bagradas, some thirty-odd years ago now I suppose. At that battle, again fought between Rome and us, there was over one hundred elephants used in a frontal assault to smash the Legions. He spoke of the ground shaking as they charged and of men going down like nine pins some being picked up and hurled through the air as the beasts entered their own battle madness. Here's hoping to Baal the Romans never use elephants." Armaco gulped the wine, wiping his hand over his mouth where it spilled onto his chin.

Baldor looked quizzically at Armaco, the elephants and wine forgotten, "You were raised in a tavern?"

"I raised myself from what I remember." He spoke bitterly, his expression matching his tone.

Baldor missed the bitterness. "Were your parents too busy running the tavern to look after you, or did you have to work too hard?" He jested.

Armaco looked away flushing slightly, his lip twisting into a snarl. The silence brought Baldor's attention back and he saw the pained look on his friend's face.

"Have I offended you Armaco? ... I'm sorry!"

"It's alright Baldor, just bad memories that's all ... just bad memories."

Baldor being forthright and naïve blundered on.

"I didn't mean any disrespect to your parents, I ..."

Armaco looked morosely at Baldor while chewing his lip as if considering his words. "I'll tell you what I've told no other Baldor, then that's the end of it, I never knew my father, I have but a name to guess at. My mother ... well I wish I never knew her, she didn't own the tavern; she was a tavern whore. I was the result of a bad business deal I guess, she left me to be raised by whoever would bother. Many's the night I stole my dinner from leftovers and that thrown to the dogs while she rolled on her back and drank herself stupid."

Realizing he'd awoken ghosts Baldor looked awkward, Armaco however continued as if needing to be rid of the tale.

"I don't blame her for what she was; Baal knows we have to make a living from the gifts the Gods give us. I do blame her though for abandoning me."

Baldor, not knowing what to do or say placed his hand on Armaco's shoulder patting it gently. Armaco's head fell forward, his face flushed with the wine and the fresh air, he looked at the ground the bitterness replaced by sadness.

"I can tell you this Armaco, Gestix told it to me when I was … other than myself and I hope it's a comfort to you. You're my friend, my very good friend and I'll never turn my back on you, hurt you, nor abandon you, come what may. I trust you with my life, have done! … You can trust me."

He offered his hand, the one-eyed warrior's face lightened and he nodded gently, the pair clasping each other's wrist and forearm. Baldor tipped the wineskin in salute.

"To us! Friends as long as we draw breath."

Armaco smiled. "Aye! And then some!"

Chapter Eighteen

Publius Scipio stood on the balcony of the Harbourmaster's offices, watching his men queuing along the wharfs and back into the narrow streets of Pisa itself, waiting to embark on the large, square-rigged transports that would take them to Spain and Africa and war with Carthage. There were four regular Legions, two for each of the Consuls with two auxiliary Legions in support, made up of subject allies from within the Republic. In total, almost thirty thousand infantry and two thousand horse formed up in their units or Maniples of Equites, Velites, Hastati, Princeps and Triari. This mixture of cavalry, light troops, heavy javelin men, heavy infantry and veteran heavy infantry respectively, which made up the Roman Legion. Publius turned to accept an offered goblet of wine from his General and brother, Gnaeus.

"Just over twenty years since we did this the last time." Publius said as he sipped the cool liquid.

"We'll finish it this time brother, Carthage will be a smoking ruin with its people enslaved ere we are done!"

"I told you Gnaeus, this Hannibal is no fool." Publius turned back to watching his troops, smiling to himself at the Optios barking men into line and the Centurions prodding and marshalling with their vine canes. "And unlike you I still have my reservations and it troubles me, I think we're starting down a long, hard road the end of which is a long way off."

"Come Publius, worry not man!" Came somewhat scathingly from Tiberius. "Gnaeus has the rights of it, they're just barbarians. You box this boy Hannibal up in Spain and crush him; I'll collect another Legion at Lilybaeum and burn this rat's nest at Carthage out and that will be the end of them I tell you. We'll be home for the harvest coming in."

"Of course … you're right Tiberius." Publius replied with as much sincerity and conviction as he could muster, hiding his true feelings beneath a forced smile, not wishing to discuss his fears with his fellow Consul. He raised his goblet to the two men alongside him, "Rome, Jupiter and victory gentlemen." All three downed their wine then collected helmets and cloaks from the table before heading to the wharfs.

Tiberius Sempronius Longus, joint Consul of Rome, a head shorter than Publius but broad of shoulder and body, strutted with all the pride and arrogance of the nobilitas class to which he belonged. His fleshy face crammed in by the cheek guards of his helmet, accentuating his hooked nose and small pig-like eyes. As the two Consuls passed their assembling Legions cheers broke out. Ragged and disjointed at first, then gathering momentum and coherence and rising to a crescendo of. "Scipio, Scipio, Scipio!"

Publius looked humble but raised his arm in salute and smiled; Tiberius huffed and glowered beneath his helmet.

The transports continued to fill with men, horses, mules, siege equipment and provisions under the watchful eyes of the Quartermasters and the ships Captains, the soldiers herded, counted and billeted the same as the animals. The three men walked amongst the menagerie that lined the wharf's, exchanging words and passing comments to old colleagues and snapping orders and threats to tardy or slack looking soldiers. The group stopped alongside a century of Hastati, the young Optio, Cornelius came smartly to attention and saluted, calling his men to the same readiness, accompanied by a rattle of metal and wood.

"Everything in order Optio?" Tiberius grunted.

"Yes sir! In order and ready to go."

The Consuls inspected the Legionnaires who stood bolt upright, looking straight ahead. Tiberius noted their immaculate turn out, the gleaming mail shirts and burnished helmets, polished harness and shields covered ready for the journey. He particularly liked the way the nerves jumped in one of the men's necks as he scrutinised him. It was good for the men to fear him he thought, keeps them in their place.

"Congratulations on your men Optio, they're a credit to you." He said almost grudgingly.

Cornelius, a little embarrassed at the attention flushed lightly but managed an unsure. "Thank you, sir."

"Rider coming through! Make way! … Make way there! … Rider to see the Consuls." A Centurion pushed through the ranks to the side of Cornelius's Century; he pointed with his cane to the command group and urged the dishevelled, weary looking rider onwards. The rider was lightly armed and dressed in a short tunic and leather armour. He was filthy and mud spattered, his face showing tear like trails where sweat had coursed, washing the dirt away. His mount was all but blown, its head lolling as it walked through the ranks of troops. The animal pushed its strong odour ahead of it, caked in mud to its belly, its flanks and neck covered with flecked sweat and spume over its bay coat. The rider dismounted, stumbling as his feet felt solid ground beneath them.

"Stand up man! What's to do?" Snapped Tiberius.

Publius grasped the man's arm firmly, aiding his balance while smiling at him. He motioned to a nearby Legionnaire for his water flask giving it to the rider. The man looked nervously between a glowering, impatient Tiberius and a quiet smiling Publius.

"Drink soldier, then tell us your news" Publius said calmly.

The messenger gulped the water as Publius led him out of earshot of the assembled men.

"Now! In your own time." He said quietly.

"Sir, a message from the senate, dire news! Thankfully I found you before you embarked fully …"

"Out with it man, for Jupiter's sake! We haven't all day." Tiberius cut in. The man lost control, worn out from the ride and overawed by the company he was in, he babbled and stuttered. "Gods above man! …"

"Tiberius!" Publius all but shouted. "Tiberius, please!" Lowering his voice again and slipping in a smile to smooth his rebuke. "Let him gather his breath and speak, else we will be here all day."

Tiberius huffed and rolled his pig-like eyes but remained silent.

"Now." Publius began again. "You've come from the senate, with important news?"

The man nodded. "Yes sir, yes! The Boii have revolted in the north, in Cisalpine Gaul along …"

"Bastard heathen savages! You turn your back …" Tiberius exploded

Publius held up his hand for peace and turned to the messenger again.

"Sir … sirs', you are both recalled! Yourselves and your Legions! You are to march northwards to quell the uprising and put yourselves between the Boii and Rome, immediately sir! That was the order from the senate." The man let out a sigh as his message was delivered, seeming to visibly shrink now his work was done.

"Hmm, the Boii eh! The largest Gallic tribe in the north." Publius cupped his chin as he spoke.

"And the Insurbes too sir, them as well! They've allied with the Boii." The messenger interceded quickly

"Stinking, barbarian bastards!" Tiberius ground his teeth.

"Tiberius! … Consul! Not in front of the men. Please, a little decorum if you will."

Publius took a step away from Tiberius, the messenger and his brother, quietly fuming but thinking deeply. He was vaguely aware of Tiberius haranguing the messenger for more details, while he busied calculating times in his head. If they needed to march north to quell the uprising then return here, it could add a month, maybe two to the campaign. That was assuming all went well. Also, his intelligence sources told him Hannibal was marching towards the Pyrenees, what was he at? Where was he going? If Hannibal continued into the mountains he felt sure the terrain and the fickle Gauls would cause him trouble en route and thus slow his progress but once on the other side of the mountains, what then? Would he then attack Massilia? He broke off from his thoughts, reasoning he should discuss it with Tiberius anyway, shaking his head at the thought of trying to explain and reason with the man. He opted firstly to get his men back off the ships.

****

With the Ebro now well behind them the Carthaginian army made its approach through the foothills of the Pyrenees, the mercenary company off-duty and riding within the main column. Talk was of the intended destination as it was now apparent they were not staying in Spain, Balaam was surprisingly quiet and seemed content to listen to them debating. The air was already noticeably cooler than that of the plain and as the sun sank behind the mountain peaks and evening came, the warrior's breath came out in huge, white billowing clouds. Malo in particular, having never witnessed such a chill nor seen his breath before, wrapped a scarf around his nose and mouth and now had little to say. Baldor on the other hand was behaving childlike and blowing his breath in all directions finding that the deeper he drew his breath to blow, the bigger the clouds, as the hotter vapour reacted with the cold dry air that surrounded them.

As the shadows lengthened, the column halted and the men set up camp for the night. The crisp, dry cold had them kindling fires as much for warmth as for preparation of the evening meal. The orange, yellow glow of thousands of tiny fires sprang up all over the hills, sparkling like stars in the night sky. Baldor dropped small sticks on the fire coaxing it into a stronger blaze, raising crackling sparks that danced and swirled upwards into the darkness. Malo, swathed in his cloak and scarf, sat as close to the fire as he could without burning, he held his hands up to the blaze then rubbed them together briskly, the friction of his dry skin loud in the stillness. Once the fire had burnt through the fresh material and died back to a glowing bed of red embers, Baldor placed circular flat stones in the fire to heat. From a dampened cloth in his pack, he produced a thick, coarse millet dough; he kneaded it with his knuckles, adding fresh water to bring it to the right texture. Content with the consistency he laid it to one side while the stones heated. He erected a small iron spit over the fire and set about plucking and gutting a rigid guinea fowl, which he'd carried suspended from his horses trappings since Malo put an arrow through it at midday.

"Do you think we should keep him on?" Armaco quipped between tearing at a stick of dried beef.

"Make somebody a good wife eh?" Marko added.

"Don't be upsetting the cook now lads, we haven't eaten yet! I'm not afraid to admit he makes a good job!" Gestix winked at the others as Baldor worked diligently on the bird.

"After the biggest portion again Gestix?" Harbro asked, shaking his head and grinning.

"Putting food in keeps the cold out, it's as simple as that. I was born in the mountains remember? I don't mind fighting or even dying if I have to but I have no intention of dying cold and hungry."

The warriors huddled around the fire as the bird went on the skewer. Before long it was sizzling and spitting juice onto the glowing timber, the tantalizing smell wafting through the air and tormenting empty stomachs.

"Do you still hold with your earlier thoughts Gestix? This of crossing the Alps?" Baldor asked while tending the cooking meat and dropping the millet dough, now formed into patties the size of his palm onto the hot stones to bake.

"Well, the General has detailed ten thousand foot and a thousand horse under General Hasdrubal to keep secure what we have gained here and to act as a rallying point for new recruitment. I can't see where else we could be headed but we're leaving Spain, that's obvious! There is nothing in Gaul that he could want; the silver mines are here in Spain and ours already. I'll wager we cross the Rhone and march for the Alps, we could be over them and into Cisalpine Gaul ere the summer finishes. Then after the winter, a march down the plains of Po will bring you to Rome itself and we all know how much he hates Rome."

"You seem to know the area well Gestix?"

The big Gaul looked suddenly morose. "I should do Harbro; I was born and raised in Cisalpine Gaul." He said quietly a trace of bitterness mixed with sadness. The men looked up their attention caught; Gestix had never said where he was from or why he'd left. He stared into the fire then continued. "When I left, I made my way over the Alps and these mountains we are in now, then down to Tarraco where I took ship for Carthage."

None of the warriors ventured to ask why but all were very curious. Baldor stopped his cooking duties, the questions forming in his mind that he wanted to ask but also mindful of the big Gaul's demeanour towards privacy.

"Was that so you could fight in the last war against Rome?" He asked tentatively.

"Yes." He continued staring into the fire, his voice monotone, his mind clearly elsewhere. "My people fought the Romans as best they could when they claimed suzerainty over us. We learned too late that reckless, undisciplined, wild charges are not the way to wage war on Rome. Despite the ferocity and speed of such tactics, they are useless against a shield wall if they don't break it but we threw ourselves at it again and again. At times it bent and buckled but the rear ranks pushed it back into shape and filled gaps in the wall of those we slew with fresh ones, in the end flesh and blood was no match for iron and wood and we broke." He shook his head in sad regret of the memory. "My tribe, ever confident in the ability of our warriors had not fled the village and the Romans having driven us from the field, fell upon it and slaughtered my people … women, children, the old and the sick, they spared none. They burned it to the ground, hunted down, and slew anyone they found. They butchered or stole the livestock, poisoned wells and even slew the dogs; they left all as they lay, food for wolves and crows. The few of us that survived joined the other tribes when and where we could but all suffered the same fate. I knew by then that the only way to defeat Rome would be with an army of a similar likeness, discipline and tactics, that's why I made my way to Carthage."

Despite their suspicions being confirmed as to Gestix's past, Baldor and the others were still dumbstruck, they could see the sorrow in his eyes and the pain he felt as he raised ghosts. Baldor wiped his hands on a cloth to hide his nervousness; he sucked in his breath and asked gently.

"Your family Gestix … what of …?" The words died in his throat as the big man, still not looking up from the fire, just shook his head gently.

Harbro pulled meat off the skewer and tasted it; nodding in satisfaction, he drew his knife cutting the meat free of the iron, offering portions around. Breaking the now pregnant silence, he volunteered his own tale as he dropped food on the men's wooden platters.

"The Romans slew my eldest brother on Sicily and my father at Dreparnum. I left the farm to settle the score after burying my mother when she died of a broken heart."

The men looked around the group for who would speak next.

"I was born Roman …" Marko began tentatively. The others looked at him bewildered, expecting some sour jest. His face however was serious and the scowl that wrinkled his brow and curled his lip spoke of a bitter tale to tell.

"My father was Roman." He paused as if waiting for the statement to sink in. "And a Legionnaire in his time, they invalided him out with a crippling thigh wound, he married my mother after his discharge and they settled on the plot of land given to him for his service."

The men ignored the food given to them. Hungry as they were they let it lie or paused with it torn between their fingers and stared intently at Marko as he continued.

"I too was a Legionnaire ..."

Baldor dropped the bread he was holding, Gestix looked dumbfounded, Malo pulled his scarf from his mouth as if to speak and Armaco's good eye seemed to grow as disbelief registered amongst them all. All looked as if they were about to interrupt when Harbro cut in.

"Let him finish!"

Marko continued. "When the last war broke out I was on leave at home in Capua with my parents. I was finishing up, having worked in the fields helping to bring in the last of the corn harvest. My mother and sisters had returned home to prepare supper and my father with them to pay off the hired help for their day's labour. Evening was drawing in when I heard shouts and screams coming from the house. I ran towards home only to be met by the stable boy running towards me, bellowing my name, crying murder, his face cut, and bleeding from a beating. When I questioned him as to what was amiss he could barely speak for the fear that was in him. Between his stuttering and shaking, I learned that some men from the nearby village had come to the farm seeking my parents. Apparently they were angry at the prospect of the coming war with Carthage ... all fired with wine and full of drunken courage." He spat the last words contemptuously. "They had seen my mother first as she was outside collecting her basket from the orchard, they began shouting and haranguing her, she railed to the taunts calling them cowards and drunkards, telling them to away home and leave a woman in peace at her own house. My father ventured out to see what the commotion was. By this time, they were hurling stones at my mother and then him when he went to protect her, calling her a whore and him a whoremaster. Even the house boy was seized and beaten but being young managed …"

"Why? … Why would they do that, if you were …" Baldor interrupted.

"If we were Roman, you were going to say?" Marko smiled bitterly. "Well my father was Roman but my mother … my poor, sweet mother was Carthaginian that was the cause of the trouble and the reason that the ignorant, stupid bastards had chosen to vent their spleen upon her. They stoned her in her own orchard and beat my father to death with his stick when he tried to defend her."

The faces of the listening men were angry and grim, the flickering light casting red then black shadows upon their features accentuating the looks. Harbro placed a heavy hand gently on Marko's shoulder in comfort.

"Well lad, you're with your mother's people now … among friends and we're glad to have you."

Marko's head had fallen forward as his tale had come out, the burden of carrying the awful secret and keeping it to himself for years all suddenly too much. Gestix passed a wineskin to Baldor intimating that he give it to Marko, the man took a long drink, breathed deeply and tried to pull himself together. No one spoke nor ate as if expecting him to continue. He began again, this time the words came slowly from between clenched teeth as he fought with his emotions not to break down.

"By the time I reached the house the drunken pigs had set it ablaze … I was too late to help my parents, they were both dead in the orchard … I could hear the screams from within as they started on my sisters. Attia, the eldest had taken a knife to one of the bastards as she tried to defend herself and our two youngest sisters from them.

To her credit she killed one before they cut her down."

His tone hoarse and bitter, Marko took a long drink dragging a hand over his mouth.

"I killed all that I could catch, drunken men can beat a woman or an old, crippled man but they are no match for a sober soldier. Still I was too late; they slew Attia and little Carla. They were busy raping Lamella as I fought outside. Three I slew in the garden with the sickle I had used to cut the corn, those inside managed to close the door on me and escaped from the rear of the house. When I finally got in I caught two of them finishing with Lamella, she was dead across the table, her throat cut. The bastards were so drunk they seemed oblivious to the flames around them; they thought me one of them and shouted that I should have said if I wanted a turn before they killed the Carthaginian slut. I buried the sickle in the first ones face, the second I hurled through the doorway into the flames, locking him in."

Marko's face turned to the fire and he stared unseeing at the red glow, the warriors about him not knowing what to say said nothing, one or two took a drink from their wineskins and like Marko just stared into the fire or at the ground.

"Five men I slew that night, one for each of my family but it was not enough. The Roman in me died forever that day ..." His voice wavered slightly and dried in his throat forcing him to drink before continuing. "My birth name was Marcus, Marcus Ventulas Cotter but I changed it to Marko and headed to Carthage and my mother's folk. Rome and anything Roman has been my sworn enemy since."

Silence and awkwardness descended on the group, the meal remained untouched, only when the crudely baked bread was ready and Baldor pulled it clear of the fire did anyone venture to speak. Armaco, as tactless and unsubtle as he was brave and honest broke the silence.

"What of you then Malo? What brings you here? What's your tale?" Malo peered over his scarf his large, dark eyes reflecting the firelight and taking on a haunted look. He said not a word, instead he opened his cloak and slipped his tunic sleeve down over his shoulder, his skin raised in a welted scar of Roman numerals where a branding iron had burnt into his skin.

"You were a galley slave?" Even the tactless Armaco sounded incredulous.

"No one survives that, Baal's teeth how did ..."

The Nubian said nothing. Holding his hand palm outwards signalling that the question was neither for answering nor discussion, he pulled his tunic back up, closed his robe and rubbed his hands together again in front of the fire. The men looked at each other and slowly began eating, no one had anything to say, all lost in their own thoughts. Armaco again began the conversation, perhaps to steer any questions from his own past.

"Well, we have all come from a world of shit, no exceptions! Each of us has a sorry tale to tell and no one other than those here to tell it to, none of us has family left other than those about him here now. All we can do is look out for each other and be a family ourselves, brothers in arms eh!"

"Armaco, you talk some shit!" Harbro replied cynically. Armaco frowned and looked at Harbro unsure as to where the conversation was going. "But that shit is the best I have heard in a while." He raised his wineskin in salute to Armaco and then the rest of the group. "Brothers!" He bowed his head then took a drink.

The sadness and tension vanished as men smiled and grabbed at their own wineskins, the repeated chorus of "Brothers … brothers." broke out amidst smiles and gulps of wine. The men relaxed and reached for their meat and hot bread.

The men awoke to a thick, enveloping fog. They rolled in stiff, frost-hardened blankets as they stretched and rubbed cramped and chilled limbs to restore circulation. The camp came to life as men packed equipment, readying themselves, their mounts and their pack animals for the days march. Guides kindled torches that spluttered and crackled miserably in the dampness before finally flaring into life, planting them along the side of the track as way markers for the army to follow. The eerie glow from the flames lit the way as the warriors shuffled past in the gloom, all colours of their clothes and equipment turned to monochrome.

As the morning passed, the watery sunlight grew in brilliance and burned off the fog, the chill start to the day replaced with a sweat-damp noon. At the higher altitude, the lush greenness was replaced by a dead, sand-coloured scrub; the soil supplanted by shale. Exposed rocks gave a barren look making the going difficult for the marching men. Trees changed from broadleaf, meadow varieties of oak, sycamore and beech to the pines, birches, larches and conifers of the high country as the army wound its way to the head of the pass. The altitude allowed snowdrops and edelweiss to linger in large irregular shaped carpets of white; they spread over the grass and around the base of the trees like snow. High above in the clear sky, hawks circled slowly, lazily riding the warm thermals in their search for prey.

Baldor had thought long and hard before falling asleep the previous night. After hearing the tales of suffering and hardship from his comrades, he realised he was far from alone with pain and heartache, in truth the others seemed to have suffered greater than he. The compassionate side of him felt deeply for the men that he now called brothers and his guilt and self-loathing deepened further when he thought of them rallying about him supporting him through his grief and troubles. He was grateful for the friendship bestowed upon him and promised himself he would return it, he owed them all that which they had given him. With his grief in perspective, he was determined to look to his friends and to make the most of the life given to him. He smiled as he remembered Gestix's words about living life, as ever he was right.

With his heart lightened and his mind clear after what seemed like eons of grief, indecision and self-hate, he felt whole once more and truly thankful to be alive. With his new view of life and the glorious summer-like day, he was enjoying the ride and appreciating the world and friends as if seeing both through new eyes.

He was in awe of his surroundings, used to the dry, hot climate and plains of North Africa, he gaped in wonder at the abundance of water that cascaded and flowed seemingly everywhere, running in small streams alongside the track and bursting out of stark rock faces. The air itself smelt different, being sharp, cool and clear, he breathed deeply of it, filling his lungs and enjoying the clarity it brought to his sinuses and head. As they rode past another stand of pines, he picked up the tangy scent of the gum before running his fingers through the low hanging branches, marvelling at the needle-like tubes instead of leaves. He found his hands pleasantly scented but also impossibly sticky with the sap that oozed from the timber and needles and which no amount of rubbing would remove.

As they continued on the narrow track, they climbed above the treeline. High up amongst the rocks where the only living thing was lichen and moss on the stones; the view to the north and east opened up below them. Tens of stades below them and as far as the eye could see, was a lush carpet of green. The tall grass swayed and moved in the breeze looking like a giant sheet of silk flapping gently in the wind. Amidst the changing shades of green the pools and streams of water sparkled blue in the bright sunlight, reflecting and dazzling like diamonds upon a robe of green. The abundance and size of the waterways giving the appearance of an inland sea with the grass as islands. Flocks of waterfowl swept into and away from this watery world, only tiny black dots in the air from this height but managing to darken the sky so great was their numbers. Baldor caught his breath at the sight.

"What on earth? It looks like a …"

"A marsh! A giant, insect ridden! Stinking marsh!" Armaco grumbled.

"He means the Rhone Delta." Gestix said with a chuckle. "It's not so bad, just huge. It will take a day or two to get down to it from here and then we have to get across it to the Rhone, if we are going where I think we are."

Chapter Nineteen

Balaam's company was the first to reach the inland sea some one and a half days after seeing it from the rocky peaks. Scouting ahead, they rendezvoused at the delta's edge looking back at the army spilling from the foothills towards them. It was easy to trace the track the army followed, owing to the colour and flashes of sunlight on metal coming from the living stream of men as they flowed in long procession from the heights to the lush greenness below. Baldor swatted at the flies for the umpteenth time, the insects buzzing about the men and horses relentlessly, the horses twitched their coats, swished tails and shook their heads as the flies circled and settled upon them.

"I thought you said it was not that bad in here Gestix, these flies will drive us mad!"

"They're only flies Baldor, wait till the mosquitoes start tonight … be brave!" The big man smiled as he kicked his horse on. Armaco swatting at the insects himself motioned Baldor to follow the Gaul.

"Nothing bothers him eh?" He said sarcastically to no one in particular.

The men rode to meet the first of the horses spilling off the mountain track, looking for Balaam to place their report. They found him in a foul mood, which wasn't helped by the flies, he flicked his scarf about his face repeatedly, muttering and cursing under his breath.

"Well! Report?"

Harbro spoke up. "My compliments sir." He saluted and nodded respectably. "There's no large area to camp anywhere, we'll have to spread out and pitch where the ground remains dry. The delta goes for as far as we can see and have scouted so far, that being almost half a day northeast sir."

Balaam tutted loudly. "Stinking, fly ridden hole! How in Hades name are we supposed to get through this?" He gazed at the thick, high grass and innumerable pools of water. "Baldor, Gestix, grab fresh rations and water and push out again, keep due east and ride as far as you can but time yourselves so that you are back ere dusk falls. The rest of you are stood down."

Although tired and sore Baldor was not averse to scouting further, the marshy vista just like the mountains was all new to him and a further source of wonder.

"Have you enough food and water to last you the day lad?" Gestix asked.

"As always! I'm learning soldiering from a good man." He bowed his head and smiled before digging his heels into Risto and trotting eastwards. Despite the flies, the delta was a beautiful place but with bogs, deep water and similar looking tracks also a treacherous one. The water sparkled as the sunlight flashed and shimmered on its surface, it looked cool and inviting, and formed pools in various sizes from puddles to lakes. Around the waters edge, bulrushes, reeds, flax and sedge grew in profusion, the tall bulrushes with their brown maceheads bending gracefully in the morning breeze. Willow and birch trees grew on the higher and drier ground amidst a thick, green carpet of tussock grass; the new season's leaves rustling like sheets of parchment rubbed together as the boughs moved with the wind. The pair learned very quickly to keep to the drier looking scrub as the green, lush grass was not always firm underfoot causing the horses to flounder, almost to their knees in places.

Taking their bearings from the sun, they rode until after midday before stopping near a large lake for water and food. Hobbling their mounts, they slipped off their helmets, glad to feel the cool air on their sweat matted hair. The lake was thickly covered with mallards, widgeons and shelducks, most of which seemed keen on seeking a mate with noisy ritual displays of water walking, flapping wings, quacking and fighting. A solitary heron waded majestically past, working its way along the waters edge seeking his prey of small fish or frogs in the shallows. So intent on his hunting that he neither saw nor heard the watching men.

"Malo would have him for the pot if he was here." Baldor said spraying crumbs, his mouth full of bread and hard cheese.

"He's too noble a bird to kill just to eat, don't you think?"

"With my stomach as empty as it's been this last couple of days I'd be damning the nobility of him and putting an arrow in him myself."

"I'd be concerned of upsetting some water spirit or Lake Goddess for killing a bird as regal and beautiful as that, surely it could only bring bad luck?"

"How do you know it's not a gift from the Gods?" Baldor replied, teasing his friend for his cautious piety.

Gestix threw a lump of bread at Baldor. "It's time you showed some respect to the Gods again young Targa, a man cannot live on bread and cheese when his soul's empty."

Gestix smiled as he chided, though he was still concerned at Baldor's Godless state. For all the mental and physical improvements Baldor had made since losing Aiticia, returning to reverence was not one of them. Being in the profession they were Gestix deemed a warrior needed his Gods.

Baldor's face changed, his look turning sour and Gestix wished he hadn't brought the subject up. Not wanting to make the lad feel awkward, he continued. "We need all the help, protection and luck we can get is all."

"I have you, Armaco, Marko, Malo and Harbro to watch over me as well as these to keep me from harm." He fingered the marble at his throat and pulled the small cameo from his armour. He kissed it gently before tucking it away. Gestix just smiled and quietly mouthed a prayer to Epona to forgive and care for his Godless friend.

Late afternoon and stades more of riding brought no changes in the terrain. The wind had dropped and the sun was in full splendour heating the glades and turning them into suntraps and cooking the men in their armour and helmets. They came to a fork in the track from which two paths led away, one into the trees and the other around the lake's edge. Gestix looked up to gauge the time from the sun.

"We haven't time to try both tracks together before we need to get back." He pulled a silver coin from his purse and flicked it, caught it and slapped it on the back of his hand covering it with the other. "Goddess or horse?"

"Horse!"

Gestix uncovered the coin. "Hah! Goddess! I'll take the trees and the shade; you take the track by the water and cook a little more! Piety lad, it grants you things." He smirked at Baldor who just shook his head but smiled warmly back.

Gestix looked at the sun. "See those trees? When the sun's above them meet me back here, then we're off back to camp and report, alright?"

Baldor nodded and turned his horse towards the lake, quietly humming a tune as he rode along the water's edge. He ducked instinctively as a wave of geese flew overhead, passing so low above him that he could feel the wind from beneath their wings; they hit the lake surface on his left, skidding and splashing with a multitude of loud honks.

Reining in to watch successive formations land, he never heard the horse and rider coming from downwind until a moment before they slammed into him, knocking him and his mount to the ground. Baldor landed heavily but clear of the flailing hooves and writhing body of his horse. The fallen animal stalled his attacker momentarily, giving him a chance to draw his sword as he tried to stand. He was badly shaken from the fall with the breath knocked right out of him and his balance askew. He drew only one weapon from the pair on his back, having to use the other arm as counter balance against his staggering gait. Recognising Carthaginian weapons and garb, he shouted.

"I'm Carthaginian! … Same as …" The husked, breathless whisper died in his throat as his wind gave out. The rider; either unhearing or uncaring cleared Baldor's horse and bore down on him. The momentum of the oncoming horse was gone but the height advantage of the rider was still great. A heavy swinging cut from a spatha beat Baldor's sword down as he raised it in defence of his head. Still unsteady, he fell again under the impact of the blow. The rider dragged cruelly on his mount's bit turning it quickly. Using his sword as a stick Baldor pulled himself from the dirt again; leaving it stuck deep in the ground he drew his second sword. Before he could raise it, the rider passed again and swept the sword out of his hands with an upward cut sending it spinning away. Just managing to keep his feet and gathering his wits, Baldor stayed close to the rider as he forced the horse about again. Hurling himself upwards, his hands like claws, he tried desperately to snatch the man from the horse's back. His fingers scraped over the smooth leather of the man's corselet, catching on nothing, then hooked into the sword baldric. The man's forward impetus pulled at Baldor's finger joints as he twisted his hands into the belt and pulled hard. Both men fell in a tangled heap, the sounds of air knocked from lungs and grunts of agony rending the air. They rolled across the grass towards the waters edge, hands scrabbling for the other's throat and fists flying blindly desperately seeking a target. Thrashing and rolling, they tumbled over the small step of land separating the grass from the shoreline of stones and brown silt. Separated momentarily they clambered to their feet amidst the crunch of pebbles beneath their boots. Their swords gone, both grabbed for their daggers.

Baldor peered at the wild-eyed, demented face crammed beneath helmet and cheek guards. "Ahaggar? ... Ahaggar! For Baal's sake! It's me! It's Baldor!"

Ahaggar laughed manically and nodded. Straightening his left arm to fend Baldor off, he retracted the right with the dagger in it back towards him, easing into a crouch.

"I know it's you boy!" The frenzied laugh came again. "I tracked you and your faithful dog but now he's gone and you're mine!"

Not understanding Ahaggar's ranting or attack, Baldor did realise the need to fight for his life. He crouched and flexed his knife arm, at the same time trying to move to better ground.

"No, no!" Ahaggar shook his head, a deranged look on his face as he closed the exit to the swords, keeping Baldor near the water's edge. "No, you stay and fight here boy! You're a good swordsman ... so they say! But what are you like with a knife? You have to dance close with a knife ... come, come!"

Ahaggar beckoned with his empty hand and cackled with insane relish when he saw Baldor uncomfortably shifting position and still trying to get back to his swords. Ahaggar closed the gap quickly and his knife hand shot out like a striking snake, just missing Baldor's arm as he dodged the heavy blade.

"You're quick boy! Quick! But can you keep it up?" He jabbed again, Baldor sidestepping. "I'm going to cut you boy! A bit at a time, the Lady said to make it slow, make you suffer. I have to earn my silver for your carcass." He stared at Baldor, his eyes large and full of madness.

Baldor had no idea what Ahaggar meant, he seemed unhinged or demented. Not daring to think about anything other than staying alive, his eyes and senses concentrated on the man and his knife. Ahaggar jabbed again, rotating the knife faster than a blinking eye from pointing outwards to pointing down. Baldor misread the move and suffered a deep backwards slash across his forearm, almost losing his dagger as the nerves reacted to the cut.

"You need to be quicker than that boy!" He cackled. "Knife fighting is different to your swords; we cut a piece at a time, just a piece."

He changed the knife from hand to hand with blurring speed while opening his guard momentarily, taunting Baldor to strike. When Baldor jabbed at what seemed like an opening, he was cut again on the other arm.

"You're not learning boy!"

Baldor felt the cold fingers of fear creeping into his gut. This fighting style was new to him, his speed as a swordsman hampered by the closeness of his opponent and Ahaggar stuck to him like his own shadow. Desperate to keep Ahaggar away, he feinted left trying to wrong foot him. He lunged quickly but Ahaggar dodged and rotating his blade again, slashed down and across Baldor's thigh. Baldor gasped as the searing pain raked his thigh muscle causing his leg to shake dangerously.

"That's three cuts boy! Bloody useless you are!" He smirked at his wit.

In that moment of over confidence, Baldor moved as if he was going to feint then didn't. Rotating his knife, he dragged the point across Ahaggar's upper arm, the point jumping clear of the flesh as it hit the man's wrist braces.

"Bastard whelp!"

Shocked at the change in fortune Ahaggar sobered as blood spilled down his forearm. Suddenly weary of his deadly game he came at Baldor quickly, hands moving fast and body twisting. Baldor stepped back evasively and stumbled over the loose, weed slippery stones into ankle deep water, He went down with a loud splash, the noise scattering the geese into a flapping, honking hullabaloo. The fall saved his life as Ahaggar brought his blade up seeking his throat. Instead, the blade slashed across his chin and mouth, deflecting away when it caught his cheek guard. Cursing, Ahaggar stepped after him to finish him. Baldor, unable to gain his feet raised his arm as a final defence. Ahaggar slapped the arm down, whooping in victory as he raised the dagger to strike.

The blow never came. Gestix drove his mount into the shallows, kicking up water spray and stones and felling a surprised Ahaggar with a heavy blow to the back of the helmet from the flat of his falcata. Ahaggar fell dazed over the top of Baldor who kicked and pushed him away as if diseased. Gestix dismounted amidst the skittering horse and entangled men, and pulled Baldor to his feet, the blood from his wounds mixing with the water and spreading it, washing the lad red.

"Are you alright?" He said frantically looking Baldor over.

"Why? … Why?" Baldor gabbled, he shook his head and stared confusedly at Ahaggar.

A semi-conscious Ahaggar groaned and rolled onto his knees just as Gestix smashed a booted foot into his face, whipping his head back violently in a spray of blood and knocking him out. He kicked him again in the ribs, the force rolling him onto his back in the shallows.

"Stay down you piece of shit!"

Hooking an arm around a very unsteady Baldor, he walked him to the step of land and sat him down. Expert fingers traced over the wounds, Baldor wincing as the Gaul's fingers touched raw flesh.

"You're lucky Baldor, or fast! Maybe a bit of both eh?" The big man smiled. "Your arms are alright, flesh wounds just. The leg is deep and needs stitching but he missed your artery. Your face …" He laughed a little, more in relief than jest. "Your face is going to scar; do you think that'll improve your looks?"

Baldor smiled wanly, his body shaking as shock and chill from the water crept in.

"I … I … thought I was dead!" He blurted as the shaking stole his breath.

"Well you're not, thank the God's!" Gestix said lightly, trying to settle Baldor's fear. "Stay there!" He walked to his mount and pulled his tack bags open, ferreting inside for clean scraps of linen. Rolling one into a pad, he pushed it onto Baldor's face urging him to keep it there. Tearing another into strips, he wrapped them firmly around the thigh.

"What in Hades was that all about? He must have recognised you as a Carthaginian, surely? " Not waiting for a reply he continued, "Take your helmet off so I can get this bandage on."

Baldor fumbled at the strap with trembling fingers and said nothing as he fought to control the shaking. The surprise had unsettled him along with the unfamiliar fighting style but it was the man's insane ranting and look of madness that had really frayed his nerves. He grimaced, clenching his teeth at the raw, burning feeling of sliced flesh being cleaned as Gestix worked on his wounds. After a while his breathing regulated and the shaking stopped, holding his hand out he found it steady once more, only then did he trust himself to speak.

"He knew who I was … though I hardly know him. … I don't know why he attacked me. He said he'd been tracking us but what have I or you got that he could want?"

"Hades knows! You-me, we're just like the others, no money to speak of, not enough food and the only gear we have is what we're standing up in. Anyway, we're not spending time watching our backs, we've enough to do that treacherous bastard dies now! I'll let the wind out of him and the lake can have him." Gestix stood and drew his dagger.

"He said … he said something about a woman …"

"A woman?"

"A woman wanting me dead and he was to be paid in silver for it."

Gestix looked thoughtful. "What woman? We haven't been near one since we landed in Spain!"

The pair fell silent as they mentally retraced their movements, Baldor struggling to think clearly.

"What about that crazy bitch you and Armaco ran into? … Remember … outside the senate? What was she called, Serfana, Serrana or something? You know, Carthalo's sister. That's the only damned woman I can think of!" Gestix answered his own questions as he strung events together.

"Serfina." Baldor said flatly, shaking his head in dismay. "Serfina! She was angry, yes but … no; no she wouldn't stoop to murder."

"Baldor! For Epona sake, wake up! Just because she's a noblewoman doesn't make her noble in her actions. It all makes perfect sense I tell you. Laws, protocol and nobility aside, what you have is a blood feud and people will fight any way they can with what they can, which means we'll have to drag that piece of shit back to camp to answer some questions." Gestix flicked his head at Ahaggar.

Baldor sighed deeply and settled his head in his hands. His arms oozed fresh blood as they bent to support his head. Seeing Baldor despondent always tore at Gestix's heart, whether it was paternal or brotherly he wasn't sure but his love for the lad wouldn't allow seeing him hurt. Sheathing his falcata, he gently eased Baldor's arms straight relieving the pressure off them and picking up the rags, finished binding the wounds.

"Next time take the Goddess when you call." He winked as he fastened the bandage. "And wear your wrist braces. Patrol or battle it doesn't matter, just wear them eh? They would have saved your forearms somewhat."

Baldor nodded dumbly and mumbled a disjointed apology. Gestix hushed him and was about to bandage the other arm when Ahaggar moaned and began crawling from the water's edge. Leaving his ministrations, Gestix strode down the beach and seized Ahaggar by his shoulder strap dragging him like a broken doll towards the horses. Pulling him roughly to his feet, he kneed him hard in the crotch.

"That's for the lad!" He growled, as Ahaggar was lifted off the ground with the impact, then doubled in agony onto his knees groaning deeply. He kicked him in the face, snapping his head back and rendering him unconscious again.

"And that, that's for me!"

He seized Ahaggar by his scarf and belt. Grunting loudly with the effort he bodily lifted him, throwing him face down over the back of his mount. The horse jumped forward as the weight dropped heavily onto it. Gestix took a pace away then turned on his heel as his temper broke and smashed his fist into Ahaggar's back twice, repeating. "Bastard! … Bastard!" After each blow. The horse skittered again at the attack and he paused making a physical effort to control himself. He pulled the leather lacings from Ahaggar's boots, using them to tie his hands to his feet beneath the animal's belly before returning to finish tending Baldor's wounds. Baldor visibly stunned at the momentary change from unrestrained violence to tenderness.

Early evening saw the pair and their captive return to the sprawling camp. To prevent unwanted curiosity and questions, Gestix covered and gagged their captive then tied equipment and blankets about him disguising his shape. They found Balaam and placed their report before producing their captive, the Captain looking at them as though they were making it up.

"If this woman is involved we need to take this matter to the General. Damn it Boy! Trouble follows you like a dog chasing a bitch in heat. Harbro! Get Armaco in here; see what he remembers about this." Balaam paced the tent as he spoke.

By the time Harbro returned with Armaco, Ahaggar had been lifted from the horse and laid on the floor of Balaam's tent. Still gagged and bound he looked wide-eyed from a pulped, blood-covered face at the group stood above him. As Armaco entered, his gaze caught Baldor who stood out by nature of his bandages.

"What in Hades happened Baldor?" His eyes dropped to the trussed Ahaggar. "You! … You piece of shit! I knew it! I bloody knew it!" He landed a boot hard into Ahaggar's chest.

"Enough! Enough, damn you all!" Balaam bellowed, spraying spittle as he roared. "Now! Armaco." He said lowering his voice again. "The boy's alright. What do you know off this dog here and a well-connected, vicious bitch in Carthage?"

Armaco recounted the fracas in Carthage with Serfina and her bodyguards and the attitude and behaviour of Ahaggar toward Baldor, as well as his previous unsolicited appearance in their section when on patrol. Balaam looked grimly at Ahaggar when hearing of the indiscretion on patrol.

"You deserve crucifying just for that, you risk all our lives when you don't reconnoitre properly."

Despite his hatred of Ahaggar, Armaco admitted he couldn't prove anything relating to a planned murder, it was only his gut feeling.

"So, at the end of the day we have no proof there's a connection between him." Balaam jabbed his finger at Ahaggar. "And this noblewoman and the pair of them wanting the boy dead?"

No one replied.

"I can't take this matter to the General on hearsay."

The men all tried to speak at once, some complaining others beseeching their Captain to do something. Balaam thumped his hand on the small table lifting the wine pitcher and goblets high in the air. The noise of breaking crockery had the desired affect and the men fell silent and respectful again.

"This isn't a bloody democracy, damn you!" Balaam glared at each of the men.

"As I was saying, I can't take the matter to the General on hearsay but I will take the matter of intent to kill by one soldier upon another." He paused to let it sink in. "Now! … Harbro, Armaco, get this offal out of my tent and under guard. Baldor, to the Physician. Gestix eat, and then report back here, we are going to see the General."

The following morning it was Hannibal himself who sought Baldor. He found him cleaning and checking his weapons by the fire in front of the tent. Hannibal watched, noting the meticulous and patient way Baldor worked despite his injuries hindering his movements. As Baldor finished he sighted the weapons edges then wiped the blades with unwashed sheepskin. Baldor, upon recognising Hannibal stood and saluted. Hannibal returned the salute and bade him be seated again, he pulling up a spare stool.

"I trust you're recovering well Baldor?"

"Yes sir, thank you! Stiff and sore is all now."

Hannibal settled himself on the stool and added more sticks to the fire, the early morning holding over the night's chill. He raised a small earthen jar and shook it gently.

"I have honey." He said enticingly "Have you some boiling water?"

Baldor grinned and reached behind for a waterskin, tipping its contents into a bronze pot, which he hung from a hook on the spit above the fire.

"It would seem you still have enemies in high places, despite your acquittal. If this Ahaggar Bola is to be believed."

"He told you?"

"Yes, with a little persuasion. Apparently, this Serfina Samilcar has put silver on your head. It seems she wants you dead at any cost."

Baldor sighed deeply. "Blood feud I think they call it?"

"Both families have lost! That should be an end to it! We're not barbarians to carry the slaughter to extinction." Hannibal exclaimed then paused, dipping his finger in the water checking the temperature before continuing. "Here's the problem though Serfina's father, Lord Samilcar opposed the siege of Saguntum and what he termed my families expansionist policies in Spain, calling for my removal from the army and recall to Carthage to answer for my belligerence. Therefore, I have no connection or sway with the family to try to stop this feud. If I go to the senate or go public with the matter, it will be viewed as petty revenge."

Baldor wiped two horn beakers as he listened, setting them near the fire to warm.

"Bola dies tomorrow at dawn; he'll be crucified for the attempted murder of you. It will serve as an example on two counts; one, it lets the army know that fighting and murder amongst ourselves will not be borne. Secondly but just as importantly; when word drifts back to Carthage, this Serfina will have to consider if we are onto her and thereby should discourage any further attempts on your life. Now, I think that water should be hot, use plenty of honey Baldor, I like it sweet."

The following dawn amidst a pale band of pink in the eastern corner of the sky, warriors representing every race, regiment, and sector within the army gathered as if on parade in the largest clearing or dry area in the delta. The surrounding lakes remained blanketed with a white mist awaiting the morning breeze to freshen and lift it. Men rubbed their hands from the morning chill as they waited; those with cloaks drew them closed about them. There was a low drone arising from the muted talk of the men while three slaves toiled to dig a hole atop a small incline. Others appeared carrying hammers, timber, rope and a basket of nails to the allotted spot. When all was ready, the labourers fell into line and looked to their General. Hannibal was dressed as if on parade in burnished helmet, bronze corselet and greaves with his Generals sash of purple wrapped thickly about his waist. He strode to the centre of the clearing facing the large semi-circle of waiting men. He looked along their ranks slowly, the men falling to silence, only the sounds of the birds disturbed the peace.

"Generals, Captains … officers and warriors!" He shouted, ensuring his voice carried to all. "We are here to see justice served upon a man who would slay his fellow warrior for money." He paused to let the statement sink in and to gather his breath. "I remind you that we are all under military law. All men, no matter what race, rank or creed are subject to that law. This man was apprehended in the act of murder and has since confessed to his crimes, I make example of him in hope that it is the last." He signalled the guards to carry on.

Ahaggar was brought from behind the assembled ranks. He fought and struggled against two huge men that led him on ropes bound about his wrists and neck, across the grass and toward the incline. He was naked and bore the bloodied criss-cross weals of a flogging on his back and red, purple blister marks of hot irons all over his body. Seeing the timber and recognised his fate he became almost deranged, straining and struggling frantically to be loose. Resisting the ropes, he stumbled and fell after which the men just dragged him. He wailed and tried to shout but only incoherent, mutated sounds came out. Baldor looked at Gestix; the big man answering the unasked question.

"They've cut his tongue out, that way he can't implicate anyone else, or cause awkward questions to be asked."

Seeing the man's terror and reduced to babbling like a child had the watching Gauls shouting insults and decrying him for a woman. Baldor stared at the broken wreck of a man as he was dragged, seeing hapless horror in his eyes. His skin crawled as he saw the men laughing and taking every chance to inflict more pain upon him. Baldor, as hot tempered and violent as he could be, took no pleasure in torture and despite Ahaggar's desire to slay him, he now pitied him. Ahaggar finally soiled himself, receiving further kicks from his captors as they turned their faces from the stink, the onlookers hurling more abuse. He was forced down onto the crossed beams and howled pitifully when the first nail was driven through his palm, his body shaking in spasms. Struggling frantically with his other arm one of his captors stood his full weight on it, keeping it in place across the timber. Ahaggar closed his hand to prevent it being nailed which resulted in two sharp hits with the hammer, smashing his fingers and raising a marrow-freezing howl as the nail was driven into his palm. Baldor turned away in disgust. Gestix gripped his wrist vice-like and spoke quietly but firmly.

"Stay where you are!" Baldor glared angrily, the Gaul returned the look emphatically. "Bear with it! The bastard would have shown you no mercy; this could just as easy have been your funeral rites instead!"

"They should just kill him and have done with it!"

"A lesson for all lad, a grim one I grant you but honest men have nothing to fear and can sleep with both eyes closed with shit like that gone."

Ahaggar was now firmly nailed to the cross with additional nails driven through his forearms and feet and he mercifully quiet. His head lolled on his chest but whether he was dead or just unconscious was unclear. The timber had been raised with the labourers hammering wooden wedges into place keeping the grim edifice upright. Hannibal stood once more in front of his troops.

"Justice has been done! The body will be left to rot as food for crows and a warning to others, the same as any common criminal. Officers! March your men past this wretch as we break camp, let this lesson serve!"

The camp returned to normal with men snatching what rest they could before the coming march with others seeing to their breakfast. Baldor had no stomach for it; he just sat with his comrades and was noticeable by his silence. At midmorning a servant arrived asking for him then presenting Ahaggar's armour, weapons and affects, stating that they were his to do with as he saw fit. Baldor looked aghast at the neatly stacked equipment, declaring he wanted nothing of it and pushed it back at the servant telling him to take it away. Gestix, seeing the exchange flicked his head to Armaco and the pair discreetly followed then intercepted the servant some distance from the tents.

"We'll take that!" Gestix said politely but firmly.

The servant looked as though he was about to argue but Armaco cut in.

"The lad changed his mind is all; several of us have offered to buy the affects so we'll take the gear back to him."

"I was told to give it to him personally sirs and no other. The General was quite clear upon it!"

The servant looking nervously from one to the other then turned on his heel walking quickly away. Gestix took a few quick paces overtaking and barring his path, the smaller man looking suddenly into Gestix's chest then slowly up to his face. He saw the hard, serious face behind the drooping moustache noting the suddenly cold eyes. Without taking his gaze from the man, Gestix fished in his purse and produced a silver coin that he held up for the man to inspect.

"For your trouble … friend!"

The man looked at Gestix then Armaco, Armaco smiled comically and held out his hands, the servant deposited the equipment into his arms and backed away. Gestix clicked his tongue to get the man's attention then threw the coin to him. The man caught it and took off like a bolting rabbit.

"You frightened him." Armaco laughed. "It's that moustache!"

"Hmmph" Was the only response.

"What do you want this for anyway? I don't think Baldor will thank you for the money we'll get for it; I take it you're going to sell it."

"It's not for sale! Well, not all of it. Come on." Gestix led Armaco through the camp towards the baggage train, following his nose to where men were busy butchering beef, others salting and hanging the meat on wooden frames in the sun.

"What the hell are we doing over here?" Armaco asked. Gestix ignored him seemingly intent on searching. "What are you looking for?"

"This'll do." He picked up a leather bucket half filled with blood and crusted with black flies. Then as he passed a cart stacked with sacks of maize, he lifted an empty sack. "Right, let's go sit in the sun." He walked away from the camp and off into the long grass.

Armaco followed with his bundle, muttering under his breath about crazy Gauls and too much sun.

Gestix found a quiet spot and set the bucket down along with its mobile halo of flies. He took the gear from Armaco laying it out on the ground, throwing the helmet, cloak and weapons back to Armaco whose brows wrinkled quizzically. He arranged the tunic carefully inside the corselet as if being worn, drawing his falcata he stabbed through both. He splattered the congealing blood over the leather, applying it thickly around the cut and staining the tunic beneath, adding a bloodied handprint for good affect and placing both in the sun to dry. Nodding in satisfaction, he washed his hands drying them on the grass then settled himself comfortably with his back against a tree. Armaco looked at him bewildered, Gestix, sensed the coming questions began.

"We leave them to dry then pack it all in the sack."

"And then?"

"Then we send it back to Carthage to this, Serfina. She won't know whether it is Baldor's gear sent by Bola as proof of his murder or whether Bolas' been caught and killed and this is his gear sent by Baldor's friends as a warning. Keeps the bitch guessing eh? And hopefully worried! Best of all, it should leave the lad in peace!"

Armaco whistled softly in appreciation of the scheme "And these?" He said holding up the remaining equipment.

"Sell them for whatever you can get but not to our lads mind, I don't want Baldor seeing them again. The proceeds can buy extra rations for us all."

"Baal save us from scheming Gauls!" Armaco sat down next to Gestix, sighing as the weight came off his feet. "You're not thinking of standing for the senate are you?"

Chapter Twenty

The Carthaginians spent a further three weeks pushing laboriously through the delta combating mud, flies, infections and bouts of dysentery from their carelessly deposited human waste. Finally, fixed water collection points were established and sanitary rules laid down to prevent further spread of the disease but not before the flux of the bowels killed many. Men puked and shit themselves until too weak to stand then slowly dehydrated and died. The dead were burnt regardless of religious conviction or preference, when it was discovered the soft ground allowed fluids from the decomposing bodies to leach back into the watercourses to cause further havoc. The funeral pyres were damp, smoky affairs, owing to the lack of dry wood to burn. All timber was living and green, else wet and rotted from where it had lain on the damp ground. Only when the fires began to consume the corpses, and oils and fats fed the flames did the pyres burn with any vigour. The acrid smoke stained the sky, the sickly smell clinging to men's clothes, coating nostrils, and bringing more hungry flies. Men suffered terribly with the heat of the day and then the bone chilling dampness that came after dark to plague chests and lungs. They were eaten alive by insects, the tiny mosquito causing the most havoc with bites that itched and chaffed beneath armour, causing men to scratch until the bites bled then became infected. Despite the demoralising conditions and hardships, the march went inexorably onward towards the Rhone.

The mercenary company were working as out-riders, allying themselves with local levied scouts to guide the army out of the delta to the banks of the Rhone. Cresting a scrub-covered rise on the river plain, Baldor reined his horse in, staring in disbelief at the river flowing in a wide green ribbon on its way to the sea.

"That cannot be!" He said shaking his head. Waiting for Gestix to catch him up he carefully pulled his legs up from Risto's flanks until he squatted on the horses back, then rising slowly and setting his balance, he stood on the animal's hindquarters to marvel once more at the view in front of him.

"It must be over two stades wide! And look at the flow; it's as fast as a running man."

"Aye lad! Wide, fast and deep!" Gestix said reining in alongside. "We're going to need boats, rafts and the help of Sequana to get over that."

"Who's Sequana?" Baldor asked from his lofty perch while shading his eyes for a better view.

"Sequana, my Godless friend, is the Goddess of rivers and streams and the patron Goddess of this river Rhone. A prayer or two to her wouldn't hurt."

"Say one for me then." Baldor teased as he dropped down onto Risto's back in one fluid move, smirking a little when he noticed black looks from the big Gaul. "I know you fear nothing Gestix, you're afraid of no man and more than a match for most, so why the constant piety, why should we pray? What do we need the Gods for?"

"Belief lad! Everyone needs something to believe in and … I still fear things, no matter how well I hide it, that's why I pray."

"Well, I don't think they listen, what have they ever done for us?"

"They stop the sky falling on our heads and that's something I fear."

Baldor laughed loudly. "What …?"

Gestix glowered, embarrassed and angered by the laughter "Well, you tell me what holds it up? I don't see any supports. Who else but the Gods could keep it so?"

Baldor seeing the anger did not reply, he looked away not meeting Gestix's eyes.

Gestix took a moment to control his temper and moderate his tone. "The Gods make us who and what we are … Don't treat them lightly!" He added in a hushed whisper. "We are but pieces on a game board for them to play with; you shouldn't be disrespectful nor tempt fate by calling them to question."

"What good has it ever done me?" Baldor replied from twisted lips as his anger rose, his tone changing from the light hearted jests moments before. "I prayed to Baal and made my offerings but he still took Aiticia from me and has tried to kill me ever since."

"How do you know he wasn't saving you from being killed?"

"Because it was you that saved me from myself and death at the hands of Ahaggar, then Armaco that time in Carthage. Before that, the skills learned from you and my father saved me, when I fought Carthalo and Adharbal. Flesh and blood forge this world Gestix, not Gods!" His voice rose to a rant. Gestix, as needled as he was listened as Baldor unloaded his anger.

"As I said then, perhaps Armaco and I were heaven sent?" He smiled trying to ease the seriousness of the conversation and cool Baldor's ire. "Anyway, we can't blame the Gods for all that goes wrong!"

"Why not? We praise and give thanks to them for everything that goes right."

The quick fire, fractious responses, took Gestix aback. Normally Baldor could be reasoned with but it seemed that religion and his devotion or rather the lack of it was not up for discussion. He sighed deeply, smoothing his huge moustache with his hand.

"Alright Baldor, I'll make a deal with you. I will respect your right to ignore the Gods; you respect my right to revere them and to pray for you, is that a deal? … And I thought I was the uncultured barbarian!" Gestix smiled broadly at his satire and winked at a now happier looking Baldor, who bowed his head respectfully.

"No more arguments over religion eh? … My young barbarian!" he roared with laughter and kicked his horse into motion.

****

In the far north of Italy in Cisalpine Gaul, on a daisy carpeted hillside, the Boii and their allies the Insurbes watched as the Legions of Publius Cornelius Scipio and Tiberius Sempronius Longus formed up for battle. It was a beautiful summer morning, warm and bright with blue skies and no breeze. The Gauls faced southeast and the sun was already casting its rays into their eyes, having the high ground however, they were comfortable with their position. Many had sat down, content to watch and listen as the Roman Centurions and Optios drew their men up ready for combat, their voices barking orders that drifted across the meadow. The thick grass muffled the sound of marching feet as the Legions manoeuvred and with no bare dirt to kick into dust clouds, the scene remained beautifully clear. The skylarks sang sweetly, the little birds hovering high in the blue, their wings beating at high speed. A hawk rose on the warm thermals wings outstretched and motionless, his piercing call announcing his ascent.

The Gauls were drawn up in huge rectangular formations, segregated by tribe and by warrior class. Some of the younger men were out front of the blocks in scattered, loose formation acting as skirmishers or light troops. Armed with light javelins and small buckler, some carried short swords or daggers, most were stripped to the waist and went barefoot. A handful of archers and slingers were mixed through the light troops, they stood singly or in pairs, no thoughts given to massing them together. The warriors to their rear were heavily armed with fighting spears and carried round or elliptical shields. All carried the long Gallic broadsword and most wore mail shirts and bronze or iron helmets, a few carried double-handed, long shafted axes. Preferring trousers to the short tunics of the Romans, they wore them in bright colours in checks and plaids.

Their cavalry had dismounted and sent their horses to the rear, the warriors preferring to fight on foot. Amongst the forest of spears, were standards in shapes of wolves and bears, cast in bronze and mounted atop wooden or metal shafts. Alongside the Standard-bearers were the musicians or signallers with the carnyx, a bronze instrument made of a straight hollow tube the height of a man in length. The mouthpiece formed from a swept curve and from which it widened gradually over its length, rising to a boar, horse or mythical creature's head, forming the orifice. The instrument was held vertically to play, issuing long harsh drones from the mouth of the animal's head.

Below, the Legions were in position and the officers falling silent. The Maniples were staggered compared to those in front and behind, similar in formation to the black squares on a chequer board. The spaces between each Maniple allowed for the movement of the one behind to reinforce or for the front line to retire its troops without disturbance to the waiting ranks.

The lines denoted troop type; in front in loose order were the Velites or skirmishing troops. Like the Gallic skirmishers, they too were lightly armed with javelins and a sword but carried a larger oval shield. Some wore a simple helmet over which was draped a wolfskin, its pelt falling over their shoulders and backs as added protection. Next were the Hastati, the first of the medium line infantry. These men were in the prime of life, experienced and battle ready, armed with the pilum or heavy javelin. A shower of these released before contact could disrupt and break up an enemy line, opening the ranks for the men following with the gladius. The gladius was the short, broad-bladed sword of the Legion. Used as a thrusting weapon from behind a shield wall it suited close quarter combat to deadly affect. The men wore mail shirts reaching to mid-thigh and helmets of bronze, sporting feathers or coloured plumage from their crest, a large shield, just shorter than the Legionnaire himself completed their equipment. After the Hastati was the Princeps, similar in dress and arms, except the pilum was replaced by a broad-headed, fighting spear, the Hasta. Finally, in reserve was the Triari, similarly armed but veteran warriors, experienced and battle proven.

Total silence fell over both armies like the calm before some terrible storm. The men arrayed in their full panoply of war took time to study their enemy, many knowing it could be the last thing they would see on earth. Some mouthed prayers else fingered and kissed effigies of their Gods or tokens of good luck. One or two shook and quietly wet themselves as nerves got the better of them, many of the youngest vomited as the tension mounted. The wait before combat was always the hardest thing of all; the fraying nerves, the regret of things left unsaid, the fear of letting comrades down and the need for courage when death was all around plagued veteran and untried alike. The ability to handle the emotions being all that set men apart.

Cornelius Scipio, standing with his Centurion felt his hands trembling; he clenched his fists to control the shake, his palms cold and sticky as fear spread its aura over him. At the tender age of seventeen, this was his first pitched battle. Like most, he prayed for the fortitude that he would let himself nor his men down and that the Gods would spare his life. His father had set a heady standard to follow, being a successful; political leader, feared warrior and accomplished General much loved by his troops. Right now, the young Optio would settle for maintaining the family name and honour and staying alive.

"Alright Optio?" His Centurion asked quietly not taking his eyes off the Gauls. "Won't be long now, you're doing well, just relax and breathe, smile a little. We're all scared shitless but being officers we can't show it else we might upset the lads."

"You scared, sir?" Cornelius said smiling, genuinely glad to talk. "I don't believe you'd be scared if Pluto and all his demons were up on that hill."

"Pluto and his demons no, but these Gauls, they scare me ...." Cornelius looked intently at his Centurion. "Haven't you seen some of their women Cornelius? You'd need to be a hard man to tame them!" Gaius Laelius, Centurion in the Legion of the Boar, friend and mentor to Cornelius laughed, his young Optio forgetting the nerve fraying tension laughed with him.

As if following some unheard command, prayers and whispered talk died away, men shook hands, wished one another well and arranged to meet later in the day, some hiding their fear with grim jests of Elysium or Hades, then fell silent.

"Stand to!" A centurion bellowed as the Consuls walked to the front and centre of the line.

The rattle of steel and wood as men came smartly to attention startled a hare secreted in the grass a spear's throw from the first rank; it bolted, zigzagging across the meadow. A shrewd, Publius Scipio noticed the hare's flighty departure.

"Soldiers, citizens of Rome! Brave men all, true sons of the she wolf!" His words carried clearly across the meadow, returning a slight echo as he paused. "Surely that is a Gallic Hare!" He pointed after the departing Coney. "And I believe he is leading the way from this field for those men up there." Some laughter broke out amongst the Legionnaires. "The men you will be sending in the same direction and at the same speed!" Publius smiled at his men, the ranks laughing back at their Consul. He raised his arms for quiet so he could speak again. "You are highly trained, you are well equipped and you are the best soldiers this world has ever seen!" His voice rose as he drove the point's home, the men responding in cheers. "We'll not be here over long! I vouch you lads will see that rabble off then we'll be back on our way to Spain to send those Carthaginians homeward too!" The men cheered loudly again. "May the Gods smile upon you and keep you! Be brave! Be strong!"

He fastened his helmet as a chant of 'Scipio, Scipio' began building along with the accompaniment of spears clashing shields. Publius turned to Tiberius. "Will you give your blessing, Tiberius?"

Tiberius huffed and glowered beneath his helmet. "They are here to fight and die if need be, that's what we pay them for! Lets to it!"

Publius was about to insist that Tiberius speak but he was already walking back to his position. Publius turned again to the cheering men; he saluted and bowed his head in respect before walking to his own position. The Centurions took over, calling for battle stations and men fell silent, readying for the fight.

Up on the hill the Gauls were on their feet and making final adjustment to shield straps and harness, war cries starting up along with whoops and shouts. The Chiefs were out front of the massed warriors and calling while pointing at the Romans below, their oration prompting weapon and shield clashing and raising the men to frenzy. Wailing blasts from the carnyx drifted down the hill and the Gauls began their advance, first one block then another, then all.

Walking at first and maintaining the clash of weapons and shields, then as eagerness overtook some, moving to a trot then to a running charge, shields held up and forward. The blocks melted together into a mass of howling, racing warriors that came at breakneck speed screaming hate and baying for blood. The Velites hurled their javelins as the Gallic skirmishers came into range, the short exchange saw the first casualties as men rolled and screamed in the grass, their bodies sprouting javelins. The Velites however had no time for further action as the wave of Gallic infantry bore down on them at the run, threatening to engulf everything in their path. Seeing the Velites about to be overrun, the Consuls ordered the recall and the signallers blew three short blasts on the cornicen. These horns, like the carnyx were of bronze but curved in the form of a letter c. Hearing the recall the Velites dodged back through the Maniples to safety. The Gauls whooped louder, the ground vibrating as thousands of feet pounded down the hillside sounding like rolling thunder. The Hastati bunched tighter, as men sought the closeness of comrades, shields began to overlap and lock. A deliberately calm, Gaius walked the line calling to make ready with the pilum, his vine cane denoting his rank tucked under his arm. Arms pulled back as the Legionnaires prepared to shower the Gauls in metal rain.

"Steady lads! Wait for the order!" He called.

The Gauls were coming within bowshot and the Roman archers, judging the speed and distance of the howling ranks loosed, sending the first of their arrows soaring high. Gaius followed the arrows judging his men's pila throw for moments after the arrows hit, the additional havoc ensuring a maximising blow.

"Hold lads!"

The Gauls came on at breakneck speed, their ranks opening as overeager, psyched warriors outpaced each other in their haste to close.

"Hold!"

The arrows were arcing downwards.

"Hold!"

Arrows struck home with thuds and clatters into bodies and shields, followed by shrieks, and screams as men went down, some rolling and sliding along the ground as their impetus carried them forward.

"Release!"

A whoosh of disturbed air mixed with grunts and gasps of exertion from the Legionnaires signalled the departure of the pila towards the Gauls. A rain of whistling, moaning death flew in low trajectory towards the charging and tumbling ranks now less than thirty paces from the waiting Romans. Men went down in swathes as the pila slammed into them, punching more gaps in the lines.

"Keep your dressing! Shields up! Let them come!" Gaius slipped into the front rank while drawing his gladius.

Despite the arrows, the pila and the casualties the Gauls came on without pause, swerving and jumping over fallen and rolling comrades. Legionnaires leaned into their shields readying for the human wave about to break over them like an angry ocean roller battering a breakwater. At twenty paces to impact, the hatred and battle madness was clear to see on the warriors faces. At ten paces distinguishing features, scars and tattoos were evident. Then an unholy crash of bodies, iron and splintering wood mixed with the grunts and screams of men announcing the arrival of the Gauls to the Roman shield wall.

****

Within three days of exiting the delta, the Carthaginian army was camped along the western bank of the Rhone. The men scattered for innumerable stades up and downstream, their tents mixing with the huts of the Volcae tribe that dotted the western side of the river. Their orders were for the peaceful and purchased acquisition of boats, rafts, timber or anything capable of transporting men and animals over the water. Gallic warriors conversant with the local dialect were tasked with dealing and bargaining with the Volcae, supported by their Carthaginian colleagues they sought the Chief or Headman of each village. Gestix, heading up one such deputation was dressed in a highly burnished mail corselet and chequered pants, his hair bound in a plait as thick as a man's wrist, a heavy gold torque about his throat and a Gallic broad sword hanging from his belt. The mercenary company, also decked in their finery, flanked him. They approached their allotted village at a respectful midmorning, in strength but without appearing too martial or threatening. Although armed, helmets had been purposefully abandoned and shields and spears left in camp.

"Why the need for all of us to come to the negotiations Gestix? It still looks a bit threatening." Balaam grumbled while mopping sweat from his brow.

"Prestige Captain! We have to find the fine line between threatening and respect. We need to make the Chief feel important and that he's worth the effort by bringing so many men but without seeming to threaten or intimidate him in his own village … tricky eh?"

"You Gauls are a tricky, prickly lot!" Balaam moaned.

"You missed out proud sir."

Before Balaam could reply, they trotted into the village square heralded by a chorus of barking as the resident dogs caught the unfamiliar scent. Tall, longhaired warriors, most complete with beards and moustaches were drawn up in ranks, all dressed in the full panoply of war. They formed a broad avenue leading to a raised timber dais, upon which rested a chair covered in bearskins, complete with a big man sat regally upon it, his thick blonde moustache reaching almost to his chest.

"Maybe we should've come better armed? It looks like they're expecting a war." Balaam grizzled.

"It's pride and prestige sir, that's all"

Balaam hooted and caught a murderous look from Gestix; he sighed. "Each to their own I guess, I meant no insult."

Gestix dipped his head accepting the reluctant apology then halted the company back from the dais and dismounted, Balaam relaying orders for the others to follow suit. Gestix bowed his head to the man on the throne-like chair and waited. After what seemed a long and uncomfortable silence he was beckoned forward, without looking back, he called Balaam to come with him. The two strode along the avenue of warriors. Balaam, despite being a head shorter than all, carried himself nobly with an air of superiority and command. He muttered under his breath about pompous, puffed up barbarians but followed behind Gestix as bidden, being on Gestix's deaf side his grizzles went unheard. When both were seated upon the dais, albeit on lower chairs or stools than the Chief, the formalities and negotiations began.

Baldor, holding Risto's bridle moved his eyes instead of his head, looking around the square at the village, the people and the warriors. The buildings were mostly of timber logs with mud plastered between the joints as weatherproofing, the roofs being bundles of thick, mustard coloured thatch. Huge hunting dogs lolled in the sun outside some of the hut doorways, watching all and panting with the heat. The people were coloured with pale or bronze skin, their hair colour predominantly fair with shades of blonde from moon-silver through to ripe wheat and ash. A few were darker, with one or two coloured vibrant copper through to rust-red, their skin strangely milky-white. The women varied from large and fierce with coarse looks to slim and strikingly beautiful, with ice blue or emerald green eyes, high cheekbones and delicate, sculptured features. Colour was in abundance in their clothing with checks, stripes and plaids of various hues, many wore gold or silver bracelets and torques about their necks. The warriors dress varied from those heavily armed in mail shirts, bronze helmet and polished shields inscribed with concentric patterns and swirls, to those in leather trousers and bare chests carrying only a round wooden shield and spear. Clothing and arms differences apart, an aura of fierce, indomitable pride emanated from all.

As the sun climbed higher negotiations continued, the waiting company sweating freely in their corselets. All, thankful of not having helmets and shields to contend with. As uncomfortable and hot as they were, they remained immobile as ordered, quietly noting the iron discipline of the Gallic warriors who suffered stoically beneath helmet, mail and heavy weaponry. A further wait saw the men on the dais stand and shake hands then share huge goblets of ale amidst smiles and some laughter. With formalities over, villagers and warriors alike began wandering amongst the Carthaginians examining their garb, weapons and horses in a manner not unlike inquisitive children. Some women pointed at Malo, one or two touching him, before backing away giggling and looking at their fingers as if expecting to see his colouring on their skin. Two younger women approached Baldor, eyes all of fire, their lips showing a feminine, sexual pout. They eyed him unashamedly as if selecting a piece of meat; his embarrassment saved by an older warrior who growled gruffly at the pair, sending them scurrying back to the other women. He in turn boldly ran his fingers over Baldor's facial scars nodding as if in approval, muttering in the same guttural tones. Baldor, unsure what to do stood unmoving. The man lifted his own arm and showed a white scar from elbow to wrist, then pointed to his other arm and another scar. Baldor realising the gist, in turn showed his scarred arms one at a time then moved his tunic aside showing the scar from the stab wound left by Carthalo. The man prodded the scar then shouted to another warrior, as the other approached he conversed and pointed to Baldor's scars. The other warrior nodded then spoke in heavily accented Phoenician to Baldor.

"My friend admires your scars, he says you are young to have so many!" He said haltingly. "He says you must have fought many times … unless you fought only once and poorly."

Baldor's smile faded, replaced by a twist of his lips as his fierce pride rankled. He replied in fluent Gallic to the translating warrior all the while keeping his tone civil.

"I admire your friend's scars, they demonstrate his prowess. He must have had a long and distinguished life … unless he fights poorly and is just lucky to have lived so long?"

The air was suddenly pregnant with tension. Warriors nearby held their breaths and hands slowly moved towards sword hilts, all having gathered the gist of the conversation. A honeybee buzzed past, seeming very loud in the sudden quiet. The scarred warrior looked deeply into Baldor's eyes then smiled and laughed heartily, nodding his head and slapping his thigh while talking.

The translating warrior spoke again, more for the benefit of the other Carthaginians than Baldor who was already smiling again.

"My friend says you must have fought many times and fought well, he also says you must have learned from a Gaul to be so good yet so young, he offers you his hospitality and would know of the two ..." The man raised two thick fingers. "Blades you carry on your back?"

The scarred warrior threw a heavy arm over Baldor's shoulder and walked him towards a hut; Armaco fell in alongside replying to the questioning look on the warrior's face.

"We're brothers." He said pointing to Baldor and himself. "Where he goes I go!" Baldor translated and the warrior looked at Armaco before touching his eye patch and nodding again, beckoning and gesturing it was time for a drink.

Chapter Twenty one

A full week of bargaining for boats, barges, timber and the building of it into rafts found the Carthaginians ready to cross the Rhone. The Volcae domiciled on the eastern bank however proved neither receptive nor friendly to the encamped army unlike their neighbours on the western bank. Whether that was because they had the river between them and felt secure or they just harboured a mistrust of the Carthaginian intentions wasn't clear. Abundantly clear was they wouldn't tolerate the Carthaginians passing through their lands and intended to dispute the river crossing, thousands of armed warriors lining the bank were evidence of that. Hannibal had sent numerous envoys bearing gifts as well as elders and Chiefs from the tribe on the western bank, advising he meant no harm and would pay for food and any goods they could supply. When the envoy's severed heads were hurled into the Carthaginian camp just as darkness fell, Hannibal moved from negotiation to action.

As dawn broke, Hannibal dispatched small boats to probe the eastern bank and assess the Volcae positions while searching for landing points. The boats were eventually driven back by missile fire, then chased off as the Volcae put to the water in their own boats. With his reconnaissance done, Hannibal ordered the cutting down of more trees to make larger rafts and called a council of war with his Generals.

The midday's heat was such that Hannibal had the meeting table placed outside his tent, conducting his briefing in the open air.

Unrolling a parchment map, he laid it on the table using small river stones as paperweights. The map showed details of the river, settlements and the huge forests that covered the eastern bank.

"Gentlemen, within six days we will be ready to cross the Rhone, we would be over there now but for the refusal of a safe passage. With the completion of the larger rafts, we can drop greater amounts of men quicker onto the eastern bank once the crossing begins. We'll be landing on an opposed shoreline under missile fire and determined attack once we hit the far bank, yes Mago?"

"Why not threaten to kill some of the Volcae this side of the river? That should make the bastards on the other bank reconsider letting us through, they're the same tribe are they not?"

"Same tribe but a different branch, General." Sergatatonix replied raising his eyebrows and laughing a little. "It wouldn't make a blind bit of difference if you slew them all. In fact, they'd probably be happy if you did!" Standing back from the table, the General of the Gallic infantry was a bear of a man, a full head and a half taller than any of the command group. His thick arms covered in gold and silver bracelets, folded across a massive chest. His drooping moustache matching the rusty orange of his hair.

"Baal's breath, Serg! Don't you Gauls ever get tired of killing each other?" Mago asked.

The bear shrugged. "Only when there are Romans to kill instead!"

As laughter broke out Sergatatonix approached the table, leaning on his massive arms he scanned the map.

"It would be easier to find a ford and force it, instead of this amphibious landing General."

"True Sergatatonix! But that means more marching and no doubt a hard fight at the end of it as the Volcae will follow us along the bank as we go, however I have a plan."

The assembled men smiled amongst themselves, knowing their General left nothing to chance and his plans were always well thought out and sound.

"There is a ford but its some two hundred stades up river from here. I'm dispatching our Spanish cavalry under General Maharabal there tonight after dark." The men's heads craned over the map. "Over to you, General Maharabal."

The older man got to his feet and spread another map over the top of the first, the seated men helping transfer the stones. He scratched his beard looking thoughtful, giving the others a moment or two to study the map.

"This map shows the upper reaches of the river in better detail and where we can cross, see here? The horse's hooves will be wrapped in sacking and they will leave the camp a squadron at a time to keep the noise down. To keep our hostile unfriends busy across the river, we will also mount a diversionary attack on their bank. Nothing serious, just enough to probe their defences and make sure they have enough to concern them other than the movements of our cavalry. This attack will take place on dark so we don't envisage too much trouble from arrows and thus few casualties. We estimate it will take five days for the cavalry to reach the ford, cross and return back down the other bank to attack." He traced his finger over the map following the river and showing his proposed route. "We'll time our waterborne attack to coincide with that of the cavalry for the morning of the sixth day."

"What of the timing General? Do we use signals or work off the sunrise?" Hasdrubal the Elder, asked.

"We'll use both; we need to be in position before sunrise and the Spaniards will raise smoke so we know the attack has begun. The difficult part is timing the crossing so we hit the bank just as the Spaniards attack. Too early and we could lose a lot of men against the full force of the Volcae, too late and they may have time to gather their wits and contend with both the Spaniards and us."

"May I?" Hannibal interrupted.

"Sir." Maharabal conceded.

"We'll conduct and time trips across the river over the next few days, then work that time against sunrise on the sixth day, we'll endeavour to land just as the Spaniards hit the Volcae rear. Any more questions gentlemen?" Hannibal waited, smiling warmly. "No questions? Right, Mago, I want wicker screens made for the front and sides of the rafts and you and our heavy assault troops up front. Force me a beachhead so the light infantry and the heavy cavalry can get ashore!"

"You'll be in command of the eastern bank by breakfast on the sixth day brother, I promise it!"

****

Dawn of the sixth day announced itself with rolling thunder and a torrential downpour. The dirty, grey-black skies refused to brighten and Hannibal watched fretfully, trying to differentiate between rain clouds and the last of the darkness as he searched for the first chinks of light. Looking to the eastern bank, he saw only curtains of rain drifting across the water obscuring his view any further, too early to look for smoke he reasoned. He already had men aboard the boats and heading across the river. To allow for the drift of the fast current the craft launched a stade or two upstream, cutting across the flow at an obtuse angle.

Despite a messenger to say the Spanish cavalry had crossed the ford successfully and unopposed, Hannibal remained apprehensive. By calculation, the Spaniards should now be in position and ready for this morning's assault but three days was a long time to be in enemy country and hidden, especially for thousands of horses. Hannibal paced the bank, though his faith in his officer's abilities was resolute, his concern was the unavoidable time span between communications. Forcing himself to stand still rather than appear anxious, he watched solemnly as the black shapes that were rafts and boats came down and across the river, his fingers however still tap, tapping on his sword scabbard. He quietly mouthed another prayer to Baal and then to Tanith for good measure, the timing needed to be exact or many men were going to die.

Balaam and his men were crammed shoulder to shoulder onto a raft made from beech logs nailed and lashed together. The men cursed and swore as they slipped on the smooth, wet bark when the platform rocked in the current, all were unhappy at being separated from their beloved horses. The horses were roped in strings behind the raft and swimming their way over amidst snorts and heavy breathing. With no breeze and the high wicker screens enclosing the raft, the rank odour of stale sweat was well contained and nauseatingly strong. Some men had vomited, either from the previous evenings over indulgence, fear or unfamiliarity on the water, the acid smell from the glutinous liquid adding to the stink. Some urinated where they stood as bladders became uncomfortably full, the liquids mixing and adding to the stink and already precarious footing.

The men were heavily armed; all carried a shield and fighting spear as well as sidearms. Helmets had been fitted, as there would be no time once they hit the bank. Balaam and Harbro peered from behind the wicker screens scanning the still shadowy shoreline. The warriors were quiet, soft whispers from mumbled prayers just audible above the noise of retching and the soft splash of paddles and poles that propelled the raft forward. Baldor was sandwiched between Gestix and Armaco; both were deep in prayer so despite his nerves giving him the need to talk, he left them to their devotions. His stomach rumbled and churned. Unsure whether the breakfast he'd eaten was a good idea and whether it was going to come back up, he tried to swallow and found his mouth bone dry. Leaning his spear against his shoulder, he eased the cameo from his corselet and rubbed his thumb over it, wishing for …

"Shit! We're coming into range." Clatters and thuds from arrows striking the wicker and the raft timbers followed the shout. Men came alive, unfinished prayers cut irreverently short. Balaam took one last look at the hazy light creeping into the sky behind the veil of driving rain then turned to address the men.

"No signal yet! We'll be in the shallows shortly and under attack. The assault troops are not ashore and it looks like the damned Spaniards are late!" His tone was grim.

An arrow slipped through a gap in the wicker screens and hit a warrior in the throat, spraying hot, wet blood in crimson arcs over his comrades as he twisted and fell.

"Get your damned shields up!" Balaam roared.

The warrior gagged and choked, grasping at his throat and the wooden shaft that transfixed it, his breath gargling and whistling as he tried to breathe, more arrows clattered against the wicker as battle cries started up from the bank.

"Horse holders to the rear!" Harbro called.

Gestix and Armaco pushed Baldor towards the rear of the raft to stand with the other horse marshals.

"Grab the horses lad, we'll see you on the bank but watch yourself you hear? Keep that shield up!" The big man wiped rain from his face and winked before grasping Baldor's forearm in reassurance, he ducked as an arrow skidded over his shield. As the raft pushed closer to shore the rain of missiles intensified with arrows, javelins and slingshot coming at it. Most rattled and banged harmlessly against the wicker like hail stones, inevitably some slipped through gaps and men grunted and screamed as metal tore flesh, adding blood and a body or two to the piss and puke.

"Steady lads!" Balaam ordered above the incessant metal hail and the screams and groans of the wounded. "Half a stade now and we'll be in the shallows so keep together! ... Shields locked! ... Horse holders! Bring the horses forward as soon as you feel the river bed beneath you, we'll have to mount under fire!" He turned to Harbro. "The bloody assault troops are not ashore yet to keep the bastards busy! And where in Hade's name's those Spaniards?"

"No signal yet sir." Harbro replied peering through a slit between the screens.

Balaam glanced to the heavens, squinting at the now heavier deluge of rain; dawn had truly broken with indigo, charcoal and purple coloured clouds showing in the pale light.

"Godless, heathen, bastard Spanish!" He muttered then looked to the riverbank once more judging distance. Drawing his sword and peering through the wicker he called to his men "Make ready! ... Make ready! .... Ready! ... Now, go, go!"

The wicker screens were hurled to one side and most of the men in the first rank fell immediately, transfixed and feathered like roosters by a salvo of arrows. From behind, warriors climbed over their wounded and dying comrades and jumped into the shallows. To the rear, Baldor mounted a still swimming, Risto holding the reins of four other mounts swimming behind. He struggled to keep his seat, slipping and floating over Risto's back as the other animals reins pulled on his arm. They strained wide-eyed, frantic to be away from the mayhem, desperate to touch hoof to ground but not wanting to head into the maelstrom out front. Finally, Risto's hooves contacted the shale of the riverbed and he ploughed out of the water in a burst of spray. Baldor clamped his thighs tightly on the wet, slippery flanks heaving on the reins of the others forcing them reluctantly after him. Just when he thought his arm would wrench from its socket, they too found the riverbed and came on in a shower of spray and foam amidst snorts and whickers. Pulling his shield in front of his body, he hid behind it while kicking Risto's flanks, driving him towards the huddle of fellow warriors pushing slowly ashore. With the water still thigh deep, men hid behind shields supporting one another against the missile storm. At the foot of the bank, battle was already joined. Many of the Volcae, driven wild with battle madness had left their defensive position and rushed down to attack the heavy assault troops who were just clearing the waters edge. Bloodlust and fury smashed into the Carthaginians, checking their advance and forcing them back into the water, men fell to be trampled, drowned and slaughtered. Mago, resplendent in black armour and purple sash, roared like a maddened bull for his men to hold. He lay about the enemy with Herculean blows with his bodyguards and Standard-bearer fighting alongside him. His men seeing his example renewed their efforts and fighting tooth and nail began holding the line. With neither side gaining advantage, the bodies piled up in the shallows, men slashing and stabbing over the heightening wall of flesh and blood.

Baldor and the other horse holders came alongside the mercenary company, Balaam pointing with his sword to the horses and shouting for the men to mount. It was no easy manoeuvre under fire, some of the first to mount being hit by arrows and javelins and falling or rolling backwards into the water. Horses too met their end as arrows thudded into them, collapsing with whinnies and snorts on top of and alongside their riders. Baldor's heart pounded, his body tensed in anticipation of an arrow thudding into him at any moment. He expected every breath to be his last as men and animals died like flies around him. The horses he held skittered and jumped as bodies drifting on the current floated into their legs. At last, Gestix, Armaco and the other warriors were mounting and the arrow storm slackening somewhat, as all along the bank more craft discharged their human cargo, giving more targets for the Volcae archers and missile troops.

"Follow me! Get out of the water! Come on! Ride the bastard's down!" Balaam shouted, pointing up the bank with his sword. Suddenly, just upstream of the mercenaries, more of the Volcae spilled from the bank towards the waters edge but they weren't attacking the Carthaginians in the water but looking back over their shoulders to the forest behind. The Carthaginians in the shallows began to cheer and bang their swords on shields, the men arriving in boats taking up the call. The noise spread down the battle line, swords pointing beyond the bank where clouds of smoke rose into the rain.

"The Spaniards! … The Spaniards are here!" Someone shouted as Spanish cavalry spilled onto the riverbank where the Volcae had exited moments before.

Without any command the stalled Carthaginian ranks hurled themselves back at the Volcae, who confused and unsettled by the attack in their rear were unsure whether to fight to the front or behind. Flames rose behind the Volcae as the Spaniards fired their village and drove towards the river. Caught in the pincer movement the tribesmen tried to disengage. The Carthaginian infantry exploited their newfound advantage and pressed the retreating Volcae closely, harrying and killing them as they ran, the cavalry riding them down and slaughtering them, as the retreat became a panicked rout. Those too proud to surrender sold their lives as dearly as they could.

Baldor and the remains of the mercenary company had driven the Volcae in front of them back over the bank and into the forest where the fleeing tribesmen scattered. Balaam wheeled his horse about in front of his men barking orders. "Form your squadrons! First one on me, the second on Harbro, third on Armaco. Don't separate! We're vulnerable among the trees if they rally. Ride them down lads, kill them all, make them pay!" The fleeing Volcae dodged ahead of the cavalry, slipping through the trees like rabbits fleeing dogs. The mercenaries, bloodied and angry from their mauling in the shallows drove the running men through the woods, herding them like cattle and spearing or cutting down any they caught. Some did rally, in two's or three's or small groups as they realised there was no escape. The mercenaries, riding close bowled the standing men over like ninepins, a litter of dead and dying bodies marking their passage through the forest.

The mercenaries reined in when they reached the village, where, despite the mornings heavy rain the diligent application of fire under the thatch and in the huts had most of the dwellings burning fiercely. Shading their faces from the heat they looked for further signs of resistance, in sharp contrast to the noise and mayhem on the beach the village was now eerily quiet. The odd shout or scream drifted back from the riverbank amidst the dry crackle of burning thatch and low hanging branches on nearby trees as they too caught fire. The place was deserted except for the dead scattered on the road and around the huts. Bodies of women and children lay amongst the fallen warriors, Baldor wanted to turn away when he saw the broken bodies and blood staining the ground in dark red pools but his eyes refused to obey. Shock at the carnage before him held his gaze, like some butchers yard the corpses were missing heads and limbs and horrendous wounds laid the flesh open, many had the iron javelin of the Spaniards lodged in them. Some had been ridden down, squashed and trampled into the ground, their bodies flattened. He lowered his spear, the battle madness fading and the bloodlust subsiding, he felt sick to the stomach. Despite his willingness to kill in retaliation for the horror inflicted upon them in the shallows he recoiled at the thought of killing women and children. A large, shaggy dog as big as a week-old calf prowled between two huts that had almost burned out. The animal barked savagely at the mounted men then sniffed and nuzzled a dead child before standing over the body snarling and baring huge yellow teeth at the mounted watchers.

"Right lads; back to the river let's see to our wounded. There's no more to do here, anything of value will have been taken by the Spaniards." Balaam called as he pulled his horse around the way they had come.

As Baldor turned Risto about he saw the dog gently licking blood from the child, the little blonde head moving as the huge animal lapped before whimpering again. He watched as the dog pushed the body with its nose then licked some more before throwing its head back to howl. Baldor sat motionless and stared; the howl seemed to go right through him, a pitiful, demented, lost howl, reminding him of his own loss. Sickened at the slaughter and wondering why the people had not left before the battle started and how men could ride women and children down, he vomited up his breakfast.

"Come on lad, lets away!" Gestix was alongside and pulling gently on his arm. "It can't always be helped Baldor, the women and children are mixed through with the warriors, there would be no time to differentiate." Gestix spoke quietly, the ghosts of his past also awakened.

Baldor wiped a hand over his lips and spat to clear his sticky mouth.

"Come on Baldor, we have our lads to see to."

Baldor turned to follow Gestix, his body working but his mind numb and eyes unseeing; sitting woodenly he let Risto follow the other horses. At the riverbank, the men found a carpet of bodies littering the ground to the waters edge and into the shallows where the fighting had been the fiercest. The dead lay in a long, partly submerged line where the ranks had fought each other to a standstill. Limbs stuck up and out, spears, arrows and swords stuck up from the mound like the quills of a porcupine. The rafts run aground in the shallows were laden with the dead, wounded and dying. Where the current eddied back on itself, bodies floated in slow circles gently knocking into each other and staining the green water a dark red ochre.

The gut wrenching work of tending the wounded and dying went on all day, the men pausing only for a drink and a brief rest, food being neither available nor looked for. Rain continued non-stop at the same heavy rate until evening drew in. The rays of the setting sun finally breaking through the brass coloured clouds casting weak, washed-out, light and forming a wide rainbow. Twilight came and as the weary men pitched their tents, word passed of a successful battle and a relatively light casualty list. Exhausted and too tired to care, men stripped off their sodden clothes and rolled in their blankets.

****

The port of Massilia in southern Gaul was choked to overflowing with war galleys and large, broad-beamed transports of the Roman fleet. Commercial shipping was ordered and in the more reluctant cases, forced to stand off from the harbours and wharves; having to drop anchor offshore and wait as the Legions, fresh from their victory over the Boii and Insurbes disembarked. The Legions had moved fast after their victory. Leaving a token force to harry the retreating Gauls and ensure they did not regroup, they had burnt or buried their dead on the field. Sleeping only one night on the battlefield, they'd marched with the following dawn, heading southeastwards to the coast and the port of Pisa. Force marching, they'd averaged almost thirty Roman miles a day under the baking sun, carrying weapons and equipment, pausing briefly at noon for food then pushing on until early evening, any water required being drunk as they marched. The seriously wounded were transported on carts with the walking casualties following in their rear at a more sedate pace, these heading directly south to their barracks and Rome.

Legionnaires, horses, mules and equipment were now emptying onto the wharves to be marshalled, formed into column and sent northwest towards Tarascon at the eastern mouth of the Rhone. Since embarking at Pisa some five days ago, the Legionnaires had been crammed and penned in the holds of the ships. Far from having the chance to rest and recuperate on board after the forced march, they had suffered a nightmarishly, rough sea crossing. The abject fear of drowning or shipwreck had courted many, along with the inevitable seasickness. Having to remain below decks in the vomit-splattered quarters and stinking, fetid air, they'd had no chance to wash or shave. Sleep had been at the best fitful until sheer exhaustion had carried men to almost unconsciousness. Now, faced with another march they formed up awaiting their orders, too tired, queasy and dishevelled to complain or care. Despite their bone weariness and the filthy, dilapidated state of them, they relished the feeling of solid ground beneath their feet and the warm, fresh morning breeze that blew over them and steadily offshore.

Cornelius, jaded and weary as the rest straightened his back, hiding his tiredness as he walked the length of his Maniple exchanging words and greetings with the men, awaiting Gaius returning with their orders. Having suffered badly with seasickness he hadn't eaten a full meal in five days, subsisting on dry bread and water only, he felt his stomach grumble and bubble as the acids ate the lining. His eyes were bloodshot and black-ringed, his skin the white, deathly pallor of a corpse, he chewed mechanically on a piece of stale bread hoping the morsel would allay the stomach pains. Gaius, pushing through the ranks marched quickly towards him with a concerned look on his face that snapped him from his misery. Quickly and painfully swallowing the bread, he asked.

"What are our orders sir?"

"We're to march westwards towards Tarascon."

"Just as we thought then."

"Yes, but Hannibal is already across the Pyrenees and approaching the Rhone!"

"He's moving fast! So, we've less marching to do and battle comes quicker." Cornelius smiled, the black rings under his eyes wrinkling.

"Ever the optimist Cornelius!" Gaius slapped a hand on the younger's shoulder; turning him away from the men, he lowered his voice. "Your father and Consul Tiberius are sure Hannibal will try to force his way here and assail Massilia. It makes perfect sense to me too, being our staging post between Rome and Spain. The difficulty for us is three fold. One, the shape we are in, two, if he closes quickly seeking battle we have little time to recuperate and thirdly … thirdly, he may already have picked his ground and we'll have no choice but to face him on it." Gaius spoke bitterly as he fastened his helmet strap.

"We can beat these Carthaginians sir!" Cornelius replied confidently. "Tired we may be, looking and smelling like shit, certainly! The finest army in the world and unbeatable, definitely!"

Gaius smiled and nodded, then laughed gently.

"You're right Cornelius, forgive me." Gaius collected himself and cleared his throat. "It's I who should be talking you up, not the other way about. Let the bastards come! We have beaten them before and can do it again." The fire returned to his voice and he turned back to his men.

"Form up you idle bastards! You've laid around long enough! Form up!"

Men pulled themselves to attention, the years of iron discipline always produced a response when a Centurion bellowed.

"Prepare to march! It'll sweat the bloody sickness out of you! A cavalry screen is riding ahead to locate these Carthaginians, we estimate a day maybe two before battle, so you will be ready!"

A few muted grumbles came back from the ranks.

"I said you will be ready! … What did I say?"

"Ready … ready sir … ready." Came back disjointedly and quietly.

Gaius slapped his vine cane hard against his greave, the whoosh then the crack of the blow focusing the men.

"Men of the Boar! What did I say?" His voice rose to a parade ground shout.

"Ready sir!" Shouted back in unison.

Gaius nodded satisfactorily. "Good, now let's get moving! Carry on Optio."

Chapter Twenty two

Two days following the battle for the eastern bank, the sun was up splitting the skies as the first cock crowed, the damp chill of the night replaced by fresh morning heat. Baldor rolled in his blankets as the scents and noises of the waking world drew him from slumber. He became aware of a deep drumming, rumbling and the ground vibrating beneath him. His nose detected the strong smell of horses mixing with his own body odour and the stuffy, musty scent of the tent walls and roof drying with the sun. His eyes flicked open as the tempo and vibration increased to see Armaco and Gestix standing at the tent entrance looking southeastwards. Framed in the doorway he saw the reason for the rumbling as Numidian cavalry passed at a steady trot. The lightly armed, black warriors on their mustard coloured ponies filed past, the men's white teeth caught in smiles, chatter, and framed against their dark skins. Unable to hear the conversation between Armaco and Gestix, he dragged himself from his blankets and went to look.

Peering over his friends shoulders, he saw it was a sizeable contingent of men but heading in the opposite direction of travel to the army. The rumble built to a deafening pounding making conversation impossible and the three just took in the passing spectacle, the elder two already counting heads. Before long the cavalcade was gone, the additional odour of fresh horse dung mixing with the baking bread and goat meat cooking on the fire near the tent.

"Near enough five hundred of them I reckon, Gestix?"

"Aye, all of that I'd say ... and all heading south."

"That's too large a party for scouting." Baldor added.

"Dead right lad, way too large! They are carrying a few days' worth of rations as well. Hmm, there's something afoot? Maybe the Captain will be able to shed some light on it."

"Breakfasts up lads." Harbro shouted above the sizzle and spit of frying meat.

They joined Harbro around the fire, all sniffing appreciatively at the smell. Malo was finishing off patties of millet dough on the firestones. He nipped each piece between finger and thumb assessing its consistency before passing one to each man. Marko was mixing up hot water, honey and cloves in horn cups. Harbro shared the goat strips onto the platters and spooned some of the fat over it, the men dipping the bread and relishing the combination of fresh bread soaked in meat juices. Nods and grunts of satisfaction were the only conversation.

With both banks now under Carthaginian control, the baggage train and the elephants were to be brought over. Hannibal, as ever was taking no chances and retained a rearguard of infantry and cavalry screens to ensure the baggage was not interfered with. Balaam's men were part of the rearguard and once more back on the western bank. Balaam was in his usual foul mood and moaning bitterly that they were, outriders not quartermasters and bloody arse wipes for the victualler's, peddlers, whores and traders that followed in every armies wake. Carts and wagons laden with timber, spare weapons, flasks of wine and engineering equipment had begun ferrying across at first light. Mules, tied nose to tail and carrying disassembled field artillery and ammunition made their way to the rivers edge. Their long, bending strings stretched back two to three stades from the barge loading points, the brown coloured lines moving slowly over the ground like giant earthworms. Herds of cattle, sheep and goats were also driven towards the waiting barges. This walking larder mustered and escorted by herders who harried the animals down the trail with shouts and whacks from sticks. At the barges, quartermasters counted the animals as they passed, an apprentice recording the numbers by cutting notches into a tally stick. Further downstream and downwind of all the activity the elephants made their way to the waiting craft.

Keeping their horses at a distance and upwind, the mercenaries watched as the loading of the great, grey beasts began. Huge rafts constructed of oak logs were tied up at the waters edge awaiting the animals boarding. The elephants followed in single file behind the matriarch with a mahout mounted upon each one, a handler, walking alongside holding a hooked stick behind one of the animal's ears or over it's trunk to guide it in the required direction. As they plodded closer to the barges the matriarch suddenly raised her trunk and trumpeted loudly raising her head up and down quickly. She slowed and stopped while the rest of the herd took up the trumpeting call, raising an unearthly din. Despite the distance from the beasts, the mercenary's horses shied and stamped at the noise. Some of the replacement mounts bucked and kicked at the unfamiliar sound, tipping their riders into the dirt. The men moved their mounts further back, fighting and struggling to calm and bring them under control. Finally, well away from the trumpeting animals and with a semblance of order restored, the men had a chance to speak.

"How are we going to operate next to them? The horses won't abide their noise let alone their stink." Baldor asked Gestix and Armaco.

"Familiarity Baldor, you gradually expose the horses to them just like when you break a horse to a rider. After a while, they'll become accustomed and will settle. The noise and smell are the weapons as you've just witnessed. To untrained cavalry the affect can be catastrophic."

"Baal almighty, look!" Armaco interrupted, pointing back to the elephants.

Near the water chaos ensued. The matriarch was rearing on her hind legs refusing to be driven onto the raft, the animals in her rear had also gone berserk and were milling around trumpeting loudly. The mahouts and guides trying to control them were knocked over, then crushed and trampled in the mayhem. Eventually the matriarch made a dash away from rafts, heading towards the treeline. The rest of the herd followed leaving broken, flattened bodies and some panicky handlers in their wake.

"Do we go down and help sir?" Harbro asked still patting and settling his mount.

"Hades will freeze over first Harbro! Leave the bloody experts to sort it out. Cavalrymen belong with horses not elephants. We're security screens not nursemaids … split the lads into pairs, patrol up and downstream, rotate them in periods until dark. I don't envisage any trouble but …"

"I know sir; we haven't lived this long by being slack."

"Damn right! We'll camp near the river at those willow trees I showed you. Send the remainder of the men after me."

"Yes sir!" Harbro pulled his mount around to organise the patrols as Balaam rode away.

Gestix and Baldor found themselves one of the first patrols and sent upstream, they elected to follow close to the riverbank.

"What or who are we supposed to be looking for Gestix?"

"Potential trouble lad, anything untoward?" Gestix replied matter of factly.

"From where though? The Volcae on this bank are friendly, if the others were to rally it would be on the other bank, surely?"

Gestix shrugged. "You're probably right but it's wise to post rearguards and screens, security of your forces is paramount, especially where the baggage train is concerned. Many an army has been caught napping and lost their baggage; over confident and comfortable is not a good state. Anyway, what would we be doing if we weren't patrolling?"

"Sleeping would be good!"

"You can't still be tired lad? You were abed till after sun up; had breakfast made for you … I don't know, the youth of today, now when I was young …"

"Spare me please! No, no let me see, you were up before it was light infact you were up before you went to bed, then you went out and caught breakfast, collecting the wood to cook it on as you went. Those were the days!" Baldor laughed heartily, Gestix raised a fist and shook it at him, unable to hide a grin himself.

The pair meandered along the bank though remaining vigilant, the sun warming their backs. They heard the call of a moorhen hidden somewhere along the water's edge and the lazy drone of honeybees working from one flower to another. The smell of wild garlic, damp vegetation and the river itself was strong in their noses and out on the water the occasional splash of jumping fish taking flies was all that disturbed the peace.

"Beautiful eh?" Gestix said passing a waterskin to Baldor.

Baldor rinsed his mouth and spat then took a long drink. "It certainly is. My father was right, there is a huge world outside Carthage and travel does broaden experience. I've seen things this last year that I wouldn't have believed otherwise."

They rounded a looping bend in the river where the water eddied, swirling into an indent in the bank, out of the main flow the current was markedly slowed. Women from the village lined the bank washing clothes, many of which already laid up the bank behind them or draped over bushes drying in the sun. Some of the older women sang as they worked, the younger ones distracted with chatter and platting daisy flowers into necklaces. The little ones played, chasing each other and the dogs that accompanied them. It was one of these dogs that announced the men's approach with deep, throaty barks.

Gestix pulled his mount up, motioning Baldor to do likewise. The women hearing the barking and seeing the reason quickly gathered their children to them, shepherding them into groups. One or two slipped small daggers from sheaths at their belts, discreetly letting the weapon filled hand fall slowly to their sides. Gestix raised an open hand in greeting and called quietly.

"We mean you no harm."

The women spoke quietly among themselves, never once taking their eyes from the two men as they assessed any perceived threat.

"Come on lad, we can ride around, give them some space eh?"

Baldor nodded but as he turned Risto away, he noticed some of the women pointing at him and chattering excitedly. As they swung wide of the women a few of the younger ones broke away and walked boldly towards them. Baldor recognised two of them from their scrutiny of him in the village. The women suddenly all smiles and giddiness approached Gestix, calling for him to halt. Gestix reined up and looked at Baldor, shrugging his shoulders. The women bunched up around his horse some stroking the animal others asking questions of where the men were going and what were they doing, their mood a mix of humour and mischief. The two that had eyed Baldor in the village stood off to one side studying him while talking and giggling, Baldor found himself blushing beneath their gaze. Embarrassed, overheating and self-conscious, he unbuckled and removed his helmet and this made the two women worse, with more smiles, giggles and whispered comments. One of the women near Gestix pushed closer and asked in husky tones.

"Does your friend have a woman?" The rest giggled as the question was asked.

"We don't really care if he has a woman! He can have another can't he?" Another said as an uproar of laughter broke out.

"How old is he?" Asked another.

Gestix looked at Baldor, raising his eyebrows and smiling when he saw his friend's discomfort.

"Why don't you ask him yourself?" He replied amicably. "He speaks Gallic as well as you or me."

This time it was the turn of the women to look a little abashed. Gestix, looking at Baldor and then back to the women, laughed heartily. The more vocal woman of the group recovered her composure and turning to Baldor, boldly asked if he was interested in a good Volcae woman for a wife. Trying to stifle a laugh when he saw Baldor's face colouring once more, Gestix snorted with the effort and burst out laughing.

"Watch out Baldor!" He managed between laughing, snorting and breathing.

The woman pointed at the two young women standing to one side.

"Reannon, the small, dark haired one there, she'll make you a good wife, if you can tame her!" The woman cackled and the rest joined in with whoops and more laughter.

Reannon stepped forward of her companion. Her small hand rolled into a fist and raised threateningly, a flash of anger across her sculptured features, her brown-black hair tumbling in lustrous cascades over her shoulder as the movement dislodged her hair tie.

"You mouthy old fishwife! I can find my own man without your intervention, if I want him I'll ask him."

The vocal woman eased back into the relative safety of the group. The others mewed like cats and made clawing motions with their hands at the exchange between the pair. Reannon ignoring the teasing, drew herself up proudly lifting her head and chin and walked gracefully to Baldor's horse. Her dark green eyes shone like emeralds against her pale skin and dark hair, her small nose finished petitely above delicate cherry lips. Baldor as embarrassed as he was, was mesmerized by her beauty and stared at her.

"Well, Bal ...dor!" She struggled with the unfamiliar name. "I am a free-born woman with a right to choose a husband." Her voice flowed soft and warm, like honey poured on a summer's day. "My father presents suitor after suitor to me, mostly they are ignorant, uncultured oafs but you … you look different! Are you looking for a good woman?"

Baldor was speechless, embarrassed and taken aback by the directness and brazenness of the woman who spoke so confidently and casually as if discussing a business deal, he could only stare. Her beauty however sent a shiver up his spine, despite the day's heat. He snapped himself from his reverie, thinking quickly.

"No … no, I'm not looking for a woman." He replied bluntly turning his horse away, hearing the other women laughing and jeering as he did so.

Gestix intercepted him before he'd ridden far. He came alongside and leaned across to speak keeping his voice low.

"That wasn't well done!"

"What do you mean? … What am I supposed to say?" He snapped, his embarrassment giving way to anger.

"It doesn't matter what you say, it's the way you say it! Remember these are proud people."

"But she doesn't even know me! It's ludicrous! What kind of woman asks a man if he's looking for a wife?"

"A Gallic woman! It's not uncommon!"

"You mean it's normal?"

"For a free-born woman yes! Unlike Roman, Greek or Carthaginian women, she has the right to choose. That aside Baldor, you know me, you should know my people? Direct, honest, proud, like children really, we say what we think."

Baldor remained quiet.

"I think you could have handled that Reannon better, right now she'll be embarrassed, not by your rejection but by the way you did it. She paid you a compliment by asking for you interest, the least you could have done was to compliment her back as you decline. Manners and prestige lad, they're a must!"

Baldor chewed his lip as he thought. He looked to where the women stood and saw Reannon was being teased and laughed at, her beauty now, shaded by anger as she defended herself in the verbal exchange. He looked back at Gestix and sighed deeply.

"Give me a moment." He turned and walked his horse back to where Reannon stood. As he drew closer, the women fell silent.

"Reannon ... lady ... a word if I may?" He asked gently.

Reannon looked at him sternly her face coloured from the teasing and the put-down. She didn't answer but stared at him directly, the anger and fire in her eyes only adding to her beauty.

"Lady, you have done me much honour with the offer you made, much ... and I thank you for it. If I were to remain here I would happily fight any suitor your father offered in my stead." Noticing the women listening and Reannon's face lightening, he paused to let his words sink in. "However, I am passing through on my way to war and though you are the best reason I could find not to go, I must. ... Forgive me Reannon, though it is my loss." He bowed his head and smiled.

Reannon's head lifted, her outraged look replaced with a smile as warm as the sun.

He suddenly felt less confident and reached for his helmet to give his hands something to do while clearing his throat as he sought parting words. Reannon beat him to it.

"Farewell then Baldor, may your Gods keep you." She beckoned him to lean down then kissed him gently on the cheek.

The women giggled and cheered as Reannon walked proudly to her waiting friend. Baldor, blushing again pulled his mount around towards Gestix and the direction of their patrol.

"Nobly done Baldor ... we could always stay here you know!"

Baldor glowered causing Gestix to laugh again.

"You're enjoying this aren't you?"

Gestix tried to stop laughing but made a poor job of it, snorting and coughing with the effort.

"Bloody Gauls, all pride and stupid games!"

"Bear up Baldor, you've made a young lady very happy, but I wonder, was it because you turned her down?" He roared with laughter wiping tears from his eyes. "You have to admit she's beautiful, think on, it could have been worse, she might have had a face like a horse's arse!" Gestix continued to laugh and soon Baldor was infected by his friend's mirth. To see the big man laugh and cry tears like a child while he did so always lifted Baldor from the doldrums or away from his injured pride and he laughed himself.

****

Early afternoon came and the sun burned skin and heated armour, boiling the men inside it like crayfish in a pot. Helmets had long since been removed, the pair draping cloaks over their armour to keep the sun off. Each dismounted in turn and scooped river water up their arms and over their heads, enjoying the tepid water on their skin whilst the other kept watch.

"Here Baldor, this helps keep you cool." Gestix undid his neck cloth and soaked it then wrung it out loosely and offered it to Baldor gesturing for him to give his cloth in exchange. "It picks up any breeze and the coolness enters your blood through the big veins on your neck. When it dries out, soak it again."

As Gestix remounted, Baldor started the conversation again.

"Does this feel more like home to you with the rivers, the mountains and the greenery? It's very different from what I grew up with in Carthage."

"Yes, I was born into such as this but home … home was what your parents gave me, may the God's bless them." He bowed his head respectably. "I've lived longer in Carthage than I did in the hills and mountains of my birth, my people and their way of life are but a distant memory now."

"You've never spoken much of that life, is it too painful? I don't mean to intrude." He added quickly.

The clip clop of hooves and the gentle gurgle of the river were the only noises to be heard for a while and Baldor wondered if he had overstepped the mark into his friend's privacy, then Gestix cleared his throat to speak.

"I was much the same age as you are now and also had a wife … until the Romans came. Life dealt to me similarly then as it has to you."

Baldor saw the sorrow appear on Gestix's face.

"I'm sorry, I didn't mean to …"

"It's alright lad." He said managing a sad smile. "It's right that you should know. After all, I have known all about you since you were a lump in your mother's belly. Comrades in arms should be familiar with each other's lives. Then if death comes, the right words can be said to warn those that have gone before of your coming."

Gestix looked ahead as he spoke, his eyes fixed on some point in the distance. It was some time before he started again.

"Her name was Brecca and if I knew her aright she'll be asking me where I've been, when my time comes that is." He laughed a little, his face lightening. "Yes, that is exactly what she'll say." They rode a little further; Baldor remained quiet, sensing that Gestix wasn't finished. The sadness returned to his face, his eyes losing their sparkle of his distant memory. He began again, picking his words as if every syllable caused him pain.

"The boys … the boys will be waiting too …"

Baldor had always anticipated a wife or a lover in Gestix's life but the mention of children surprised him.

"The boys?" He said softly. "Your boys?"

"Yes, twins. Cadeyrn and Caedmon … my fine strong boys, they too will be waiting with their mother for me. They would have been four years older than you are now … as tall as you are … I surmise. And good men … good men, just like you." Gestix turned to look at Baldor, his eyes watery but he smiled.

Baldor coloured. "You do me much honour Gestix and … and I am truly sorry for your loss, it must be hard to bear?"

"No harder than your own."

"But I've had you to help me with my grief, who did you have?"

"Your parents' lad, they filled the void for me and your father was my true friend. Your mother, may Epona bless her! Your mother cared for me and accepted me unquestioningly into her home, loving me like a long lost brother."

"And you … you never looked for another woman?"

"No … no." He said slowly. "No one could replace Brecca, not as far as a companion or a wife goes, no. She was the one, the only one for me." He looked straight ahead as he spoke. "As the years passed and when I was lonely or the need took me I'd visit the brothels in the city but mostly I was content on my own."

"I feel the same. Women, the right women that is, they leave gaps that can't be filled."

"You're young yet Baldor, you should let someone try." Gestix offered tentatively.

"Like Reannon?" Baldor grinned trying to lighten the sadness.

"Nooooo, but there'll be someone sometime and you should give them a chance."

"We'll see … we'll see, but right now I am happy the way things are."

Gestix smiled and nodded. "Fair enough lad, as long as you're happy then I'm happy." He was pleased at what he'd heard; being able to talk to Baldor about women, his loss and the future, without him becoming moody or angry told Gestix the lad was almost whole again.

The pair made their way back to the camp their patrol over; as they approached, they met Malo and Marko.

"Nothing to report lads. Just watch out for the women, they're a handful." Gestix called as they passed.

Baldor and Gestix found Balaam resting with his back against a tree, honing the edge on his sword and enjoying the sun. He was clearly in better humour for he listened intently as they delivered their report, asking his questions in a civil tone. Report done, they tethered the horses leaving them to crop the lush grass. They joined Harbro and Armaco in the shade of the other trees, Harbro passing them some bread and fruit.

"That's all we have till we're re-supplied. Don't say anything to the Captain but Malo's on the look out for meat as they patrol … he took his bow." He winked as he spoke.

"We'll eat well tonight then!" Gestix said confidently. "I've never known him miss." He bit into an apple. "Did you find out what was to do with the Numidians the other morning?" He munched loudly as he spoke.

"Romans!"

"Where?" Gestix and Baldor answered together.

"Word is they'll land at Massalia so the General dispatched the Numidians to take a look. There could be a battle coming."

"Well then, let's make the most of the peace at the moment!" Gestix sat down heavily, sighing in contentment as his back found the support of the tree trunk.

****

The following morning saw the last of the supplies and baggage safely over the river, with only the elephants still to cross. Since the last debacle with the animals, the engineers had manufactured more raft sections but made them much larger using logs from the tallest and straightest pine trees. When completed, these huge sections were lashed together forming a causeway some thirty cubits wide and which stretched almost a third of the distance across the river. Ropes tied to the floating platforms were pegged into the bank upstream, holding them from moving and drifting in the current. Over the timber, labourers had spread and leveled earth and rushes, giving a flat, natural seeming platform upon which to walk and reassure the animals they were still on solid ground. At the end of the causeway, the raft itself waited, also covered in earth and rushes but with a heavy, corral type, holding fence and gate, encompassing it. In front of the raft, small boats complete with oar crews were ready with towropes running from their vessels to the raft. Once the elephants were aboard, these boats would tow the raft over the river.

The mercenaries lined the bank to watch. Baldor in particular, having an appreciation for the time and labour involved for such construction, marveled at the scale and speed of the work done.

"How did they build that so fast? There was nothing there two days ago!"

"Organisation lad, combined with technical ability and manpower." Gestix answered.

"Bloody elephants! They're not worth the trouble." Balaam muttered.

No one argued and the men watched as the animals were walked to the causeway. Again, the matriarch led with the rest following in pairs, she curled her trunk upwards as she walked sniffing at the air. She walked onto the causeway with no sign of panic. Despite her weight, the sections hardly moved as her huge feet slapped down on the earth and rush strewn timber, the rest of the troop happy to follow in her wake.

"Looks like they're going to manage alright this time." Baldor said.

"Aye, we should be able to follow now as they're the last of the baggage train. What do you think, Captain?" asked Harbro.

"Just waiting for our orders and we're off." Balaam swatted at a fly as he answered.

As the elephants filled the first barge to capacity the rest were held back from starting up the causeway. The Bosuns in each of the boats shouting orders to ready oars and for the men on the causeway to cut the raft loose. The elephants still on shore trumpeted to those afloat, the separation of the troop causing anxiety to some of the beasts. As the first raft slipped clear of the bank, the second was quickly maneuvered into place and the next batch of animals herded up the causeway. In contrast to the previous attempt, the elephants tried to trot up the makeshift road so eager were they to follow their herd mates, the mahout's and handlers trying frantically to slow and control them.

The second raft loaded quickly and set off across the river following the first; the third and final group being herded and loaded in the same fashion.

"All done!" Armaco said.

"They're not over yet." Balaam put in, grudgingly.

All three rafts were on the water and the first more than half way across. As it hit the main current it began to swing quickly, causing the matriarch to trumpet in alarm, immediately bringing a cacophony of calls back. The animals jostled nervously and the raft rocked, their shifting weight exaggerating the platform rise and fall and causing further alarm. The cries of the mahouts trying to calm them came back over the water, while on the following rafts the other animals took up the calls of distress and also began panicking. On the first raft, one of the beasts lost its footing and went down heavily on its hindquarters smashing the fence rail. The animal next to it falling and rolling over the half-sitting beast then off the raft, trumpeting loudly as it hit the water.

"Oh shit! I thought it was all going to well!" Harbro said shaking his head.

"Told you, bloody stinking monstrosities!" Balaam sneered.

The panic spread to all three rafts and the animals trumpeted, pushed, reared and broke the rails penning them in, the mahouts tipped into the water or crushed in the panic. The elephants in the water were at least swimming towards the opposite bank, their trunks raised above their heads. The animals still on the rafts hurled themselves into the river, not wanting to be separated from the rest of the herd.

"What a bloody mess! Still, its one way of getting them across. The poor bastards handling them didn't have a chance." Armaco shook his head. "I can't see any of the handlers swimming either, drowned or crushed? What a choice."

"Not our problem!" Balaam interjected coldly. "Right, the performance is over, you're all stood down till we receive our orders. Harbro, carry on!"

"Form column … fours! Back to the camp." Harbro bellowed, the mercenaries falling in behind him, riding four abreast.

The men dozed and lazed through the hot afternoon. Some slept and others diced while a few honed their weapon blades or cleaned equipment. The drumming of hooves broke the peace, the men rousing themselves to see a lone horseman galloping along the bank raising dust in his wake.

"This looks like trouble."

The horseman reined up making an impressive halt, the horse's hind legs sliding on the grass, the trailing dust cloud drifting around them.

"I'm looking for Captain Balaam, I have dispatches!" He called as his sweat-lathered horse skittered and sidestepped.

"That'll be me!" Balaam was on his feet and halfway to the horse.

"Captain Sir!" The messenger handed Balaam a leather tube from which Balaam shook out a parchment scroll.

"Wait you!" He turned his back on the messenger and stepped away a pace or so, reading. The mercenaries watched their Captain's face intently, trying to interpret the news from his expressions. After what seemed like an eternity, they saw Balaam's face cloud.

"It's trouble alright!" Harbro said under his breath.

Balaam folded the parchment quickly and pushed it into his corselet turning to the messenger.

"Give the General my compliments and tell him we'll be over directly, all's done here."

With a brief salute, the messenger sawed on the reins pulling his now, dust covered horse about, kicking savagely at its flanks sending it leaping forward spraying divots and dirt in its wake.

"Harbro, to me! Break camp! Mount up! Mount up! We're moving out."

Men leapt to their feet, possessions quickly gathered up, helmets strapped on and weapons loosened in sheaths as they grabbed their horse's reins. The small campfires had dirt kicked over them.

"What's to do sir?" Harbro enquired as he presented himself in front of Balaam.

"Romans! There's been a contact between them and that Numidian division we saw leaving the other morning. The bastards cut the Numidians up badly, some three hundred dead the message said. The Romans hounded them all the way back to our main camp and had time to assess what was going on before being chased off by the heavy cavalry. We're ordered to cross immediately; the camp's breaking on the other side, the whole army moves now!"

"To where sir?"

"Up the valley to the bloody Alps, we're taking the war to Italy!"

"Yes Sir!" Harbro saluted and headed to his horse calling for the men to form up as he went.

"Out of the mountains of rock, ice and snow came forth a river of flesh, blood and iron, for to make Rome a nation of widows."

Anon

Part 3

Chapter Twenty three

The Carthaginians headed north following the Rhone upstream. Like some giant silver serpent, the column stretched back thirty-five stades following the contours of the river. It was arrayed traditionally with scouts and screens out front, the infantry forming the vanguard and the baggage train secured by the cavalry in the rear. Keeping near the riverbank the going was flat and relatively easy, however the marching pace was not. Hannibal was unsure whether the Numidians had encountered a similar probing force or whether the Roman cavalry were part of their van with the Legions following close in their rear. Not wanting to fight an action in southern Gaul he pushed his men along at double pace, wishing to put as much distance between them and the Romans as possible.

The country through which they passed was beautiful and open; the flat river meadow covered in lush grass, yellow flowering ragwort and an abundance of blood-red poppies and other late summer blooms. Hazel, apple and walnut trees dotted the meadows and which the passing troops stripped bare of their ripening fruit, some eaten as they marched some stored for the journey. Swallows and swifts were collecting in flocks and filling the trees, the occasional dead or denuded tree seeming the preferred assembly point for them. To the east, the tree line of ash and beech grew thickly as they climbed from the meadow to gentle hills, in the distance the mountain ranges showed purple and blue. With only the north and eastern flanks to patrol and the west protected by the river, the mercenary patrols were halved, most of the men now riding in column behind their Captain.

The weather remained settled and dry and though the afternoon sun was still hot there was a noticeable coolness as evening drew in, darkness crept in quicker too, heralded by a chorus of late season grasshoppers and crickets.

The army continued through similar country for another three days, their march remaining brisk but uneventful and peaceful. They passed no settlements along the way, only the occasional shieling or herder's hut. These simple folk telling them they were now leaving the land of the Volcae and entering the land of the Cavares Gauls.

They came to a fork in the river where the Rhone was joined by the smaller tributary, the Isere. This mountain born river thundered out of the Alps, boiling and roaring as it surged into the Rhone. As the two rivers mixed and widened, the brown torrent of the Isere slowed its flow and dropped out its mountain minerals, slowly changing colour from tan to olive green, becoming one with the Rhone.

Here the scouts came galloping back reporting a large gathering of Gauls up ahead. This gathering however, was not armed resistance opposing the Carthaginians but a meeting between two factions who were in vociferous dispute with one another. Hannibal reluctantly called a halt and dispatched emissaries requesting peaceful passage through the land.

Anxious at the enforced delay but being four days north of their previous camp and no further news of the Romans, he reasoned he'd lost them. As a precaution, he set a substantial rearguard and dispatched scouts back southwards to watch the trails and relay news to him on a regular basis. If the Legions did follow him this far north, they would find him ready.

****

Back in the empty Carthaginian camp near the Rhone crossing, the Roman infantry were arriving and spreading out over the well-trodden earth and old fireplaces. Damaged and discarded equipment, animal bones, droppings and the remains of funeral pyres littered the area, the Legionaries silently taking note of the size of the camp area and calculating potential troop numbers as they deployed. Publius walked his horse around the camp making his own calculations, confirming to himself the numbers his cavalry had reported.

"We're too late Publius! Just too late!" Gnaeus thumped his fist on his thigh as he spoke. "We should've pushed harder from Massilia then we may have caught them."

"To what end though brother? The men were exhausted from the sea crossing and with this four day, forced march from Massilia, fighting a battle straight after would not be good odds to be taking on the Carthaginian. As you can see, they have been well rested." He gestured to the signs of the camp.

"Sir … sir, we have some prisoners!" A cavalryman reined up to the side of the Consul and the command group. "Deserters sir!"

Publius undid his helmet, holding it in the crook of his arm. "Get me some answers soldier; I want to know when this army left and where they're going, quickly!"

"Yes sir!" The rider kicked his mount away.

Publius turned to his command group. "Have the men set up camp here, Jupiter knows they will need a rest."

"Rest! Rest! Gods above man! We should be pushing on to catch these savages and have done with it!" Tiberius objected.

Publius wiped a hand over his eyes smudging the sweat and the overlaying dirt crusting his skin, making an effort not to snap at Tiberius.

"Tiberius … Consul … its pointless pushing on until we establish when this camp emptied and in what direction they went, though I think I can guess. It's late in the day, the light fading and the men need to rest. As you can see our enemy have been well rested and I don't want to take the Carthaginian on when he has the dice loaded so much in his favour, Jupiter knows he's dangerous enough."

"Hah! If you're tired Publius, stand back man. Let me sort this out."

Publius moved his horse alongside Tiberius, his face suddenly grim and his jaw set. He leaned over speaking quietly so not be overheard.

"Consul Longus!" He hissed through gritted teeth, the formal naming catching the man's attention. "This is a joint command; we do this together, now use your head man! If we could catch the Carthaginian and finish this successfully, you would have my support.

Open your eyes, the men are exhausted, they need rest, not another march then battle."

Tiberius tried to interrupt but Publius gripped his forearm hard and continued.

"And unlike us, most have been marching as well as carrying their equipment since we left Cisalpine Gaul twenty days ago."

Tiberius shook Publius's hand loose, his face flushing in anger. Publius however was not finished.

"These Carthaginians are not some barbarian tribe that will fold and run under the first flight of pila! I'll not fight them until we're ready and able and can win! I won't let you drag this army to destruction along with my career, aye, and your own, for that's what you risk if you force a battle at the moment."

Tiberius glared; he seemed ready to argue but the dark, ruthless look on Publius's face told him the matter was closed. Despite being a professional soldier himself, he didn't have the combat experience of Publius nor had he fought the Carthaginians before. Too stubborn to admit he was wrong and too proud to defer to his fellow Consul he kicked his horse away, calling for the prisoners to be brought to him.

Gnaeus came alongside Publius. "May I ask what all that was about?"

"No! You may not!" Publius snapped. Gnaeus knew his brother well enough to leave it at that.

He brought himself to attention, immediately reverting to the formal protocols of command. "Your orders sir?"

"Have this camp fortified. Post sentries and issue the men with extra rations. Bring me the information from the prisoners."

"Yes sir!" Gnaeus relayed the orders as Publius dismounted and walked his horse to where his tent was being erected.

****

The courier trotted his horse up the white dust road to the Samilcar villa. Before he reached the gate, the sentry on the wall recognised him and called for the gates to be opened. The gatekeeper waited in the shadow of the gate arch, holding out his hands for the messages and goods as the rider entered the darkened archway. As the two men exchanged pleasantries, the courier passed over wax-sealed scrolls and folded parchments, then reached behind him to unfasten a sack slung over the horse's hindquarters. The gatekeeper grunted at the weight lowering the sack quickly to the floor. With the packages handed over, he offered a drink to the courier, leaving him in the shade to enjoy it as he made his way to the house with the deliveries. Unable to read, he deposited the parchments, scrolls and the heavy sack at the scribe's office for him to sort and distribute.

By early evening, the scribe had answered the trivial missives and usual business undertakings, placing the personal or items beyond his scope of work for the family to open at their leisure.

Returning to her private rooms from a day in the city, Serfina called for her handmaidens to prepare her bath. Collecting her messages from the small table just inside the door, her nose wrinkled as it picked up the strong smell of hessian. Looking around she saw the sack leaning against the table leg, despite her curiosity she opted to open her messages first. With a weary sigh, she flopped down on the settle, kicking off her dusty sandals and pushing a silken cushion into her lower back before opening her correspondence. Slaves dashed in and out of the room with pitchers of steaming water, tipping them into the rectangular, marble bath sunk waist-deep in the floor. A girl added scented oils to the water then agitated it with a wooden paddle, the sweet scent of the infusions drifting on the rising steam and filling the room with the perfume.

Serfina was still reading when the handmaiden called her for her bath. Dropping the papers and completely forgetting the sack, she padded across the tiles to the steaming bath. The handmaiden helped Serfina out of her dress and fastened her hair up into a bun, then slipping off her own dress, offered her hand to Serfina, helping her down the steps into the pool, quietly mouthing a prayer that the water temperature would be acceptable. Serfina let out a contented sigh as she eased into the bath, lowering her body under the surface to her neck. The maid picked up a small sponge, awaiting her mistress rising from the water so she could begin washing and massaging her skin.

As the water cooled, Serfina demanded towels. The maid moving quickly to fetch them and feeling the evening chill raising goosebumps on her wet skin as she hurried. Remaining naked, she wrapped Serfina in soft towels while patting her skin gently dry. When all was finished and Serfina wrapped in clean robes she dismissed the maid, the girl wrapping herself in a towel and picking up her dress from the floor before bowing out of the room.

Feeling relaxed, Serfina was about to retire when she remembered the sack. Suddenly curious, she lifted it but surprised by the weight, it slipped from her grasp clattering loudly on the floor. Suddenly suspicious, she was about to call the maid to open it when a voice in her head told her to look herself. Undoing the leather tie, she upended the sack tipping the contents on the floor. A warrior's corselet clattered onto the tiles with a dirty, stained tunic falling silently alongside. She stared, her brow furrowing in confusion. Bending down she tentatively turned the corselet over. Twisting her mouth in distaste at the dirty leather, she recoiled quickly as the front of the armour and the dark stained rent came into view. The smell of hessian replaced now with a stink of stale sweat and ingrained filth; she stared at the gash that perforated the leather facing and the dark staining. Recognising blood, she jumped back in horror, wiping her hands together trying to rid them of the dirt and flakes of dry blood left on her skin. Recovering from the shock her temper flared, cursing Ahaggar for a fool and a halfwit. Tanith in heaven! She didn't need to see Targa's armour! Why not send word by letter, advising of his demise, dispatches marked for the Samilcar house would be secure enough from prying eyes; no one would dare interfere with them. Even if they did, the death of a soldier was a common enough occurrence, murdered or otherwise and had nothing to do with people of her class.

In control of herself once more, she picked up the knife used to open her messages and carefully lifting the tunic with the point, turned it to the front. She nodded and smiled with relish as she noted the cut and deep staining on the tunic. Dropping the tunic back on the floor, she allowed herself a gleeful laugh, which accompanied the warm satisfaction and feeling of triumph. She felt complete again, as if a weight had been lifted from her shoulders. Her spirits soared; Targa was dead, dead and rotting. With Carthalo avenged and Adharbal's pride restored, not that he would know it, she was excited and suddenly alive with the news. Her tiredness forgotten she poured herself another drink and sat on the settle to enjoy it, sipping appreciatively at the sweet wine she raised the goblet to the corselet.

"Rot in Hades, Targa!" She mouthed quietly, taking another sip.

As she lowered her cup and sunk back into the settle enjoying her moment of triumph, the glow of the lamps caught on the corselet and it sparkled momentarily despite its filthy state. Distracted by the flash she looked again, as she moved the light blinked once more. She squatted next to the armour for a closer look, seeing brass stars and crescent moons emblazoned in symmetrical groups beneath the dirt her memory began to recollect. She'd seen this armour before … where? Why would she notice armour? Ignoring the filth now, she rubbed her finger over the metal, cleaning some of the brown staining from the tarnished bronze. As her mind finally recollected where she'd seen it, she let out a wail like a wounded, demented animal left in a trap. It was Ahaggar Bola's armour. The armour he'd worn the night he'd visited her with his offer of murder. In a fit of temper, she hurled her drink across the room, the goblet bouncing, ringing and spraying its red contents as it hit the wall then the tiled floor. She snatched the armour up and despite its weight, threw it as hard as she could back to the floor cursing and swearing. Breathless with the effort she stamped her small, slippered foot repeatedly against the leather, working herself into a hysterical frenzy. Finally, gasping for air and dizzy with the effort she fell back onto the settle and cried bitterly.

Eventually, coming to terms with her thwarted schemes and her frustrations, she dried her tears and gathered her wits. If that was Bola's armour then whoever sent it knew about her and the arrangement! She felt a cold shiver down her spine and her bowels contract as the realisation and fear gripped her. Who'd he told? He must have named her! Someone knew something. Panic took her. With a trembling hand, she poured another drink, quaffing it quickly and pouring another. As powerful as her family was, to be implicated and charged with murder could see her tried and executed like any common criminal. Trying to think she poured yet another drink, downing it as swiftly as the others. As the wine calmed her nerves she reasoned the scenario, someone knew of her connection to Bola and possibly of their arrangement. However, if they had any proof, the city guard would be here arresting her now. Therefore, her plan may be discovered or just suspected but proof was another matter, she'd have to be more careful is all. Gripping the goblet tightly until her fingers turned white and ached, she cursed Ahaggar for a bumbling, yapping fool and then Targa with all the vehemence she could muster.

She'd find another way; somehow, supposing it took a lifetime, she'd have her vengeance. Targa would pay in blood for what he'd done. No one! Not even Tanith herself would stop her having her revenge. With the hate-filled thoughts abound in her head and the copious amount of wine fuddling her senses; she laid full length on the settle. Drinking the last of the wine she rested her head on the cushions, a single tear dampening the smooth fabric against her cheek, a tear this time not from fear but frustration, born from cold, hard hatred.

****

The Carthaginian camp stretched along the riverbank, from the confluence of the two rivers southwards into the distance. Hannibal finding himself immersed in the tribal dispute as a non-biased mediator. Though not wishing to linger, he'd reluctantly accepted the invitation, deeming it wise not to offend the Gallic sensitivity. He reasoned that a few days rest for his troops would not go amiss. Moreover, if he could make allies of this Cavares tribe rather than enemies, then it was time well spent. His scouts returning from the south reported the Romans had occupied the old Carthaginian camp and apart from their scouts, the Legions had not ventured further. Therefore, with the Romans a comfortable four days march away, he decided he could afford to halt for a day or two.

He made his usual precautionary measures with a rear guard but to allow for rest and recuperation he had half the army stand to, ready for combat whilst the other rested and relaxed, the role being reversed on a half-day basis.

The tribal dispute was based around the succession of a new Chief. The choice lay between two brothers each with a valid claim to the position, for in the laws of this particular tribe the eldest did not automatically inherit. Hannibal listened for two days to the arguments from both sides; the difficulty lying in the correct choice according to politics and the avoidance of bloodshed, not so much, in who could lay the best claim. By the third day, the deliberations were complete and a decision reached. Hannibal chose the eldest brother for the Chiefdom. Ready for the disappointment of the younger, he offered him a Captaincy and the chance to carve a new kingdom of his own with riches to match. Astute as ever, he had picked his men aright. Nominating the elder as Chief brought contentment and settlement to the tribe, showing the younger the army and stimulating thoughts of adventure in him, saw him relinquishing his claim and enlisting along with a contingent of one hundred of his own warriors.

The tribal elders, thankful of the settlement without bloodshed threw the village and their hospitality open to the dark skinned strangers and their allies. Something of a festival atmosphere prevailed, sheep and goats were slaughtered and roasted, beer and wine flowed and commerce between the peoples commenced. An edict was swiftly passed throughout the army that the locals were to be treated with respect and traded with fairly, anyone caught in contravention would be crucified and there would be no exceptions. With the route over the mountains confirmed and autumn already here, soldiers looked for furs in the form of cloaks, hats and gloves. They traded silver coin, bracelets, rings and cooler summer fabrics for the winter wear of this upland people. Gestix helped his comrades select the best and most useful items, drawing on his experience of winters in the mountains in his youth.

His colleagues readily accepted the bearskin cloaks and mink hats, even the cowls and stoles of wolfskin but having them accept the long trousers of the Gauls met with stoic resistance. Trying to explain snow to men who'd never seen it, nor felt it's chilling, skin-numbing cold was impossible, a hard winter in North Africa being a far cry from a European winter in the mountains. Finally, feeling he was wasting his breath, he waved away the protests. He was trading on two pairs of lined, leather trousers for himself and Baldor when Balaam appeared behind him.

"Is that what you reckon we'll need for the mountains, Gestix?"

"Aye Captain, at least! There'll be snow high up already."

Balaam fished in his purse and pushed some silver into Gestix's hands.

"Get me some, same size as the boy, but not so bloody long in the leg!"

Harbro and the rest of the reluctant purchasers looked at one another, then their Captain. Soon hands were dipping into purses or offering goods to Gestix to barter for trousers for them.

With the army rested and re-supplied, they began their march again the following day. With local guides from the Cavares leading them, they turned from the Rhone following the Isere northeastwards into the foothills of the mountains. With scouts reporting no movement from the Romans, Hannibal eased the pace of the march to normal, surmising that having not moved they wouldn't follow him into the mountains. Now the race was on to get his army over the Alps onto the northern plains of Italy before the Legions could retrace their steps homeward and bar his way. He wanted, needed, a battle. However, it must be on his chosen ground, at his time and he must have victory. The outcome of the first battle in Italy would decide much.

****

The Romans too were enjoying a rest from marching. Comfortably ensconced in their enemy's old camp the men looked to their health and wellbeing, bathing and bandaging blistered feet, strapping strained joints and catching up on their sleep. They ate cooked food instead of the dried marching rations they had suffered for nearly three weeks and like soldiers anywhere they enjoyed their wine, albeit sour and poor quality. They repaired and washed their tunics, cleaned and polished armour and honed their weapons, their Centurions and Optios still turning them out for parade daily, ensuring they remained on a war footing.

The now square shaped camp was surrounded by a waist-deep ditch with an earth rampart above it, complete with sharpened timber stakes protruding spear-height from the top of it. There were four gateways, placed to each point of the compass and avenued internally with curtain walls some twenty paces in length, making them easily defendable. The muleskin tents, housing eight men in each were pegged equidistantly in straight rows. Latrines had been dug; watering points established and a field hospital set up, roads and parade grounds completing this temporary military citadel.

The prisoners or their remains were left outside the camp. They had talked quickly in an attempt to save their lives, telling of the planned march over the Alps. The Romans, having their suspicions confirmed then demonstrated their contempt for deserters and executed them along the roadside. Weary of marching and bitter at the prospect of having to turn about and march again, the execution party vented their spleen on the hapless men. With time on their hands, they protracted their prisoners suffering. They crucified some, gambling on which prisoner would last the longest while competing to see who could inflict the most pain while keeping the prisoner alive. Men were hung on crosses by nails through their skin instead of their bones, some they hung upside down, nailed only through their feet. Tiring of crucifixion, they turned to impaling; stripping the men naked, they lowered them onto vertical timber spikes, the point of entrance being their anus. The pleading for mercy and subsequent blood chilling howls reached new heights but the time of suffering was short before the victim expired. The soldiers, ever-resourceful then threaded their victims onto timber poles, the wood pushed through skin like a needle through cloth. This produced the grimmest results as far as time was concerned, with no vital organs pierced or arteries ruptured, men lingered in a semi-conscious, pain-wracked state. The soldiers doused them with water to restore consciousness or gave enforced drinks to keep them alive and win their wagers.

Publius called his staff to a briefing, assembling in his tent after supper he laid his plans in front of them. Darkness arrived prematurely heralded by iron-grey rain clouds that rolled across the sky blotting the sun. The temperature dropped quickly, the drastic change provoking a deep rumble of thunder in the hills. Birds disappeared heading for their roosts in the trees; even the ravens and crows left their picking at the dead and dying prisoners to seek shelter. Men busied themselves securing guylines and moving equipment under cover. Publius had the brazier in his tent raked, exposing the glowing embers and radiating more heat; he called for mulled wine to warm his officers as he talked.

Publius had requested a meeting with Tiberius prior but to no avail, the man remaining aloof since his rebuke; dismissing it, he made his own plans. Thus, he was somewhat surprised when Tiberius appeared along with his Legate, ever the peacemaker, Publius welcomed him warmly ushering him personally to his seat. The slaves quickly served the wine, the officers, swathed in campaign cloaks cupping their hands around the steaming goblets breathing in the vapour of cinnamon, nutmeg and cloves.

Publius raised his goblet but before he could propose a toast, there was a protracted bright flash as lightning arced across the sky, followed a moment later by thunder that crashed and rolled in a hollow peel over the hills and forest. The rain came, instantly heavy, pelting the tent and drumming the ground in such force that it drowned his words.

"The senate and the people of Rome!"

The men's faces told him they hadn't heard him and he repeated louder:

"Gentlemen, the senate and people of Rome!"

The sentiment echoed back followed by slurps and sighs of contentment as the wine warmed and comforted the men. One or two of the more superstitious amongst them rolled their eyes and sunk a little lower in their seats, reading the outburst from nature as a portent of doom for either Publius, the army or Rome. However, apart from a few wary glances none chose to air his concern.

"Consul." He bowed his head to Tiberius. "Gentlemen, a change of plan. The Carthaginian is at least four days ahead of us. I won't chase him further." He paused to let the statement sink in. "Even if we were to catch him our men would be exhausted again, he'll have the advantage of being able to choose his ground and in this nature will help him. You've seen the land changing?" He paused, looking for understanding and agreement. "The higher we go the worse the terrain becomes for our tactics, there are no open, flat places up there to allow our Legions to deploy. He has Spanish mountain troops with him and no doubt, locals giving him further advantage. He's heading for the mountains and intends crossing into Italy."

"At this time of the year sir! Surely the winter will catch him before he's over?"

"Agreed! However, without doubt that is his intention. As you know the idea is not new, it's been done before by the Gauls. He'll exit into Cisalpine Gaul onto the plains of the Po with no one to bar his way."

"The Gauls crossed at the height of summer though! Is this Hannibal mad?" Ventured the Legate.

"Let's pray the mountains do our work for us and finish the bastards!" Grumbled Tiberius, his comment drawing laughter.

Vibrant talk commenced around the table for many had expected Hannibal to turn and fight, believing him boxed in. The idea of an army crossing the roof of the world with a fast approaching winter seemed like madness. Publius drained his goblet and banged it on the table for order.

"Gentlemen! Gentlemen! One at a time, Gnaeus?"

"Will he not just go to ground sir? Reappearing once we're gone."

"No, there's nothing in southern Gaul for him; I believe this trek has been his intention all along. I thought originally he coveted Spain for her silver mines and manpower but I was wrong."

Talk burst out from the assembly, Publius having to bang his goblet harder for silence.

"I should've seen it earlier as it makes perfect sense. Hannibal won't settle for his father's mantle as overlord of Spain, he wants more. He has no Navy or at least any that will dare put to sea for we control the Middlesea, so the only way is to march and he's marching for Rome!"

Chairs knocked over as men jumped to their feet, anger on their faces, curses in their throats and fire in their bellies. Publius was quietly content, knowing he would be able to ask what he would of them now.

"Here's the plan! Contrary to good military sense we'll divide our forces but …" He had to quieten them again before he could continue. "But … we'll do so without danger and it'll be to our advantage." The men fell silent, hanging on his every word. "Tomorrow I'll take my Legions back to Massilia. From there we'll take ship for Pisa again, then march northwards to Cisalpine Gaul. We'll stop the Carthaginian as he enters the plains of Po. General Gnaeus, you will take a legion and head to Spain, this will unsettle the Carthaginian rear. Begin reconsolidating our interests there; I'll see you are further reinforced once I'm back in Italy. Suppress any recruitment for the Carthaginians and cut off their silver supplies, they'll find it harder to wage war without men and money."

"Yes sir."

"Consul Tiberius." He waited politely until the man nodded ascent. "Consul, yours will be the most important command and the most difficult." Publius deliberately played on the point and to the man's prickly vanity. Tiberius listened, his look impassive. Publius however saw the unconscious lightening of his features, as his vanity and pride were sated. "Consul, will you hold your Legions here? Bolting the door if you like. I don't think Hannibal will return this way with you to block his path but it'll ensure that he moves one way or another; he can't keep an army up there indefinitely with winter coming. Once you're sure he's moved well into the mountains and too far to venture back, march after me and meet me on the plains of Po."

Tiberius nodded, saying nothing.

"Gentlemen, together we'll crush him!"

Fists drummed the table in appreciation of the strategy, the men raising goblets in salute.

The torrential rain continued unabated throughout the night, washing out some tents and forming ankle deep pools on the ground. The river rose to full flood, the water level flush with the top of the bank and mud brown in colour. Dawn arrived as a pale pink wash in the east though the charcoal clouds refused to move, keeping the light subdued and making for a miserable autumn morning. The rain lessened in intensity but continued to fall without signs of respite. Publius was already on the move, trotting his horse along the waiting column of silent men, his campaign cloak draped from his shoulders and over the horse's hindquarters. The men were arrayed in their Maniples their Optios to one side; the Centurions all ranked together in front. The leopard skin mantled Tribunes and forest of brass standards at the columns head. Taking his position at the front of the column, he signalled them forward. A long wailing note from the cornicen drifted over the camp and men put their first foot forward on their march back to Massilia and homeward. Tramping out of the gate the column swung past the prisoners. Publius cast a distasteful, sideways glance at the broken bodies. He abhorred torture, despite the sometime necessity of it, repulsed by what he saw he wondered at what made men revel in it. Looking from body to body, he was shocked to see one move. Hiding his revulsion, he ordered a Centurion to see to the dispatch of any that still drew breath. The Centurion in turn detailed two Legionnaires to check all the bodies and kill any that remained alive. The men in the column, oblivious to the prisoners dropped their heads forward against the driving rain marching on along the road that was fast becoming a muddy track.

Chapter Twenty four

The Cavares guides led the Carthaginians northeast for four days through the foothills of the Alps without event or trouble. On the fifth day, they advised they were nearing the limit of their territory and thus their knowledge, up ahead they said was the lands of the Allobroge tribe and they could go no further. Hannibal asked for as much information as possible concerning the Allobroges, only to be told they were much like any other Gallic tribe except these were particularly territorial and warlike.

With no response from the Allobroges to his requests for a peaceful passage, other than the curt dismissal of his emissaries, Hannibal called up his outriders. Balaam's company was the first summoned with Gestix and Baldor one of the first pairs dispatched on patrol. Leaving at first light, Baldor was already wrapped in his furs, trousers and wearing gloves. Gestix laughed heartily at the sight of his cocooned comrade.

"Come Baldor! It's not that cold! Not yet! There is a touch of frost I grant you but it's just a nice, fresh day in the mountains. Wait until we are up amongst the snow." He carried on laughing and shaking his head as he led his horse from the picket line.

Gestix, as ever seemed impervious to the changes of weather. Breathing deeply he exaggerated his breaths as if relishing the morning chill. He whistled softly to himself as he threw his blanket over his mount followed by his newly acquired black sheepskin, adjusting and fastening the holding strap beneath the horse's belly.

"So, you're only interested in keeping your arse warm?" Baldor sniggered.

"Oh, it's not for my benefit lad, I'm only thinking of the horse." Gestix laughed again, Baldor smiling in amusement.

"Here's something Baldor, serious now!" As Baldor looked, Gestix slid his sword a hands width clear of its scabbard then pushed it back repeating the action with his dagger. Baldor furrowed his brows not understanding.

"Do this every so oft now we're in the mountains. It stops the frost freezing the blade to the scabbard."

Baldor tried both his swords then his dagger and found they moved easily.

"Good!" Gestix nodded. "It's not so much a concern at the moment but form the habit eh? Once we're above the snow line it becomes vital."

"How cold's it going to get?"

"This time of the year, above the snow line, after dark? Cold enough to freeze your moustache and beard!"

"I can't comprehend such; it's so bloody cold already!"

"You'll get used to it lad, honest. It'll take a week or two but you'll harden to it! And I'd consider growing a beard if I were you, I'm going to!" Gestix rubbed his hand over his already stubble jaw. "Mine maybe a little greyer than the last time though. Come on, we'd better get out there."

At midmorning, the track led them into a wide, high-sided valley. The floor covered in tufted, brown grass and scrub and dotted with trees and grey boulders of all sizes giving restricted views. Riding deeper, the cliffs grew in height leaving the valley floor in shadow and at a chilled, tomb-like temperature, the ground still white and hard from the night's frost. Gestix looked about as they rode, studying the terrain and the shadowed walls, calling a halt every so often just to listen. Baldor saw no signs of life other than some rabbits and a few small finch's that chirped and fluttered from tree to tree in front of their horses. He chewed on a tough, dried beef strip as they rode, he was hungry and could think only of the hot breakfast he was missing, he couldn't imagine anyone being about in here. As they stopped again, Gestix slipped from his mount and bent down to lift his horse's front leg, drawing his dagger he probed the hoof. Baldor looked down to see what the trouble was.

"Don't look away from me lad but up on the ridge, to your right, we have company. They've been following us for a little while, at least that I've seen anyway."

Baldor resisted the urge to look.

"Trouble?"

"Could be, there's four of them I think? I haven't seen any bows so it's not too bad." He carried on with the pretence of checking the hoof.

Baldor felt his stomach knot. He felt suddenly vulnerable and very uncomfortable. He wanted to draw his weapons, just for the reassurance of their feel in his hands. Gestix, sensing his friend's trepidation lowered the hoof and patted Baldor's thigh before remounting.

"Don't worry lad, it may be nothing and with no bows and on foot, we're a match for them. We'll just play it steady and carry on."

"Carry on! Shouldn't we go back and report?"

"Report what? Four men in the valley?" Gestix grinned. "No! We'll carry on but without letting them know we've seen them." He winked at Baldor and walked his horse on. "Chew some more beef and relax!"

Amazed at Gestix's nonchalant behaviour Baldor fretted, this cat and mouse game didn't appeal to him at all. Along with his rising fear he now had to continue scouting but without alerting the men who watched them, that they'd been seen. Continuing up the valley the terrain began to change again. The sides tapered inwards dramatically, narrowing the valley floor before falling away steeply to the right leaving a tree lined, precipitous path against the left side. Letting the horses pick their own way, Gestix chatted as they went while reminding Baldor to relax. They saw no one else until the sun climbed high enough to shine into the massive gorge. As the light crept over the darkened ground like the opening of a curtain, there was a momentary flash from metal up on the cliffs. Baldor was about to speak but Gestix cut him short, placing a restraining hand on his arm in case he went to point.

"I saw it lad, the bastards are thicker than flies around shit!"

"How many have you seen?" Baldor asked incredulously.

"Two other groups on the left high up and one larger group on the right just before the path narrowed." He heard Baldor's sharp intake of breath. "I didn't want to worry you!"

"Too late, I'm worried! What do we do from here?"

"Well, we've a good idea of the terrain now and know the Allobroges are occupying the cliffs in some force." He looked up at the sky. "Hmmm, going by the sun I think now's a good time to go; but slowly mind, as if we've finished another boring patrol." He dismounted again as he finished speaking.

"What in Hades?"

"I need a piss!"

Baldor groaned, wanting to be gone. He fretted further while Gestix took his time. As Gestix remounted, he paused for a drink, offering the flask to Baldor. Seeing he was about to refuse he said firmly.

"Take a drink! And take a look as you do. Only at the ones on the left mind, we can see the others when we turn back."

Baldor swigged the water, rinsing his mouth and spitting. "I still can't see them." He took another drink.

"High up, past those white looking larch trees, right on the escarpment. Don't look too long mind!"

"I can see where you mean but can't see them."

"Don't worry about it, let's go. When we turn back, watch for the other party, they're back down the trail but making their way up the valley side from those huge boulders we passed near the pines. That's the ones I've seen but there could be more! Come on."

Baldor turned his horse, relieved to be advancing no further, he still expected at any moment to hear whoops and screams of the watching men as they came after them. The silence continued however, putting him more on edge. Hearing his heartbeat pounding in his ears, he felt his stomach knot and the 'empty pit' feeling growing in his bowel. He also felt somewhat useless; he had seen nothing and had no inkling of anyone being in the valley, but for Gestix he would have carried on regardless. He vowed he would take patrols more seriously in the future, though they weren't out of this mess yet. Keeping a deliberate, easy pace, they rode back down the trail, Gestix talking quietly over the thump of the hooves.

"You're doing well!" He smiled as he spoke. "If they were going to attack they'd have done so by now. I'm gambling they want us back to camp to report nothing amiss so we then bring the army up."

"Why do they want to fight anyway? We only want a safe passage."

Gestix shrugged. "Why does the sun come up every morning? Anything they can take from the baggage train will help them through the winter I guess and this ones coming early, even for this far north. And, Gauls being Gauls, they probably have nothing else better to do." He grinned and Baldor relaxed a little. As they neared the valley mouth Gestix whispered again, his tone a little more urgent.

"There's more of them now than when we entered and they're still making their way higher up. This has the makings of a huge ambush, if we clear the valley mouth we're safe, if they try and stop us just ride at them, don't stop!"

"Make sure you can keep up!" Baldor quipped grimly.

They were neither attacked nor followed as they made their way back to Balaam and the army to report. Drawing the valley shape in a smoothed patch of dirt with his dagger point, Gestix advising estimated travelling times from the valley entrance to where it narrowed. Baldor converted the time into distance as best as he was able, while Gestix marked the positions where he'd seen the Allobroges congregating. A scribe copied the sketch onto parchment, double checking measurements and details from the pair as he worked. Armaco and Marko watched and listened, taking the exercise as a briefing, as they were next on patrol and would not return until dark.

The following morning, muster sounded. The horns brassy notes carrying in the crisp stillness seemed to echo as they relayed the length of the column and the army struck camp. The haphazard city of tents and awnings disappeared and fires were extinguished. The milling, chaos of men were shouted into order, forming themselves up by company, regiment and then division, all dressed in the full panoply of war. Before the sun was clear of the crags the once sprawling column was replaced by neat, rectangular blocks of infantry and horse, with the baggage train of carts, wagons, slaves and servants safely ensconced in the centre. Hannibal placed the elephants in two sections, one to the front of the column behind the cavalry vanguard but in front of the main body of infantry, the second bringing up the rear. The animals would make shock weapons, hopefully deterring attack from tribesmen who would never have seen such beasts. The orders were to advance up the valley to the beginning of the narrowing of the trail. If there was no contact with the enemy, they were to pitch camp and wait. Moving at the pace of the slowest, the column would take most of the day to reach their destination.

Expecting trouble, the small patrols increased to company strength and the whole mercenary company fell in as one, being led away to the right flank of the army. Having not seen the whole company together for a long time, Baldor glanced back along the small column as it peeled away in fours from the main one. The company was a cosmopolitan mix, predominately Carthaginian but with Greeks, Spaniards, a Nubian and a Gaul represented, all with differing cultures, fashions, Gods and in Malo's case skin colour. His ebony face stood out from the rest and in sharp contrast to his white leather corselet and tossing white helmet plumes. The warriors were adorned in myriad colours from cloaks and tunics through to corselets and painted shield faces, some wore plumed bronze helmets, others plain leather and some painted. Their shields were circular in shape but differed by pattern or device on the face; their weapons also differed according to personal preference. Individual and different as they were; all were well armed and carried the look and manner of hardened, professional soldiers. Baldor was proud to be part of the company but wondered at how his life had changed in just over a year from businessman to mercenary soldier. He'd fitted in well, respected for his skill with his swords and despite his self-denial and modesty, for his courage. He enjoyed the camaraderie and adventure it had bought him and the experience of the countries he had passed through with their peoples and customs, fondly remembering his father's words of travel broadening experience. His pleasant musing was cut short as his memories went to his mother and his promise never to go soldiering; the guilt for his broken word punished him, turning his previously warm nostalgia suddenly cold. The cold turned to bitterness as the guilt he felt over Aiticia's death also assailed him; he added an additional scourge for not thinking of her for sometime. Before he could torture himself further, the order came to move to the gallop and his concentration forced back to the present.

Morning had slipped into a cloudless, bright, autumn afternoon but when the column entered the valley, the sun was already low in the sky leaving the valley floor in shadow again. The change was dramatic, from sun-warmed trail to tomb-like temperatures, the warriors feeling sweat drying on their skins with the cold chill. The cavalrymen pulled cloaks from backpacks swathing themselves to the neck as they rode deeper into the shadow. Gestix kicked his horse alongside Harbro's while indicating with nods of his head where he'd seen the Allobroges during patrol. The Allobroges were still there but in greater numbers than before, and now made little attempt at concealment. The sun flashed from weapons and shields all along the escarpment showing their positions and highlighting their numbers. The Carthaginians looked upwards as they marched, watching the watchers. Unease spread along the column and a low grumble became audible unrest as men talked, wondering why they were marching into what appeared to be a trap. Officers came back along the lines barking men to silence and driving them onward.

By late afternoon, the army was at the narrowing of the trail. The unease they felt at being within the confines of the valley and close to an enemy in a strong position, had them abandon the pitching of tents. Instead, they placed bedrolls around the fires and to further aid readiness most remained in their armour, few thought they would sleep.

Darkness fell and the men settled to their evening meal. Hannibal appeared with a contingent of five thousand Spanish mountain troops in his wake. Despite the evening chill, both he and the men wore only short, cotton tunics and lightly armed with short swords, daggers, and wearing neither armour nor helmets. Most were barefoot and carried ropes looped over their shoulders some with grapnels attached. As they worked their way through the camp towards the rear of the column, officers called their men to a briefing, Balaam sending Harbro to summon the company.

The men found him pacing in front of the fire, his silhouette casting an unsettling giant shadow against the rocks amidst the dancing red glow from the flames.

"Come close, closer!" He waved them towards him. "I'm not going to shout."

The men formed a circle around him, shuffling and edging close, when he had quiet he began.

"You all saw the Allobroges on the way into the valley. Well, they won't be there in the morning! Armaco, Marko, explain."

"Yes sir." Armaco cleared his throat. "We were in here last night as darkness fell; keeping well-hidden owing to the information gained by Gest ..."

"Get on with it man! Cut to the chase." Balaam chided.

"Yes Sir! Anyway, when darkness falls the Allobroges abandon their positions and return to their settlement leaving no one on guard. The General has taken the Spaniards up there to occupy the heights ready to drive them off as they return in the morning. We can all sleep well."

Smiles of relief spread around the group, easing some of the tension. Before they became too complacent, Balaam interjected sharply.

"We can sleep better, not well!" The General and the Spaniards may be up there." He pointed skywards. "And the Allobroges may be over there." His thumb pointed behind him and up the valley. "But we're taking no chances. So, no drinking, gambling or whoring tonight! Get some sleep, we move at first light and it may yet be into combat. Harbro, weapon check, Armaco, set the watch, questions?" With nothing forthcoming Balaam dismissed them, rolling in his blankets armour and all, leaving Harbro and Armaco to relay his orders.

Dawn found light signals flashing from both sides of the escarpment advising that Hannibal and his Spaniards had control of the heights. With a huge cheer at the securing of their flanks, the army began its advance with the Spaniards moving parallel to them. Scouts reported the Allobroges retreating northwards in front of the advancing column with no signs of resistance. Further on, the column was forced to slow it's pace, having to thin in width as it moved onto a narrower track, men and wagons bunched up and stopped.

It was midday when the attack came. A third of the column including the baggage train had moved onto the track when shouts and the rumble of hooves saw the remains of a badly mauled patrol burst from the trees to the left telling of enemy contact. The cavalrymen were looking and fighting to their rear as they hit the trail, rider-less horses announcing casualties. Somehow, the Allobroges had quietly regrouped and were now advancing quickly through the trees. Their war cries carried echoingly from out of the forest, the noise of breaking bracken and the rumble from thousands of feet heralded their coming, to the men on the track it sounded as if all the demons from Hades were loose.

The blare of war horns along the column called for a stand to while officers and line closers bellowed to form men into coherent ranks, physically pushing the slowest into place. Men threw off cloaks and bunched up. Shields quickly overlapped and locked together; spears bristled outward over shield rims. A few stray arrows and slingshot came out of the forest gloom, wounding or killing the slow or unlucky, the lead slingshot causing horrific wounds as it tore flesh and smashed bones, unprotected faces bursting open like rotten fruit. Then, erupting from the treeline amidst screams of hate and unrestrained bloodlust came the Allobroges. Balaam immediately turned his men from column to line but with no space to gain speed the line could only trot forward. Some fell from their mounts, killed by missiles, else the horses went down in neighing, rolling heaps as arrows feathered their chests and slingshot broke legs and smashed heads.

The attack was fast and ferocious, the battle-mad tribesmen hitting the column at different times and varying strengths. The column bent and flexed with the impact, some units held while others split open with the defenders knocked down in swathes. The Allobroges pouring into the gaps hacking and slashing, trampling or jumping over the injured. The heavy infantry within the column stood their ground, first checking then pushing the tribesmen back, slowly straightening their ranks after the first rush. Their better equipment and steady discipline helping them cope with the initial shock. The impetus of the attack forced some men off the track, driven screaming, fighting and dying over the edge, some of the Allobroges going down with them as men fought hand to hand, berserk fury replacing reason.

The pack animals were unaccustomed to the noise of battle and terrified from the mayhem and stink of blood. Braying and whinnying they strained wild-eyed at their tethers, rearing and kicking, hooves crippling or killing some of their handlers. Some broke loose, careering wildly into others, knocking them over or pushing them off the path as they ran berserk. A desperate pushing, shoving battle ensued as the Allobroges tried to force the column off the road.

Baldor and the mercenaries rode headlong into the charging Allobroges. The tribesmen in full battle fury, hurling themselves fearlessly at the oncoming horses. Many fell under the hooves, others died on the mercenary's spears. Undeterred, the rest swirled around the horses like floodwaters around rocks. Baldor lost his spear in a warrior's chest as the man spun around with the impact. Blades clattered and deflected off his armour while hands came up to grab at his shield trying to tear it and him from his mount. Chopping and stabbing downwards, he forced Risto about in a circle, scattering the milling tribesmen driving them back from his horse.

Suddenly, he was seized from the rear by his scabbard strap, pulled backwards, and down, over Risto's hindquarters. Another tribesman, taking advantage of his exposed position and stalling mount, tore his shield from his grip, hands snatching his arm as it flailed for balance. Clamping his legs to retain his seat, Baldor struggled with his rearward adversary while crosscutting to his left killing the shield taker. The man behind was climbing over the top of him, the pair too close for either to bring swords into play and hands dropped weapons to grapple, punch or choke. The man roared his war cry whilst struggling to pull Baldor loose, the pair close enough for Baldor to smell the man's foul breath and feel the hot spittle on his face. Losing the struggle Baldor began to panic, as he was dragged from his mount, the pair falling backwards and landing heavily. Flailing and twisting atop his assailant, Baldor tried desperately to break loose from the man's grip about his neck and shoulders. Risto stumbled backwards, trampling his assailant's leg. The man grunting in agony and slackening his grip momentarily, Baldor snatched a hand loose, clawing the man's face, gouging eyes and soft tissue bloody. The warrior howled in agony and released him. Baldor recovering first, rolled to one side then head butted him repeatedly, smashing his helmet rim into the bearded cheek and nose. Hot blood sprayed across his eyes and cheeks as the man's face burst then collapsed. Blinking the red haze from his eyes, he pulled himself to his knees and snatched up his fallen sword, driving it deep into the heaving chest beneath him. Breathless from the struggle, his chest and throat tight from fear, he threw himself over Risto's back as others pressed in to attack again. Kicking Risto hard he applied pressure with his legs, left then right, causing the horse to lunge and wheel, the action scattering the tribesmen from around them.

Balaam and Harbro rallied their men as the initial attack subsided. Men gasped for breath and took a moment, the two sides eyeing each other like rutting stags. Some, finding their breath cursed and harangued their enemy as the fury built again. The ground was littered with bodies of Allobroges and mercenaries alike. Horses thrashed on the floor some hamstrung with their legs flopping uselessly, others disembowelled and losing their lifeblood and guts onto the grass.

The odds were not good; the tribesmen's ranks were swelling quickly as more appeared from out of the woods, while the mercenary's ranks were depleting with no support available, the units to their right and left being also heavily engaged. Reinforcements from the column could only trickle onto the narrow path a handful at a time, thus Balaam reasoned the best form of defence was attack.

"Kill the bastards! Kill them!" He roared pointing his sword then kicking his horse forward. His men, understanding their desperate position roared their defiance and rode after him. Some of the braver tribesmen rushed to meet them; most were ridden or hacked down as the horses passed. Some dropped low beneath the sword strokes and either tripped or slashed the horse's bellies bringing animals and riders tumbling to the floor in bone-crushing ruin. Battle joined again, with a thundering crash and a low groan as flesh and blood collided with shields and tightly packed ranks, screams rang out as men were stabbed and trampled. The melee continued with unabated fury and despite the height advantage of the mercenaries they slowly grew less as the Allobroges separated them out and pulled them down. Seeing the tactic, Balaam used his riding skill and sheer ferocity to herd his men into a tight group once more. Yelling to close ranks, he forced his horse around the broken lines, bowling tribesmen over and killing any that barred his path. With exhaustion claiming many on both sides, fury lessened and men fought in silence with only grunts and gasps accompanying the clash of metal, recklessness replaced with dogged, methodical fighting. The tribesmen, sensing victory began to value the chance to enjoy it, the mercenaries fighting for time and the hope of reinforcements.

The mercenaries were now almost stationary, the ground around them so deep with dead and dying they could no longer move. The horses damp with sweat, splashed with blood and weary from the manoeuvring and pushing. Their heads hung low and though they still skittered and jostled, they were near exhaustion from the stress of battle, the smell of blood and the uncertainty of stepping on corpses. The mercenaries were also exhausted. Bloodied and soaked in sweat their armour battered, helmets dented or missing, their weapons blunted and notched. With grim, blood spattered faces and injuries from flesh wounds through to mortal they looked as though they had walked through Hades.

It seemed they wouldn't ride away from this battle. To their left and right combat still raged with all units committed, the trickle of reinforcements continually pushing onto the track being readily soaked away. Despite their plight there was no fear now, the men strangely calm and quiet but their heads held high that spoke of defiance and the promise of a hard fight for those coming to take their lives. They saluted each other, words un-necessary to show their feelings. Balaam called across the carnage to the Allobroges.

"Come on you heathen swine! Come, if you think you can take us! We'll send more of you to Charon ere this day is done!" He hawked deep in his throat and spat at them.

A horn sounded from deep in the forest, the note repeating again and again, drifting through the trees. Fresh war cries were heard and the Allobroges looked back over their shoulders suddenly unsure. Horns droned again followed by the thunder of feet and breaking bracken, shouts echoed through the canopy followed by the sounds of battle joining again. The mercenaries looked on waiting for the attack to come; Balaam began to laugh then roared:

"It's the General! The General and the bloody Spaniards, to the savage's rear! … Not so brave now you bastards!"

As he shouted, the Allobroges ranks rippled and jostled forwards towards the mercenaries as the Spaniards attacked their rear back in the trees. Balaam's men cheered then hurled themselves into the fray with renewed ferocity. The Allobroges, shocked and bewildered from being attackers to the attacked and caught in the pincer movement broke, their fire and bloodlust replaced by panic and flight.

With no need for prisoners, there was no interest in sparing lives and the fury of soldiers that had looked certain death in the face only a moment before was released. Surrendering and wounded tribesmen were slaughtered where they stood; cries and pleas for quarter answered with blades as bloodlust took over.

In the end, discipline and exhaustion was all that prevented the Allobroges being wiped-out. As early afternoon came, the weary, gore spattered Carthaginians were brought to order, their officers pulling their men back and the few Allobroges that still drew breath were spared. Hannibal as tired and as blood covered as his men, called for his mount and for reserve cavalry units to be brought up from the rear.

Balaam regrouped his company and a grim, bloodied Harbro, still sitting atop his horse began the roll call. He scratched marks on a wax tablet against men's names depending upon their state, there were many silences as the names were called. The lightly wounded were treated by their comrades, the more serious being taken to the surgeons and orderlies at the rapidly erected tents and awnings that passed for a hospital. The pitiful, chilling screams as they were lifted and carried off the road, fraying men's nerves and setting the tone for vengeance.

Hannibal and the reserve cavalry units threaded their way through the carnage pushing ahead to secure the road. The fresh, un-blooded warriors gawped at the broken, gore-spattered bodies as they passed, some looked quickly away while others saluted or bowed their heads.

Chapter Twenty five

Hannibal and the cavalry scattered the Allobroges who'd escaped the slaughter harassing and slaying any they caught. The chase continued until they came in sight of the Allobroge's Township where without pause Hannibal led his men straight to the attack. There was no real defence, all the warriors of combat age having being involved in the morning's battle; the place full only of women, children and old men. Despite his anger at the ambush Hannibal forbade further slaughter, instead the town was stripped bare of anything of use and value before being raised to the ground and the terrified inhabitants driven off. Trotting into camp after dark beneath flickering torches they drove herds of goats and sheep before them, followed by carts laden with furs, wine, weapons and grain as well as some of their own men whom they'd found as captives.

The day following the battle was given over to rest. Sore and aching from combat and chilled from the night's cold, the men warmed oil and liniments over the fires rubbing it into their stiff and aching muscles. They sharpened weapons and repaired damaged equipment whilst the spoils from the town were distributed amongst them. The captured animals were slaughtered and roasted whole over huge fire pits. The smell of the roasting meats drifting tantalisingly on the cool mountain air; all were given their fill of food and the captured wine and beer. As the sun climbed higher so did the men's spirits, full bellies and wine-warmed wits no doubt aiding the process.

Putting aside the previous day's horrors, they paid respect to their departed comrades saluting them and the Gods with offerings of wine and beer tipped on the ground. Living for the day, they toasted themselves and their survival and settled to talk or sleep again, making the most of their day's respite.

A further two days march northeast passed without event, the only trials being the steepening terrain and the lowering temperatures. The shortening autumn days, though still dry and sunny brought little warmth, leaving the shaded areas in perpetual frost and the night skies clear and tomb-cold. The third day after the battle took them into the broad valley of the Durance. This ice-blue river was not a single flow but numerous streams of fast flowing water that formed bubbling shallows and eddying pools of varying depths, all of which spread widely over a grey-shingle riverbed. Harbro, Malo and Marko were already on the far bank having swum their mounts over. With orders to press on and reconnoitre, they signalled their intent back to Baldor, Armaco and Gestix on the west bank who were still searching for the safest and easiest fording point for the army to cross. They worked their way upriver checking low banked or level accesses' for shallows, inevitably finding the way blocked by deeper pools behind. Baldor walked Risto into what appeared to be shallows only for the water to rise suddenly up his calves and he pulled his feet up clear. Risto stumbled on the stony bed, tipping the precariously balanced Baldor into the river with a splash. He surfaced a moment later, the water at chest height, blowing like a whale and gasping for breath as the chill stole it away. Gestix and Armaco roared with laughter, the big Gaul beside himself in mirth when Baldor growled and cursed splashing water childishly in their direction.

"Best let him cool off Gestix; he can be hot-headed at times." Armaco buckled with laughter.

"Too deep for infantry then, Baldor?" Gestix added while laughing and wiping his eyes.

The pair continued up the riverbank still laughing, leaving Baldor cursing, shivering and stripping off his soaking tunic. By the time Baldor caught up with them they'd selected a fording point, their horses wet to their bellies where they'd waded them across and back, testing depth and current.

"We can cross here lad ... without swimming!" The pair snorted and looked at Baldor who managed a smile then broke into laughter as he forgot his injured pride.

"It looks as though it deepens in the middle there?" He pointed. "And the currents fast!"

"Aye, but manageable, if we rig ropes across the flow and downstream a little, that should serve to catch anyone losing their footing and drifting away." Gestix drew in the air demonstrating his point.

Leaving Gestix and Baldor at the ford, Armaco galloped back to the column seeking the engineers and to advise of the crossing point. Settling down to wait Gestix ushered Baldor back into the shadow of the trees, seeing the quizzical look he answered before Baldor asked.

"Too open out there! Better to stand in the cold and watch, than sit in the sun and be seen ... We're still on patrol!"

"I haven't seen anyone ..." Baldor's voice trailed away as he remembered the last valley and the lesson learned. "Have you?"

Gestix smiled. "Now you're thinking! Thankfully no, I haven't seen anyone ... yet! What else can you remember?"

Baldor looked about, thoughtful and serious, then at Gestix who raised his eyebrows questioningly. Baldor quickly lifted his hands to pull at his swords. One wouldn't move while the other came free but only after agitated tugging. Gestix already had his own blade clear of its sheath and pointing at Baldor's chest, his point made.

"The water lad, when you took a swim this morning, in these temperatures it takes little to form ice." Gestix sheathed his blade as Baldor's face took on a crestfallen look.

"I checked them, I did!"

"Good ... but check more often, especially after swimming practice!"

By mid-afternoon ropes had been stretched taut across the river and anchored to large rocks or pegged with iron spikes. The elephant troop had already waded over and the cavalry vanguard was mostly across, some being detailed to act as lifeguards. These were placed downstream of the ropes, dotted across the river to help fish out any infantry losing their footing. On the far bank, the rest formed four rank deep screens, at oblique angles to the ford's exit, giving protection to the infantry as they cleared the ford and formed up. With the crossing underway Gestix, Baldor and the now returned

Armaco forded the river themselves and began further reconnaissance of the land ahead.

Two dry, crisp days east of the Durance saw the army marching through the land of the Tricori, so far without trouble or harassment. Hannibal sent envoys seeking the tribal elders and permission for passage but though the envoys ranged far they found no sign of a township or anyone of importance. Unwilling to dally with autumn slipping into winter Hannibal pressed on, however to reduce risk if attacked, he reorganised the column's order of march. Heavy and light cavalry made up the vanguard with the mule trains behind followed by the baggage train, non-combatants and the elephants, who were now heavily laden with equipment. Light infantry, acting as protective screens escorted the baggage. Next came the medium class infantry and the African pikemen. Lastly, he placed his best heavy infantry, if he was to be attacked from the rear the enemy would find a sledgehammer waiting for them.

They passed a few small settlements and the odd croft nestled into the hillside but saw no one that offered any threat, catching only glimpses of shepherds and farming folk. All of whom vanished quickly, along with their possessions and livestock as they approached. The terrain had steepened and grown to giant scale about them, dwarfing them with cliffs that rose steeply from the valley floor to boulder strewn, escarpments and craggy peaks. The track however remained grass covered, albeit dry and dead looking, dotted with clumps of gorse, and stunted broadleaf trees, most of which were losing their leaves. The few that remained offered yellow, orange and russet colouring to a drab, dying landscape. Only the hardy pine and fir varieties seemed to prosper in the thin soils and rising altitudes and though of a good size, they too had lost their summer lustre with their needles drab-green or a golden-brown. Their, fist size, grey-brown fir cones were collected from the ground by the passing soldiers, this easily obtainable fuel supply burnt readily and gave off a large amount of heat.

One of the local guides reined up in front of Baldor speaking quickly in Gallic. His head and face hidden beneath a grey, wolf pelt that fell away over his neck and back, his body wrapped in a tattered bearskin cloak, heavily stained about the neck and matted with dirt. The light breeze carried the musty smell of the furs along with the stench of the man's body odour; Baldor held his breath as the closeness amplified the stink. The man pointed eastwards as he jabbered, showing rotting teeth beneath a thick red beard, then held out his hand. Baldor replied fluently while passing over a small disc and pointing back in the direction of the column. The man looked at the token, grunted and dropped it into his pouch then trotted off.

"I hope that was a token for the bath house?" Armaco wafted a hand in front of his face as he spoke.

"We may smell that bad soon! I don't know about you but I'm not taking a bath in these temperatures." Baldor replied, using a gloved hand to scratch at the few days' growth of whiskers on his face.

"What did he say anyway?" Armaco yawned and passed a beef strip to Baldor.

"Well, he wasn't too happy about having to take the token to the quartermaster; he was expecting payment in coin now."

"Not that! What did he say about where we are?" Armaco sounded irritable, Baldor laughed and Armaco tutted, realising he was being teased.

"He said this is the limit of Tricori land and thus the limit of his knowledge. Up ahead is the land of the Nantuates, apparently they are a numerous people and from what he has heard not to be trusted."

"I don't trust any of the bastards!" Armaco grumbled.

"You're bad tempered when you haven't been fed Armaco. It's a beautiful day and it's peaceful … well, so far anyway … enjoy the scenery!"

"Spare me the philosophy Baldor, you sound like Gestix."

Baldor fell quiet; it was unusual for Armaco to be so tetchy. Before he could probe further as to the reason for his mood, he noticed movement in the distance. Suddenly very alert, he intimated to Armaco what he saw; the pair unconsciously checked their weapons as they looked for signs of trouble.

The movement turned out to be the Nantuate; they approached on foot and unarmed, carrying olive branches and late autumn flowers woven into garlands and wreaths. A deputation of elders led the procession and came towards the pair who listened to their entreaty. They came in peace they said offering their thanks, having heard of Hannibal's prowess and victory over their enemies the Allobroges. They wished no trouble from him and offered none, he could pass freely over their land and they would trade with him if he so wished. They offered gifts of cattle and would bind themselves to him with hostages. They also offered guides to help the Carthaginians through their lands.

After receiving word of the deputation, Hannibal and Mago came forward of the column. They listened as the tribal elders reiterated their offer, Mago muttering under his breath about treacherous Gauls. Hannibal turned and glowered and Mago huffed but fell silent. Hannibal sat for a long while after the interpreter finished, reasoning and thinking the best way forward. The silence was heavy as the Gauls waited for their answer while watching Hannibal and the heavily armed Carthaginians intently. Horses twitched and stamped their hooves as if impatient, tails flicked rattling harness, other than that the silence was that of the grave. Despite Mago's misgivings, Hannibal accepted the offer. A refusal he deemed would only bring trouble from the Nantuates injured pride and he had no desire to fight another un-necessary battle or lose more men before he reached Italy. He asked for the hostages and guides to be brought to him, turning away he summoned his commanders to a council.

****

Gestix placed another log on the spluttering fire, adding fir cones to help the green timber take hold, he listened to the banter between the men as they discussed the day's happenings and their own interpretations of what they thought would happen next. Harbro gestured him to sit near him, offering a cup of hot water, honey and cloves.

"What do you think Gestix?" He sipped his drink as he asked, wrapping his hands around the goblet for warmth.

"I don't like it!" He replied quietly, while inhaling the sweet and spicy steam appreciatively. "And I don't trust them! All those offers and that garland shit, it doesn't ring true to me."

Harbro nodded and took another drink. "Aye, I think you've the rights of it!" He said, almost resignedly.

"Listen here lads! Listen!" Balaam called the group to order as he approached. Faces peered from fur wraps and hoods, when he had silence he began. "The order of march stays as it is. Despite these local guides, we're ordered to continue operating as screens. So tomorrow we look out for each other but even more so than usual.

We don't separate into ones and two's, we stay in groups, minimum of sixes, you hear?" He looked round the men as they nodded their assent. "Watch these Nantuates lad's; they're not to be trusted."

The following morning brought a heavy frost. The warriors awoke in white dusted furs and stiffened, frozen blankets, the skies covered with smoke-grey clouds with the promise of rain or most likely snow. Dragging themselves sloth like from their furs and heavy cloaks, they rubbed hands and bodies to restore warmth and kindled fires to prepare breakfast. With the light full in the east, horns droned across the stillness and slowly the column came to life. The Nantuates guides were waiting as promised and led the column down the valley.

For the next two days, although in high country the going become easier with the weather remaining dry but bitterly cold.

The wind picked up and gathered force as the days progressed, now it howled down the valley with an icy edge that cut to the bone. Men covered extremities in gloves and scarves, faces too wrapped to below the eyes as the wind took moisture from any exposed skin leaving it dry and cracked. The biting cold was a terrible experience for men used to the warm air of Africa or southern Spain and most had never experienced temperatures like it. The Moors and Numidians especially suffered, despite the furs and cloaks they wrapped themselves in, their darkened skins losing body heat faster than the others. Armaco was particularly miserable, far from his usual blunt and honest self he became quiet and withdrawn, huddled in his furs with his thoughts. The third day saw the terrain change dramatically again; the wide valleys and easy marching disappeared, replaced by narrowing defiles forcing the column to thin its width, thus almost doubling in length. As midday approached, they turned into a narrow river gorge with steeply sloping cliffs rising above them. The stream, running parallel to their march was small and shallow but flowing at tremendous speed such was the steepness of the land. One side of the track was heavily wooded whilst the other remained bare of foliage, dotted sporadically with boulders and rocks of all sizes. Gestix looked about taking in the terrain and their position.

"What's wrong Gestix?" Baldor asked. Receiving no answer, he asked again.

"Well, by tomorrow we'll be up in the crags and peaks of the mountains and there is no space up there for an ambush. If they're going to lead us into a trap then this is the best place I've seen."

"But we haven't seen anything suspicious whilst on patrol? No one has?"

"Exactly! Seen nothing! No people, no animals. We've passed plenty of empty dwellings but seen no one."

"But you know what happens; the locals melt away as the army approaches ... always!"

"Aye, but we always catch a glimpse or two. I checked two huts yesterday, they hadn't been abandoned but vacated and quite recently, the fires were cold in the hearth yet there was plenty logs outside and the grain pits were full! Considering we are passing through peacefully and no threat, it's a strange time of year for folk to be moving around don't you think?"

Baldor looked thoughtful, if Gestix suspected trouble it was worth taking note.

"Have you spoken to Harbro or the Captain?"

"Yes, but all we can do is watch and wait. We have their hostages I suppose. I just don't like it is all! We can't see far owing to those damned trees and these high cliffs give too good a vantage point over us and the path. Our left flank is against the stream which gives some protection but also hems us in, you see my concern?"

By mid-afternoon, the column was making good progress through the gorge until the track narrowed further, where it passed around a giant rock spur, which seemed to grow out of the path. Approximately half of the army had passed this point when the Nantuates erupted out of the forest like a tidal wave on the right flank of the marching soldiers. On the left, men appeared on the heights and began hurling rocks and levering huge boulders over the edge. Horns blared along the column calling men to arms and ranks closed up. Rocks bounced and careered down the slope, smashing and tearing others loose as they thundered down the incline, bouncing over the stream hitting the men below. The warriors on the track pushed to get out of the way of the incoming debris; some formed a shield wall against it and paid a heavy price. With the speed the rocks had gained, even those of fist size caused a devastating impact; the larger stones smashed shields and men off the track, breaking them like matchwood. Coinciding with the attack to the

Carthaginian flanks the Nantuates also attacked the column's rear and cut the army in half at the rock spur. Thus, the cavalry screens, vanguard and mule train along with the escorting infantry were separated from the baggage and the rearward infantry divisions.

Balaam recalled his men. Shouting to Malo, he pointed at the two, quickly departing Nantuates guides, drawing his finger across his throat. Malo snatched his bow from its case and had an arrow nocked to the string before the men had ridden fifty paces. A moment later an arrow hit the nearest one between the shoulder blades, snapping his head back as the impact knocked the breath from him, he dropped his spear and tumbled from his horse. The next arrow hit the other horse's rump causing its rear legs to fold under it; the animal collapsed pinning its rider beneath it then trampled him as it tried to stand.

"The bastard should be crippled at least! Come on, back to the column!" Balaam growled.

Back at the spur, the light infantry were attacking the Nantuates that divided the column but with the tribesmen defending only a narrow frontage, the chances of a breakthrough looked grim. The front of the column could do nothing to help the rear, except keep pressure on the Nantuates at the spur. The few men with bows loosing at any tribesmen that became visible on the top of the giant rock. Battle raged until darkness fell and exhaustion took over. As the moon rose, combat became sporadic as both sides sought to disengage. Only when the moon disappeared behind banking cloud and it became too dark to see did the fighting finally cease.

The dead of both sides lay piled around the spur, choking the path and preventing access or exit for either half of the column. In the blackness the wounded cried and moaned like tortured spirits, their comrades unable to see couldn't help, the risk of carrying torches made the bearers easy targets for any bowmen still lurking. Steeling themselves to the screams and pleas, men settled down to wait for dawn. As well as contending with the blood-curdling cries and the occasional howls of wolves, both halves of the column were left to contemplate the fate of the other.

Professionalism from the officers helped allay panic and steady men's nerves. Despite the darkness, they quietly collected their units about them preparing to fight a rearguard action in the morning. Balaam and Harbro collected their company, Harbro even managing to count the men. To bolster resolve and confidence Balaam gave a liturgy from history, *'The retreat of the ten thousand'* telling how during the Persian wars, Greek mercenaries had found themselves trapped, similar to the way they were now. Despite overwhelming odds and deep in enemy country, they'd fought a rearguard action against the Persians all the way back to the coast and escaped safely to Greece. His point being, if Greeks could do it, what had Carthaginians to fear? With some quiet agreement and even subdued laughter, the men's spirits raised a little.

Chapter Twenty six

The Nantuates did not reappear with the following dawn and the badly mauled column began extricating itself from the gorge. Regrouping and continuing eastwards they left their dead beneath rock cairns and smouldering pyres. The thick smoke adding to a brooding, storm-promising sky, already black dotted with circling kites and ravens. The placing of the heavy infantry at the rear had saved the column from more serious damage, perhaps even annihilation. Turning about face, they'd borne the brunt of the attack and held the majority of Nantuates at bay. Despite this measure and stoic resistance, the casualties amongst men and animals had been substantial.

After a long and gruelling day's march from the battle, the column left the tree line far below and were up amongst the crags and patchy snow, approaching the highest point of the pass. Their morale low from the stalemate battle, the never-ending march and downturn in the weather. Their enemy now was the freezing temperatures and the constant dry, biting wind. The men were almost unrecognisable as warriors, swathed in furs and cloaks from head to foot, horses too had covers and blankets draped over them for protection from the elements, only the elephants with their thick hides seemed impervious to the weather. The men remained vigilant for trouble as it was found stragglers or small parties were attacked. Sometimes the bodies were found, usually stripped of their weapons, armour, and anything of value, else men, animals and equipment simply disappeared.

Hannibal changed the order of march again, scattering the elephants throughout the column and pulling small companies together into division sized concentrations for safety. He formed flying units of cavalry that ranged the length of the column herding and guarding it like sheepdogs, ready to respond to any attack upon it.

Balaam and his men continued scouting operations but as one unit. Reaching the summit of the pass, they reined in amidst leaden skies and a howling, blustery wind. Holding flapping cloaks and blankets closed about them they took in the breath-taking view, the men quite in awe as they looked over the northern plains of Italy or as the Romans termed it, Cisalpine Gaul, stretching below them. Baldor for one had never seen anything like it.

"We must be at the top of the world! Surely, there's no place higher?" He exclaimed, shouting above the wind. Despite the cold and being bone weary, his voice had an excited tone to it, even Balaam seemed impressed by the view?

"Aye, a man shouldn't go higher than this, else he finds himself amongst the Gods before his time."

"That may not be a bad thing sir, for I imagine we're all destined for Hades?" Harbro commented dryly.

"Pah! Hades is for Romans and barbarian bastards, Harbro! We're the sons of Baal Hammon and he'll have a place for us at his table."

"The Lord God, Baal better make room for one more then Captain, barbarian or not, I want my place!" Gestix interjected, raising muted laughter from beneath face scarves.

"Alright! Alright!" Balaam called the men to order as small talk sprung up. "Baldor! Armaco! Malo! Marko!" He rapped the names out. "Back to the General! Tell him we're just over half a day ahead of him at the head of the pass, with Italy in sight, go!"

The men turned their horses about, Baldor calling to Armaco who was stood off from the group, slouched on his mount. Baldor hailed him again but to no response, riding over he shook him.

"Come on misery! You can't sleep yet!"

Armaco slumped across his mounts neck, his shield and spear clattering on the frozen ground as they fell. Baldor dropped his spear and hooked an arm around his friend preventing him falling while calling for Gestix.

Armaco was lifted down and propped against a rock. His breathing fast and shallow and his skin strangely hot. Gestix shook him gently and called his name trying to wake him.

"You men! Back to the General I said!" Balaam barked.

"But sir! ..." Baldor interjected.

"Damn you boy! I won't repeat myself again!"

Realising there'd be no negotiating, Baldor mounted quickly and sawing on the reins kicked Risto around heading down the track at frightening speed. Malo and Marko following but at a safer pace.

"Harbro! You go too; three's too small a group and that boy's mind is not on the job in hand!" Balaam ordered.

"Sir!"

The hoof beats faded as the men rounded the corner of the track on their way back to the column.

Before darkness fell, the lookouts Balaam had posted reported two riders heading up the track at the gallop. One of which appeared to be Baldor leading the other horse behind him with a terrified man on its back.

"Impossible man!" Balaam snapped. "He hasn't had time to be there and back! The column was at least half a day behind us."

Moments later the two riders thundered into the small camp. The horses steaming in the chill air and lathered with sweat, they blew hard as Baldor brought them to a skidding, sliding halt. He'd dismounted and was hauling the other man from his horse before the animals stopped, the man shouting and protesting the moment his feet touched the ground. Ignoring the protests, Baldor dragged him stumbling and struggling to where Armaco laid. The mercenaries looked on in interest while Balaam made his way over to see what the commotion was about.

The man was stooped over Armaco and starting to examine him while shouting at Baldor.

"My bag! I need my bag you fool! I can't help him with my bare hands! I'm a physician not a conjuror!"

"What's to do here?" Balaam roared.

"You're damn soldier over there!" The man pointed to Baldor returning with the bag though he continued to assess Armaco as he spoke. "He demanded I come and tend his friend! Demanded! ... I told him, I have others to see to. What's he do ...?"

Baldor offered the bag to the physician, who snatched it while cursing under his breath as he rummaged in it.

"He seizes me! That's what he does! Sticks a sword under my chin and threatens to add me to the casualty list if I don't come with him!"

Balaam's face creased into a smile, placing a hand over his mouth to hide it he huffed instead.

"How long's this man been like this?" The physician asked.

"We're not sure sir." Baldor replied.

"What would you know? You're a raving madman!" He turned towards Balaam. "Mad he is! Mad! Riding up the damn path as if we can sprout wings should we fall! I want charges brought!"

The man continued to rant between wanting Baldor crucified, hung or stoned and asking questions about Armaco. The gathering mercenaries all stifling laughs as they listened to the man's bluster while watching him work.

"Captain Sir!" Baldor addressed Balaam; suddenly remembering his mission. "The General sends his compliments and advises he'll camp tonight and bring the column up in the morning. We're to camp here to await him and any stragglers that come in."

Balaam nodded and grunted acknowledgement then placed his arm around Baldor's shoulder turning him away from the physician and whispering quietly.

"You're a bad lad, Baldor! Kidnapping physicians at sword point!" He tut, tutted as he smiled mockingly and shook his head. "You've been around us lot too long." He winked at Baldor then raised his voice again, talking again to the physician. "We'll have him flogged sir, if that'll suffice? The ground hereabouts is a little hard to plant a cross and we're short of trees for a hanging. Stoning is an option, though the ones here are large and heavy to lift!"

The man paled as he listened while pouring the contents of a small earthenware flask between Armaco's lips and stroking his throat to help him swallow. "Flogged?"

"Aye sir, we'll have the skin off his back for you!"

"Are you mad as well, man? That's more work for me when I've to treat him! Do I look like I need more work? Idiots! You soldiers are all bloody idiots!" He pointed to Baldor. "You, fool! Bring some hot, fresh water and clean cloths. Clean mind! If you know what that is!"

Gestix produced his package of clean linen as Baldor went for water. The Gaul squatted beside the physician offering the cloths.

"At last, someone with some sense! Now, see here?" The physician turned Armaco's head towards Gestix as he unwrapped the last of the scarves and removed the eye patch, exposing the empty socket. The area was ingrained with filth, the skin angry and puckered; where it had been rubbed raw, it leaked pus and watery, brown blood. Looking closely at the wound the Physician's nose wrinkled at the smell emanating from it. "He's had problems here; I think the dirt's come from his hands rubbing at it." The Physician held up one of Armaco's hands, which was black with dirt and old blood. "He's carried an infection into the socket and it's festered, poisoning his body. Hence the fever."

Gestix nodded sagely. "I suppose we've all been a little tardy with the washing of late … and the shaving." He rubbed his hand over his beard.

The physician ferreted in his bag again, producing a pestle and mortar and a small, muslin bag of powder.

"Where's the fool with the water?"

Baldor returned with a pot of steaming water setting it down near the physician. Shooing Baldor away he wet the cloth and carefully washed in and around the wound, Armaco twitched and mumbled as the hot swab touched broken skin. Nodding in satisfaction when the cleaning was completed, he ground the powder while demanding more hot water, mixing both into a thick, sticky paste, which he spread over the wound. Placing a cloth pad over it, he bandaged around Armaco's head holding it in place.

"Acacia?" Gestix asked, pointing to the powder.

The physician nodded. "Clean the wound daily and reapply the compress! Use a new, clean pad! The fever should pass in a day or two, let him rest and keep him warm." He passed the bag to Gestix then repacked his bag and stood to go.

"By your leave?" He said sarcastically to Baldor.

Baldor fished in his purse pulling out a handful of silver coins. Taking the man's hand, he tipped the coins into it, filling it while bowing his head and offering his thanks. The physician looked at the coins and picked out two then raised his eyes to look at Baldor.

"One for the treatment and one for the travelling time." He took another before pushing the rest back into Baldor's hand. "And one for the years you took off my life on the way here!"

Baldor pushed the remainder of the coins at him but he waved them away.

"You're a madman and a fool! But an honest one it seems." He turned away. "Anybody else need my services while I'm here?"

****

The army camped for two days on the summit, the men grateful for the break in the march and a chance to recover from the battle. Horses and mules that had bolted during the action drifted into the camp, arriving in ones and two's or the occasional group. Some still carried their packs intact, others trailed their load tangled in the ropes when it had become dislodged from their backs, most however had lost their load altogether. Some were injured either from the battle or from their flight and despite their efforts to catch up had to be destroyed. Stragglers of the human kind also arrived; the lost and the injured limped in, as well as some non-combatants that had fled the attack then managed to pick up the army's trail again. The men's morale was low as they huddled around their fires, intent only on trying to keep warm and fed, their mood worsened when the leaden skies began dropping huge flakes of snow. Driven on the wind the snow began to drift, depositing in depth against rocks, tent sides and the sleeping men who'd swapped shelter of the tents for the warmth of the fire. Baldor however, was fascinated with the snow. Like a questioning child, he picked it up, studying the texture and tasting it, marvelling at how it melted on his tongue then discussing it with Malo who was also mystified by the strange phenomenon. They moulded it in their hands making balls, one or two of which were aimed in Gestix's direction. Malo was most interested in the crisp, detailed tracks left in it, more so when they froze and were still there two days later.

Hannibal spent his time moving between the regiments and divisions as they arrived and pitched camp. He spoke to all in turn, while pointing to the plains below. Telling them the way to Italy was now open, the worst of the journey over and that with a battle or two more down on the plains, both Italy and Rome itself would be theirs for the taking. By passing over the mountains, he said they were literally passing over the walls of Rome itself, who would be able to stop them now? They'd fought and marched together these many months, forging into an elite force, proving their worth as both warriors and men.

Baldor listened intently as Hannibal spoke and he felt his spirits rise and confidence bolstered as he told them of what was to come. He wondered what it was about the man that made him so readily believable. He didn't shout or rant he just talked, men seeming content to listen. Some questioned him though none seemed to doubt his words nor try to contradict. Was it the common touch he displayed in his actions or because he shared his men's hardships? He dressed no better than they did, he ate and slept amongst them and fought alongside them, demonstrating personal courage and his ability to command. Perhaps it was this capacity to be a General and a soldier but above all a man. He had, Baldor concluded, a persona that transcended race, language and culture, binding men to him.

Yes, there was the promise of plunder, always dear to soldier's hearts but in truth; the men had seen little of that since the fall of Saguntum. Baldor surmised that in a fickle world where very little was assured Hannibal stood out, what he said or planned came to pass and despite his youth, his list of victories condoning his words was impressive. Like Alexander before him, he inspired and led from the front but differed in that he remained real and ordinary in the way he conducted himself, claiming neither royal blood nor divine lineage. Baldor knew he would follow this man come what may.

The army moved off the summit on the third day and for the first time in weeks began marching downhill. The snow made things difficult, especially for the wagon drivers as the downward slope twisted and turned sharply, making controlling the draft teams tricky and cornering a precarious task. The previous day's snow had hardened and crisped overnight, turning it to ice and with the fresh fall on top of it, was now treacherous. Where the track dropped steeply, any application of the wagon's brakes sent them sliding, sledge-like under their own weight. The wagons had to be slowed using ropes and men acting as anchors, they heaved and slipped, being dragged even, as they fought to hold the wagons back. Sometimes the animals panicked from being forced onwards by their load and thus drove forwards to get away from it, this in turn further increasing the load for the men. More than a few wagons slid over the edge as they went out of control. Some of the drivers, too slow to move or caught on the wrong side of their driving platform also went over, their screams mixing with those of the falling animals and echoing across the mountains as they fell. The thickening snow hid potholes and rocks, causing sprains and broken bones as men and animals slipped and fell when they encountered the hidden hazards. Many fell to their deaths when part of the track crumbled away dropping dirt, rocks, men and animals to the valley far below. Those at the rear of the column fared the worst as the snow became compacted by the thousands of feet and hooves, turning it to a polished, mirror-like ice. The march reduced to a crawl, Hannibal detailing working parties to clear the snow ahead of the column and to hack up the compacted ice that was forming from their passage over it. When the supply of shovels and adze's ran out men used their shields to scoop the snow away.

The day remained crystal clear, the wind eased, and the skies though overcast allowed chinks of watery sunlight to break through. As men worked, they looked and pointed at the plains below, flat and snow free and no doubt warmer, and more hospitable than where they were now. Many dreamed of sprouting wings and flying to the plains away from the bitter cold and the nightmare struggle to descend the mountains. When darkness fell, they camped on the road making small fires from the kindling and fir cones they carried with them. After cooking their evening meal, they wrapped themselves cocoon-like in blankets and furs, huddling around the fires and together for warmth. Armaco was on the mend, the two days halt on the summit had given his body chance to fight the infection and fever. Gestix had reapplied the acacia paste and changed the dressings daily, the wound drying and scabbing over, the redness fading. His skin no longer burned, and his sleep was no longer fitful. His character too was returning to normal and though still weak, he sat his mount and rode with the company.

Another day of struggle brought the column head below the snowline and back onto bare ground. Cheers went up as the snow petered out. Baldor could not remember being happier to see barren ground or commit to manual labour, as he took his turn in the squads detailed to the back breaking work of clearing debris from the track. They pushed fist sized stones to one side of the track or used them to fill potholes so the wagons could pass unhindered, the larger boulders they hurled over the edge. As slow and painstaking as the work was, it reduced accidents and further losses of both men and animals. The work warmed the men's bodies, driving some of the cold induced lethargy and stiffness from them, the progress helping lift morale as each stade cleared, and downward, was a stade nearer the plains.

****

The mercenary company carefully picked their way over the rock and shale on the track but eventually had to dismount as the stones multiplied in numbers and depth forming a belt of scree. Too treacherous for the horses to walk on, they left them so to view the track where it took a sharp turn up ahead. As Baldor rounded the corner, he stopped abruptly, a low groan coming from his lips.

"What is it Baldor? … Baldor!" Gestix called, receiving no response.

Baldor's head dropped and his shoulders sagged as if in defeat. Gestix caught him up and looked to where Baldor was pointing.

"For the love of Taranis!" Gestix exclaimed despairingly.

In front of them, the track was completely gone where a landslide had wiped it from the side of the mountain. Above, where the track had been, the land laid open like a giant, gaping wound. Hundreds of tons of earth and rock had broken away from the mountainside, crashing down on the track, the force of the impact carrying all before it. The men stared at the gouge where the track had been, looking into fresh air and down to the valley floor. Apart from a few mumbles and curses, no one had much to say, despair and sudden weariness etched into their features. Balaam came to his senses first and dispatched messengers back to find the General and inform him of the predicament. He sent the usual team of Baldor, Malo, Marko, Gestix, Armaco and Harbro, to see if there was another way around the damaged road.

Just as darkness fell, Harbro and his team were back at the ruined road and relaying with heavy hearts that there was no other way forward, not even mountain goats could pass they said, they would need wings to get down from where they'd looked. Hannibal and his engineers arrived and walked out to the edge of the road assessing the damage. The men waited quietly in the gloom shivering a little after the exertions of the ride, their breath ballooning in white vapour clouds while the horses steamed. Balaam spoke quietly to Harbro then strode out to join Hannibal and the engineers.

"Dismount! Rub the horses down then get some rest." Harbro called.

Grateful for the chance to move again and keep warm, the men saw to their mounts then kindled fires for the evening meal. As before, with no ground suitable for pitching tents they settled down to sleep on the road. Just as they rolled into their blankets, labourers and slaves began filing past with shovels, pick-axes and adzes, heading towards the damaged road.

"We might be short on sleep tonight looking at that lot." Marko grumbled.

Shortly, the tapping of pick-axes and sounds of earth and stones being shovelled drifted back to the mercenaries, thankfully, the corner of the road muted the majority of noise and the exhausted men were soon asleep. The following morning saw the whole column backed up and camped along the road behind the mercenaries with the crisp, cold wind freshening. As the winter light brightened in the east, men huddled around the fire rubbing their hands and pulling furs and blankets about them.

"Another day in paradise lads!" Harbro quipped.

"Not if you're a horse!" Gestix replied. "They had the last of their feed three days past and there's still no sign of any grazing for them."

"True." Harbro sighed. "They were already a bit thin to start with, that highland grass they managed to get had no goodness in it. Hopefully another day or two and we should see some greenery. Trouble is, this late in the season everything is dying off." He shook his head and scowled. "We should have been out of these mountains and down in better country long since."

As Baldor and Malo prepared breakfast they saw more units of labourers coming and going to the excavations, the noise of the digging however never stopped. Balaam appeared as they ate and hunkered down beside them warming his hands and accepting the plate of greasy, fried meat that was offered. Picking at the sizzling food with his fingers, he ate with relish as he talked.

"The labourers have cut into the hillside to form a new road; they've been at it all night."

The men looked up from their meal, hope and tinges of excitement on their faces.

"They've hit a seam of rock though; it's bloody huge and hard as the heart of a damned street whore!" The men's hopes faded as quickly as they had come.

"We all need to take a turn at digging and we also need timber, lots of it! All are to help cut and gather it, then split it into burning size."

"Timber sir? Why'd we need that?" Marko asked.

"Damned if I know! Nevertheless, that's the order. There's no scouting to do, so after breakfast we all become woodcutters."

"Well, it'll save us freezing our arses off sir." Harbro quipped, raising a few smiles and chuckles from the men around the fire. Shortly, the sounds of axes, saws and the creak and crash of timber falling mixed with the noise of digging. Warriors became labourers, woodcutters and builders as they strived to forge a road and cut timber into burnable sizes. The larger boles required splitting lengthways before they could be moved or cut into shorter lengths. Baldor found his experience from the shipyards helped. Having seen men breaking down huge timber ready for sawing into planking, he was able to advise and demonstrate to his comrades the methods of wedging it along the grain to force and burst it apart.

As they worked, Hannibal moved amongst them, directing, encouraging and taking a hand at the heavy labouring. His presence had the same positive affect as if he was fighting alongside them, whereby they worked harder and longer without rest. As weary as they were of the mountains, the marching and the freezing cold, there was a renewed vigour in them. Many reasoned the young General would remove them from their predicament, he always had a plan, he'd brought them this far.

The cut timber was carried or dragged to the exposed pinnacle of rock blocking the road. Placing faggots around it first, they stacked heavier logs on top, building what looked like a huge pyre. When the rock was completely covered in timber, the engineers set it alight. The flames were poor, miserable affairs at first, the timber green and damp. Adding what little oil they had left to help the flames take hold, they carefully and patiently grew the fire spreading it from place to place. The gusting wind helped, forcing air through the logs and fanning the flames, soon they crackled and roared, growing in strength and appetite and devouring the wood. As the flames spread the heat intensified, soon the timber was sparking spitting and whistling as sap boiled and bubbled out.

"What are they trying to do Gestix?" Armaco stared and shook his head as he spoke. "You can't burn rock!"

Gestix shook his head slowly, watching intently at the goings on. "Baldor! Any idea?"

"None! I've never seen the likes of this."

"Bring more timber! Keep it coming, we'll need more heat." One of the engineers called.

Already, he had to stand back and shield his face from the blaze as it grew hotter. Men were sorted into shifts, some cut while others carried and others rested, the work continuing non-stop throughout the day and night, the flames lighting the sky like some giant signalling beacon to the Gods. By this stage, the engineers and men feeding the flames were covered in dampened blankets, their faces bound in scarves to ward off the immense heat emanating from the blaze.

The mercenaries awoke the next morning to cracks, bangs and cheering. Leaving their blankets and without pausing for breakfast they ran down to the fire, elbowing their way through the assembled crowd to see what was afoot. The heat was still incredible. The burned timber left a layer of red embers four cubits deep around the rock base, from which fluttering grey-white ash rose on the hot air drifting like snowflakes on the wind. The rock seemed to shimmer and wobble, similar to the heat haze that rises from a paved road on a hot day. The engineers stood atop small wooden platforms, which had been pushed close to the rock but towering above it. They emptied casks of wine over the roasted stone, the cold liquid steaming and hissing as it boiled off on contact, causing loud cracking and shattering as the rock reacted to the massive changes in temperature. Fissures appeared as if by magic as it contracted too quickly, small pieces flew off like missiles, zinging and whining through the air like demented insects, some hitting the assembled men. Despite some howls of pain the men cheered while others capered and danced with delight, more than a few sniffed appreciatively at the heady aroma of vaporised wine carrying on the wind.

By midday, the rock was cooled sufficiently for men to stand on it, though they still felt the heat through the soles of their boots. A cacophony of hammers, chisels and picks saw the weakened rock attacked from all angles, the men reducing the obstruction piece by piece breaking it into manageable bits, which they hurled over the edge to the valley below. Tough as the warriors were, their hands were unused to manual labour and before long blisters grew then burst, secreting sticky fluid over the tool handles. Hands were bandaged or those that had gloves put them on, the work never ceasing. Hannibal found rotating the men in shorter shifts gave the best results as the men worked feverishly before exhaustion took them. Those returning for their second shift were heartened when they saw the rock diminished from when they'd finished work earlier. A further day and half of non-stop labouring saw the rock gone and the newly cut road clear of obstruction.

The mercenaries were readying their mounts to begin scouting again but as Baldor tried to fit Risto's bridle the horse pushed his head into his chest, sniffing and whinnying at him. Baldor stroked Risto's head speaking softly as it continued nuzzling.

"They're hungry lad! Poor buggers have had nothing for over four days now, their feeds gone and we've no bread left to give them."

Baldor bent down to the tack bag at his feet and fished out a bruised apple. Risto caught the scent and pushed closer, curling his lips exposing long yellow teeth; he eagerly took the offered fruit munching loudly on it. Baldor produced another, which he cut in half in a bid to lengthen the meal for his horse.

"Steady boy! Steady now." He stroked Risto as the animal ate.

"Where did you get them from?" Gestix asked in wonder.

"From the fat Greek quartermaster, with the last of my silver." Baldor smiled. "There's more in the bag, enough for your mount and the two re-mounts, two apples each."

Gestix smiled. "You're too soft and kind lad! You should've kept your silver. They'd have survived until the morning you know, we'll pick up grazing for them then."

Baldor shrugged and patted Risto. "As long as we and the horses can eat I don't care about the money." He smiled wistfully. "It's my new outlook on life, live for today and enjoy every moment!"

Gestix roared with laughter. "That's it lad! That's it! We'll make a Gaul of you yet!"

By late afternoon the following day, the mercenaries were down on the plain and Balaam dispatched a patrol to bring the column onwards. The sky was blue and cloudless and despite the chill wind, the sun offered some midwinter warmth to the men as they sat their mounts while they cropped hungrily at the grass.

Gestix had become strangely quiet throughout the day. Baldor noticing it, badgered him gently for conversation. He always felt disconcerted and somewhat uncomfortable when the big man was quiet or melancholy, as there was usually trouble just around the corner.

"Are you sure you're alright Gestix?" He asked for the umpteenth time.

Gestix didn't reply immediately, as Baldor watched waiting for an answer, he saw him chew his lip as if considering his response.

"I'm almost home lad! Almost! … I was born and lived just over a days ride from here."

"We should go and …" Baldor remembered Gestix's tale and stopped himself short, Gestix however didn't appear to be listening.

The awkwardness was cut short by Armaco reining in alongside.

"The Captain says we're to camp here and await the column." He settled his horse as he spoke. "It's open and wind swept but a damn sight warmer than the bloody mountains eh?"

The mercenaries prepared their evening meal pooling the last scraps they had, Malo adding to it with a rabbit, albeit a thin one. Behind them, the greatest army ever to cross the Alps poured from the mountains and began setting up camp on the plains of the Po.

Chapter Twenty seven

The ice-edged breeze blew flurries of snow that settled against the bundles of blankets and furs on the ground that were sleeping men. Baldor stirred as the white crystals melted on his face, dawn was breaking and allowing slivers of grey and pink light to creep into the world. He was about to bury his head beneath the furs once more, desperate to sleep longer and rest his weary body when light footfalls disturbed him further. From bleary eyes, he saw Gestix slipping quietly from his bedroll. Baldor surmised he was going to relieve himself and was about to curl up again when he saw him ferreting in his pack and removing particular items and his spare sword from its sheepskin wrappings.

"Gestix! Is everything alright?" He asked in a hushed whisper, trying not to disturb the sleeping warriors.

Gestix carried on obliviously, Baldor's low toned question having fallen on his damaged ear. Baldor called again, as loud as he dared without risking waking the others but still to no response. They were all exhausted from their ordeal in the Alps and this had been the first night in over two weeks, when they'd slept without fear of attack after what had been a nightmare journey. Half starved, chilled to the bone and almost physically broken, too weary to erect tents or awnings, they'd rolled in their blankets and furs as soon as their meager supper was over.

Gestix slipped away, taking the sword and chosen possessions still unaware of Baldor and his concern. Baldor pulled his furs tighter around him closing his eyes again, reasoning Gestix was just up and about early. A heartbeat later he sat bolt upright blinking and rubbing his eyes trying to make them work, something was wrong, very wrong! Gestix had unpacked possessions Baldor hadn't seen in months, what was he doing with them at this time of the morning?

He tried to stand and found his leg numb. Stumbling and falling backwards, he forced clumsy, stiff fingers to rub life back into it, before picking up his swords to follow Gestix, who moving swiftly, was already disappearing into the trees almost a stade away.

Attempting to run to catch up, Baldor fell again as his legs refused to work, the muscles still sleepy and unfeeling, his worn out body already pushed beyond endurance. Cursing, he regained his feet but with his balance still askew was forced to follow at a more sedate, limping pace while loosening both swords in their sheaths as he went. He slipped quietly into the small copse at the same place Gestix had entered.

The morning light was growing, pale yellow replacing the rose pink; it filtered through the branches dissolving the shadows. Following the rough trail downward he stumbled over hidden roots, his feet kicking up fallen leaves that covered them and releasing a damp earthy smell. He was about to call for Gestix again when he saw him through the trees, sitting back on his knees by the edge of a small lake. The water was the colour of old limes and partially covered in pond weed with dead looking reed stems lining its edge. The water surface was undisturbed, the light morning breeze held at bay by the drooping willows that surrounded it. His head was bowed forward, chin resting on his chest, his hands palm down on his thighs. He rocked backward and forward gently, eyes closed and his lips moving in silent prayer and despite the cold, he was stripped to the waist.

Secreting himself behind one of the thicker trunks Baldor crouched, his stiffened body complaining as muscles and ligaments were forced to work and bend. Realising Gestix was praying and feeling he was intruding, he was about to retrace his steps when he noticed the broadsword, a gold neck torque, some small figurines of deities and a finely crafted broach laid in the grass. Intrigued, he decided to stay.

Gestix ceased rocking and raised his arms skyward. He began to chant quietly the words mostly unintelligible to Baldor other than the odd names of deities such as Epona and Sirona, whom Baldor had heard him mention or call upon in the past. He paused every so often picking an item from his belongings, holding it aloft as if offering a gift before casting it out into the pool. Baldor had seen Gestix pray many times but usually it was a quick word or two over food, with a little wine spilt on the ground or a morsel of food left as an offering and lately the asking of blessing before combat. He'd never seen him offering treasured possessions. Gestix left the sword till last, holding it horizontal and level to his shoulders by tip and hilt he continued praying before lifting it high above his head offering it skyward. The rays from the rising sun danced and shimmered on the blade and after pressing the finely wrought hilt to his lips, he threw it. The weapon whooshed and hummed as it spun and somersaulted through the air before disappearing with a splash into the water, his head once more bowed in reverence.

Despite his concerns, Baldor quietly backed away, not wishing to betray his presence or intrude further. He made his way out of the trees and waited some distance from the path watching for Gestix emerging. Time passed and he pulled the furs about his shoulders, blowing into cupped hands to warm them as the wind swirled about him. Eventually he saw Gestix coming through the trees, his shirt back on. Baldor began walking towards him as if he'd been searching for him.

"Gestix! Where have you been? Are you alright?"

Gestix waved in acknowledgement. "Just having a look around is all, lad!"

The usual conviction however was missing from his voice and when Baldor looked at him questioningly, he tried to bolster his previous reply.

"I'm fine lad, honest! And you, did you sleep well?" He slipped his arm around Baldor's shoulder turning him back towards the camp. "I hope you've come to tell me the fire's on and breakfast's cooking?"

"Er, no... I was concerned when I woke and you were gone."

It was Gestix's turn to look questioningly as he was always up and about early, long before Baldor.

Baldor felt guilty for not starting the fire and for the intrusion, however he felt sure not all was well, Gestix had not mentioned praying, why didn't he just say he needed to pray? They walked back towards the camp, the big man hugging the younger closer affectionately. Baldor looked for something to say to break the silence.

"We must have lost thousands of men in the mountains with the cold, plus the desertions and all those killed from un-necessary battles just to get here, how are we going to take on and defeat the Legions?"

"Well, let's hope recruiting improves now we're down on the plains. At least we are alive and here lad, which must prove something? It also says much for the quality of the General eh, successfully taking an army over the roof of the world this late in the year and a multi-cultural army at that! And despite the cost, we have fought together as one and won! The Romans will be bearing all that in mind when we close with them, believe me. We're not quite in the 'she wolf's' den yet but certainly close enough to make her think her tail may catch fire! Now, if these Gauls would just stop fighting among themselves and us, we could really give the Romans something to think about. Anyway … what did you say you had cooked for breakfast?" Gestix chuckled as he spoke.

Baldor smiled back a little relieved, this sounded more like his friend.

Three cold but restful days later found the Carthaginians advancing southeastwards over the plain towards the Po river. The plain continued as far as the eye could see, carpeted in short tufted grass, pale wintergreen in colour where it grew near streams and pools and ochre on the flats where moisture was stolen on the wind. Tiny streams cut through it like arteries in a warrior's forearm, exposing gravel beds and where the ground lowered further; water collected into bogs and pools with stands of sedge and reeds about their edges. Numerous small woodlands and copses were scattered across it with a mix of pine, larch, oak and poplar growing alongside one another. The plain seemed endless as it merged and faded into a green-blue haze on the horizon but after the harshness of the mountains, the early winter beauty seemed like paradise.

It was now easy going for both horses and men, the cavalry again in the van with outriders in front, the infantry still breaking camp and following on behind. Scouts reported Scipio and his Legions to be pushing northwest at speed, following the Po towards them but approaching over the smaller tributary of the Ticinus and the bridge they'd built across it. It seemed Scipio was anxious to annex Hannibal in the north and was spoiling for a fight. Hannibal was more than happy to oblige, hungry for a victory to bolster his men's confidence and bring the tribes of hesitant Boii, Insurbes and Ligurians to his side.

With the plain opening before them and the traumas of the mountains behind them, his men were in better spirits. Though still recovering they were rested and had hot food in their bellies.

Despite the sun, the morning remained bitterly cold, the skies a pale ocean-blue and cloudless. The unseasonably dry autumn and early winter had left rivers low in height and the streams nothing more than trickles. Thus, the breeze whipped dust from the riverbeds blowing it in clouds along their course and onto the plain itself where the advancing army added to it. Balaam's troop was in the van, alongside divisions of Spanish and Gallic heavy cavalry and advancing in wide column at a gentle trot. Flanking them in loose order on their small ponies were the Numidians, these lightly armed, somber warriors wrapped beneath robes and blankets of dirty white or black. Suffering terribly with the cold they hid hands and feet in any material available, many had wrapped their faces with scarves covering mouths and noses leaving only dark, hawk-like eyes on view. As a fighting unit, they looked laughable; by reputation however, they were deadly and in truth were without equal, the finest light cavalry in the world.

The Gallic heavy cavalry were in stark contrast with flamboyant clothing of checks and plaid and heavily armed. All wore helmets of bronze or leather, some crested with spikes or effigies of animals. Most wore mail shirts and all carried a large shield, circular or oval in shape, faced with painted devices or patterns. They also differed markedly in character from their Numidian allies, being raucous, gregarious and fiercely proud.

Baldor and Gestix were helmeted as much against the cold as in readiness for combat, bearskin cloaks wrapped about them over leather corselets. Baldor wore fur lined, leather gloves and a thick scarf about his neck as he still suffered with the cold climate; Gestix as ever seemed impervious to the chill, just as he had to the heat extremes in Carthage. Baldor quietly marveled at him, he suffered hardships and changing situations with casual indifference, his pride and love for Baldor were the only things that couldn't be compromised and if a threat was made to either he would fight the world if need be. Baldor remained quietly concerned for him, especially since the morning he'd found him by the pool; though Gestix never spoke of it he'd seemed troubled, pre-occupied and a little withdrawn since. He was making an effort to appear normal and to others he seemed no different. Baldor knowing him best, noted the lack of humour in him and the time spent in deep thought, his mind clearly elsewhere. Baldor raised his concerns more than once, only to have them politely disregarded as 'nothing wrong nor to worry about' he was well he said and could even blame his deafness on his injury instead of old age. Baldor had his good name back and they were out of the mountains, the Gods were good!

Outriders galloping back to the column and reining up sharply in front of Hannibal and the command group snapped Baldor from his thoughts, they pointed back at a huge dust cloud in the distance. Before Baldor could speak, Gestix did. "Romans!"

Before orders were issued, men were removing restricting cloaks and furs, rolling and stowing them in bags or strapping them with other gear over their horse's back. Helmet straps were fastened, weapons loosened in sheaths, shield straps and corselet bindings checked. Gestix indicated for Baldor to remove his scarf, then tugged at his gloves and had him remove them when he decided they were too slack to wear in combat. Orders came that Roman cavalry was indeed approaching, at the trot and in a wide frontage. Also, their Velites were accompanying them in open order, their formations indicating they were seeking battle and the estimated time before contact was before noon.

Orders barked from troop commanders and Captains with mounted messengers and interpreters racing between units relaying instructions. The Numidians were to stay out wide on the flanks of the heavy cavalry, who would continue their advance as they were. Their frontage however, should prepare to widen or narrow to match the Roman line once it was in view. They were not to attack the Roman flanks, that task left solely to the Numidians. There would be no pause for talk between Generals of the two sides; a hammer blow to the Roman centre at high speed was the command. At two stades out from the Roman line, they should move to full gallop, watch for the signals!

With preparations done and under orders warriors shook hands as they trotted on, calling to their Gods for blessings for their comrades and themselves. Gestix leaned across and hugged Baldor strongly.

"You stay by me, you hear! May Epona and all the Gods be with you lad! Your father would be proud of you! I'm very proud of you!"

As Gestix eased away Baldor noticed a sadness in his eyes, it was more than just the usual look of concern before battle, a look rather of loss, departure and grief. Baldor felt uneasy and with panic rising in him, he grabbed at Gestix's forearm holding it tight.

"Are you alright? What troubles you?"

The Gaul shook his head slowly, a wan smile on his face. He patted Baldor's hand lightly and sighed deeply. He looked Baldor in the eyes, speaking very gently. "I'm alright lad, honestly! … I'm alright now, so don't worry. You look after yourself mind! This is going to be a hard, fast fight, give no quarter to these bastards for you'll receive none."

Baldor knew Gestix was not telling the whole truth and something was definitely worrying him. However, before he could ponder further a blast on a war horn and the command to move to the canter saw the horses urged on. The drumming hooves grew louder. Weapons rattled and leather creaked as eight thousand cavalry flowed over the plain. Men pulling back on the reins as the horses, sensing action and with subsequent adrenalin release tried to quicken their pace further. Out on the flanks the Numidians slipped into thinner columns, the lithe desert ponies keeping pace comfortably with the larger Gallic and Spanish mounts.

Across the plain, the Roman ranks materialized from a blur of colours to become individual men and horses. Brightly painted shields, uniforms and flashes of sunlight on metal heralded the approaching dust cloud. Slipping from between the horses in loose order and at a loping run came the Velites preparing to hurl javelins once the range closed.

Balaam glanced back to his men before drawing his sword. Pointing it groundward, he looked to Hannibal and the command group watching for their command, ready to relay it.

The rumble of hooves became thunder as the horses surged. Some pranced while others whinnied and shook their harness, straining to be given their head as they felt the terrible excitement and trepidation of the riders. Balaam's arm began to rise. He brought it up slowly until vertical from his shoulder, the sword pointing skyward.

"Hold! ... Hold!" He called as one or two horses pushed forward of the line.

"Hold!"

A heartbeat later, he dropped his arm forward pointing straight at the advancing Romans.

"Charge!" Balaam's scream was lost in the noise but from out of the ranks; whoops, screams and battle cries rose to a crescendo, blood lust and adrenalin taking over from trepidation and fear. Like a huge dam finally bursting, the horses went to the charge. Their speed eating up the ground, raising the thunder of their hooves to a deafening, ground shuddering level. Men adjusted position; spears raised above shoulders pointing forwards. Thighs gripping their mounts flanks tight as the horses stretched beneath them.

Both armies were on a collision course, like two great waves they rolled over the plain, raising billows of grey dust as they came. The final Stade closed quickly. The Velites were unnerved by the Carthaginian speed and most failed to release their missiles. Choosing instead to fall back through their oncoming cavalry's ranks.

The Roman cavalry differed markedly in appearance from the Carthaginians, being uniform in dress and all similarly armed. Mail shirts covered crimson tunics and they carried a fighting spear with a spatha at their belt.

With less than a javelin throw before impact, men finally lost any hesitation, rationale or thoughts of their own safety. Almost overdosed with adrenalin they eyed their targets, desperate to kill, ride down, and destroy the other.

Like thunder and lightning rolling and striking simultaneously, the two sides clashed. Animal and human becoming battering ram and buffer as Carthaginian and Roman collided head on. Horses went down in scores, some from the impact, some from spears, others tripping over other fallen animals. Men were catapulted through the air from their mounts or dashed to the ground to be trampled and crushed. The air rent with the loud crack of spear shafts splintering, metal clanging and scraping. An awful groan came from hundreds of throats like breath knocked from a giant's lungs. Metal sliced and ripped flesh, bones splintered and broke and the killing began.

The resulting carnage from the first wave's collision gave a momentary pause, the following ranks unable close with the enemy. A swathe of dead and dying horses and men littered the field for the full length of the line. Horses whinnied in pain, many rolling on the ground wild-eyed with legs smashed. Some tried to stand, others gasping as they bled and died with spears sticking from their bodies. Warriors broken like rag dolls crawled from the mess, some regaining their feet and looking about to remount, others just wandered dazed and concussed, some fell again as their injury took over, most however, stayed were they lay.

As the following waves of warriors crossed the carnage to engage the enemy further, the Numidians swooped. Attacking the Roman flanks, they rode down the scattered Velites that were caught in the open. Galloping towards the Roman wings the Numidians swerved away before impact while hurling javelins into the massed ranks. The barrage continued relentlessly with fresh warriors riding in to replace the ones veering away. Like wasps stinging a maddening bull they drove the Romans to distraction, causing ranks to break, loss of order and bloody chaos while evading every sortie made against them.

Baldor and Gestix were in the centre of the line but in the third rank, thereby avoiding the preliminary impact, they now pushed over the carnage seeking the Roman line. The battle broke into swirling melees of various sizes that spun round about with men hacking and slashing at one another. Those unhorsed fought on foot, trying to drag their enemy from their mounts or seeking others already on the ground. Balaam led his men headlong towards one of the largest melees. Their rank crashing into the almost stationary Romans and sending more earthward, the Romans slowly giving ground as flesh and blood neared its limit.

Publius, resplendent in bronze cuirass, horsehair crested helmet and his Consul's purple sash rode about attempting to make order from the carnage. He called to his men, urging his trumpeter to signal a regroup. Mounted on a chalk-white horse he laid about the enemy as he called his men to him. He seemed to lead a charmed life as more than one javelin thudded into his shield rather than hitting him. Anyone who engaged him face on was either hacked to the ground or killed outright. Slowly his troops began to rally. By the time Balaam saw him, he had a sizeable contingent about him, and consequently Balaam led his troop directly at him.

The resulting clash again emptied more men from their mounts. Those that did not fall set about the enemy hacking and thrusting as individual, almost personal combats began. Baldor was driven to one side of the melee, fighting savagely with a Roman Decurion. With spears gone, the pair wheeled about trading sword blows. The blades clashed and scraped as the horses slipped and stumbled over the corpse strewn, blood-wet grass. The Roman drove in hard at Baldor, using his horse's weight in an attempt to push him and his mount over. The Roman cursed and grunted, raining fast, heavy blows with his spatha that split Baldor's shield, rendering it useless. Casting it away, Baldor caught the Romans weapon on the hilt of his own, the pair now straining at full arms stretch above their heads. The Roman grabbed for his dagger with his empty hand, intending to blade Baldor in his unprotected side. Unable to twist away, Baldor punched the Roman hard in the throat, crushing his windpipe. Gagging and spluttering the man instinctively grabbed at his neck, his sword arm relaxing. Baldor swung his weapon down chopping the man's neck through to his spine. Hot blood sprayed his face and sword arm as the Roman collapsed. Ignoring the dying man and blinking through the blood, Baldor looked around the chaos for more adversaries. He saw Gestix attacked from the side by a purple sashed Roman. Shouting a warning, he drove Risto towards the pair trying to intercept them. Gestix, his damaged hearing towards the Roman did not hear his approach nor Baldor's warning.

Looking and fighting to the front, he was unaware of his attacker until the Roman's spatha entered his armpit beneath his shoulder strap, pushing deep into his chest. The big man dropped his sword as the spatha drove the breath from him. Attempting to turn his mount and protect himself with his shield, the Roman wrenched the sword free and rained blows on him. Baldor was driving Risto across the grass at lightning speed, screaming a challenge at the Roman trying to draw him away.

The Roman, intent on his adversary only looked up at the last moment as Baldor rode into him unchecked. The three men and their mounts went down in a chaotic heap of animals, shields, weapons and bodies. Gestix fell clear of the horses, the Roman falling under them with Baldor on top. The horses writhed and twisted, whickering while trying to regain their feet, hooves flailing, kicking the air. Baldor was on his feet first, the Roman's horse struggling to its feet next but only after severely trampling its rider. As the horse stumbled clear of the Roman, Baldor stepped in to attack him. Snatching up his fallen sword from the grass, he reached behind his shoulder drawing his second weapon as he advanced. Attacking with both blades, he rained blows on the dazed, concussed man who was struggling to stand and defend himself.

Risto also tried to stand but with a hind leg broken fell backwards instead, rolling into and knocking Baldor sideways. The Roman, given a moments respite, snatched a broken spear shaft from the ground using it along with his sword to defend himself as Baldor regained his balance and attacked again. With both swords striking quicker than cobras, he drove the Roman back. The Roman stumbled; dazed from his fall and sorely injured from the trampling, was weakening fast. Baldor, enraged beyond reason, his blood lust driving him, pushed the attack harder.

He knocked the spatha from the Roman's hand sending it spinning away. His other blade chopping the wooden spear shaft in two and the man sank exhausted onto one knee. With his battle cry loud in his throat, Baldor pulled both weapons back ready to drive them into the Romans chest. The breathless, defeated man just looked up at him, resigned to his fate. However, before the blades could strike home, a blow to the head from behind knocked Baldor to the ground again.

The blow came from a horseman galloping past at high speed. The rider, having difficulty slowing the horse to turn about gave Baldor a moment to regain his feet. His head ringing from the impact, his vision flashing and flickering, he tore off his helmet to let the cold air at his head. Picking up his weapons again but stumbling and staggering from the affects of the blow, he went to attack the Roman once more.

The man was still on one knee, exhausted; his head slumped on his chest. Baldor ran at him determined to kill him. The rider meantime had forced the horse around in a tight, hoof sliding, whinnying turn, kicking it into motion again coming back to ride Baldor down. Seeing the rider at the last moment Baldor sidestepped and dropped low, narrowly dodging the swinging gladius meant to decapitate him. He slashed one falcata along the animal's legs and belly and stabbed with the other as it hurtled passed, losing the weapon as it caught in a rib and snatched from his hand. Tipping it's rider into the dirt, the horse went down bellowing and snorting. The rider jumped from his dying mount as it buckled beneath him, landing on his feet with only a stumble. He stepped between the exhausted man and Baldor, his gladius pointing forward.

Chapter Twenty eight

Baldor was badly shaken from the blow to his head. Feeling as though it would burst, he staggered and tottered as his balance and senses slipped in and out of co-ordination. His movements and those of the advancing Roman appearing to change from normal speed to slow and laboured, then back again. Desperate to clear his vision and befuddled senses he blinked and shook his head. Ignoring his intended adversary who had slumped to a sitting position on the grass, he turned to face the new threat. Flexing bloodied, sticky fingers on the hilt of his remaining sword, he checked his grip and prepared to defend himself.

The Roman sidestepped then lunged low only to raise the sword quickly trying to catch Baldor with the up thrust. Baldor mirrored his moves, the blades clanging loudly as though beaten on a blacksmiths anvil, scraping together along their length like the screeching of a banshee. The pair pushed apart, blades slicing air as each man swung and missed. They attacked again each seeking an opening, swords coming together at stomach height as Baldor warded off a disemboweling thrust. As the hilts locked, he brought his knee up aiming for the Roman's groin but missed and hit the man's thigh muscle instead. The Roman grunted in pain and responded by head butting him. The embossed helmet ridge hitting Baldor on the bridge of his nose, breaking it and snapping his head back violently. His head seemed to explode, his vision replaced by tiny flashes of bright, white-yellow light as his senses and body began to close down. He swung wildly with his falcata as his legs folded beneath him. By chance, the falcata's edge caught the Roman's blade hard, sending it spinning away. The force of the blow however vibrated through his own weapon tingling and deadening his fingers causing him to drop it. Baldor sunk semi-conscious to his knees, the Roman grabbed for his throat whilst drawing his dagger stepping in close for the kill. Struggling to see through the tears, coughing and choking on his blood, Baldor caught the Roman's dagger hand as the blade forced down towards his face. The Roman's hand tightened over his throat, fingers clawing then squeezing vice-like on his windpipe shutting of the air. Battered senseless and unable to see properly or breathe through his smashed nose, Baldor began to panic. The subsequent adrenalin rush took him above the pain and numbed senses, supercharging his body imbuing colossal strength into his muscles. Like a lightning bolt, his fist drove up hard towards the Romans groin and this time connected. The Roman groaned loudly, bending double and dropping his dagger. His grip loosened on Baldor's throat as the numbing, sickening pain gripped him stealing his breath. Baldor snatched at his harness dragging him to the ground.

The pair clawed, punched and grabbed at each other, hands seeking to rip throats and gouge eyes. Rolling and wrestling on the ground, Baldor's longer arms found the other's throat and he forced the Roman into the dirt and rolled astride him pinning him down. Locking both hands about the base of the man's neck he pushed in hard with his thumbs to crush his throat. The Roman's hands instinctively closed about Baldor's wrists, pulling and tearing, trying to force them away as he gagged and choked. His body bucked and thrashed like an unbroken pony trying to throw Baldor off. Their eyes locked as they struggled. Hands shaking, arm muscles tensing and straining, lips curled into feral snarls baring teeth gritted in effort and savage hate. Holding the smaller man down with his body weight, Baldor leaned forward adding the weight of his shoulders to his hands as he choked the life from him. Blood fell in heavy, syrupy drops from his smashed nose landing on the Roman's face. The eyelids flickering and blinking from the splashing blood now bulged in panic as the air supply closed off.

"Die! … Die, you bastard! Die!" Baldor growled loudly with the effort to slay him while shaking his neck as if throttling a chicken.

As the man weakened and succumbed, Baldor saw he was of similar age to himself, perhaps younger. The bloodied face pale and dotted with freckles, the eyebrows curiously blonde. His lips moved and gasped small breaths as if trying to form words a hollow, dying rattle in his throat.

Baldor's stare was distracted by a flash of sunlight reflecting from a bracelet on the man's wrist. A small, simple bracelet of copper and bronze wire twists, polished and worn from age ... a child's bracelet ... his old bracelet! Baldor stared hard, not believing his eyes, his hands though continuing to squeeze the life from the Roman. He looked again at the bracelet then back to the man's face. The eyes had rolled back and the grip slackened while the body shook in violent spasms from air starvation as death approached.

Baldor released his grip, using one hand he grabbed at the bracelet to examine it closer. It definitely was or had been his, so who was the man who wore it? Surely ... surely not the small blonde boy he'd pulled from the sea all those years ago? Despite his battle rage he was shocked and suddenly curious and he let go of the man's throat altogether. Seizing him by his mail shirt, he shook him violently.

"Where did you get this?" He shook the wrist with the bracelet on it. "Where? ... Who in Hade's name are you? ... Talk ... damn you!"

He shook the man like a doll as he shouted. The Roman coughed and gasped as the motion helped restore air to his lungs and aided the return of consciousness. In his numbed, semi-conscious state the Roman lashed out feebly with his fist, hitting Baldor in the chest; Baldor knocked the arm savagely away.

"Where did you get this?" He shook the arm and bracelet harder. "Where? Tell me or I'll tear your throat out!"

The Roman coughed and tried to speak but only croaks and mumbles came from the tortured throat as he sucked air in rasping breaths. Baldor undid the man's helmet strap pulling it off, throwing it to one side. Steam rose from the blonde, sweat matted hair. Just visible above the right eye beneath the wet fringe was a thick, raised white scar. Baldor seized him by his shirt again this time pulling him up towards his face.

"Bastard! How did you get this bracelet?" He snarled through tight lips, bloody spittle spraying the pale face in front of him.

The Roman looked at him with bleary, flickering eyes, a strange smile playing briefly on his lips. He tried to speak but again only incoherent mumbles and dry sounds came out. He swallowed hard sucking in precious breath, slowly lifting his hand to point to the marble encased in gold filigree about Baldor's neck.

"Th... the... same way ... you got that, Bal ... Baldor!" He gasped.

The pair stared at each other, a long searching look. Each in his own mind remembering the other and that day long ago on a wharf in Spain, when play had turned to tragedy. An unseen bond made between them. Sadly, the friendship that should have blossomed, dashed away by anger and hatred before it could flourish. Each scrutinised the other, mentally rolling back the years, seeing and remembering one another as boys. Boys without a care in the world other than winning a game of marbles, how had it come to this? Two men tied by the precious gift of a life saved, now ready and in the process of trying to kill one another. Baldor slowly, almost gently lowered the Roman back to the ground, letting go of the mail shirt. Bewildered and shocked he un-straddled his chest and sat back heavily on the ground alongside him. Holding his head in his hands, he shook it gently, his mind lost in a whirl of bloodlust, savagery, confusion and madness.

He was distracted from his shock and reverie by the rumble of approaching hooves and looking up he saw cavalry were swinging back his way. Leaving the Roman, he wearily pulled himself to his feet, hawking and spitting strings of glutinous blood as he tried to clear his nose and throat. The Roman, also recovering, rolled onto his side and pulled himself to his knees still sucking in air in huge, noisy gulps. Baldor ignored him as he saw the new trouble he was in. The small group of approaching cavalry were clearly Roman judging by the red-faced shields and un-bridled mounts and they were riding straight towards him. There was no one near him for support, Balaam and the troop had galloped on, chasing the retreating Romans pressing them hard. The Carthaginian infantry were still marching someway behind and had yet to appear, leaving him alone with the dead and the dying.

With nowhere to run and too weary and hurt to care, he searched among the carnage for his falcata and a shield. He watched the cavalry, now less than a stade away and closing fast. Suddenly mindful then panicky amidst his jumbled, confused thoughts, that he hadn't checked Gestix since he fell; he walked back towards where he lay. Confused, head pounding and sick to the stomach with worry for his friend, he stepped over bodies of men and horses towards him. Tripping and stumbling over the dead then slipping on the blood soaked grass, he looked back again at the approaching cavalry, they had not changed their route. Glancing from the cavalry to where Gestix had fallen, he gauged the distance and time it would take him to get there. He saw the blonde youth helping the sashed Roman to his feet while frantically waving the cavalry closer. Determined not to let the sashed Roman escape, Baldor quickened his step back towards them, if he was to die on this field he would not die alone. He shouted at the pair who also struggled and stumbled over the fallen. The younger helping the elder who was having trouble standing, he held his ribs and staggered drunkenly, head lolling as he was steered towards the arriving horsemen.

"Leave him! ... Leave the pig be! ... He dies here!" Baldor's head pounded with the effort of shouting.

With bloodlust rising once more, he closed on the pair, stumbling clumsily as he came raising his shield and sword ready to attack. The younger man hearing Baldor's challenge and advance glanced frantically behind him gauging distance. With his own weapon and those of the elder man gone, he could do nothing but increase his pace, hauling the injured man with him towards the oncoming horsemen. Baldor was almost on top of the pair when he lost his footing as a body rolled beneath his boots. His falcata swung wildly as he fell, just missing the elder man's head and shoulders but raking hard down the rear of his corselet hacking the purple sash away. The pair hurried on as Baldor struggled to his feet again.

A javelin thumping into the ground in front of him stopped his advance. He looked up just in time to deflect the next javelin with his shield before it hit him in the side. Sheathing his sword, he snatched the javelin from the ground hurling it back at the cavalryman. More javelins flew past him, he ducking and sidestepping them. He silently cursed himself for his predicament; he was going to die here.

Two cavalrymen dismounted to aid the older Roman onto the back of an empty horse, two others riding in with a spare mount for the blonde man. The rest turned their attention to Baldor and kicked their mounts over the fallen towards him. Another javelin thumped into the carcass of a horse next to him. Pushing his foot against the animal, Baldor snatched at the weapon twisting and pulling it free.

Hefting it into a throwing position, he sent it back at the nearest cavalryman hitting him in the chest. At such short range and hate-fueled force behind the throw, the small iron head burst through the rider's mail shirt smashing ribs apart burying deep in his chest. He rolled backwards off his horse like a circus tumbler. His comrades drew their spathas and rushed Baldor screaming death. Snatching up another discarded javelin, he stepped onto the flanks of a dead horse to give him more height and even the fight a little. Realizing he couldn't win and that this day would be his last, he roared his defiance as they closed on him. His javelin flew across the remaining distance, hitting an oncoming horse in the base of the neck just above the front legs. The power behind the throw took the javelin deep into its body bursting its heart, killing it outright. The horse collapsed to its knees, hurling the rider some ten paces in front of it rolling and bouncing over the ground. The next rider was almost on Baldor when another horse intercepted, forcing them apart.

"Hold!" The Blonde Roman called. Shouting as best he could through his damaged throat, his hand raised palm open to halt the attacking men. "Hold, I say!" His horse reared at the abrupt stop and pranced in a small circle on its hind legs as it tried to balance. "Leave him!" He rasped at the cavalrymen, his voice dry and gravelly.

The riders looking confused at the order and sour at missing the chance of a sure kill, struggled to settle their horses as they jostled from the sudden halt.

"Leave him now! ... Help; help my father off the field and to the surgeon immediately! See to it! This man is mine."

The riders turned away from Baldor back to the older Roman and their comrades who supported him atop his horse. The blonde man turned towards Baldor, patting and settling his mount so he could speak. Baldor drew his falcata and raised his shield in ready defense.

"Enough Baldor! I pray you ... enough!" He shouted, though his voice tailed off as his damaged throat refused to work. "Enough!" he said again pleadingly, almost in a whisper as he walked his mount to where Baldor stood upon the dead horse. The pair stared at one another, Baldor slowly lowering his falcata and wearily throwing down the shield. He wiped a hand across his face trying to remove some of the thick blood blocking his ruined nose. Diverse emotions of anger, hate, fear and sorrow battered both men's minds and tore their hearts. As adrenalin slowed and rationale returned they just stared, like two little boys, lost and confused.

"You would have slain my father, Baldor and for that I should kill you." He said evenly.

"Come ... try then! If you think you can." Baldor raised his sword beckoning with his other hand, his anger flaring again.

The Roman refused to be drawn and shaking his head gently continued quietly. "You saved my life Baldor, when we were children. Are you so keen to take it now? I could no more kill you than kill my own brother! For that is what we are, is it not ... brothers?"

Baldor lowered his falcata again. Embarrassed at his anger and deeply touched by the sentiment, he could think of nothing to say.

"Your countrymen have the field and the day. I must retire but I have ensured you leave with your life." The Roman paused as his voice dried in his throat again; he rubbed the bruised flesh gently before reaching for and uncorking a waterskin. He offered it first to Baldor, who as parched as he was, stubbornly shook his head. The man shrugged and took a long drink.

"So Baldor..." He began; pausing to tip some water into his hand rubbing it over his face. "My life debt to you is finally paid, that makes us even now. The next time we meet and there will be a next time, of that I am sure; the Gods have not thrown us together this twice for no reason. Then ... well, I will leave it to you to choose our destiny. Whether we fight or make our peace. But remember my friend, countries and governments make wars, not men, not brothers. Until we meet again." He bowed his head lifting a closed fist to his heart in salute.

Urging his mount around he was about to kick its flanks when Baldor found voice.

"Who are you? ... You know me but I have no name to call you."

The Roman had to bring his mount around once more to face Baldor; it whinnied and tossed its head as it picked up the scent of other horses returning across the plain. Drawing himself upright and with a regal look on his face he answered.

"I am Cornelius Publius Scipio, second son of the Consul, Publius Cornelius Scipio, the man you would have slain."

With that, he kicked the horse's flanks and was away, leaving dust in his wake.

Baldor was still trying to take it all in, he was shocked, confused and somewhat overawed at the events that had occurred. He shivered, suddenly feeling the chill of the winter wind, his battle weary body having cooled and the sweat dried upon him, his wet tunic sticking to his skin. Rubbing his brow trying to collect his befuddled wits, he looked about unsure as to where he had seen Gestix last. All around him, men and horses lay tangled in grotesque heaps like offal in a butcher's yard. Bodies torn and twisted in death, some without limbs or heads and many with spears or swords sticking in them. Discarded and broken weapons littered the ground amidst strings of blue-red intestines, limbs, excrement and dark red blood, which pooled and mixed with the dust or stained the grass. Some men still twitched and moaned; one or two had dragged themselves to a sitting position and sat holding wounds closed while they waited for help, one man staggered about in circles as if drunk. Crows and ravens alighted from their lazy circling and marched cautiously about the dead. Merciless, ebony eyes checking for signs of life before hopping onto the bodies to begin their feast. Their coarse squawks drifted over the plain as they fought and flapped while beaks pecked at the lifeless, staring eyes and exposed flesh, pulling at and squabbling over strings of bloodied intestines. The Carthaginian infantry drifted onto the field, their arrival scattering the carrion birds skyward again in black, squawking clouds. The infantry immediately began searching the dead and dying, those of the enemy that were not dead were quickly dispatched, their bodies stripped of anything of value. Through this madness, Baldor began the search for his friend.

Bone weary, he searched the carnage, trying to retrace his steps to where he had seen Gestix last. He came across the remnants of the purple sash; still knotted, it lay bright and stark against the ochre coloured grass. Stooping and groaning with the effort he scooped it up, his lip curling and twisting his face into a snarl as he pushed it into his belt alongside his dagger. Steeling himself to the whimpers and moans of the dying, he dared not stop to help, being very conscious now of the elapsed time since Gestix had fallen.

Would he find him crippled, dying or dead? He wondered as he worked himself into a panic, would he be able to find him at all in this sea of bodies that seemed to stretch endlessly over the plain. After what seemed like an eternity of searching, he saw Risto, laid on his side with his red blanket still strapped over his back. The animal panted, a broken leg hanging at an obtuse angle to its body. As Baldor drew nearer Risto picked up his scent, his head moving up and down as he recognised then tried to stand to see his master. Collapsing back in a heap the horse let out a bellow as though the wind had been knocked from him. Baldor felt his stomach knot, his skin flushed hotly and the nausea came, his eyes filled as he looked at his horse twisting in pain. Risto's eyes bulged hugely exposing their whites, the mouth all frothed with foam as the lips curled back to whicker. Close by and laid on his side, face down, was Gestix. His wounded arm uppermost his body deathly still. Blood, the colour of ripened plums stained his tunic at the shoulder and soaked the grass next to him.

Not wanting to believe what he saw, Baldor's heart sank and his stomach heaved. "No! ... no ... no ... oo!" With his mind numbed and his body pushed beyond endurance, his legs folded beneath him and he fell heavily to his knees behind and beside his friend.

"Gestix! Gestix!" He uttered in a rushed whisper.

With dread rising in him like a devouring disease, he reached out with shaking hands, gently rolling the Gaul towards him, leaning him against his thighs. Gestix let out a long moan as he was moved; his eyes flickered but did not open. Baldor undid the helmet strap and slipped it off. Gestix stirred slightly as the cold air dried the moisture on his brow and cooled his wet hair, he opened his eyes but they closed again quickly.

"Gestix ..." Baldor stopped short as his hands contacted wet-warm blood from the soaked tunic. Touching blood-slicked hands to Gestix's skin, he found it cold and clammy, his breathing shallow and irregular. He looked about frantically for help. The infantry were still too far away to hear his shouts and too engrossed in their robbery and murder to care. He was unsure of what to do, though he had seen plenty of injuries to know the big man was very badly hurt. He was frustrated further as he had no means of helping, for he had neither water nor bandages and was too frightened to leave his friend to search for them. Swallowing his horror and fear, Baldor eased the big man close.

"I'll get you out of here ... just hold on ... just hold on!" He mumbled through tears that mixed with blood and mucus from his nose.

Baldor probed his fingers tentatively beneath the tunic to assess the wound and wished he hadn't. The flesh was sliced deeply and lay flap-like, open to the bone, the blood as thick and warm as winter's gruel. Remembering the sash in his belt, he pulled it out. Folding it as best he could with his free hand, he gently but firmly pushed it under the tunic to plug the wound, Gestix twitched and gasped at the contact.

Finally snapping from the strain of the combat, the shock and horror and now the condition of his friend, Baldor broke down, sobbing and hugging the wounded Gaul close to him.

"Gestix … Gestix, I'll get you well! Just hold on, can …can you hear me? … Gestix, please?"

Gestix moaned deeply, his face twisting in pain. He sucked in a deep breath and blinked his eyes open. He stared unseeing into space and smiled.

"Asmilcar? Asmilcar, is that you? …" He laughed a little before the pain cut him short.

"Its me, Gestix! … Baldor! Me! … It's alright, I'm here now."

As though unhearing Gestix continued, albeit slowly and raggedly.

"Asmilcar, I've missed you …where…where have you been? It's been too…" The pain gripped him savagely, strangling his words.

Distraught at his friend's plight and powerless to do anything to help him, Baldor held him tighter, rocking him gently.

"Gestix!" Baldor shook him gently as the Gaul seemed to lose consciousness "It's me! … Baldor! … Baldor, just me!"

Gestix moaned then twitched violently as though a nerve spasmed. His eyes flickered open again but still held a distant unseeing stare. He mouthed words but only broken, inaudible whispers came out mixed with frothing blood.

"Gestix, Gestix … I'm sorry! … Sorry! This is all my fault! Mine! We should never have come; I should have listened to you … listened."

Baldor pulled Gestix closer resting his bloodied, broken face on his head. His tears washing blood and sweat onto the blonde crown as he sobbed broken-heartedly.

"Asm… Asmilcar." Came out in a hoarse whisper. "The boy has done well … see! … Baldor … Bal … dor your father is here …"

Gestix shuffled his body placing his good arm on the ground trying to rise to his feet.

"I'm coming, Asmilcar ... coming ... I'm just a little slower than I was ... wait you!" The Gaul smiled as he gasped the words.

Baldor was still holding him, trying to prevent him moving. "Gestix, please be still, don't move, don't move! Wait till I can get you out of here ..."

"Baldor? ... There you ... are! I have ... to go, your father's here ... see!"

Gestix slumped back as his muscles refused to lift him, the movement seemed to knock more wind from him and his eyes closed again.

Baldor looked up as the sound of hooves came across the field once more; he squinted through tear-filled eyes to see who approached. Finally, having to rub bloodied hands over his eyes to clear them and wincing at the pressure on his broken face, he recognised the foremost rider.

"Armaco! ... Armaco! Help! ...Over here! ... Over here, for the love of Baal!" His head pounded as he shouted, his throat sore and parched.

"You'll be alright now, Gestix ... alright, just hold on, we'll get you to the surgeon."

The group Baldor had seen reined in momentarily before splitting into two. The larger riding in the direction of the retreating Scipios while three riders headed towards him and Gestix.

A moment later Armaco, Marko and Malo reined in hard just in front of Baldor, the men dismounting before the horses stopped, their dust cloud drifting past them to settle on Baldor and Gestix. The look on the warrior's faces when they saw the pair said all they did not.

"Armaco, help me... for Baal's sake help me! He's hurt bad!"

"It's alright ... we're here now." Armaco said as he squatted next to the pair.

"Help him Armaco ... please help him!" Baldor beseeched his tone frantic.

Whilst Armaco reassured and helped Baldor, Marko and Malo gently lifted Gestix from him, propping him upright against a dead horse. Undoing the corselet shoulder strap and side lacing to better access the wound; they eased the blood soaked sash to one side assessing the damage.

Armaco caught the grave looks from both men as they finished their examination. Trying to assess how much blood had been lost, he picked up the sash thinking it to be a piece of cloth used as a bandage. As it unfolded from his hand, he recognised it for what it was.

"Where in Hades has this? … Baldor, where did this come from?"

"You've got to stop him bleeding, for …"

"Baldor, where did this come from? Do you know?" Armaco persisted, holding the sodden sash towards Baldor.

"For Baal's sake, make it stop! Make it stop!" Baldor babbled, oblivious to the question, his mind engulfed with the horror of it all.

Realising he would have to wait for coherent answers, Armaco crumpled the sash in his hand wringing the blood from it then pushed it beneath his corselet. Baldor tried to stand but Armaco held him where he was. Removing his neck cloth, he tipped water from a flask onto it, gently cleaning the blood from Baldor's face. He turned it slowly from side to side looking at the damage, tutting softly at what he saw.

"The lads will do their best, you know that." He said reassuringly smiling as best he could. "Any more damage anywhere? … Baldor?"

Baldor shook his head, his eyes firmly held on Gestix, watching as the men bound the wound as best they could.

"It's lucky we found you so fast. I lost you after the charge. I thought you were in front of us. Harbro has taken the others after those Romans riding away from near you. One of them looked important, the one in the bronze corselet, he must have been a General or something."

Not listening or caring, Baldor shook and sobbed. His bloodshot eyes staring at Armaco with a lost, heartbroken, wits-end stare of a man pushed too far. His tears fell heavily and Armaco leaned forward, hugging Baldor's head to his chest as the lad finally gave way and cried pitifully.

Armaco held him as he broke while motioning the others to get Gestix onto a horse. The men eased him gently onto the animal's back but had to tie him in place when he slumped sack-like over its neck. With Gestix secured, Armaco caught Malo's eye and gestured towards Risto. The Nubian nodded and padded over to the horse. Risto snorted and twitched as Malo crouched, stroking him and speaking softly while he ran his hand over the fetlock deftly examining the leg. Sighing, he stood and slipped an arrow from his quiver nocking it to the string.

"Come Baldor, we need to get you both off the field." Armaco hooked his arm under Baldor's armpit easing him to his feet. "The day's ours at least, we're hounding them to Hades … come now… come."

As Marko and Armaco helped Baldor towards a horse, he saw Malo pulling back his bow, the arrow aimed down at Risto's head.

"No! … No!" He cried his voice trailing off as he tried to struggle free.

Armaco held him firmly. "We have to Baldor! His leg is broken … he's in pain. There's nothing we can do."

The thud of the arrow striking home with great force brought a sharp sigh from Risto and a wail from Baldor as he was bundled, wilting, onto a spare mount and Armaco led them from the field.

The five made their way back towards their advancing army weaving around and through the carnage of broken bodies of men and horses. The cries and screams of the wounded were pitiful, the sight and smell nauseating. Baldor for once seemed not to hear or see it, so caught up in concern and grief at his friend's state. As they guided the horses down across a small, steep-banked stream Gestix fell forward over his mount's neck again. Baldor kicked his mount alongside quickly, taking hold of his body preventing him from falling further. Armaco dismounted, running to the other side of the horse to help while calling for Malo and Marko. As he steadied Gestix, his hands contacted fresh blood where the wound had opened and bled again. On inspection he found the bandages soaked, he cursed viciously beneath his breath.

"Help me lift him down! Marko cut the ropes."

"We need to get him to the surgeon Armaco, we can't stop here!" Baldor shouted, highly agitated.

"Lift him down!" Armaco barked back.

Marko and Malo looked from Baldor back to Armaco.

"Lift him down damn you!" Armaco's face twisted in anger.

Marko pushed a knife into Baldor's hands. "Cut the ropes Baldor, Malo help me here."

Gestix groaned softly, his head lolling as the men eased him to the ground laying him with his back against the stream bank. The men looked at the blood all over their hands and chests and stood back as

Armaco knelt down with a waterskin, pushing it gently between Gestix's lips. The big man was only semi -conscious and most of the liquid dribbled back out of his mouth. Armaco gently tilted his head back and managed to get some down his throat. Tipping the rest onto a neck cloth, he bathed his face. The water seemed to bring him around and his eyes opened. Armaco called over his shoulder to Baldor. He stood as Baldor came forward while turning his back on Gestix and whispered softly.

"He hasn't got long Baldor; he's lost too much blood."

Baldor wilted and dropped heavily to his knees alongside his friend, more tears running through the dried blood and dirt on his face. In his mind, he'd known, but to hear it said aloud brought it home to him, making it terribly real.

"I'm s ... sorry, Gestix" He said between huge sobs that racked his frame. "I'm sorry ... sorry for, for all of this! For not listening! For not being Godly. For ..."

Gestix gasped for breath, shaking his head gently whilst looking intently at Baldor. He lifted his good arm his hand grasping Baldor's and squeezing affectionately.

"Shhh lad ... shhh." He gasped again then coughed and slavered blood and his eyes closed.

"Don't go ... don't ..."

"It's ... it's my time is all."

"No ... no!"

"It's ... not for us to decide lad ... remember ... remember to say the words for me." He managed a smile.

"I will ..." Came out in a rushed whisper. "Don't go ..."

"You're ... a ... good, good lad." The words faded to a whisper.

Baldor leant forward hugging Gestix tightly to him. With his body shaking, he didn't feel Gestix go limp in his arms.

The three men standing behind Baldor bowed their heads in respect; clutching right fists to their hearts, they mouthed prayers. The irregular breathing and gasping of Baldor suddenly seeming very loud.

Armaco let a respectable time pass before motioning the two others to bring the horses. He tentatively placed a hand on Baldor's shoulder.

"Baldor!" He said quietly. "Baldor ... he's gone. Come, we need to get him away from here and do things right ... come on."

He eased Baldor and Gestix gently apart and signaled Malo and Marko to take the limp body. Raising Baldor to his feet, he led him to his mount. Baldor walked woodenly going where he was bidden, his face ashen, eyes sunken, lifeless, and overflowing with tears and his heart broken.

*

Historical Note

After recovering from his wound, Hannibal did leave the siege at Saguntum to quell the insurrection amongst the Carpetani and Oretani tribes who resided in the central uplands of Spain. However, little is known of the punitive expedition he mounted, other than it was swift and decisive. Thus, the battle in the forest in which Baldor came to his notice is my own invention. However, all the other battles and their outcomes described in this book are as they were in history.

The battle of the Ticinus was the first locking of horns between the Romans and Carthaginians on Roman soil. It was no great, set piece battle but rather a large, fast moving skirmish fought by the cavalry arms of both sides. Hannibal needed a quick victory to both impress and bring the local tribes to him in alliance against Rome, Scipio also sought speed, desperate to check or destroy Hannibal before his presence spread further insurrection and revolt.

The battle appears at first hand to have been a rushed, haphazard affair with both sides chancing much on the outcome. For Hannibal however, the outcome was as sure as the coming of the next day. He knew the Roman strength lay in their heavy Infantry and disciplined formations, not in their cavalry. The Roman cavalry were predominantly heavy and lacked sufficient light units to support and protect it properly as it operated. The leadership of it also lacked the elan, experience and individuality that was to be found abundantly in Hannibal, Maharabal and his subordinates. The Roman negation to adapt and change tactics to suit the terrain or their enemy, also reduced their effectiveness along with their large cumbersome shields and still bridle-less ponies.

By sharp contrast Hannibal's own strength lay in his heavy and light cavalry units, both of which he had an abundance of. Operating both arms in close support of one another was a deadly combination of which he was a past master and one that would help him lay waste to the Roman Legions and occupy Italy for a further sixteen years.

The Roman Consul, Publius Scipio was badly wounded at the Ticinus and was only saved and rescued from the battlefield by the intervention of his son Cornelius, (the future Scipio Africanus) a youth of only seventeen years at the time. It is said that with the swift routing of the Roman cavalry the Consuls bodyguard feared to return to the field to save their commander, the selfless and brave act of Cornelius eventually shaming them into returning to help carry their Consul from the field.

Very little is known of Cornelius prior to this action and thus his rescue from the sea as a boy by Baldor is also my own invention

In the aftermath of the Ticinus, the Romans fell back across the river Po destroying the bridges as they went. They took up a defensive position in the foothills of the Apennine Mountains on the eastern bank of the river Trebbia near Placentia. Demoralised and shocked from their defeat and with their beloved leader injured, they refused further offers of combat from the Carthaginians, choosing instead to wait for the joint Consul, Tiberius Sempronius Longus and his Legions to reinforce them.

The well planned ambushes and huge, set piece, decisive battles are yet to come that will bleed the Roman armies white and bring the mightiest empire on earth almost to its knees. The theatre of war will cover Italy, Spain and finally North Africa and Carthage itself, with the conflict lasting for a further sixteen years and claiming tens of thousands of lives. The war of the giants had begun.

Thus, Baldor must march on. Injured and broken heated, a war to fight and a blood feud to settle.

Printed in Great Britain
by Amazon